First Glimpse

Janet sighed and turned to retrace her steps. It was getting darker, but the air was still now. She stood looking through a dusty window into a room piled with boxes, trying to orient herself. Around the next corner, gravel crunched.

Janet stooped for a rock, shoved her hand into her pocket. What are you doing? she asked herself. It's only another lost person.

The gravel crunched again and the other lost person came around the corner. She was tall, taller than Tina. She wore a long red cape so heavy that it hardly moved as she walked, and red boots. She had red and black hair, the red like her cloak and the black like coal. On her broad forehead and high-boned face was no expression at all. She walked past Janet in a waft of some bitter smell like the ivy's, only more complex. Janet opened her mouth as the woman walked right at the faded sign, and left it open. The red cloak, the long mass of streaked hair, mingled with the ivy and, rustling, disappeared.

FIREBIRD
WHERE FANTASY TAKES FLIGHT™

Beldan's Fire	Midori Snyder
The Blue Girl	Charles de Lint
The Blue Sword	Robin McKinley
The Changeling Sea	Patricia A. McKillip
Crown Duel	Sherwood Smith
Ecstasia	Francesca Lia Block
The Faery Reel: Tales from the Twilight Realm	Ellen Datlow and Terri Windling, eds.
Firebirds Rising: An Anthology of Original Science Fiction and Fantasy	Sharyn November, ed.
The Green Man: Tales from the Mythic Forest	Ellen Datlow and Terri Windling, eds.
Hannah's Garden	Midori Snyder
The Hero and the Crown	Robin McKinley
The Hex Witch of Seldom	Nancy Springer
The Hidden Land	Pamela Dean
New Moon	Midori Snyder
The Outlaws of Sherwood	Robin McKinley
Sadar's Keep	Midori Snyder
The Secret Country	Pamela Dean
Singer	Jean Thesman
Tamsin	Peter S. Beagle
Waifs and Strays	Charles de Lint
The Whim of the Dragon	Pamela Dean
The Winter Prince	Elizabeth E. Wein

TAM LIN

PAMELA DEAN

INTRODUCTION BY TERRI WINDLING

FIREBIRD

AN IMPRINT OF PENGUIN GROUP (USA) INC.

This book is for Terri Windling

FIREBIRD
Published by the Penguin Group
Penguin Group (USA) Inc., 345 Hudson Street, New York, New York 10014, U.S.A.
Penguin Group (Canada), 90 Eglinton Avenue East, Suite 700, Toronto, Ontario, Canada M4P 2Y3 (a division of Pearson Penguin Canada Inc.)
Penguin Books Ltd, 80 Strand, London WC2R 0RL, England
Penguin Ireland, 25 St Stephen's Green, Dublin 2, Ireland (a division of Penguin Books Ltd)
Penguin Group (Australia), 250 Camberwell Road, Camberwell, Victoria 3124, Australia (a division of Pearson Australia Group Pty Ltd)
Penguin Books India Pvt Ltd, 11 Community Centre, Panchsheel Park, New Delhi - 110 017, India
Penguin Group (NZ), Cnr Airborne and Rosedale Roads, Albany, Auckland, 1310 New Zealand (a division of Pearson New Zealand Ltd)
Penguin Books (South Africa) (Pty) Ltd, 24 Sturdee Avenue, Rosebank, Johannesburg 2196, South Africa

Registered Offices: Penguin Books Ltd, 80 Strand, London WC2R 0RL, England

Grateful acknowledgment is made for permission to quote from *The Lady's Not for Burning* by Christopher Fry, © 1950, 1956, 1977 by Christopher Fry. Published by Oxford University Press.

First published in hardcover in the United States of America by Tor Books, a division of Tom Doherty Associates, 1991
Published by Firebird, an imprint of Penguin Group (USA) Inc., 2006

1 3 5 7 9 10 8 6 4 2

ISBN 0-14-240652-X

Printed in the United States of America

ACKNOWLEDGMENTS

I am grateful to Patricia Wrede and Caroline Stevermer, and to Steven Brust, Emma Bull, Kara Dalkey, and Will Shetterly, for their ability to be both honest and encouraging; and to my husband, David Dyer-Bennet, kindest of project managers.

INTRODUCTION
TERRI WINDLING

Pamela Dean's enchanting *Tam Lin* has been captivating readers since its first publication in 1991 as part of a series of novels based on classic fairy tales. But in fact, the traditional story of Tam Lin wasn't originally a fairy tale at all. Although it did appear in fairy tale form in Joseph Jacob's *More English Fairy Tales* and other nineteenth century collections, in its original form it was an old folk song (a ballad) from the Border country between Scotland and England. No one knows just how old the ballad is, since few ballads were written down prior to the sixteenth century. It wasn't until the nineteenth century that folklore became a serious area of academic study, and by that time, many manuscripts recording old ballads had been tragically lost. "Tam Lin," however, managed to survive, and is still performed by folk musicians today, widely regarded as the finest fairy ballad of the British Isles. The ballad appears to come from Selkirk, a town very near the area where Scotland's famous author and folklorist Sir Walter Scott once lived, and its story is deeply rooted in the fairy lore of ancient Scotland.

I don't want to say too much about that story here lest I lessen the suspense of Pamela Dean's novel for readers unfamiliar with her source material—but at the end of this book, you'll find the old Scottish ballad printed in its entirety. Or rather, I should say that you'll find *one* version of the ballad—for there are numerous variants of it, many of which were collected and published by the great ballad scholar Sir Francis Child in his famous five-volume work *The English and Scottish Popular Ballads* (1882–1898). The Child Ballads, as the 305 ballads printed in Child's massive collection have come to be known, are still sung by folk singers all across the British Isles, America, and Canada. These ballads are full of wonderful stories about elfin knights, fairy kings and queens, monsters who turn into beautiful maidens, doves who weep blood red tears and other images of the fantastic. Other Child Ballads are less supernatural but often dark, spooky, and tragic; they are tales of murder, seduction, and love brutally betrayed.

"Tam Lin" is one of the best known of the supernatural ballads, or fairy ballads. It is loosely related to another famous fairy ballad called "Thomas the Rhymer," which comes from the same history-rich Border region between Scotland and England. "Tam Lin" is also related to similar ballads in the Swedish and Danish traditions, as well as to stories ranging from "Thetis and Peleus" in classical myth to a Cretan fairy tale about a shape-shifting neriad (water nymph).

I don't think it gives too much of the plot away to say that legends surrounding Halloween (All Hallow's Eve) are important to the tale of Tam Lin. In past times, Halloween was known as Samhain (pronounced *sowwain*), which was New Year's Eve to the ancient Celts, who started their seasonal cycle at winter's beginning on November 1. Samhain was a powerful, dangerous time—a time when the gates between worlds opened, when ghosts of the dead came to haunt the living and fairies road across the hills on horses as fast as the wind. It was at this time every seven years that Scottish fairies paid a "teind," or sacrifice, to Hell. This wasn't the Hell of Christian lore, ruled over by a devil with horns, but a darker side of the fairy world, sometimes known as the Unseelie Court. This was the realm of treacherous fairies who delighted in causing harm to humankind. The winter months between Samhaine and Beltane (May Day) belonged to the rule of Unseelie Court, while the Seelie Court (the "light" fairies, who were less malign but could also be dangerous to mortals) held sway in the human world from the first of May to Halloween. The usual teind that was paid to Hell was the life-blood of a mortal man; but if no such creature could be found and lured into Fairyland at the right time, the Seelie Court would then have to sacrifice one of their own number.

Even during years when the teind was not due it was dangerous to spy upon the fairy court as it rode the hills on Samhain night. One glimpse of this magnificent parade could leave a man blind, or addled in his wits, or cause him to follow after and be lost to the mortal world forever. Samhain, therefore, was a time for mortals to exercise particular caution—particularly at twilight, when the boundaries between the human world and the fairy realm grew especially permeable.

In some parts of Scotland, hearth-fires were distinguished and houses kept safely hidden in darkness while communities gathered at bonfires built with ritual spells of protection. As the sun came up again in the morning, each household would take a brand from the fire to light their own hearth-fires again; this would keep their homes safe from fairy mischief during the six dark months to come. Certain places were particularly loved by the fairies and were best avoided on Samhain night: the dark of the woods, stone circles, barrows, bridges over running water, wells, springs, and all cross-roads—particularly at the stroke of midnight. Of course, if for some urgent, desperate reason you *wanted* to find the fairy court, then Halloween would be the time to do it. As Janet does, in the ballad of Tam Lin. But more on that, and on brave young Janet's plight, in the pages ahead. . . .

Pamela Dean has taken the story of Tam Lin and transplanted it across the ocean, setting her tale on a college campus in the American midwest. All of the ballad's major characters are here, along with its ancient, traditional themes of love and courage, sacrifice and transformation. This is a highly original retelling of one of the world's great fairy legends, rich in folklore and literary elusions, steeped in Shakespeare, balladry, and magic. It is an honor and a pleasure to introduce this wonderful novel to readers once again.

If Pamela Dean's *Tam Lin* whets your appetite for other treatments of the ballad, I recommend the following (all of which are very different from the novel in your hands): *The Perilous Gard* by Elizabeth Marie Pope, *Fire and Hemlock* by Diana Wynne Jones, *Winter Rose* by Patricia A. McKillip, *Red Shift* by Alan Garner, *A Dark Horn Blowing* by Dahlov Ipcar, and *An Earthly Knight* by Janet McNaughton. Also try Joan Vinge's story "Tam Lin" in the anthology *Imaginary Lands* (edited by Robin McKinley), Delia Sherman's "Cotillion" in *Firebirds* (edited by Sharyn November) and Liz Locchead's fabulous poem "Tam-Lin's Lady" in her collection *Dreaming Frankenstein*. For children's picture book versions of the story, try *Tam Lin* by Susan Cooper, with illustrations by Warwick Hutton, and *Tam Lin* by Jane Yolen, with illustrations by Charles Mikolaycak.

Other good fantasy novels inspired by ballads and folk

music from the British Isles: *Thomas the Rhymer* by Ellen Kushner, *Through a Brazen Mirror* by Delia Sherman, *The Little Country* by Charles de Lint, *War for the Oaks* by Emma Bull, *Swim the Moon* by Paul Brandon, and *Moonwise* by Greer Gilman. Finally, don't miss *The Book of Ballads* by the award-winning artist Charles Vess, a terrific collection of ballads (including "Tam Lin") told in comic book form, with stories by Charles de Lint, Neil Gaiman, Jane Yolen, Midori Snyder, and other top fantasy writers.

To hear the ballad of Tam Lin performed, I particularly recommend Fairport Convention's famous folk-rock version on their *Leige and Leaf* CD, Pyewackett's evocative version on *The Man in the Moon Drinks Claret*, and Frankie Armstrong's more traditional version on *Ballads*.

CHAPTER 1

The year Janet started at Blackstock College, the Office of Residential Life had spent the summer removing from all the dormitories the old wooden bookcases that, once filled with books, fell over unless wedged. Chase and Phillips's *A New Introduction to Greek* was the favorite instrument for wedging; majors in the Classics used the remedial math textbook, but this caused the cases to develop a slight backward tilt, so that doughnuts, pens, student identification cards, or concert tickets placed on top of them slid with indistinguishable slowness backward and eventually vanished dustily behind. The generally harried air of most Classics majors was attributed by their friends and roommates entirely to their reliance on an inferior wedging system for their bookcases. Janet's father said he doubted that this pervasive student theory accounted for the actions of the Office of Residential Life in replacing the bookcases, if only because the Office of Residential Life had only once paid the slightest attention to any student opinion or request, this once being in the spring term of 1969, when their three cramped rooms were appropriated by a group of students who felt that the war in Viet Nam bestowed on all those of draft age the right to coed housing.

Janet doubted this account of the students' reasoning; her father's opinion of the Office of Residential Life was, however, woefully accurate. One look around the room they had given her confirmed it. She had the names of two roommates. The room had three closets, three desks, three chairs, three bureaus. But it had two sets of bunk beds (enough, that is, for four people), and it had, replacing the three (or maybe four) tall, solid bookcases with five shelves each, a measly four shelves, warped boards wobbling a little on their brass brackets, which had not been inserted into their strips evenly, probably because the strips themselves were installed crookedly on the wall.

"How many people are supposed to be in here?" demanded her mother.

"Three," said Janet, tragically.

"Open that box of books, then, and grab two of those shelves. Nobody else is going to bring six boxes of books to college.

"I don't even think they read," said Janet, still tragically.

"What makes you think they don't?" said her father.

"One of them didn't write me back at all, and the other one talked about beer and Bach and *tennis*."

"Which one did which?" said her mother, slamming two handsful of Heinlein juveniles and a fat chunk of Hermann Hesse paperbacks onto the lowest shelf.

"Mom, if I'm stealing two shelves they shouldn't be the lowest ones."

"Your roommates are probably taller than you are."

"Everybody is," said her sister, who at twelve was, and blond to boot.

"Which one did which?" said her father.

"The Chicago one wrote; the Pennsylvania one didn't. Mom, don't bang that one around, it's coming apart."

"That's *mine*," said her sister.

"Lily-Milly, it is not. I never gave it to you."

"Don't *call* me that!" shrieked her sister.

"Apply to your parents," said Janet, wrestling her footlocker along the carpeting into the alcove that held one of the desks. It featured a window overlooking, down a long slope tangled with rough grass and dandelions, a round and self-conscious lake full of ducks and algae.

"Where's Andrew?" said the male parent, with good timing but genuine concern.

"Talking to some of the girls in the hall," said Lily. She wandered back along the room's long narrow entrance, where the three closets were—and where had that fourth roommate kept her clothes, for heaven's sake? thought Janet—and after a moment could be heard proclaiming happily, "Jannie, he's telling them about the time you put the garlic in the—"

"God damn it!" howled Janet, lunging for the door. "I should have gone to Colgate! I should have gone to Grinnell! I should have—"

"Don't say it," said her mother, "or I'll throw *The Wind in the Willows* right out the window."

"I should have gone to *Harvard*!" shrieked Janet, recklessly diving into the crowd of girls in the hall and laying impetuous hands on her only brother. "You get in here now!"

"Jannie," he said, as solemnly as only an eight-year-old could, "they say there's a ghost in your room."

"Oh, of course," said Janet brightly. "What a relief. I couldn't think what that extra bed was for."

"She's very quiet," said the Resident Assistant, a tall and round-faced young woman who had written Janet a perfectly responsible and sane letter about the college, just as though Janet's father had not taught here for twenty-two years.

"Who was she?" said Janet, still tugging her brother along

but aware of the necessity of being civil. Luckily, Andrew was cute and redheaded, and the four girls in the hall were regarding him benignly.

"Classics major," said a short black student, as if that explained everything. Everybody at Blackstock who was not a member of the Classics Department talked like that. Janet had never met a Classics major; the professors she had met from that department seemed no more peculiar than those of any other. But it was one of Blackstock's tenets. They will never fix the Music and Drama Center; it always snows on Parents' Weekend; Classics majors are crazy.

"What class?" Of course, they might have chosen her as the butt of one of the innumerable jokes played on freshmen; faculty brats were favorite targets.

"Ninety-nine," said an even smaller girl with glasses.

"Janet Margaret Carter," said Lily from the doorway, "come unpack these books."

"I'll see you at the meeting tonight," Janet said generally, lugged her brother back into the room, and banged the door shut.

Her mother was leaning out one of the windows; her father was sitting on her desk. "Look what you made your mother do," he said.

"You made her do it," said Janet, more or less automatically. She let go of Andrew but stayed between him and the door. "She couldn't stand to hear any more about how nobody in the entire Department of Humane Letters at Harvard—not that there is one—is doing anything but painstakingly reconstructing Aristotle." Having delivered her standard speech, she absorbed what her mother had threatened—to throw *The Wind in the Willows* out a fourth-floor window. She said with much more force, "Mom, how *could* you?"

"Colgate," said her mother, not turning from the window. Her voice was unnaturally calm for the subject they were discussing. The morning sunshine haloed her red head. "Or Cornell, maybe—the little one, that is."

"It's too late now," said Janet. "Why don't you all just go home now, and I'll come for Sunday supper in a month or two."

"Walk down with us and get your book," said her mother.

The book had landed flat on its front in a clump of dandelions. Janet brushed it off and felt the binding tenderly. It had been so battered already, any new damage was hard to locate. Her mother had given it to her on her eighth birthday, and if Janet had ever thrown any book anywhere her mother would probably have put her on bread and water and Eugene Field for a week. It must be very stressful after all, sending your oldest child off to college, even if college was about ten blocks away.

Andrew, fidgeting about and scuffing his feet on the sidewalk, said, "Dad, those girls say there's a ghost in Jan's room."

"On Fourth Ericson?" said her father. "Is it the same old story, or a new one? What sort of ghost?"

"Classics major!" said Andrew, and laughed immoderately.

"Ha ha," said his father. "You know it's time to replace the campus joke when small boys find it funny."

"Better the Classics Department than yours," said Janet's mother. "I shudder to think what they could find to say about the English Department if they put their minds to it."

"Now, Janet," said her father, oblivious, "don't take English 10 from Brinsley."

"I know," said Janet. "Senior Seminar from Brinsley. English 10 from Evans if I want to do it right, or Tyler if I want to be usefully irritated. And Chaucer *only* from Brinsley, and if I'm very, very good, I can take the Romantics from you next year. Go away now, I have to unpack."

She hugged her parents; gave Andrew a chance to hug her, which he surprised her by taking; and looked speculatively at her sister.

"I hope you get roommates worse than me," said Lily.

Well, that was that. She ran up the four flights of red-carpeted steps and encountered another group of girls in the wide hall of the fourth floor. The RA was among them. What was her name, for heaven's sake. Irma? Norma? Nora, all right.

"What can I expect from the ghost?" Janet asked her. If they were having fun, you might as well let them have it.

"Not much," said Nora. "She throws books out the window."

"That could get annoying in the winter."

"Not your books—ghost books."

"Whose? All the ones she hated?"

"It's hard to read the titles when they're flying around," said Nora dryly. The three other girls, all clearly new students as well, giggled a little, in a hopeful way.

They either knew nothing, or were dreadfully unimaginative. "I'd better get unpacked," Janet said, and went into her room.

There she sat on her desk and surveyed it all. Ericson was one of the older dormitories, which meant high ceilings, slightly scarred oak woodwork, wide windowsills, and an old white porcelain sink, with mismatched faucets, in what might once have been the fourth roommate's closet. The carpet was red, like the stairs'; the walls and ceiling were clean white. You could paint them if you wanted to, but it would be a lot of trouble, and the Office of Residential Life was stingy in its allowance of colors. The iron bunk beds were painted white, too; the other furniture matched the woodwork, though it was rather more used-looking. The room had southern, eastern, and northern exposures; the four largest windows looked eastward, and Janet had claimed the desk that looked north. It was all warm, clean, and pleasant. Janet looked at the tumble of books on the bottom shelf, and sniffed.

She had given up this useless exercise and was putting writing paper and sealing wax and typewriter ribbons into the drawers of her desk when someone knocked on the door and then came in.

"Hello!" called Janet, so as not to startle the newcomer.

"Hi," said a comfortingly midwestern voice, and the first of the two roommates—unless there were three—came around the corner. Janet went on smiling, but her stomach protested a little. This roommate—probably the Chicago one, who had written, since she had a tennis racket under one arm and a tape player under the other—was about six feet tall and looked perfectly pleased with this condition. She was dressed more or less as Janet was, except that her blue corduroy pants had been ironed; her Oxford-cloth shirt was not only ironed, but pink, and tucked in, too; her tennis shoes were of a dazzling blueness. She had a nice healthy face with large blue eyes, and a head of straight blond hair, cut just above the shoulders, that put even Lily's to shame. Why doesn't she grow it long? thought Janet. All over the country were girls wearing Indian cotton dresses and Earth shoes who would kill for hair like that.

"Hi," said the roommate, a little less certainly. "I'm Christina. Which—no, let me guess. Are you Molly?"

"Why, do I look like somebody who doesn't answer letters?"

"Janet, then. Didn't she answer yours? She sent me a nice one, but it was a little strange."

Janet bit her lip on the next obvious question; Christina looked earnest, and would therefore probably take it the wrong way. "I was glad you wrote, anyway."

Christina dumped the racket, the tape player, and a bulging shopping bag onto the nearest lower bunk, and looked at the contents of the bookshelves. "Are all these yours?"

The dangerous question. "Yes."

"These are kids' books."

She sounded more puzzled than disapproving, but whatever tone it was said in, that remark boded no good. Janet held her tongue. "Oh, well," said Christina cheerfully, "I brought my teddy bear." She extracted a gray floppy object from her shopping bag and propped it up against the brown-paper package of bedding provided by the Office of Residential Life.

Useless, Janet decided, but tolerant. Whether this made her worse than Lily was a question that would bear a deal of examination.

"Did you have a nice trip?" said Christina.

"I live in town," said Janet, who had said as much in her letter. "Where's the rest of your stuff?"

Somebody else knocked. Janet and Christina both called, "Come in!" Janet thought she could grow to hate that hallway with the closets; you always had to wait for who was coming.

Who was coming, as it lumped around the corner, appeared to be composed largely of scuffed blue suitcases. It dropped these, panting, and emerged as another tall person, maybe five eight, with curly brown hair, a sharp, freckled face, and the clothes that should have gone with Christina's hair. Not the Indian cotton, but well and truly faded blue jeans, old sandals, a denim shirt with a peace symbol embroidered on one pocket and a rose on the other.

"Hello, Molly," said Janet.

"Hi. Which of you is—oh, far *out*!" She lunged at the bookshelves, brought up with her nose an inch away from the books, and tilting her head sideways read her way down every spine there, nodding and exclaiming. "I *hate* Hermann Hesse," she said, wheeling around, "but the rest of these are my very favorites."

"They're mine," said Janet, beaming at her.

"So you're Janet. Can you really read Hesse?"

"My best friend likes him," said Janet, "and he's very intense."

"I thought he was boring," said Molly, "but never mind. What else have you got in here?" She folded herself to the floor and looked expectantly at Janet. Janet, feeling unfairly that Christina would have just ripped the boxes open, supposing she was interested at all, sat down too, and reached for the one containing the new books, the ones getting ready for college had not left her time to read.

"I left my stuff down in the lobby," said Christina. This was merely a statement of fact, Janet thought, intended to explain why she was going out the door instead of joining in the examination of the box; but both Janet and Molly, without exchanging a glance, scrambled to their feet and accompanied her down the four flights of steps, and toiled back up them again with suitcases, footlocker, and four cardboard boxes. These last were too light to contain books.

Christina promptly ripped the brown paper from her bedding and made up one of the bottom bunks. Janet and Molly unloaded the box of new books.

"I haven't had time to read these," Janet said.

"Well, let's see," said Molly, turning the books over one by one. She had very long fingers. *Till We Have Faces, All the Myriad Ways, Jack of Shadows, The Children of Llyr, More Than Human, The Daughter of Time, The Crystal Cave,* and *A Tan and Sandy Silence* fell through her searching hands, accompanied by exclamations of approval and puzzlement and anticipation. Janet watched them, and wished for a quiet corner with any one of them. They would let her read here, all right, until her eyes fell out of her head and she babbled of green fields; but they wouldn't let her read any of these.

"Oh, do you read mysteries?" said Christina, peering over Molly's shoulder at the entirely misleading cover of *The Daughter of Time*. "I love Agatha Christie."

You would, thought Janet. She said temperately, "I used to like the Tommy and Tuppence books a lot." Christina looked as if she, too, were thinking, you would.

She turned to Molly, looking, Janet thought, martyred, and said, "Which desk do you want?"

"I don't care," said Molly. "I work on my bed. At least"—and she cast a jaundiced eye at the bunk beds—"I did at home. Do we have to have these things?"

"You can't type on your bed," said Christina. "Do you want the desk by Janet's bookshelves or the one by my bed?"

"Wanna bet?" said Molly. "I don't care, really; but you do have a point. Do we want to clump up in little corners, or go wandering through each other's territory all the time?"

"We have to dress all in a row in the hallway," said Christina, rather wearily. Janet looked at her for the first time since the conversation began and saw that she was clutching a Smith-Corona portable typewriter case, presumably with typewriter inside it.

"Put Molly by my books," she said hastily. "You take that desk."

Christina thumped the typewriter down on the desk indicated, the one under the eastern windows. Janet walked over and considered the view: a bit of lawn, a circle of asphalt with a bed of geraniums in the middle of it, and the square brick building, like an elementary school, that the asphalt provided access to. Forbes Hall, one of the modern dormitories. Boring, but at least not distracting. Janet tried the southern window: a large lawn spattered with dandelions, bordered by a line of large pines where it met the street, and presently the site of two Frisbee games and a futile attempt to teach a large brown dog to fetch a stick. Janet thought her lake was probably more conducive to reflection; but it depended partly on what subject one had to reflect on. "What are you majoring in?" she asked Molly.

"Biology," said Molly.

"So am I," said Christina, as if she were reconsidering it. "Premed?"

"God, no," said Molly. "I want to study tidepools."

"I'm premed," said Christina.

"Be sure to tell us good-bye when the term starts," said Molly kindly. "And we'll give you a welcome-back party just before vacation. Unless Janet's premed too?"

Janet hooted, until she saw Christina's face. "I'm not a Biology major at all," she said.

"Well, what?"

"English."

"What for?" said Christina.

"Look," said Janet, irritated, "if the thing you liked best to do in the world was read, and somebody offered to pay you room and board and give you a liberal-arts degree if you would just read for four years, wouldn't you do it?"

"But what will you do after that?"

"Go to graduate school and read some more."

Christina sighed. Janet relented. "I guess I'll teach," she said. You did not, clearly, tell Christina that you wrote poetry. You might tell Molly later; or you might not.

"Well," said Christina, not visibly placated, "what are we going to do about this room?"

Molly kicked the nearest bunk bed lightly, then said, "Ha!" and dived into her pile of possessions again. She came up with a battered wooden thing like a misshapen boomerang, with a few flakes of red and white paint still clinging to its surface.

"What's that?" said Christina.

"My teddy bear," said Molly, rolling onto the bottom bunk Christina had made up and staring fixedly at the underside of the upper bunk. "Yep," she said, with considerable satisfaction. She got up again, gripped the wooden thing firmly, and smacked one of the uprights of the bunk bed with it.

"What?" said Christina in her weary tone.

"It's a field hockey stick," said Molly.

Janet began to laugh. "And you think Hesse is boring."

"Field hockey is the quintessence of skill and dispatch," said Molly, and took another swing at the bed. There was an ungodly bang—she had used a great deal more force this time—and the bunk wobbled.

"Do you sleep with it?" said Christina.

Molly said, "No, I keep it under the bed to repel boarders. It's still my teddy bear. Stand back, Tina, I don't want to get you on the backswing." She swung again.

Between the thumps of the hockey stick Janet could hear echoing thumps on the door. She staggered to her feet and went and opened it. It was one the girls from the ghost discussion. She was as short as Janet, and much thinner, with gold wire-rimmed glasses, huge brown eyes, and brown hair in braids. She was wearing a red Blackstock T-shirt so much too big for her that the lion and the snake of the Blackstock seal were touching noses and the dove had disappeared entirely in a fold. She said with some asperity, "What is going on in here?"

"We're taking apart the bunk beds," said Janet, with her best semblance of demureness.

"Really? May I watch? We've got them too, and they're nothing but trouble." She eyed Janet dubiously, and added, "My name's Peg Powell; I'm in four-ten. Sophomore. Classics."

Janet introduced herself and led Peg Powell down the room's little hallway. She was possessed of an intense desire to ask, "Are all Classics majors really crazy?" She said instead, "Do you know anything else about the Fourth Ericson ghost?"

"Oh, certainly. She throws Chase and Phillips and B. F. Skinner out the window."

"But then what does she use to prop up her bookcase?"

"Skeat," said Peg, with every evidence of sincerity.

Janet, who had spent the past month in a somewhat overwrought state and been up most of the previous night packing—for why hurry when you had only half a mile to travel to college?—collapsed upon Molly's desk, whooping.

"You didn't look like a giggler," said Molly, shaking her hands briskly and gripping the hockey stick again. Christina's bed was beginning to resemble a drawing of an irregular geometrical solid.

"Sorry," said Janet, with the tears running down her face. Her stomach felt as if Andrew had jumped on it.

"No, no, that's a good thing. Nobody wants a stuffy

roommate, even if she does read Madeleine L'Engle. Hello, what can we do for you?"

"Carry on," said Peg Powell. "If that works, I want to borrow your hockey stick."

"See?" said Molly, generally. "She knows what it is."

"I went to a pretentious Eastern girls' school," said Peg apologetically.

"So did I," said Molly.

Christina and Janet looked at one another with what Janet recognized as complete sympathy, the first moment of it that they had experienced. Neither the apologetic tone nor the deprecatory adjective alleviated their reaction in the slightest. For two seconds the Midwest was arrayed against the East. This threesome might work after all. Then Molly hit the bed again.

With a prolonged screeching, the upper bunk slid down its uprights and landed on the lower bunk, on Christina's pink-and-blue patchwork quilt, with a force that made the springs groan. A collection of dust and anonymous bits of stuff sprang out and suffused the sunny air of the room. Peg Powell said, "O moi egoh." Christina made a pathetic but muffled noise, as if somebody had stepped on her foot in church. Janet managed not to laugh again; if that had been her own quilt, she would have been furious. Molly, utterly unperturbed, dropped the hockey stick and examined the joints that connected the bed. "Uh-huh," she said. "Now that they've been loosened, these just twist off." And she twisted them off. The uprights swayed.

"What you ought to do," said Peg, "is put up a notice on the bulletin board in one of the new dorms with the tiny rooms—Dunbar or maybe Forbes. They've got normal beds and no space, so maybe they'll trade. May I borrow that hockey stick?"

"Well," said Molly dubiously, "I don't know. I think I've cracked it."

"Try women's Phys Ed," said Janet. "There's a field hockey course this term; I saw it in the catalog."

"If I can get one," said Peg to Molly, "will you come and apply it to the bed?"

"Sure," said Molly. "If you help us lift Christina's top bunk off her bottom one."

"Peg's not very big," said Christina. "We can do it, Molly."

"Though she be little, yet she is fierce," said Janet.

Nobody paid the slightest attention to this; Peg merely remarked, "You need four people to balance it," and the four of them, gasping, moved the upper piece of the bed off the lower and let it fall, which it did with an unmelodious groan and a thump that bounced dust out of the rug.

"The downstairs neighbors'll be up here next," said Christina.

Peg went off with a remark about meeting them at dinner if they wanted to eat in Taylor Hall. Christina brushed the bits of bed off her quilt and resumed her unpacking.

"What did Peg say that was so funny?" said Molly to Janet, sitting down on Janet's desk.

Janet laughed again, and told her.

"What's Skeat?" said Molly

"It's the standard Chaucer text," said Janet.

"Why is that funny?"

"It's the same size as the remedial math book."

"What?"

"That's what I say, too," said Christina.

Janet filled them in on the campus folklore about the old bookcases; they were polite but puzzled.

"Tell you what," said Molly, delving about in Janet's sealing wax and trying to fit the signet onto her thumb, "we'll use it as an index of college-induced madness. You tell us the same thing next fall, and the fall after, and see if we laugh."

"All right," said Janet. She put the unread books up next to the Hermann Hesse. Something was perturbing her; something was wrong with the joke. A member of the class of 1899 would not, of course, have had a remedial math book, the educational system having been better organized back then. And if she were a Classics major, she would need the Chase and Phillips for other things, even if she hadn't thrown it out the window. So it made sense for her to prop up her bookcase with Skeat. If she would have had Skeat. But would she have had Chase and Phillips?

"Excuse me," said Janet; and she went along to 410 and knocked on the door.

It was opened by the other member of the hall discussion: a round and somber young woman the color of soy sauce. Her hair was very short. The shape of her skull was beautiful, but something in her expression made Janet wish not to know what went on underneath it.

"Is Peg here?" she said

"Gone for a hockey stick."

Janet introduced herself. The other girl was called Sharon Washington. She was polite, but did not smile. Janet said, "I wanted to look at her Chase and Phillips for a moment; could you tell her?"

"Bottom shelf, one that's falling apart," said Sharon, standing back to let her in.

Peg's shelves were over her bed. Janet knelt on the blue-and-pink-and-purple Indian bedspread and took down a familiar thin black volume. Its binding was hanging by three strings. She found the copyright page. It was in its seventh printing, God alone knew why; but the earliest copyright date was 1941. Janet returned it carefully to its place between *Homer and the Heroic Tradition* and Liddell and Scott's *Greek-English Lexicon*, and stood up thoughtfully.

"Anything else, I'd say borrow it," said Sharon, "but it's worth my life to let that one out of here."

"Are you a Classics major too?" Janet asked cautiously.

"Fat chance. Geo. Nobody in the department is crazy, and there are more men than women. What about you?"

"English," said Janet.

Sharon looked judicious. "Won't hurt you, probably."

"Look, do you know about the Fourth Ericson ghost?"

"Sure. I'd throw Skinner out the window too. Drove Peg crazier than she is, last year."

Skinner. "But how could the ghost have Skinner? And how could she have Chase and Phillips, either, it was published in 1941?"

Janet was sorry the moment she said it. But either this was not in fact a story made up just to confound new students, or Sharon was a consummate actress, because she looked judicious again, then grinned. "Guess some later ghost gave 'em to her. Young ladies didn't throw books in the 1890's, did they? Somebody had to teach her to be unruly."

"Uh-huh," said Janet, unresentful. Sharon was probably a consummate actress. "Thanks; and good luck with your hockey stick."

She went back to the room. Christina had spread one of her towels on Molly's desk and was ironing shirts. Molly was lying on the unmade bottom bunk, reading *Magister Ludi* and scowling.

"Don't let them tell you about the Fourth Ericson ghost," said Janet.

"They already did," said Christina; Molly made a vague noise of the kind intended to persuade people you have heard them when in fact you haven't. Janet knew all about those. She was smiling as she went to shut the window her mother had thrown *The Wind in the Willows* out of.

CHAPTER 2

Three days later, emerging from a maelstrom of picnics, discussion groups, encounter sessions, hikes, tours, lectures, and demonstrations of everything from the shortcut through the library to the proper maintenance of one's bicycle in the climate of Minnesota, Janet trudged across campus to meet her advisor and discuss her first term's schedule.

It was raining, the kind of untimely rain you got in Minnesota one fall out of three. It would bring the leaves down before they had even finished turning, making October barren to the sight and the name of Indian summer a mockery. All the elms were giving up already, showering wet yellow leaves on the black asphalt of the sidewalks. The wind picked them up and plastered them to the reflecting glass of the Music and Drama Center. They did not improve that building's appearance; it was not ugly, but it sat between the pseudo-Gothic brick splendors of Ericson and the pure limestone lines of the chapel like a shoe box among jewelry chests. The rain pooled in all the low spots of the clever brick walks and terraces surrounding it, showing clearly all the flaws in its execution. Much of the Music and Drama Center was underground, and it leaked, and was going to cost a great deal of money to repair. Janet's father called it a perfect example of Modern Maladroit.

Janet resented it the more because it stood on what had once been a fine field of wildflowers, crossing which had taken far less time than going around so large a building. At least all the reflective glass of its entrances showed you the lovely middle of campus. Janet stared instead at her passing image, between the leaves: a figure too small and too sturdy, with a too-curly cloud of very pleasing red hair.

It was perhaps a mistake, she thought now that she could see herself whole and from a distance, to wear mint-green pants and an emerald-green shirt with a dark green jacket. Christina had looked at her oddly, and Christina always looked not only tidy but appealing, so her opinion on dress was worth considering. Always granting, of course, that the opinion on any subject was worth considering of somebody who had made three earnest efforts to read *A Wrinkle in Time* and pronounced it "silly."

Well, at least she had Molly. And Peg Powell turned out to be possessed of a complete set of the works of E. Nesbit, which had been foolishly left at home, but which Peg promised to bring back after the Christmas break. Janet's mind, wandering fuzzily back to her first meeting with Peg, presented her suddenly with a picture that halted her in the middle of a puddle. "Peg and Sharon haven't *got* bunk beds!" she said aloud.

A gust of wind blew into her eyes, and she began to walk again, carefully not talking to herself. No, it really had happened. Peg had distinctly said that she and Sharon had bunk beds; Sharon, in fact, had said Peg had gone for a hockey stick. But Janet could see with perfect clarity the blurred geometric pattern, purple and blue and dark pink, of Peg's bedspread, on the single bed with the four bookshelves above it: Chase and Phillips; Liddell and Scott; Whitman; the little red volumes of *The Iliad* and *The Odyssey*, two per epic; and a minor collection of books on music history crammed sideways at the end of the shelf. She had really seen that. She remembered the alarming dip of the bed under her knees, so that the lower shelf was almost too high for her to read the titles on it. No bunk beds. Sharon's bed had been across the room, covered with a white spread trimmed in eyelet lace and scattered with red pillows.

Janet gave up. She must have misunderstood something; or Peg had. Right now there was a class schedule to fight for, supposing she could ever find the office of her advisor.

Her advisor was one Melinda Wolfe, an instructor in the notorious Classics Department. This did not mean, of course, that one could find her in the building that housed that department. Classics and Music had been fighting it out for sole possession of Chester Hall since 1954; the only visible result of many bitter battles was the housing of the minor members of both departments in a huddle of temporary buildings put up behind Masters Hall during World War II.

Janet accordingly went on past Chester Hall where it glowered, among its ancient larches and its young maples, at the chapel surrounded by treeless lawn. She turned right and ducked around Masters Hall—another pseudo-Gothic splendor that moreover boasted a number of fat white columns. It was somewhat smaller than Ericson and pocked with window air conditioners. Once behind Masters, Janet began wandering the muddy gravel between the buildings of Masters Annex. Melinda Wolfe was in something called A40-6.

Janet found F, B, G, R, and Q. At this point she put her head into the Admissions Office and asked directions. Building A was between N and G, but set back; its address was concealed by a good growth of ivy. Room 40 was a small square room with doors opening off it, and one of these doors was numbered 6. There was no name tag, only a little wreath of dried plants: the downy gray-green feathers of southernwood, sage with its blue flowers, spiky rosemary, the carrotlike leaves and yellow flowers of fennel. The mingled smells were sharp and rather jolting. Janet was ten minutes late. She stopped woolgathering and knocked, and when a deep, pleasant voice invited her, she went in.

Melinda Wolfe had a green metal desk, stacks of books and pamphlets, a coffee maker, and a dazzling presence. Janet barely managed not to gape at her. This was the first person from the adult world she had seen in a week. No, that wasn't accurate. The professors who had conducted the discussion groups, the college employees who had provided advice, even some of the RA's, were all adult. The outside world, maybe; or maybe just the world of fashion. Janet vowed to tell Christina all about Melinda Wolfe, who had smooth, short red hair; who wore makeup so artful it made you think twice about your sensible decision not to use the damn stuff; who was slender and graceful and wore a gray wool dress that argued all too persuasively that no redhead should ever wear any other color. She had green eyes, too—or tinted contact lenses.

"I'm so glad you're late," she said. "The last one thinks he wants to be a doctor but he won't take any physics courses. Your file looks a lot more promising. Are you completely bewildered, or do you have some idea of what you want?"

Janet passed her the worksheet provided for this purpose. Melinda Wolfe read it and frowned. "English 10, Philosophy 12, Anthropology 10," she said.

"I want to get started on the English courses, since that's my major," said Janet. "And I need the other two for distribution. I thought the Philo sounded wonderful and the Anthro awful, so it makes a good mix."

"It's an intelligent schedule," said Melinda Wolfe, "if you're sure you want to be an English major. Wouldn't you like to look around a little first? You've got six credits from your AP course, and you're exempt from Freshman Composition, which is what most of your fellow English majors will be taking this term. You said in your entrance essay that you're interested in languages?"

Janet nodded. She was half impressed and half alarmed that Melinda Wolfe had bothered to notice all this. That was, of course, what good advisors were supposed to do, and all those exams and credits were a matter of public record. She still felt, obscurely, that her privacy had been violated.

"Well," said Melinda Wolfe, with a sharp look at Janet, "you might be better off majoring in Classics. Latin and Greek will give you an enormous advantage in learning any other Indo-European language, and introduce you to much of the work that's the basis of English literature. You could still get a Master's degree in English if you liked." She made these practical suggestions in a voice that sounded like Lady Macbeth urging on her reluctant husband. She couldn't help it, perhaps, any more than people with thin voices could.

"What would you recommend?" said Janet, trying not to sound wary.

"Greek Literature in Translation; that's how we snag most of our majors. Keep the Anthropology; you aren't going to like anything that department offers, and you might as well get it over with. I'd advise against this section of Philosophy—it's our visiting professor, and while his books are brilliant, he has a heavy Czechoslovakian accent."

"But I'm interested in the philosophical problems of classical science," said Janet. "I can sit in the front."

"All right. What about the Greek course? You can always take English 10 this winter or spring."

"But I want it from Evans," said Janet, "and he only teaches it in the fall."

"Are you sure you want it from Evans? He's reduced more students to tears than any three other professors put together."

"But he's good," said Janet, half as a question.

"Oh, he's magnificent, if you can stomach him. Don't sit in

the front of *his* class, that's all. You can wait until next fall, surely, with all these extra credits?"

"But I'd be a year behind in my major, if I decided I didn't want to switch to Classics," said Janet. She thought it over. Something about Melinda Wolfe put her back up; she hoped it wasn't just that Wolfe made her feel grubby. She asked, "When's beginning Greek offered?"

"Winter term."

"Well, that might work. Because I want English 11 from Evans, too, and he only does that in the spring."

"I really hate to see all you kids limiting your choices so soon," said Melinda Wolfe.

Janet discovered in herself a desire not to disappoint her advisor. She wanted to seem intelligent, not stubborn. She took a deep breath and said, "But if I can start an English major my sophomore year, why can't I start a Classics one then, if I decide I don't want the English?"

"True, O King," said her advisor, with perfect mildness. "All right. Let me sign that. But if any of those classes are closed before your number comes up, remember Greek Literature in Translation."

"Okay," said Janet. "Thanks."

Melinda Wolfe wrote her name with economy, no flourish; and looked up at Janet. "If you read science fiction," she said, "you'll like Herodotus."

Now how did she know what Janet read? "I'll bear it in mind," Janet said, collected her signed schedule, and got herself out of there.

It had stopped raining. It seemed very dark for eleven in the morning. The wind was breaking the clouds up, and the whole sky was taking on the luminous grayish-yellow that always gave Janet a headache. The ivy rasped against the corrugated iron of the temporary buildings. There was no other sound.

Janet was puzzling over Melinda Wolfe rather than looking where she was going, and found herself blinking at a dead end.

A faded handwritten sign half grown over with ivy said, "Greek 2 will meet in Library 406 from now on."

Janet sighed and turned to retrace her steps. It was getting darker, but the air was still now. She stood looking through a dusty window into a room piled with boxes, trying to orient herself. Around the next corner, gravel crunched.

Janet stooped for a rock, shoved her hand into her pocket, and backed herself up against the ivy. What are you doing? she asked herself. It's only another lost person.

The gravel crunched again and the other lost person came around the corner. She was tall, taller than Tina. She wore a long red cape so heavy that it hardly moved as she walked, and red boots. She had red and black hair, the red like her cloak and the black like coal. On her broad forehead and high-boned face was no expression at all. She walked past Janet in a waft of some bitter smell like the ivy's only more complex. Janet opened her mouth as the woman walked right at the faded sign, and left it open. The red cloak, the long mass of streaked hair, mingled with the ivy and, rustling, disappeared.

Janet threw her rock at the sign. It bent the fragile paper back and disappeared. Fine, thought Janet. The ivy hides a doorway. She went the other way, quickly.

Janet came around Masters Hall again and looked across the wide green space, set randomly with young oak trees, that separated Masters from the chapel. Between the green grass and the pale glowing sky, the chapel's gray stone looked white. The deep red of the oak leaves was as rich as blood. The day wasn't dark at all. It was just those narrow walkways full of the bitter smell of the ivy that seemed so. Janet rubbed her eyes briskly, and went to meet Christina and Peg for lunch.

Peg had a perverse fondness for eating in the dining hall that cowered under the mass of Taylor Hall. Since she also possessed a much stronger will than you would expect from her size or the meek way she blinked at you from behind her glasses, Janet had already spent a great deal more time than she liked in the dim vastness of Taylor.

It was especially bad today; three of the fluorescent fixtures were flickering and two were out. The light seeping in through the high, barred basement windows looked left over from the previous century, like Fourth Ericson's ghost. The dark wooden tables, round and square and rectangular, that made Eliot Hall charming to eat in, sank into the gloom here as if they had something to hide. The red or green coverings of the chair seats looked like gray that had been bled on or brown that had grown mold over itself. The smell of vegetable soup seemed to be last week's, and the general air last year's.

Janet got herself a bowl of soup, a grilled-cheese sandwich, and a couple of apples to smuggle out again, and went looking for Peg and Christina.

They were at a square table that had been set too close to the line of people waiting for lunch, but Janet knew already that budging either of them was almost impossible. She sat down with her back to the steam tables and hoped nobody would trip over her.

"How was your advisor?" she said to Christina, who had expressed enormous apprehension at the discovery that her advisor was a member of the Religion Department, as if he might require her to eschew learning evolution.

"He was just fine," said Christina. "He tried to get me to take some Latin, but that was all. I might take some next year."

"Who is he?" said Peg.

"Fields," said Christina.

"Oh, you should have asked me about him; he's great. I'm taking New Testament Greek from him this term. He has a wonderful sense of humor. Sharon said you had some nut in the Religion Department, and I thought it must be Olsen."

"Why'd he want you to take Latin?" said Janet.

"Oh, you know, because of medical terminology and biological jargon and all that; he said it made them easier to figure out."

"My advisor tried to get me to take Greek," said Janet.

"Who's your advisor?" said Peg.

"Melinda Wolfe."

"Well, she's in the Classics Department; what d'you expect?"

"Fields didn't try to get Tina to take any Religion courses, did he?"

"No; but Classics is full of demon recruiters. Wolfe is okay, though. She lives in Ericson Apartment, and gives a big party each spring."

"You've got to get a look at her, Tina," said Janet. She was halfway into her description of Melinda Wolfe, and was actually holding all Christina's attention, when Molly arrived with a tray that contained nine little china bowls of tapioca pudding.

"Bleah!" said Peg, edging away from her.

"I'm having my period; I can't eat anything else. Talk about something distracting."

"I'm telling Tina about Melinda Wolfe," said Janet. Molly looked dubiously at her tapioca, which Janet decided was a license to continue. "She made me think gray was the only color for redheads."

"It depends on your complexion," said Christina. She was wearing gray herself; it made her eyes look very blue, which was most unfair. "You could get one of the Blackstock T-shirts in gray, and see how it looked. It might wash your eyes out; I'm not sure." She had been picking all the pineapple out of her fruit cup as Janet spoke; now she speared a bleached and wrinkled grape with her fork and scowled at it. "Oh!" she said. "I thought that name was familiar. Some of the kids on the Bio Tour were talking about Wolfe. They said she's a —"

Molly's head came up like a dog's that hears unfamiliar footsteps. Peg said, "A lesbian? They say that about everybody who lives in Ericson."

"And what do they say about the guys who live in Dunbar?" said Molly.

Peg grinned at her. "They say they're all jocks," she said.

"What a blessing for them," said Molly sourly.

"Well?" said Christina to Janet.

"Well, what?"

"Did she act like—"

"How the hell should I know?" Janet snapped, and immediately felt guilty. She was reacting not to what Christina had said or almost said about Wolfe, but to the fact that neither Molly nor Peg had liked it. She added more temperately, "She tried to get me to change my major to Classics. That's all." Was that what had put her back up? No, surely not; Melinda Wolfe had been perfectly impersonal: she had just seemed to know too much and to be using it to push her notions of what Janet should do. None of this would enlighten Tina. Janet said, "Peg, I wanted to ask you—"

"Speaking of which," said Peg, very softly, "coming in the door this very minute are five wonderful reasons to be a Classics major. Don't stare at them, Janet, wait till they come around the corner."

Janet heard a crowd of boys pass, laughing, and obediently waited until they shoved their trays around the corner and began helping themselves to milk or soda and making obscene comments about the remaining tapioca pudding. She had intended to glance up casually, but she found herself staring. Two blonds, two with dark hair, one redhead. If anybody had asked her, she would have said they were in Theater, not Classics. They had beautiful voices, and a presence that warmed and lit the dingy hall as if all the lights had been repaired instantaneously. Janet looked up, but the dead lights were still dead and the flickering ones still pulsing.

She looked at the five boys more carefully. They had a full complement of long hair, beards, and mustaches; but she thought of the theater again, of historical drama. They were far too tidy to be her contemporaries. But they wore jeans and T-shirts, or muslin smocks with embroidery, or unironed sports shirts, just like anybody else. They talked like other college students, if those jokes over the tapioca were any example. They removed themselves and their trays to the next room, where they could smoke. And that took care of that, thought Janet, half displeased and half relieved.

"Too skinny," said Molly, stacking four empty bowls and looking thoughtfully at the rest.

"Can you introduce me?" said Christina.

"Sure you don't want to major in Classics?" said Peg to Janet.

"What is this obsession?" demanded Janet. "Sharon says she's a Geo major because there are more men than women, and now you—"

"Hah," said Peg. "When Sharon was eleven, she had a rock collection so huge she had to sleep in the basement. She just likes shocking the young."

"What about you?" said Molly, also sounding rather irate.

"I just thought, Wolfe had provided the intellectual bait, and I'd provide some other sort," said Peg, peaceably. "Just doing my share for my department. Every teacher in it is wonderful, really." She looked at Christina. "If you take Latin, you'll meet two of the boys," she said. "They're really into Greek, but you've got to have two terms of Latin for the major, and they're running out of time."

"I guess it'd be a change from math and science," said Christina. "Which two?"

"Thomas Lane," said Peg, "that's the tall blond one. And Jack Nikopoulos, that's the tall one with dark hair."

"Both the tall ones! How can I resist? Who were the other three?"

"The short one with the curly dark hair was Nicholas Tooley. He's just a freshman, but I know he's going to take Latin."

"How?"

"He lives down the hall from Sharon's boyfriend. The

redhead's Robert Benfield and the short blond one is Robert Armin. Benfield is Rob and Armin is Robin. Benfield plays tennis. Armin's great love seems to be beer, but he must do something besides drink because he's the only freshman in the history of the department to be exempted out of all the beginning courses. They let him go straight to Aristophanes." She turned to Janet.

"What did you start to ask me, Jan, before the boys came in?"

"Something about your bedspread," said Janet. She sat very still, summoning up the threads of the conversation; she almost had it.

"You can get them at Jacobsen's," said Peg.

"We have to go anyway," said Christina, "to get the material for the curtains. Do you guys want to go now, if it's not raining?"

"Can I come?" said Peg. "Sharon broke my big mug and I'm afraid she'll buy me a new one."

"Why not let her?" said Molly, standing up and stretching alarmingly. "Stupid body," she said, picking up the tray. "There's no point in all these histrionics."

"I'm not being histrionic," said Peg, with mild indignation. "Sharon'll buy something with some sick Hallmark verse on it."

"I meant my period," said Molly. "I wouldn't have pegged Sharon for the sentimental type."

"Huh," said Peg, also standing. "Just you wait."

When they got outside, the sun had come out and was making rhinestones out of the raindrops. Janet wished it were still raining; what she wanted to ask Peg, she had thought of first in the rain.

"Do you really want a pink-and-blue Indian bedspread?" said Molly to Janet. They had lagged behind the other two; Peg was a brisk walker and Christina had long legs.

"No," said Janet. She walked faster; Peg and Christina were almost out of sight. The backs of her legs hurt from climbing to the top of the observatory yesterday. When she was in grade school, she had gone up there every day. "Oh, hell," she said. "I forgot to sign up for any Phys Ed."

"So did I," said Molly. "This time of the month the mere thought of exercise makes me homicidal. What were you thinking of taking?"

"Fencing," said Janet.

"Because you're fierce, I suppose. Everybody will have the reach on you; why don't you take Archery with me?"

"I'm fast," said Janet, rather nettled. She stopped under the ancient cedar trees that marked the main entrance to Blackstock College, averted her eyes from the brick box, the color of tomato soup, that was Blackstock's newest dormitory, and held out her hands to Molly at waist height, palms down. "Try me," she said.

Molly grinned unnervingly, positioned her own hands about an inch under Janet's, palms up, and began rattling out, "There was a boy named Eustace Clarence Scrubb, and he almost deserved it." She snatched her hands away suddenly, but Janet slapped them smartly.

"Not bad," said Molly, with a kind of grudging pleasure. "Try again. Shit! I can beat all my brothers at this. Come on. Well, hell. You *are* fast. Okay, give it to 'em for me, too. But I want a rematch when my body's not in rebellion."

"Oh, come on, take fencing with me." said Janet. Janet started walking again, off the grounds of Blackstock and along Church Street with its collection of tall, narrow, cut-rate Victorian houses. "Didn't you play Three Musketeers when you were little?"

"Pirates," said Molly.

"That's swordplay, too."

"We used clubs," said Molly. "No, I want to take Archery, because what I always wanted to play was Robin Hood and they said if we did, I'd have to be Maid Marian and be rescued."

"Maid Marian didn't need rescuing," said Janet, shocked.

"My brothers thought she did," said Molly. "My God, look at

that house. I didn't think you had houses like this out in the Wild West."

"Minnesota became a state in 1857," said Janet, patiently. "That's the President's House; that reception thing for supper tonight is there. They'll give you a guided tour." She had always thought the President's House was profoundly ugly, but there was no denying that it was impressive.

"Is it haunted, too?"

"Not that I know of."

"Why is the trim that ghastly pink?"

"Like Peg's bedspread. Henry Barker's wife painted it that color in 1911, and now it's a tradition."

"Just like the language requirement," murmured Molly. "We'd better move, or Tina will buy pink curtains with little flowers on them."

"I thought she was talking about red stripes."

"Only to placate me."

"We could get a calico print," said Janet, "with red stripes *and* little pink flowers."

"Excuse me," said Molly; "I have to beat you both there." She took off running at a speed amazing in somebody who was suffering from cramps. Janet ran after her for perhaps a block, which was enough to prove that Molly's legs were faster than her hands. Janet then went sideways around the Methodist Church, and took the shortcut.

She arrived in front of Jacobsen's plate-glass front before the rest of them, with a stitch in her side and a sensation that the weather was a great deal hotter and damper than she had thought. What had she been doing with herself this last year? This run had been nothing to her as recently as her sophomore year in high school, when she had raced Danny Chin from River Street to the high school, and beaten him by a yard.

Peg and Christina were coming along the sidewalk now, peering into the window of the music store; making oh-how-cute faces at the little bookstore, which meant the cat George

Eliot and her latest litter were wallowing all over the window display; and then, seeing Janet, they looked puzzled and walked faster.

Molly came pounding up behind them, passed them while narrowly missing a light pole, and skidded to a stop next to Janet. Her face was perfectly white, and with the freckles looked more like a chocolate-chip cookie than anything else. Her breathing was much easier than Janet's. Her gray University of Pennsylvania T-shirt was dark with sweat under the arms and between her breasts, and her hair had gone fuzzy with damp.

"Show me how you did that," she said without gasping.

"Later," wheezed Janet.

"Look at Peg and Tina," chortled Molly. She wrapped her arms around her middle. "Shut up," she told it firmly.

"What's the matter?" said Peg.

"She was afraid Tina'd buy curtains with flowers on them," said Janet.

"Only because you threatened to help," said Molly. "It's just cramps."

"Have you taken anything for them?"

"Nothing works."

Peg dug in the pocket of her denim skirt and produced a tiny enamel box with an iris on it. "Want a Happy Pill?"

Molly's big blue eyes narrowed instantly, and a look of the most glowering suspicion spread over her cheerful face. Janet was alarmed; Peg, however, was not only unperturbed, but appeared to understand. "It's perfectly legal," she said. "It's codeine and aspirin. The Health Service gives them to people when they have flu or strep throat, and we all hoard them for when we really need them. If you don't need to use your brain for anything this afternoon, you should take one."

Molly accepted the pill and they pushed open the doors and went into Jacobsen's. It smelled of cloth, beef jerky, and rubber, and looked as the labyrinth of the Minotaur might have if it had been built by the owner of a nineteenth-century general store. Half an hour later they emerged with heavy material of striped cotton in red, blue, and green that was going to clash dreadfully with Christina's quilt.

The sun had gone behind the clouds again, and a twisty damp wind was rattling discarded paper cups in the gutters, since it was not strong enough to pick up the sodden leaves. The light was a diffuse version of the greeny-yellow that precedes a tornado, but the sky was more confused than threatening.

When they reached their dormitory and opened the door of their room, they found a folded paper lying on the carpet, addressed to Janet. In a stiff backhand full of peculiar s's, it said, "We forgot your Phys Ed. Write in whatever you want, but think about either Swimming, which you need to graduate, or Outdoor Fitness, which is good in this weather. Archery and Fencing are rumored to be bad choices this year; the usual teacher is on sabbatical. Melinda Wolfe."

Janet sat on her bed looking at this epistle for some time. Then she unearthed her schedule sheet from under a box of typing paper Christina had bought yesterday, and wrote in, "Fencing, Swifte, 2a," under the list of her other classes.

"Hey, Molly," she said. "Wolfe says Archery and Fencing aren't a good idea this year because the usual instructor is on sabbatical."

"Are you taking Fencing?"

"Yes."

" And I'm taking Archery. At least I am if I can find my schedule."

"It's under the curtain material."

"Seems like a funny thing for an advisor to tell you," said Molly, heaving herself off the top bunk and shoving the package of material from her desk to the floor.

"Don't get that all dusty," said Christina's voice from the hallway, where she was piling boxes in search of her sewing basket.

Molly, grimacing, put the material on her desk chair and took her schedule back to Janet's bed.

"How are you feeling?" said Janet.

"Dopey," said Molly, sitting down with a force that made the springs creak. She scribbled on her schedule and flung it on the floor. "I still hurt, but I don't care as much."

"Maybe you should try whiskey."

"No way. If I'm going to feel like a nineteenth-century consumptive, I demand port at the the very least." She lay back until her head dangled off the side of the bed, and sighed heavily. "I miss my ex-boyfriend," she said. "He was a jerk, but he had wonderful hands. I told him he should be a vet, but he wants to be a CPA. He used to rub my back."

"Why was he a jerk?"

"Oh, he thought reading fiction was a waste of time, and he thought I couldn't be a scientist if I was rendered miserable once a month by misapplied female hormones, and he was rude to my brothers."

"Why'd you go out with him at all?"

"He kissed very well," said Molly, still upside-down.

"Why'd you get to know him well enough to find that out?"

"He had a very large vocabulary," said Molly. She rolled over, banged her elbow on the end of the bed, and tucked it under herself, making muffled sounds.

"What in the world's the matter?" demanded Christina, emerging with a quilted sewing basket appliquéd in pink and yellow ducks.

"Hit my funny bone," said Molly.

"You're turning red," observed Janet.

"Peg says one of the Roberts—Armin, I think—gives good backrubs," said Christina. She made for her own bunk and tripped, as usual, over its discarded upper portion.

"You bump your head on the upper bunk as you stand up," said Molly to Janet, "and we'll all be casualties. Tina, maybe we could lug that down to the basement and hide it somewhere."

"Not with you all full of codeine and aspirin," said Christina. "After supper, maybe."

"How *does* alcohol mix with codeine and aspirin?" said Molly. "I can't remember."

"Nora's got a *PDR*," said Christina.

"A what?" said Janet.

"*Physician's Desk Reference.* It lists a lot of drugs and their side effects."

"Why?" said Molly.

"Somebody killed herself a couple of years ago with an overdose of sleeping pills. Nora thought if the RA'd known what to do maybe the kid wouldn't have died."

"They don't tell you *that* when they're trying to persuade you to come here," said Molly. "Did Nora say why?"

"Academic pressure," said Christina. "She had some problem with her boyfriend, Nora said, but it wouldn't have mattered if she hadn't been under so much pressure."

"Premed?" said Janet.

"Classics," said Christina.

"I want you guys to promise me something," said Molly, sliding herself, again alarmingly, into a sitting position on the floor with her back against the bed.

"What?" said Janet, obligingly.

"If any of us is thinking of doing something like that, we have to tell the other two first. I mean it. Even if we don't room together all four years; even if we haven't seen one another for months; even if we think we hate each other. And the other ones have to promise to listen, no matter what, if one of us calls and says it's important."

"You'd better assign us a password," said Janet. She caught Christina's eye, trying to gauge her reaction. Christina shrugged; Janet recognized, already, her you-guys-are-weird-but-I-guess-this-is-harmless gesture.

"I'm serious," said Molly.

"So am I. Something we won't forget in two years."

"The Snark is a Boojum."

They smiled at one another. Janet said reluctantly, "That doesn't mean anything to Tina. It should be something we'll all remember."

Christina, still delving around in her sewing basket, gurgled suddenly and said, "Pink curtains."

Molly rolled her eyes. Janet said to her, "Will you remember?"

"How could I forget?"

"All right, then. I swear."

"And I," said Molly.

"Me, too," said Christina.

CHAPTER
3

Registration was held on a Thursday. It was raining, which meant that anybody with the slightest worry about getting into a particular class stood in long lines, outside the old gymnasium where Registration took place, and became damp and disgruntled. Janet got into all her classes.

Out of what she could only view as the College's customary perversity, said classes began the next day, instead of waiting decently until Monday. She had Fencing first. Two-A felt earlier than she had hoped it would; to get up at nine-thirty was not so dreadful, but to be up and dressed and fed by then left her still a little bleary, and not inclined to physical effort. She supposed that, after the class, she would feel invigorated but not inclined to intellectual effort, just in time for her first class in the philosophical problems of classical science.

It was, of course, since everybody was fated to spend it indoors, the most beautiful of autumn days, full of cloud shadows and piercing blue sky and the hope that some of those maples might hold on to their leaves long enough to turn them red before they fell. "Do it, trees," said Janet softly to the nearest clump, which held two healthy young maples and a rather straggly ash.

Janet dodged out of the chilly shadow of the decaying Student Union and went along past the chapel and the Music and Drama Center, trying to walk briskly and feeling like a film that somebody had slowed down. She turned her head away from the reflecting glass of the M&D Center, and looked across the little natural amphitheater in which, next week, the Classics Department would be staging *Lysistrata*. They would do so in the shadow of Olin Hall, a nondescript brick building trimmed with metal strips that made it look like a radiator.

That was where Molly and Christina would be spending most of their time for the next four years. Janet turned away from that, too, wandered down the middle of the asphalt road between the M&D Center and the north end of Ericson, and moved a little more quickly for the Women's Phys Ed Center. There were enough people heading for it that the time must be close to nine-thirty.

Somewhere to her right, a husky tenor sang, "'I have heard the mermaids singing, each to each. I do not think that they will sing for me.'"

Janet stopped short. She was, just for a moment, annoyed. Like to see you do that with *Murder in the Cathedral*, she thought grumpily. Then, as the voice performed a great leap into some other tune entirely and sang, "'I have lingered in the chambers of the sea'," she became wildly intrigued. Why shouldn't he sing T. S. Eliot? And where, oh, where, had he gotten the music?

She stood waiting, and though the song stopped, a small and wiry young man with wild curly hair emerged suddenly from the shrubbery, his arms full of books that looked as if they had already seen four years' use, and plunged past her in the direction of the Women's Center.

"Excuse me," called Janet, sprinting after him.

He turned, looking alarmed. He had huge blue eyes, behind a lopsided and dilapidated pair of horn-rimmed glasses, and a blunt face decorated with mild acne. "Hello?" he said.

"You were singing 'The Love Song of J. Alfred Prufrock,'" said Janet, falling into step beside him. He had begun walking again as soon as she caught up to him.

"A point for you, lady," he said.

"Where'd you get the music?"

"I wrote it."

Janet experienced a treacherous upwelling of instant adoration, and quashed it violently. "May I hear it sometime?"

"When it's done," he said.

"Have you put a lot of poetry to music?"

"Not really—look, I have to go in here—what's your name?"

"I have to go in here, too. Janet Carter."

"Are you taking Fencing?"

"Yes."

"Thank God. If I finish the song soon, will you be my partner? Everybody else in this class is six feet tall."

"Yes, of course, if you tell me your name."

"Nick Tooley," said the dark-haired boy, and smiled as, propping his huge load precariously in one arm, he held open the door of the building for her. He was one of the Classics majors Peg had pointed out in Taylor dining hall, the one that Molly thought too skinny and Tina had not taken note of because he was short.

Everybody else in the fencing class was not six feet tall, but certainly they all exceeded five feet eight, except for the instructor. She was shorter than Janet, but very sturdy, with gray hair in two braids, a sharp chin and nose looking incongruous in her round, wrinkled face, and a crisp voice.

She sat them all down on the polished gym floor and treated them to a half-hour lecture on fencing, its history and nature, followed by a half hour's demonstration of stretching exercises that, she intimated, if performed faithfully everyday, would, by the time she actually let any of them have a foil, prevent undue injury. Next time, she finished, they would be allowed to put on masks and protective jackets.

Janet, accustomed to high-school physical education classes wherein it was tacitly assumed that everybody already knew how to do everything and was simply panting to start doing it right now, was extremely pleased. As they finished their prescribed stretches and got up, she looked sideways at Nick Tooley and caught him shutting the notebook he had been scribbling in during the lecture. He had not been taking notes, unless he always took them in sonnet form. He not only put poetry to music, he wrote it.

He caught her eye. "This will never do," he said. "I'm going to ask her if she'll give me an accelerated program."

"And what about your partner?" said Janet.

"Oh, I'll still come to class. I just need a foil this weekend. Where do you live?"

Janet just managed not to give her parents' address. "Fourth Ericson."

"I'll call you if I finish the music before Monday," he said, and marched determinedly across the floor to the fencing instructor.

Janet thought she knew a dismissal when she heard one. She went outside. The Women's Center stood on the top of a steep hill overlooking a vast playing field, the stream that fed the lakes, and, on the stream's far side, the tamer part of the Arboretum attached to Blackstock. The willow trees along the banks of the stream were bright yellow. The woods were still mostly green, with here and there a tinge of yellow. All the sumac had turned red. It might be a good autumn after all.

Janet had an hour for lunch, after which she would get a solid block of Philosophy and Anthropology; her English class would reign in lonely splendor on Tuesday, Thursday, and Saturday mornings. She had half promised to meet Christina and Peg in Taylor. She watched the wind ruffle the smooth-cut grass of the playing field, and considered the ducks sailing on the stream, and turned abruptly into Eliot Hall, where one could dine in a building set into the hill, and watch the ducks while one did it.

She found Nora and Sharon occupying a round table for eight in the spot with the best view, and decided they were unlikely to be having a private conversation. She managed to catch Sharon's eye while she was still several tables away. Sharon didn't smile, not a muscle moved in her dark face; but she did wave and pat the back of the chair next to her. Janet carried her tray over there and took the seat offered her.

"I was beginning to think you never ate," said Nora, who did smile. Janet wondered if they had chosen her to be an RA because she looked so wholesome and ordinary, with her round face and straight brown hair and glasses. "Or Molly or Christina, either," added Nora.

"Peg's got 'em used to Taylor already," said Sharon.

Nora rolled her eyes. Janet spread the paper napkin on her lap, picked up her dish of stewed tomatoes, and said, "Now don't look. I'm going to mush these into the macaroni and cheese."

Sharon covered her face with her hands. Nora said, "I've already watched Sharon pepper her cottage cheese until it turned gray; what's a few tomatoes to that?"

"How are you and your roommates getting along?" she added.

"Molly's great," said Janet. This was not tactful, but she knew what Nora was probably wanting to say, and they might as well shorten the process.

"Tina feels left out, you know," said Nora, apparently agreeing with this desire.

"She *is* left out," said Janet. "It's not our fault."

"She expected better, from your letters."

"It's the Admissions Office," said Janet. "I said I liked folk music and Molly said she went to rock concerts and Christina said she liked Bach, so they said, oh, look, three people who listen to music, and stuck us in the same room."

"Same thing happened to Peg and me," said Sharon. "She used to make jewelry and I had a rock collection. Bingo. We had to put a clothesline up in the middle of our room fall term, with sheets hanging from it; and Peg climbed in and out the window 'cause I had the door in my half."

"So why did you room together again?"

"That's what I'm saying," said Sharon. "Give Tina a chance."

"She may be athletic," said Nora, "but that doesn't mean she's stupid."

"I'm athletic," said Janet.

"Well, go play tennis with her, then."

"I hate tennis. And she hates Ping-Pong, because I asked her."

Nora sighed, and to Janet's considerable relief appeared to relinquish her post as lecturer. "Just think about it, okay?"

"Sure," said Janet. If Christina had complained to Nora, she probably did feel unhappy; unlike Molly, Tina did not favor you with any details at all of her history, her private life, or her opinions. "I know she can't be stupid if she's here," said Janet, "but I don't think she has any sense of humor."

"She has so," said Sharon.

"It's just not verbal," said Nora.

Janet, her mouth mercifully full of macaroni and tomato, gazed at them with what she hoped was an enlightened and tolerant expression, while wondering how in the world you could possibly have a nonverbal sense of humor if you were over the age of two. She hoped they didn't mean Christina was a practical joker. There hadn't been any sign of it so far.

"That reminds me," she said, having swallowed, "can we store the top part of Christina's bunk bed in the basement?"

Sharon chortled and Nora looked horrified. "Don't tell me another thing," Nora said. "You want to get pregnant, you want to get arrested for selling dope, you want to fail all your courses because you've been playing poker for six weeks straight, you want to go broke on the pinball machines in the Student Union—fine, I'm your man, I'll help you out. But don't you talk to me about College property and especially don't you talk to me about removing it from the rooms it's supposed to be in."

"Gosh," said Janet, "thanks, Nora, I'll remember that."

"And don't talk to Melinda Wolfe about it, either," said Nora, unsmiling.

"I wouldn't have thought of her," said Janet, reflectively. "I know she's the Resident Advisor for Ericson, but she's not the kind of person you run to if you're in trouble."

"Too shiny," said Sharon.

Janet grinned. "Polished," she agreed.

"She'll eat you alive," said Nora.

"Not me," said Sharon. "I'd choke her."

Nora laughed. Janet wanted to ask a number of questions, but all of them were indicative of an unhealthy and inappropriate curiosity.

Melinda Wolfe had advised her not to take the philosophy section she attended after lunch, but Melinda Wolfe had been wrong. Professor Soukup did indeed have a very heavy accent that made Janet think, the first time she heard it and always, of spy movies. But he could, it appeared, see very well, through his thick bifocal glasses, the particular kind of puzzled expression generated by an inability to understand what he was saying, as opposed to what he meant by it. When he detected this expression on any of the twenty-two students in the class, he would first repeat what he had said and then paraphrase it. This was not nearly so wearying as Janet had been afraid it might become after she had heard him do it once or twice. Partly this was because, if you were not the one puzzled, you could make a game out of how exactly he would choose to rephrase himself. And partly it was because the material he was offering in his slow, blinking, bald way was both complex and fascinating.

Janet emerged from her first seventy minutes of him with a heavily scribbled syllabus—because of course the list posted in the bookstore was quite wrong, it always was, Professor Soukup supposed it must be his handwriting. She felt the same kind of euphoria she had experienced when she opened *The Worm Ourobouros* at random and read, "O Queen, somewhat I know of grammarie and divine philosophy, yet must I bow to thee for such learning, that dwellest here from generation to generation and dost commune with the dead."

Anthropology 10, in the uncertain grasp of one Mr. King, boded no such delights. If Janet had met Mr. King as a fellow student, she would have liked him. He was tall and thin, with unruly brown hair, a long nose, glasses almost as ramshackle as Nick Tooley's, and the nervous, earnest air of somebody who knows a great deal but is at a loss as to how to impart it.

He did not look old enough to be teaching; and in fact taught nothing, taking instead half an hour of his seventy minutes to go over the syllabus with the class, and to explain how many papers they would be expected to write and when said papers would be due. Nor did it seem that he communed with the dead—the dates on all the books except one showed that the authors were either still alive or but recently dead, and their titles did not make communion sound worth the trouble anyway. The exception, *Argonauts of the Western Pacific*, did have an intriguing title. Janet hoped she could make the best of it all.

She had forty extra minutes to make the best of right now, emerging from the dim hall of the old library into the sunlight. She could go to the bookstore, which had been a palace of wild delight to her from the age of seven; except that her checkbook was in her room. She could go for a walk.

She marched along the campus's central sidewalk, under the huge yellowing elms, past the pale chapel with its spiked tower, past the Music and Drama Center, its sides full of Olin Hall and little fluttering trees. She dodged around Forbes Hall's uninspiring square, skidded down the dusty gully in the steep hill that both Forbes and Eliot sat on, and arrived in a flurry of dead leaves at the point where the lower of Blackstock's two small lakes met the stream that she had watched the ducks sail on at lunch. There was a weathered wooden bridge here, with a pleasing arch to it, and on its right on the near bank of the stream an enormous half-dead willow in whose hollow trunk a duck would usually lay her eggs in the spring. Janet peered into the hollow, out of habit; and four ducks that had been diving desultorily in the middle of the stream righted themselves and sped in her direction, making mild and hopeful comment.

When they arrived in the shadow of the willow and she still had not thrown anything into the water, their remarks became ruder. Janet felt in the pockets of her pants and discovered the last of her stolen apples. She bit a few pieces from it, spat them into her hand, and flung them onto the green, moving water. The ducks billed them morosely and went back to their diving.

Janet took a bite for herself and crossed the bridge. She could now turn right and follow the stream through the Upper Arboretum, emerging eventually in her own neighborhood; or she could follow the sidewalk between the lower lake and Dunbar Hall, climb a hill, scramble through the lilac maze, cross a highway, and plunge into the Lower Arboretum, from which, if one did not eventually retrace one's steps, one would not emerge for three days.

A squirrel streaked down the lawn of Dunbar Hall, stopped in the middle of the sidewalk just in front of her, and looked hopeful.

"You'll be sorry," said Janet, biting off a chunk of apple and dropping it onto the sidewalk. The squirrel snatched it up, took it into the long grass on the shore of the lake, dropped it, sniffed it, ran up a tree, and regarded Janet upside-down with a cold rodent stare that made her rather uneasy. She had been feeding animals on Blackstock's campus for eleven years, and although always impudent, the squirrels had never behaved quite like this.

"I had no idea you guys were so fussy," she said to it.

"Are you addressing us?" said a nice southern voice.

Janet jumped a little and looked back at the sidewalk, where an entwined couple stood smiling at her. The boy was stocky and brown-haired and burned red by the sun; he suited his voice. The girl was a head taller, as blond as Christina but ethereally built. She was probably from California.

"No, to the squirrel," said Janet; the truth was easier. "I bit it off a piece of apple with my own teeth, and you'd think its mother told it never to eat after anybody."

"They're all spoiled," said the boy. "They like godawful things—that pasty bread the Food Service gives you, or I saw some dumb freshman feeding one of them a Twinkie the other day, and the little bugger just gobbled it down."

"The ducks wouldn't touch the apple either," said Janet.

"Well, that's more reasonable," said the girl. "Apples don't grow in the water. There's a couple of swans down on the river that eat anything, if you want to try them."

"Thanks," said Janet, "but I don't mind eating it myself, it's just they all expect to be fed."

"Spoiled rotten," said the boy. "Make stew out of them, that's what I say."

"He's a Physics major," said the girl pityingly to Janet; "he gets these notions." She propelled the boy on down the sidewalk, where he seemed perfectly pleased to go.

Janet looked after them, and the squirrel began to scold her, The girl had the kind of shining charisma that the boys Peg had pointed out in Taylor had; but she talked like a Bio major. Well, it was silly to generalize on the basis of what people were majoring in, anyway. She went on past Dunbar toward the Upper Arboretum, past several students sprawled on beach towels, reading *Paradise Lost*, *Ulysses*, and Volume I of the *Norton Anthology of English Literature*. English majors studying for their comprehensive examinations, probably; it was really too early to be doing mere classwork so assiduously. None of them looked up as she went by.

She had forgotten what a mistake it was to come to the lilac maze in the autumn. The twenty-foot-high tangles of unpruned bushes, glazed with powdery mildew and hung about with dead blossoms, enclosed her in a cheerless world of trampled grass, unfruitful brambles, and seeding dandelions. Janet moved faster, but the ground was lumpy and the bent-over grasses like snares. In the center of the maze she came across another couple, flat on the grass and oblivious. Both of them were tall, with long dark hair. Janet backed quietly away and became entangled in the byways of the maze, which the College never seemed to prune the same way two years in a row. By the time she burst out onto the mowed slope that separated the maze from the highway, she was breathless and sweaty and more than half inclined to go back.

She could at least have brought a book with her. Just across the highway was a clearing with flat rocks in it; she could have sat there. Janet untucked the tails of her blouse, tied them around her waist, and marched down the hill; the walk had become a duty rather than a pleasure; but having decided to do it, she would. She waited for two pickup trucks to go by, and then darted across the highway. There was a square gravelly space for visitors to park their cars in; a narrow, dusty path that plunged steeply down between rows of spirea bushes gone wild; a wide rocky space scattered with burdock; and a minor branch of the river, with another weathered wooden bridge over it.

Janet made a ceremonial stop in the middle of the bridge. She knew this stream in all its manifestations, from cracked mud set about with slimy green rocks to the foaming mass that covered the knees of the trees and lapped at the concrete wall that separated the parking area from the woods. Today it was about midway between those two. All the rocks were covered, and the grass that overhung the banks like combed hair drifted sideways in a mild brown current. The air was full of dusty sunlight and a slow fall of yellow elm leaves. The woods decay, the woods decay and fall, thought Janet, recalling favorite poems with a pleasurable melancholy. Season of mists and mellow fruitfulness. When icicles hang by the wall.

No, thought Janet, not just yet. She pushed herself away from the railing and went on across the bridge. She hesitated between the sandy path that plunged aimlessly about in the evergreen plantation and the gravel road that led to the river, and chose the latter.

The river was full too, and much more violently so. It raged between the tree roots that snaked down its banks, and hurled sticks and dead leaves up and down. A few ducks huddled in the backwaters and made noises at Janet that seemed to expect the answer no. She offered them the apple core, but they billed it aside. She threw it into the nearest foaming circle the river offered, climbed along the muddy banks for a short time, found another gray wooden bridge, a much larger version of the previous two, and walked across it to Forbes Island.

Nobody had been pruning out here, either, and the entire place was overgrown with wild raspberries. Janet edged along the shores of the island, which was shaped like a capital L drawn by a kindergartner, until she found one narrow path. This led to the island's center, where there were a number of flat rocks, a tumbledown stone fireplace, well blackened, and a wobbly picnic table, gray grown over with green lichen. Janet lay on her back on the largest rock and watched the oak and willow branches scouring out the bowl of the sky. The wind had risen while she toiled about in the woods. It was probably going to rain again. Janet said over to herself as much as she could remember—which was most, but not all—of "The Love Song of J. Alfred Prufrock," trying to extrapolate from the fragments of music she had heard the sound of the finished piece. She knew nothing about music, but it was a pleasant exercise. When she had gone right through to "human voices wake us, and we drown," a shiver overtook her; the sort of feeling people must mean when they said that somebody had walked over their graves. The sky was darkening rapidly. Janet got up and went back to campus.

She climbed the long hill to Forbes and, sneering automatically at its shoe-box shape, turned her back on it and went into Ericson.

The door to their room was open, and voices and laughter came from it. Janet walked in, calling, "Hello!"

"There you are!" said Molly, as Janet came around the corner. "We've been waiting and waiting."

One of the Roberts—Armin, Janet thought, of the straight blond hair and reddish-blond beard—was sitting on the floor with his back to Molly's bed. Nicholas Tooley was sitting on the end of Christina's bed. They both looked perfectly at home. Christina, also sitting on her own bed, was the one who looked nervous.

"This is Janet," said Molly. "Jan, this is Robin Armin, and that's Nick Tooley."

"How do you do?" said Janet to Robin.

"Very well," he said gravely. He had a beautiful voice and a mouth that looked as if it were on the verge of making a joke, or had perhaps already made one nobody had noticed.

"And we've met," said Nick, grinning at her. He got up and walked over to her bookshelves. "Tina says all these are yours."

"I'm afraid so," said Janet. She was peripherally aware that Tina was less than pleased. That Nick Tooley was six inches too short for Tina was no excuse for not feeling guilty, let alone for feeling smug. "Do you read children's books?"

"I'm afraid so," said Nick. "I started when I was young, you know, and never got out of the habit." He touched the black spine of *The Worm Ouroboros*. "How's this?"

"Gorgeous," said Janet. "Eddison wrote at the beginning of this century, but my father says it's written in something very like genuine Elizabethan English. The beginning is a little distracting, but the main story is just like the language."

"Elizabethan English, hmmm?" said Nick. "Think I could manage that, Robin?"

"Not a chance," said Robin, still gravely. "You can't even manage Samuel Johnson."

"Give it a try," said Janet, pulling the book out and handing it to him. He flinched a little, probably at the garish cover, but took it and opened it at random.

"What," said Janet to Molly, "were you waiting for me for?"

"Robin and Nick want our bunk beds," said Molly, "and they'll give us two single beds in exchange."

"Listen to this," said Nick. When he began to read, his voice altered and grew stronger. The broad vowels of his Iowan accent moved a little sideways into something half-Southern and half-British in sound. Christina, who had been fidgeting, stopped. "'O Queen,' said Juss, 'somewhat I know of grammarie and divine philosophy, yet must I bow to thee for such learning, that dwellest here from generation to generation and dost commune with the dead. How shall we find this steed? Few they be, and high they fly above the world, and come to birth but one in three hundred years.'" His glasses had slipped down his nose, but the gaze he bent on Robin when he finished reading was not vague or myopic. "How's that, then?" he said.

"Well spoken," said Robin, as gravely as ever, "with good accent and good discretion."

"May I?" said Nick to Janet.

She nodded, and he fetched a brand-new blue knapsack from Christina's bed and tucked the book into it. Human voices wake us, she thought. Do we always drown?

"Let's go, then," said Christina, standing up, "and get this over with."

"This" turned out to be the dismantling of Janet and Molly's bunk bed; the carrying of it down four flights of steps, all the way across campus to Taylor; the carrying of it up three flights of steps; and its bestowal in Robin and Nick's room. This was one of the odder rooms in Taylor, being L-shaped. Robin, apparently at his own request, was crammed back in the bottom of the L, with hardly enough space between his bed and his desk to fit the chair in. He did have a nice view, out the narrow window, of Blackstock's few remaining elms and the delicate tower of the chapel. He had no discernible possessions, unlike Nick, who had piles of books, sweaters, socks, and magazines all over the place, not to mention a guitar case, a banjo case, and a welter of broken strings hanging off various convenient doorknobs and picture hooks.

After a brief rest and a drink of water, it was of course necessary to take the box springs, mattresses, and metal frames of the single beds back along the same route. Then they finished taking apart Christina's bed and lugged it up to the fifth floor of Taylor, where Robert Benfield wanted it. He did help them carry his two single beds back to Ericson, where they bestowed one in their own room and the other in the basement storage room, the piece that said FIFTH TAYLOR in black marker carefully turned to the wall.

Everything was just barely not too heavy. Janet was hungry and already tired from her walk. She remembered the entire experience for years as extremely unpleasant. But what she noticed more than her sore back, her aching legs, or the creases made in her hands by the metal frames of all the beds was how everybody was acting.

Christina had clearly set her sights on Nick, who had no notion of what to do with her. Robin seemed to be taking much more notice of her than Nick did, but she was oblivious to this. Molly had on a sardonic look, which made Janet wonder how she herself was behaving. Having considered it on their second trip past the Music and Drama Center, the chapel, and the Student Union, she decided that if she stopped giggling quite so much she would make a creditable account of herself. Since Nick reacted to Christina's attempts at conversation largely by making puns at her, this was difficult. Christina obviously thought that Janet was laughing only to be ingratiating.

When they had carried the last metal frame up the four flights of steps in Ericson and collapsed on the floor, the sky was the color of pewter and the wind was what Janet's family called a wolf wind—it would huff and puff and blow your house down.

"I'm starving," she said. "Let's go to supper."

"Taylor's closed," said Robin, mournfully.

"Good; I don't want to eat in a dungeon with a storm coming on. Let's go to Dunbar. We can look at the lake."

A vast spattering outside proclaimed the arrival of rain.

"Eliot," said Molly, firmly. "We can take the tunnel."

They went, not very quickly, down five flights of steps and into the basement of Ericson, past the recalcitrant soda machines and the steel racks, painted with the Civil Defense symbol and filled with empty barrels marked, "Water." "Dehydrated water," Janet's mother always remarked. "Just add water." Janet's father said the remark lacked symmetry, but the children always laughed.

They passed the door of the laundry room, whence came a noise like somebody taking apart a bunk bed with a hockey stick underwater; went down a short flight of steps, and entered the system of steam tunnels that underlay the whole east side of campus. On the bright red covering of the steam pipe at eye level, somebody had spray-painted in white, "Abandon all hope, ye who enter here."

It always irritated Janet. "All hope abandon," she muttered.

"Why is it always the people who use paint that get their quotations wrong?" said Nick Tooley, bounding up on her right. "Last year somebody wrote out the whole of 'Childe

Roland to the Dark Tower Came' in Holmes Tunnel in water-soluble marker ink, not a mistake in it, down to the very commas—and when a pipe burst and flooded the tunnel it was all washed out."

"I thought you were a freshman," said Janet.

"My brother attended Blackstock too."

"Does he make puns?" said Christina, edging up on Nick's other side.

"No," said Nick gravely. "He goes in for more practical jokes."

Christina looked sidelong at him and said nothing. They rounded a corner and walked past the entrance to Holmes Tunnel, which was much newer and glared with fluorescent light. They passed the entrance to Forbes Tunnel on their left. Ahead on the same side was a very old block of Greek that had puzzled Janet for years. "Robin," she said, "what's this?"

Robin squinted at the faded blue letters, which looked as if they had been put on with a fine paintbrush. "First ten lines of *The Iliad*," he said. "That's been there long and long. Somebody ought to touch it up."

"What does it say?" asked Christina. "Translate it for us."

"No, read it first," said Janet.

Robin cleared his throat, opened his eyes wide upon the peeling wall of the tunnel, and rolled out of his tidy beard huge assonant syllables in a rocky rhythm, punctuated with thumps where he came down hard on two syllables in a row. Janet, having seen that his expression was going to remain blank, looked at Molly. He's got her, she thought; I'm enchanted by Eliot, and Molly's done in by Homer. Or maybe just by that voice. I wonder what would get to Christina. Christina was looking bored.

Robin finished, and after a small silence Nick began to applaud. "Shall I change my major?" he said.

"What does it mean?" said Christina.

Nick said, "'Achilles' wrath, to Greece the direful spring Of woes unnumbered, heavenly goddess, sing.'"

"Don't give me these newfangled translations," said Robin. He closed his eyes. He said what came next in a much quieter voice than he had given to the Greek, but it made Janet's spine creep.

"Achilles' baneful wrath resound, O Goddess, that imposed
Infinite sorrows on the Greeks, and many brave souls losed
From breasts heroic; sent them far to that invisible cave
That no light comforts; and their limbs to dogs and vultures gave:
To all which Jove's will gave effect; from whom first strife begun
Betwixt Atrides, king of men, and Thetis' godlike son."

Like Nick's, his vowels changed when he recited. Whoever taught them theater must have had an accent.

"What *was* that?" said Janet.

Nick gave her a crooked and charming smile. "'Much have I travelled in the realms of gold,'" he said, "'and many goodly states and kingdoms seen.'"

His tone was rather sardonic; but it hardly mattered. Lost, thought Janet. He quotes Keats, too. Well, let's enjoy it, then. She said, "'Round many western islands have I been Which bards in fealty to Apollo hold.'"

Robin rattled, "'But never did I breathe its pure serene Til I heard Chapman speak out loud and bold,'" and began walking again. "We'll miss dinner," he added.

"*That* was Chapman's Homer?" said Janet, moving after him but keeping her eyes on Nick, who came along too. "The translation Robin said?"

"Will you guys stop babbling and tell me what the damn Greek means?" said Christina.

They turned into Eliot Tunnel and passed an awe-inspiring array of vending machines full of every vile concoction anybody studying at three in the morning could ever hope for, and moved a little faster for the other end of the hall the tunnel would become, where the entrance to the dining hall was. A faint smell of tomato and frying came down it damply.

Robin said, "'Sing, goddess, the wrath of Peleus' son Achilles—baneful wrath, that brought woes unnumbered upon the Greeks, and sent many strong souls of heroes to Hades, to be the prey of dogs and the feast of birds, for thus the will of Zeus was accomplished, since there first stood apart in division of conflict Atreus' son Agamemnon, lord of men, and brilliant Achilles.'"

He made the everyday English roll almost as well as the Greek. They all stopped in a clump at the double glass doors of the dining hall. The bulb above the doors was burned out. In the gray light coming down the stairs that led less subterranean diners to their meals, Robin's face was as stern as a statue's. Janet shivered, and looked for comfort at Molly, who was digging in the back pocket of her jeans for her ID card with a remote expression almost as unsettling as Robin's.

"*The Odyssey* is happier," said Nick's husky voice.

Robin did not exactly start, but his face softened a little, and showing his card to the drowsy student worker behind the table, he said quietly, "'Sing in me, Muse, that man of many turnings, who very many wanderings made, after he sacked the holy city of Troy.'"

"Oh, sure," said Molly, presenting a card already as scarred and bent as any senior's. "That's really cheerful, Nick."

"But he got home in the end," said Nick.

"I hope they fed him better than this," said Molly, gazing with large eyes and wrinkled brow at the limp and unidentifiable masses, one red, one brown, one green and white, and one all white, that offered themselves at the steam table. The girl behind it grinned at them. "Veal parmesan, hamburger casserole, vegetarian casserole, potatoes au gratin."

"Sorry," said Nick, "I don't eat vegetarians."

"The veal parmesan is the red stuff?" said Christina.

"The parmesan sinks to the bottom," said the girl cheerfully.

They made their choices and moved on. Janet, balancing a plate of potatoes au gratin and several bowls of canned grapefruit, caught up with Nick where he was waiting for somebody to refill the canister of chocolate milk. Everybody else had sat down. "What do you need a foil this weekend *for?*" she said.

"Shhh," said Nick. "Schiller."

"You've got him?"

"Shush. Rob Benfield has him right now, and I'm going to *get* him. You want to watch?"

"*Yes,*" said Janet. Two Chemistry majors in the class of 1910 had stolen a bust of Schiller from the library and insinuated it into their graduation ceremony. A Classics major and an English major had stolen it from them, kept it all summer, and brought it to Convocation the following autumn. From that time on, there were always students for whom the possession of the bust, and its showing at college events, concerned them more than their studies. Janet had never known anybody who had Schiller, and had seen him only once, at a concert of Renaissance music. She schooled her face: Christina was looking at them.

"All right. He's got him in Chester Hall, in one of the practice rooms. I'm going to meet him tomorrow afternoon to practice a duet."

"Where does the foil come in?"

"To keep him at bay."

"You're going to back down four flights of steps with a plaster bust under your arm and a foil in the other hand?"

"Benfield doesn't fence," said Nick, filling his glass.

Janet got some chocolate milk too, to add verisimilitude to an otherwise compromising position. "Well, neither do you."

There was a brief pause. "Well," said Nick, "Benfield doesn't know that."

"What time?" said Janet, following him to the table the others had taken.

"Five or so."

"Five or so what?" said Christina.

"Classes per term, to do a double major," Nick improvised and sat down next to her.

"Don't be an idiot," said Robin.

"Full of sound and fury," said Nick, reflectively. "Anybody taking Shakespeare this term?"

"Molly and I are taking it in the winter," said Janet, sitting down between Molly and Christina.

"Robin flunked it last year," said Nick.

Robin, looking unperturbed, lobbed a roll at him. "Too modern," he said.

"Shakespeare?" said Christina.

"The professor," said Nick.

"Who'd you take it from?" Janet asked Robin.

"Tyler."

"Well, then. I'm surprised they let him teach it."

"He's read it a million times," said Robin, fielding the returning roll, tearing it open, and buttering it lavishly. "If you hate Shakespeare, he's a fine one to take it from. Just like Tolstoy."

"Tolstoy taught Shakespeare?" said Christina.

Janet looked quickly at her. She might have been making a joke. Nick was looking at her, too, with his ingenuous eyes wide open. Put him and Molly together, thought Janet, and you could persuade anybody of anything.

It was Robin, however, who answered Christina. "No; hated him," he said. "He thought he was vulgar. No dignity in his language, he said. Russians, fie."

"Dostoyevski's vulgar," said Christina. It took Janet a moment to realize what Christina's remark implied. The girl who thought Madeleine L'Engle silly had read Dostoyevski.

"Do you like him?" said Robin.

"Well," said Christina, "no. I liked Freud's essays about him, so I read the books; but they weren't nearly as interesting. But he *was* vulgar, at least I thought so—so some Russians are vulgar, even if Tolstoy didn't like it."

Robin looked at her thoughtfully, and then concentrated on his meal. Nobody else said anything for some time. Janet had framed and discarded several remarks when an enormous crack of thunder smacked the air outside.

"Oh, good," said Robin. "If everybody's finished, let's go out onto the porch. The wind's in the east; we won't get much wet."

"Fine," said Christina, dropping her fork with a splat into her uneaten veal. "This stuff's like leather."

"I'll buy you a hamburger later," said Robin.

They disposed of their trays and left the dining hall.

"That's right," said Nick as they climbed the stairs. "Robin and Rob and I are going to catch the ten o'clock movie. Would you ladies like to come with us?"

"Sure," said Christina.

"What's the movie?" said Molly.

"Olivier's *Othello*," said Nick; he was looking at Robin with an expression Janet could not decipher.

"I have class early tomorrow," she said. "I was going to go tomorrow night."

"I might be up for seeing it again," said Nick.

"I mightn't," said Robin, firmly.

They passed down a long red-carpeted hall and went out onto the wide veranda that overlooked the playing fields and the stream and the Upper Arboretum. It was pouring. They were sheltered by an overhang from the rain itself, but a fine spray hit them as they approached the balustrade.

Janet leaned her arms on the damp stone and stared at the dark. It resolved itself gradually into the smooth field, the dark trees, a darker sky, and a few gray gleams from the water.

"It's cold out here," said Christina.

Nick took off his sweater and gave it to her; she draped it

over her shoulders and smiled at him. "You need a larger chevalier, lady," he said to her.

"This is fine," said Christina.

"I don't think she needs a chevalier at all," said Molly, dreamily.

"*Autre temps, autre mores,*" said Nick, not sounding at all put out. Christina, Molly, and Robin separated him from Janet; she couldn't see his face.

"I'd be thrilled to have a chevalier," said Christina, rather sharply.

"Yes, I know," said Molly. "That's why you shouldn't have one."

"I suppose you should?"

"Nope," said Molly. "I did have one. It was bad for me. Oh, far out, look at that lightning."

The thunder that followed made answering her impossible. They stayed, leaning in a row on the balustrade, silent except for an involuntary exclamation or two. Janet stood next to Robin. She became gradually aware that he smelled of lavender. She wondered if he was gay. That would put a spoke in Tina's wheel. And in Janet's own, too, maybe, depending on what, if anything, Robin's choice of roommate meant. Maybe Tina could take up with Rob Benfield instead, if she insisted on taking up with somebody. Janet thought briefly of Danny Chin, whom she had made sure to kiss before he went off to college, since she did not want to go unkissed to college herself. It seemed a foolish action, now. She had kissed Danny not because he aroused any romantic feelings in her, but because they had known each other so long that her attempt was unlikely to turn out to be embarrassing. She hadn't thought it had—but he hadn't written her from Dartmouth, either.

Kissing Robin would be odd; he had that beard. Kissing Nick might be pleasant. On the other hand, she had a great deal to do in the next four years; that much was obvious already. Staying offshore of the entire country of love might be pleasant also—or, if tonight was any example, at least amusing.

"If we want a choice of seats, we'd better be going along," said Robin. "Are you sure you won't come, Janet?"

"No, I've got an early class and a lot of reading to do by Monday."

"That's what Sunday evening is for," said Nick.

"I'm having dinner with my family on Sunday."

"Oh, are you a townie?"

"Afraid so," said Janet. "My father's Professor Carter, in English."

"Oh, the expert on the Romantic poets," said Nick. "Is that your morning class?"

"No—English 10, with Evans."

"My brother says Evans is hellacious, but worth it," said Nick. "He's better of a Saturday—he doesn't want to be there either, so he's kind to those who show up."

"We'd better go," said Christina.

They walked around the veranda to the steps, and set off past the Women's Center and Forbes Hall. Movies were shown in Olin; Janet stopped beside Ericson. "Good night, everybody." She wanted to add, "Behave yourselves," but managed not to.

"I'll call you tomorrow," said Nick in her ear, and bolted off after the others.

Janet went upstairs and read Aristotle with a distracted mind.

CHAPTER

4

Mindful of Professor Evans's reputation, Janet got up early enough on Saturday to eat breakfast. Christina snored gently; Molly slept with her head under her pillow, a habit, she said, acquired when her sister complained that she talked in her sleep.

Outside a mist like gauze was on the lakes, full of the small noises of ducks. Janet made her way to Masters Hall feeling cheerful and virtuous; this was a mood she knew could shatter in a moment into irritability, but perhaps this once it wouldn't. The English 10 classroom was the smallest she had been in so far. There were five people in the room when Janet arrived, and she sat well to the back, remembering Melinda Wolfe's stricture. By eight-thirty there were nineteen people, most of them yawning and all of them looking apprehensive. At eight thirty-six Professor Evans walked in.

He and Janet's father did not get along very well. He had been over for dinner a few times; he had worn jeans and a Chemistry Department T-shirt, and talked politics with her parents and elephants with Andrew. He was a slight, fair man in his forties, with a sharp face, pale eyes, and reddish hair. Today he was wearing a tweed jacket and a tie, whereas most of his students looked as if they had been lucky to remember to put their clothes on at all. For one wild moment, Janet wished she were wearing a skirt, which was completely foolish.

Evans looked the class over impartially; his voice when he spoke was mild.

"Are all the front-row seats broken?" he said. There was a stirring, and one laugh. Professors Evans smiled. "This room's too small to hide in," he said. "Furthermore, I'm going to oppress your free spirits and abridge your civil rights by seating you in alphabetical order; I have a hard time with names and it will help me to keep you straight. Please start with the leftmost seat in the front row, fill that up, and then start over on the left of the second row. If somebody's not present, leave a seat for him anyway. We don't throw people out this early in the term." Nobody laughed at that. Evans pulled a flat green book from under his arm and opened it. "Andrews," he said. "Atwater, Barge, Broden, Cannon, Carter, Darrish, Dixon, Dobas, Engel, Harris, Hecht, Johns, Michaelson, Minge, Reinstra, Schneider, Senneth, Shepherd, Zimmerman."

When everybody had scrambled and milled about and finally sat down—Janet had the leftmost seat in the second row, by the window—Nick Tooley, whom Janet had not even seen come in, stood by the door looking obliging, with a green Drop-Add slip in his hand. "In or out?" Evans said to him.

"In, please. Tooley."

Shepherd stirred; Evans said, "Just sit next to Miss Zimmerman, Mr. Tooley." Miss Zimmerman, a diminutive blonde in a pair of red overalls, looked pleased. Nick sat down, grinned at Janet over Zimmerman's head, and dropped his notebook on the floor. Evans walked over to the long table in the front of the room, leaned his elbows on the lectern there, and waited while Nick picked up his notebook and the whispered conversation subsided. It did so fairly quickly.

"I'm Professor Evans," he said. "This is English 10. Is anybody in the wrong room?" Nobody, it appeared, was. "Does anybody else need a slip signed?" Nobody, it appeared, did. "Good," said Evans. "The catalog describes this course as 'Introduction to English Literature, I.' They used to call it 'Survey of English Literature, I,' and in terms in which the course did not begin on Saturday morning, I used to ask the students to tell me what they thought a survey of English literature was. I have my suspicions about the change in the course description, but no proof."

Janet grinned, and several people snickered.

"I don't intend to introduce you to English literature, as if we were at a polite party," said Evans. "Parts of it certainly resemble one; and indeed my specialty is in those parts. But as some of you perhaps know already, it's rude to cut anybody to whom you've been introduced—" Janet giggled in spite of herself, and behind her she heard an unfamiliar female chortle and Nick's abrupt chuckle. Recognize it already, do you? she said to herself, and stopped grinning. "—and we will certainly find it necessary to cut some of the offerings on the syllabus this term. This does not," said Evans, leveling a severe gaze at them, "mean that I will look kindly on missed classes or missed reading. It means that negative commentary on the works in question, provided that it is intelligent and organized, will not be frowned upon. We shall be surveyors, not gentlemen." He considered their faces one by one, until Janet could hardly bear to sit still. "Not ladies and gentlemen," he said, finally, and a little grimly. The class was very quiet. "Surveyors in the more technical sense," said Evans. "To survey may be to look out over a landscape from a height; or it may mean to tramp around in the mud with heavy, fragile, cantankerous instruments. Some of my colleagues favor the view from a height; I myself feel that to consider the twentieth century a height of any sort, except that of folly, is in fact foolish. So we will wander in the mud. I think that when you come home again you'll find that the mud has been on the slopes of mountains. Your instruments you'll acquire along the way."

He considered them again, as if waiting for a question. Janet couldn't resist. She raised her hand. "Miss Carter," he said, without either consulting the list or looking as if he had ever seen her before.

Janet said, "What will our instruments be?"

"Intellect," said Evans gravely, "without which, I hope, none of you would be here. Linguistic aptitude, without which none of you should be taking this course; poetic sensitivity, which I hope to instill even in the dullest ear; moral stature, which is none of my business; and serendipity, which will be bestowed by grace. Any further questions?" Nobody had any. Janet could feel the entire class staring. She made sure her own mouth was closed. None of the dire stories about Evans had said anything like this. Maybe this was a treat he saved for the first Saturday morning.

"I will now pass out the syllabus," said Evans, and did so. When everybody had the four stapled sheets covered with purple type (and half of them, Janet observed, had sniffed it for the familiar, comforting, and no doubt narcotic whiff of ditto fluid, just as everybody had done in high school), he said, "Every year, one publisher lies to us about the availability of a textbook. This year, it's the Medeous edition of the *Roman de la Rose*. This is a French poem written by two different authors forty years apart. We are concerned with it because there is a Middle English translation of part of it, pieces of which were probably composed by Geoffrey Chaucer, of whom we'll have much to say; and also because it had a profound effect on medieval English literature. We'll be discussing the fragmentary Middle English version in detail; the text for that is available. But as background, I want you to read a modern translation of the French text. I've reserved two copies of the

Dahlberg translation and one of the Medeous for you at the library. We won't be discussing this for two weeks, but I advise you to do your background reading before the rush begins. Reserve reading materials may not be removed from the library, which closes at midnight."

He looked over Janet's head. "Yes, Mr. Tooley?"

"Which translation do you recommend?"

Evans smiled. "The Dahlberg is the standard," he said. "The Medeous is much livelier, you'll find. It occasioned considerable controversy on its publication, but is not in fact more inaccurate than any other poetic translation. Follow your heart, Mr. Tooley." Mr. Tooley didn't answer, which Janet thought wise of him. Evans walked around to the front of the table with the lectern on it and perched himself on the table's edge. "English literature is usually held to begin with *Beowulf*," he said.

A hissing of pens filled the room. Janet dutifully noted this piece of information down, though she was fairly certain that nobody would be asked to repeat it. Evans said, "We will dodge the entire question because of everybody's linguistic ineptitude. We can't really begin much before Chaucer if we want to deal with original texts, which is the best way of looking at literature. We'll be reading 'Sir Gawain and the Green Knight' in translation, because it's written in a dialect of Middle English that didn't survive. But Chaucer we will read in the original Middle English, edited for clarity and consistency, but not for spelling. After Chaucer you should find the language plain sailing. Now for some historical background," said Evans, and launched into a rapid lecture about the fourteenth century that occupied the rest of the class period. Janet's hand and wrist ached by the time he stopped.

She was still occupied in shaking the cramp out of her fingers when Nick Tooley appeared in front of her. He was wearing the same yellow sports shirt and jeans he had had on yesterday, the shirt was buttoned crookedly, and his hair had not seen a comb since he got up.

"Hello," said Janet. "How was the movie?"

"I have no idea," said Nick. "Robin took one look at Olivier in blackface and burst into hysterical laughter. He couldn't stop. He couldn't even walk. Tina and I had to help him out of the auditorium. Molly said she would never go to a movie with him again, and stayed to watch. We took him over to the Tea Room and soothed him with ice cream. If Benfield doesn't impale me over Schiller, do you want to go see the movie tonight?"

"If I get my philo reading done by then," said Janet.

"Do you have to go do it right now?" He looked at his watch. "I hate this," he said. "It's nine-forty on a Saturday morning, and I'm dressed, washed, and fed, and my appointment with Swifte's not till eleven-thirty. It's more than a poor player can cope with."

"Are you majoring in Theater?"

"What? Oh. No. I'm just exaggerating my stature. I do it constantly; you'll have to beware. I've acted in a lot of local productions, that's all, and Robin's probably going to employ my dubious talents in some experimental stuff in Ericson Little Theater later in the year."

Janet finished restoring her fingers and tucked her various pens and papers away in her knapsack. Everybody else had left.

"Do you want to go for a walk?" said Nick. "The sun should have burned the mist off by now. We can wander in the Upper Arb and pick the loosestrife."

"Sure," said Janet. "Molly and Tina probably aren't up yet; I wouldn't want to wake them turning pages."

They went from the empty classroom into the vast, airy hallway of Second Masters. The walls above the oak wainscoting were painted institutional green; but the floor was polished hardwood, scuffed over already with dusty footprints, and the vaulted ceiling was decorated with a riot of plaster molding.

"I love this building," said Janet.

"I rather like the science ones," said Nick. "All shiny black and white and silver."

"And plastic," said Janet disgustedly.

"Oh, well; I like it. You know that people built it; it didn't grow by itself."

They went down the worn marble steps, and over the worn marble floor of the first-floor lobby, and emerged between Masters's two huge Corinthian columns into a fragile sunshine and a brisk wind.

"What experimental stuff is Robin going to do?" said Janet, not feeling up to a discussion of the merits of plastic or of buildings that looked as if they hadn't just grown.

"We haven't decided," said Nick. He kicked at a dandelion on the edge of the sidewalk, and added, "We thought maybe a production of *Pygmalion* with an all-black cast."

"You can't blame Olivier, can you?" said Janet. "One of the best tragic roles ever written? He did all the rest of them."

"You didn't see that makeup," said Nick. "And he didn't have to roll his eyes. Good God, old Dickon himself never—"

"What?" said Janet.

"Somebody I knew once. Never mind. All right, you pity Olivier, and I'll pity all the black actors who'll never play Hamlet."

"That's harder," said Janet, thinking it over. "Because *Hamlet*'s a family play. All the rest of the tragedies are."

"I saw *Lear* with a black cast," said Nick, "a most gorgeous production—and I remember thinking, afterwards when I'd recovered myself, how absurd it was. They thought that because the actor playing Lear was black, his daughters must all be too. But it wouldn't have mattered. That's such an isolated play, it's got no cultural context, if Lear were black and his daughters white, it would just show up, in the proper time, the ways in which they were unnatural."

Janet thought of Molly, and Molly's brothers, and the Robin

Hood game. "I'll feel sorry for all your deprived black actors," she said, "when I'm allowed to play Hamlet." Belatedly, she remembered Sarah Bernhardt; but Nick didn't seem to.

"What, do you want to?" he said.

"No, I don't want to be an actress."

"That's refreshing."

"Why, does everybody you know want to be in theater?"

They passed between the back side of Olin and the tiny, charming brick observatory with its huge silver dome from which Janet had used to help hack the ivy every spring. Somebody shot by them on a bicycle, bumped madly over the high curbs of the asphalt road just ahead, and slammed down the hill to Dunbar in a rattle of baskets.

"Young idiot," said Nick. "More college students are killed in bicycle accidents than commit suicide from despair."

"That's not true."

"No, probably not."

"How many do commit suicide from despair?" said Janet, thinking of pink curtains and Nora's *PDR*.

"I don't keep count," said Nick, rather shortly.

They crossed the road themselves and took the steep path, made gloomy by a collection of gigantic larches. Janet kept an eye out for an overturned cyclist, but the maniac seemed to have passed safely through.

"I used to roller-skate down this hill," she said. "Before they put that new concrete bridge in."

She was used to a certain degree of wonder in response to this remark about roller-skating, but Nick said only, "It was a wooden one before; I remember."

They crossed the new bridge.

"Yes," said Janet. "We've come the wrong way, we're going to end up in the Lower Arb."

"No, I just wanted to go the long way around; I've got a friend in the woods here." They took the curved path in between Dunbar and the lake; Janet had taken it in the other direction on her walk yesterday.

On the spot where she had met the Californian and the southerner, Nick stopped and made a chittering noise between his teeth. He was answered from a spindly elm tree, and after a moment a squirrel came headfirst down its trunk, stopped at eye level, and considered Nick with interest. He dug a tattered heel of brown bread out of his back pocket, reminding Janet of Molly's ID card, and held it out. The squirrel stretched its neck like a goose and nibbled rapidly until most of the bread was gone, then snatched the remaining piece and bolted back up the tree, flirting its tail as they all did.

"Did you ever try them on apples?" said Janet.

Nick had already started walking again, and he did not turn around for this question. "They're fussy," he said. "Spoiled, I suppose." Janet caught up with him, and he started. "Sorry," he said.

"It's all right," said Janet.

They turned off the sidewalk just before the wooden bridge, crossed a small meadow of goldenrod on a dusty path, and passed into the green shade of the woods. The Upper Arboretum suffered a certain amount of maintenance every year, though nobody had ever gotten the College Council to agree to spray the poison ivy. The path they walked on was broad and partially graveled. On their right, the low banks of the stream had been shored up here and there with railroad ties and large flat stones, to prevent the stream's natural tendency to spread out through the woods and convert them to marshland. The artificial lakes were also evidencing a tendency to silt up and turn into marsh; this was hailed with delight by the Biology Department and with dismay by almost everybody else, and was at present a matter of hot dispute.

"Do *you* think they should dredge the lakes?" said Janet to Nick's back. His shirt was sticking to it; he looked to be mostly bones.

"Certainly they should," said Nick. "If they want a marsh, they can go out to Rice Lake. *Our* lakes are manmade, and they should stay made."

"My father thinks so too," said Janet. "My mother says that when nature takes hold so aggressively, you should let it have its way."

"I'll wager she didn't say so the last time you had ants," said Nick.

"No—she put mint all over the kitchen counters and the windowsills and the threshold." Nick turned around and leaned on an oak tree. With eyes like his, he would always look a little startled. "And why did she do that?"

"She'd read it repelled ants."

"And did it?"

"Somewhat. There weren't as many of them. But it made it hard to cook dinner, and everything seemed to end up with mint in it."

"She should have recited the rhyme," said Nick.

"What?"

"There's a rhyme that goes with all these herbal remedies. 'Breathe, breathe, thou merry mint, until I may see nary an ant.'"

"You've got to be kidding," said Janet cautiously.

Nick grinned at her, and the bottom fell out of her stomach. "If you say it, lady," he said. "Let's go a little farther; I know where there are Indian paintbrushes blooming still."

He did, too. Janet had assumed he was mistaking bee balm or maybe even Indian blanket, which was supposed to stop blooming in July but often did not, for Indian paintbrush. But a little farther along the path was a round space where the stream made a loop. Three ailing willows had been removed from it this summer, and it was a meadow of grass and flowers. Next year the brambles would take it; but now it blazed with goldenrod, Devil's paintbrush, the luminous blue of chicory, and the biggest Indian paintbrush flowers Janet had ever seen.

"There," said Nick, with great satisfaction, as if he had planted them all himself. He moved lightly through the knee-high grasses, picked one of the bright yellow flowers with their bristling red tips, and held it up to Janet, who had followed him. The meadow still smelled of summer, dust and baking grass and greenness.

"Just matches your hair," said Nick.

"It does not; it clashes. Try the hawkweed."

"The Devil's paintbrush? Oh, no, lady, not that one. Here, look." He tucked the flower behind her right ear. He smelled like sage. "Now, see?"

"How can I see?"

"I'll be your mirror," said Nick.

His eyes were enormous. Janet tilted her head the small amount necessary to look squarely at him, meaning to make some sharp remark; and he kissed her. He took his time about it, and unlike Danny Chin he seemed to have had some practice. This—or something—made a remarkable difference in the entire sensation. Janet was wondering in an abstracted sort of way about how long her knees were going to hold out when Nick moved his mouth about half an inch from hers and said, very softly, "'Underfoot the violet, crocus, and hyacinth with rich inlay 'broidered the ground, more colored than with stones of costliest emblem.'"

Janet did not know the poem, which, she thought later, must have been the reason that, instead of melting, she thought with awful clarity, oh, no, I'm not lying down in the flowers with somebody I don't know well enough to talk about contraception with. Nick, as if he had heard her, pulled back a little farther and smiled beatifically. "There, that's over," he said.

"I beg your pardon?" said Janet, in the tone of one who thinks the party addressed should be begging hers instead.

"The first kiss," said Nick, cheerfully. "Always best to get that one out of the way—it's so awkward."

Janet thought of Danny Chin, and chuckled. "Come on," she

said, and took Nick's hand. The sensation was peculiar. She remembered taking her mother's or father's hand when she was small; she remembered taking Andrew's hand as recently as last month. (Lily-Milly was a standoffish child who wouldn't even hug you on your birthday.) That was family—but what was this? She cleared her throat. "I'll show you a place that's unprepossessing, now, but every spring it's covered with bloodroot. We can come back past the tennis courts and the house I'm going to buy after I get my Ph.D. and come to teach at Blackstock, and that'll get you to the Women's Center a little early for your appointment."

"Lead on, MacDuff," said Nick. Janet started to correct him, and thought better of it.

Standing between Eliot and the Women's Center after Nick had gone into the latter, Janet considered and rejected lunch, company, and another walk. She was still, now that the momentary excitement had passed, in a fever after the lecture this morning. She would go to the library and get a jump on all her classmates, who would have made the fatal calculation that two weeks is a long time.

The library was a square, flat building of yellow brick, built into the side of the hill that Masters Hall sat at the top of. The library was one story tall in front, and looked, between Masters and the even more gargantuan brick bulk of the old Chemistry building, as if somebody had stepped on it. But down the hill behind, it sank for four stories, packed with books, crammed with knowledge; and scattered with odd cushions and strange padded built-in furniture added a few years ago to placate the rioting students of the time, who could never seem to make up their minds whether they were angriest about Viet Nam, about being made to learn a foreign language, or about being made to sit at a hard wooden desk while they did it. The College, being unable to do anything about Viet Nam and unwilling to do anything about the language requirement, had reformed the furniture in the library.

Janet pushed through the revolving glass doors, strode through the stark lobby with its Klee prints, turned right to the warped wooden counter that guarded the Reserve books, and asked for *The Romance of the Rose*, reserved for Professor Evans's English 10 class. The young man behind the desk shoved his glasses up his short nose and looked sheepish. The expression didn't suit him; he was pale and dark-haired and ethereal, like a romantic vampire, an impression that his open-necked white shirt and mellow voice did nothing to dissipate. Janet wondered if there had been some gigantic influx of Theater majors this year. That department did not usually have many majors.

"I just this minute gave out the last copy," the young man said. He gestured over his shoulder; Janet turned, and saw Miss Zimmerman bending her sleek yellow head over a huge folio volume. She seemed to be concentrating on the illustrations.

"Well," said Janet, "how long has she got it for?"

"Till three. The first one's due back at one and the other one at two-thirty."

Janet grimaced; the young man said, "Okay, look. There's one more copy. Professor Evans wouldn't let us put it on Reserve. It's about a hundred years old and he doesn't think we should be allowed to put our grubby fingers on it at all. Here's the call number."

"Well, thank you," said Janet, startled. "But—"

"Don't check it out and lose it, that's all."

"Okay, but—"

"Shall I say I have a weakness for redheads?"

"No, please don't," said Janet, and beat a hasty retreat. The number on the slip of paper he had handed her led her down to the bottom floor of the library, to be absorbed among the Close Rolls and the Patent Rolls and other large and improbable collections of historical documents. She passed these, and wandered, head tilted at the angle that always gave her a headache, past a flurry of French titles and a flurry of Latin ones, and bumped with alarming violence into somebody—or more precisely, into a corner of the huge book he was holding.

"What the hell are you doing?" said the possessor of the book, in a voice not at all suited to a library.

For heaven's sake, thought Janet, looking up the considerable distance to his face, it's another one of them. This place is haunted by beautiful young men with lovely voices. She rubbed her forehead and said, "Excuse me."

"Yes, all right, watch where you're going."

"Could you move out of my way, please? You're standing right where—oh. You've got the book I want."

"What could you possibly want with this?"

"I'm a student," said Janet, sweetly. "Do you want to see my ID card?"

"Go find one of the nice translations, there's a good girl."

You keep a civil tongue in your head, there's a good boy, thought Janet. She took a deep breath. "Are you going to check it out?"

"Of course not."

Lovely voice, dreadful temperament. Any rational person would walk away from him and go reserve one of the nice translations for later this afternoon. But why should he get away with being so rude? Because he had gorgeous gray eyes and yellow hair and a thin, thoughtful face? Nonsense.

"How long will you be using it, then?"

He rolled the gorgeous gray eyes at the ceiling and said through his white, white teeth, "What fucking difference does it make to you? I've got it; go away."

"Is this a nasty translation?"

"What?"

"As opposed to the nice ones?"

The young man made a noise in his throat that was just short of a growl. "How old are you?"

"Eighteen," said Janet, startled into the simple truth.

"If you want to live to be nineteen," said her antagonist, "go away."

Janet burst out laughing; this was really too much; neither of them was acting a day over twelve. From a little distance away, where the carrels were ranged under the windows, a harried voice hissed, "Shut up!" Janet could not stop laughing, and did not, in fact, greatly want to. She leaned on the cold metal shelf and chortled until the young man, who had turned very red, held the book out at arm's length, opened his long brown hands, and strode around the end of the stack before the book hit the floor. It did so with a resounding flat smack, like a car backfiring. The harried voice, now much louder and clearly female, burst into furious expostulation. The young man's voice, answering it in standard college terminology, echoed like that of somebody playing a madman in the theater.

Janet snatched up the book and ran for the stairs. When she returned the book to its place at four o'clock, there was nobody on the lowest level of the library at all. Janet had a headache, partly from the poem, which she devoutly hoped Evans was going to explain to them, or she was doomed from the start, and partly from the fact that she had had no lunch.

Nick's abduction by sword of the bust of Schiller was scheduled for five. Janet crept up the broad, well-lit stairways of the library as if she expected people to materialize out of the cinder-block walls at her, scooted through the deserted lobby, and emerged blinking into a much stronger sunlight than the earlier part of the day had suggested. She lingered on the sidewalk that led to the library, checking for the presence of tall, beautiful young men with foul tempers.

She wished she had not forced the encounter with the mad Theater major. He had been rude, and had deserved some rudeness in return; but she was not pleased with her own part in the conversation, which felt in retrospect more like flirtation than reprimand. What had been the matter with him, though? It was much too early for people to be burning out on their studies and turning obstreperous. Of course, if he'd been standing there for some time, trying to read that damn poem, then almost any wild behavior could probably be excused.

As she crossed the campus, the figures of the poem were still in her mind—the precise walled garden; the red roses; the one half-open flower that the poet had, God knew why, set his heart on; the flat, formal characters with their peculiar names: Jalosie, Amis, Biautez, Reason, Bialacoil, Franchise, Pite. All harping on the rose, one rosebud in a garden full of the flowers. Janet's mind's ear presented to her her mother's voice, in the Scottish accent she remembered from Janet's great-grandmother, reading Burns on a winter's evening when the power was out. "My luve is like a red, red rose That's newly sprung in June."

"Oh," said Janet, stopping short under one of the remaining elm trees. "It's inside out, that's what it is." Those weren't characters at all, they were attributes of the heroine; the rosebud was, not her sled, but her love, or maybe something a little more specific than that. It would be interesting to see how Evans dealt with that, given a classroom full of adolescents whose instinctive dimwitted responses to the mention of sex did not seem to have been altered in the least by the sexual revolution, their own intelligence, or anything else.

Janet started walking again, more slowly. The entire elegant intent of the poem unfolded itself in her mind like—well, like a flower. It wasn't what she would call fiction at all; it wasn't what she would call poetry, either, exhibiting, even in the lively Medeous translation, a dampening inclination to get on with the story—which wasn't a story, really, but the inside occurrences for which, in most love stories, you would see only the outside manifestations. Was *that* what they meant by allegory? It was going to be a long time until Evans's lecture on this poem, she could see that already. She wondered how much of it Nick might make pass quickly.

There was a little clump of students loitering outside the

main doors to Chester Hall, including Robin Armin and the young man from behind the Reserve Desk. An ethereal blonde who might have been the one Janet had discussed squirrels with was hanging around Robin's neck. Janet marched up to them anyway.

Mercifully, Robin grinned and said, "Nick let you in on it, too, did he?"

"Foolish boy," said Janet, rather put out. "Doesn't he know how news spreads around here? He's probably got at least two Benfield adherents in with his loyalists."

"Well, and where would be the fun if he hadn't?" said the girl.

"Oh," said Robin. "Janet Carter, this is Anne Beauvais. Freshman undecided, junior Classics."

The tall girl unwound her arms from around Robin and said to Janet, "What are you hesitating among?"

"English, English, and English," said Janet. Anne Beauvais raised an eyebrow. "Well," said Janet, "I did vaguely consider a special major with a lot of different languages in it, but it takes four terms before you get to the interesting literature; and I haven't read most of what's been written in my own language, so I'll probably just stick to that."

"Not in Classics," said Anne, coming around Robin. She was wearing a short green dress in crinkle gauze that, most unlike that material's usual behavior, clung to her and revealed that, without much doubt, she was very muscular and had no use for underwear. Janet feared for Molly's chances.

"In Classics," said Anne, fixing Janet with a stern, pale eye, "you read Xenophon in Greek I and Herodotus in Greek II, and you read Cicero in Latin I and Virgil in Latin II. It's the immersion method they used to try with the modern languages, except the students rebelled."

"And Classics students don't?"

"Have you met Medeous yet?"

"Not in person," said Janet, considerably startled. "I've read her translation of *The Romance of the Rose*."

Anne and Robin looked at each other. There was a moment of sudden and curious tension; then, as if he were offering a theory for examination, Robin said, "That must have been her grandmother."

"Yes, of course, how stupid of me," said Janet, laughing. "The date on that book was 1887."

"You don't rebel against Medeous," said Anne, grimly, "you suffer her, or you flee into exile."

"Melinda Wolfe didn't tell me about her," said Janet.

"She tried to sell you on Greek Lit in Translation, right?" Janet nodded; Anne went on, "That's the usual strategy. Soften the students up with Ferris, who's a perfect doll, and then smack them with Medeous when they're not looking."

The young man from the Reserve Desk loomed over Robin's shoulder and said, "That's not fair, Beau. She's a brilliant scholar."

"She's a bitch," said Anne, without any particular heat.

"This is Kit Lane," said Robin, "who always stands up for the downtrodden."

"Why is he defending Medeous instead of me?" said Anne.

"Excuse me," said Janet, having considered carefully Kit's long hands and slightly hollow face, and the charming way his dark hair grew away from his forehead, "do you have a brother here?"

"He's got two," said Anne, "but you mean the rude one, don't you?"

"What's Johnny done now?" said Kit.

"Flung the 1887 edition of the Medeous translation to the floor because I asked him how long he'd be using it. Oh, and used opprobrious epithets at the top of his voice in the library."

"How curious," said Kit. "He usually goes in for sarcasm."

"It couldn't have been Thomas, could it?" said Robin to Anne.

"Not a chance," said Kit.

Robin still held Anne's eyes. Janet wondered irritably if they thought they were communicating telepathically. Then a couple of students who had been swinging the main doors of the building open and shut called, "It's five of!"

Everybody moved in a rush for the doors. Inside was a short paneled corridor with the Music Library on one side of it and the offices of the Music Department on the other. At the end of this passage was a set of glass doors that led into a domed hall set with six skylights. Its plaster effusions were painted institutional green, but the marble floor still impressed Janet mightily. She and Danny Chin had once sneaked in here after dark to try roller-skating on it, and Danny had broken his arm.

Two marble staircases endowed with vehemently carved wooden balustrades led to the two branches of the second floor, where the practice rooms were. It was deathly quiet; the soundproofing up there was excellent.

Then the sounds of everybody else coming in after Janet set up echoes. The group collected in the middle of the hall, under the skylight, not speaking. There were nine of them, all very much in the theatrical mold except for, of all things, Miss Zimmerman, who might not be statuesque but was certainly as cute as a button and knew it. She was the only person present wearing red; more oddly, she was the only female not wearing green. It didn't seem to bother her; she was happily making eyes at Kit Lane. Kit, having considered her for a moment, introduced her to another of the beautiful young men, this one very dark, with features like a statue, named Jack Nikopoulos. Miss Zimmerman greeted him brightly and then fell silent.

It grew quiet again, except for the shuffle of feet. Robin, standing between Janet and Anne, breathed, "Shall we go up?"

"He says if we do he'll kill us," said Miss Zimmerman.

Everybody except Robin and the other short boy present looked at her. They looked as Janet looked, except that as far as she knew none of the rest of them had any right to look at Miss Zimmerman so, as if she had usurped their prerogatives, as if she had information appropriate only to somebody on closer terms with Nick Tooley than she appeared to be. Maybe he's kissed every last one of them in the Arboretum, thought Janet madly.

"Well," said Robin, after a long pause, "we can't have that, can we?"

Both the previous scrutiny and Robin's tone would have made Janet furious, but Miss Zimmerman smiled serenely and leaned her shoulders against the wall.

Silence descended again. The light coming through the skylight dwindled. Shafts of sun still came in the doors, but they only made a few lines of dazzle in a huge space increasingly dark. Janet went and leaned next to Miss Zimmerman, because after some consideration, Miss Zimmerman made her less uncomfortable than the rest of them. Except for Robin and the other short boy, a thin black one who looked too young to be in college and was dressed rather like Christina, everybody else was at least six feet tall, and slender, and dressed in either green or white, and possessed of interesting bones.

As the light lessened, their pale faces took on strange lines and the modern outlines of their dress—jeans, a wrap skirt, sneakers, Anne's crinkle gauze—blurred into strangeness. They looked dressed for a play. Robin and the black boy did not partake of this transformation, but neither did it seem to bother them. Miss Zimmerman was the only person who looked nervous.

Janet said quietly, "You're in Evans's English 10, aren't you?"

Miss Zimmerman jumped slightly and said, "Yes. I can't remember your first name."

"Janet."

"I'm Diane."

"Hi."

Upstairs there was a hollow boom underlaid with a crunch, as if somebody had flung a heavy wooden door back against a plaster wall and done in the doorstop. The lights in the southern half of the second floor went on. There was a scurry of feet and some breathless laughter, and suddenly two ghostly insectlike figures came clanging onto the landing. Nick had managed not only two foils—why in the world would he give Benfield a foil?—but the white jackets and screened masks as well. He had the bust tucked under his left arm, and looked, in the strange light, like a man who had taken off his head for safekeeping and was using the mask to fight with.

They fought at the top of the stairs for what seemed like forever. Nick beat Benfield back into the hallway twice, but whatever advantage he hoped for from this never materialized. They were both incredibly fast. You could hear the foils better than you could see them.

What the hell's he doing in a beginning fencing course? thought Janet; and Nick jumped backward down three steps. Thank God they were broad ones, and carpeted wood, not slippery marble. Nick made another leap; he was going to break his neck.

Anne and Kit raised a cheer. Nick lunged at Rob Benfield with a force that bent his foil into half a circle, and as Benfield sat down suddenly on a step, Nick turned and hurled the bust of Schiller straight at Janet.

Even as she shoved Anne and Kit out of the way, backing rapidly across the marble floor, trying to gauge where the wobbly thing would end up—it was a lot less stable in its flight than any ball she had ever dealt with—she thought, so clearly that it seemed for a moment she had said it, I'm going to kill you. The bust was going to go over her head and smash itself into a marble bust of Bach in the wall.

Janet made one last desperate leap backward, and hit the dip in the floor where Danny Chin had lost his footing. She fell flat on her back, arms outstretched, and caught the bust in both hands. Both her wrists felt sprained, but she had not jammed a finger.

"Holy Mother," said somebody, in a dramatic voice that the

hall made into echoes. Janet lurched to her feet and ran like hell down the hallway that led to the side door. She heard Nick shout, "Stop!" and then an assortment of yelps that persuaded her, though she would not have stopped anyway, that he had not been talking to her.

She burst out the emergency exit and ran across lawn, sidewalk, more lawn, another sidewalk, and into the welcoming labyrinth of the Fine Arts building. It would be fatal to stop; Nick couldn't possibly hold off eight people, and the sight of Schiller had been known to change allegiances abruptly. The Fine Arts building, like the library, was built into the hill and went down instead of up. Most unfortunately, it was not connected into the steam-tunnel system.

Janet galloped down four flights of steps, clutching Schiller under one arm and knowing from the way it rasped the skin inside her elbow that it had broken an ear or a nose or a curl. She pushed open the bottom door and stepped outside again, breathing hard. To her right was the grove of larches; to her left was the dismaying open space of the playing fields behind the line of Masters Hall, library, and the old Chem building; before her, across a narrow asphalt road and down a long open slope, were the lower lake and the wooden bridge to Mai Fete Island. Janet started for it, then plunged across the asphalt road, rolled halfway down the hill, and scrambled into the shelter of the larches.

It was cool in there, but extremely prickly. Janet crawled along as fast as she could manage, bumping her head and cursing Nick Tooley and his children unto the *n*th generation, until she found a suitable hollow by catching her knee in it. She removed the knee, saying, "Shit, shit, shit," under her breath because there was no time to think of anything creative, and scooped leaves and dry needles out of the hollow. She dumped Schiller into it unceremoniously, covered him over, limped on through the larch grove to the sidewalk, trudged down it to the bottom of the hill, and took off running in plain sight along the edge of the lake just as the chase came howling past the Fine Arts building.

Janet took one look at them and wadded one side of her smock up under the arm they couldn't see. Then she put on considerably more speed and pounded over the wooden bridge to Mai Fete Island, her heart racing. She had planned to let them catch her, but the way they loped after her with their long legs, like hounds to the hunt, was far too unsettling. She plunged recklessly into the underbrush, and emerged scratched and breathless on the island's other side. She could hear them coming after her over the bridge.

She looked at the green lake water. I'll get hepatitis, she thought desperately, the water will get in the scratches and I'll die a lingering death. The chase came rustling along the narrow path that ran along the shore of the island. They were not breathing hard; their steps were light, their faces intent. Janet plunged into the water. She had to swim, in the end. The water was not deep, but the silt was, and the dreadful slow-motion effect of slogging through it was not to be borne.

She achieved a brisk if lopsided dog paddle, keeping her face and the arm gouged by Schiller's broken ear out of the water as best she could, and clambered gasping up the tangled grass of the far shore. She turned and looked back at the island. There were six of them, Kit and Anne and Jack and three more very like them. The sun was in her eyes, and she could not make out their expressions. They stood up against the blazing sky like huge statues, utterly still.

She disappeared from their sight into a thin strip of woods and out again onto the asphalt road that ran down from the lilac maze to Dunbar. There were people here, on bicycles and on foot, converging on Dunbar for supper. Janet found their presence comforting, until they began to comment on how wet she was, to speculate on how she had ended up in the lake, and to make various dire predictions of exactly what diseases she would come down with.

She scowled at them impartially; then, breathing hard, she followed the clump of them into Dunbar and walked down its first-floor corridor, leaving them to stand in line for dinner. The carpeting was brown; nobody would notice the mud. And this would keep her out of sight for a little longer—or, if the chase had seen her go in, give the hunters one more place to think she might have hidden the bust. Now that she was inside, with the fading smells of dinner behind her, she became aware that she exuded a strong odor of rotting vegetation, algae, and wet dog. She was also feeling rather cold.

She paused at the glass door at Dunbar's other end, looking down the hill to the wooden bridge that crossed the stream, with the great brick bulk of Eliot Hall looming over the bridge and the lake. The reflection of sunset on its upper windows sparkled the lake with gold squares. The bridge and the sidewalk leading down to it were beginning to look rather dark. Once safely inside Eliot, she could take to the tunnels—if she wanted to. The thought of being pursued through them, or caught there, was not pleasing. Well, getting as far as Eliot was a good plan, anyway. The more buildings she went into, the more puzzling it would be for the chase. If they caught her, she would simply show them that she no longer had the bust. It was against the rules to use coercion or threats to find out the bust's location; only guile was permitted.

Janet took a deep breath, pushed open the door, and ran again, pelting down the sidewalk, over the bridge, past the hollow willow, and up the hill alongside Eliot, until she came to a door, which she yanked open and bolted through. A few dinner-goers looked at her oddly, but nobody actually commented this time; her expression just now forbade it.

She turned and squelched down the first-floor corridor to the other end of Eliot. Now she must decide which it was to be, outside or the tunnels. She peered through Eliot's side door; it was mostly oak, and gave less view than the modern glass one of Dunbar.

She could see the entrance to the Women's Center; and out of it, by God, even as she watched, paced Rob Benfield and Nick, shorn of their masks and jackets, in what looked like perfect amity. Janet put her hand angrily on the bar of the door, intending to go out and tell Nick what she thought of him. No, not like this. Even though she had done all this on his behalf, there was too great a chance that he would laugh at her; and then she would probably break his nose.

Janet went down the stairs to the basement of Eliot, and down the next flight to the tunnels. In their arid and slightly dusty depths, the rotten-lake smell of her clothes was stronger than ever. Janet moved as fast as she could without actually running. Her knee was throbbing, and her scraped arm screamed at her. She wanted to look at it more closely, but not enough to stop in the tunnels to do it.

She passed the opening of *The Iliad*, the dim tunnel to Forbes and the ghastly bright one to Holmes, hearing nothing but her own footsteps. Bright patches of poetry and invective swam at the edges of her vision; there was always something you had missed, beckoning you to stoop under a pipe or stand on one, to read what was inserted into a far corner or scrawled on the ceiling by a dedicated graffitist. Janet ignored them all, and, pursued by fragments of Tennyson and Ginsberg and a piece of Euripides that she was certain she had never seen before, turned the last corner, bolted up the steps past the dehydrated water, and ran for all she was worth up all five flights to the top floor of Ericson. She was still oozing slimy water.

She stopped outside her own door, panting, and banged on it. It was opened in a moment by Christina, who looked first annoyed and then surprised and then flabbergasted.

"What happened to you?"

"I went and jumped in the lake," said Janet, shortly.

"You'll get hepa—"

"Look, you don't want me dripping on the carpet. Could you get me my bathrobe so I can take a shower?"

Christina disappeared down the interior hallway, returning in what seemed like a long time not only with Janet's green chenille bathrobe, but her toiletry kit, her week's supply of towels, and a large paper sack from Jacobsen's as well. She was stuffing the first three into the fourth as she approached, and held out the bulging bag to Janet.

"You won't have to touch the clean stuff now," she said, "and you can put those clothes in the bag when you're done."

"And burn them," said Janet, accepting the bag. "Thank you, Tina."

"I don't think you have to burn them," said Christina. "Soak them overnight in detergent and some bleach and run them through the washer a couple of times."

"Sure," said Janet, who had not been speaking literally. "That's a good idea."

Mercifully, the bathroom was empty; very few people took showers at dinnertime. It took three latherings with herbal shampoo and four soapings with peppermint soap to get the smell of the lake off of Janet. She was about to do a fifth round with the peppermint when she realized that the remaining smell was from the sodden heap of clothes she had removed.

She bundled herself into her bathrobe, wound a towel around her head, and disposed of the clothes as Christina had recommended, putting, in addition, a large sign above the sink that said, "No, I DIDN'T forget about these; touch them at your peril." In a mixed dormitory that would just be asking for trouble, but in a girls' dorm it was probably all right; and it vented a little of her remaining spleen.

When she came upstairs she found Nora, also in a bathrobe, a red silk one with a blue dragon on the back, and her hair not in a towel but in dozens of little braids, sitting at Molly's desk and waiting for her. Christina was sitting on her own bed and looking vastly concerned.

"Christina said you fell in the lake," Nora said.

"Well?" said Janet.

"Did you swallow any water?"

"No, I don't think so."

"You'd know," said Nora. "Well, you could go in on Monday if you wanted and ask for a tetanus shot and a blood test, but there's probably nothing to worry about."

"I wasn't worrying," said Janet.

"No, I'm sure you weren't," said Nora, getting up, "but somebody has to."

She went out. Janet, still irked, began to dry her hair. As soon as she had got it so it wouldn't drip on the book, she ought to do that philo reading. She was not hungry anymore.

Christina sat on her bed, doing nothing, but having the wit not to say anything. As Janet shook herb-scented water from her right ear, somebody began to whistle in the staircase. In the room the women come and go, Talking of Michelangelo.

"It's Nick!" said Christina, starting up. "Do you want me to keep him out in the hall till you get dressed?"

"Certainly not," said Janet. What she wanted was for Christina to go away so she could scarify Nick properly; but it was Christina's room too, and Christina was being remarkably decent about everything.

The whistle came on down the hall and stopped, and Nick knocked hugely. Christina let him in; he greeted her cheerfully, saying something in a low tone that made her laugh. Janet sat down on her bed and shook out her damp hair, scowling. Nick came around the corner, pleasure and approbation evident in him from his unruly dark hair to his scuffed loafers.

"Oh, well done," he said to her. "Did I keep them occupied for long enough? I saw Kit looking quite disconsolate, but I didn't care to speak to him somehow."

Janet gathered herself carefully, and Christina said, "She ended up in the lake. What have you two been doing?"

The way she said "you two" made Janet grit her teeth.

"Schiller," said Nick, apparently unaffected. He grinned at

Janet. "That was very bright of you. That whole lot hates water. Look, do you want to have dinner before the movie?"

"I have to do my philo reading," said Janet darkly.

"Come to dinner anyway."

"If you'll promise me one thing."

"It's yours."

"*Never* do that to me again."

"But why? You managed it beautifully."

"I don't care," said Janet. "The point is not how well or badly I manage surprises like that—the point is that I hate them. Don't do it again. All you had to do was ask; I'd have agreed to take Schiller and run like hell. But *don't spring things on me.*"

"What'd you do with him?" said Christina with wide eyes.

"Nicholas?" said Janet, her eyes on Nick's blunt face and those ingenuous blue eyes, which were looking at Christina and not at her.

"I understand," said Nick; and then looked at her. "Well, what *did* you do with him? Since Tina's had to witness this uproar, she might as well be in on the secret. I need a new cell, anyway."

"A new what?" said Christina.

"Cell," said Janet. "As in conspiracy to commit revolution. We're going to have to conspire to put him in a better place, actually; he's not very secure where he is."

Nick, on hearing Schiller's location, agreed with this assessment; he and Christina and Janet then removed Schiller from under the larches and deposited him with a friend of Nick's in Dunbar. Then they ate dinner in that modern, airy, glassed-in dining hall, with its fine view of the green lake. Then they all went to see Olivier roll his eyes in *Othello*.

It was not until Nick, sitting between them, took Janet's hand and, looking to smile at him in the dim light, she saw that he was also holding Christina's hand that she remembered Tina had seen this movie last night. She did not know whether the dual hand-holding was diplomacy or impudence, but she thought she knew what to call what Tina was doing. It was appropriate, though hardly comfortable, that the theme of *Othello* should be jealousy.

Nick walked them back to Ericson afterward and left them on its front steps. "I'll call you," he said, straight to Janet, and walked off briskly, whistling "Greensleeves." It occurred to Janet that he always said that, but he never did; he just showed up.

"Isn't he cute?" said Christina placidly, and opened the main door of Ericson.

"Perishingly," said Janet, and they went upstairs.

CHAPTER

5

Janet woke up for no reason. It was very dark in the room, except for the dim rectangles of the windows, letting in some of the light of the street lamp between Forbes and Ericson. All the windows were open, and a faint breeze blew the new curtains, but it made no sound. Tina wasn't snoring. Nobody was racing motorcycles up and down Mile Street; nobody was having a beer party in Forbes. If she had been dreaming, she could not remember it. One moment she had been not awake, and now she was awake.

She shook out her pillow and lay down again. Into a mind full of negatives, one more stole. Good heavens, thought Janet, quite clearly, it wasn't Tina who saw *Othello* Friday night. Tina helped Nick soothe Robin with ice cream. It was Molly who stayed for the movie. And I've been fuming at Tina all evening for coming to see it twice just because Nick was there; and she didn't do anything wrong. My mind is going and it's only the first week of classes.

"What was that?" said Molly's voice, softly.

"I don't know," said Janet, also softly. "I woke up, but I can't hear anything."

"Shhh. There it goes."

Janet sat up and listened. Far away on the edge of hearing came a vehement sobbing and wailing. Janet went all over goosebumps. The sound drifted and died and came back more strongly, and suddenly it was not sobbing at all, but music. Somebody was playing bagpipes. "It's a piper," she breathed.

"Far out," said Molly; after a moment, she added, "Why does it have to sound like somebody killing a lot of cats?"

"I think he's only warming up; give him a minute."

"Let's go outside."

"It's three in the morning."

"Lucky for the piper," said Molly. Janet heard her get out of bed and pull her jeans on. She slept in a T-shirt, so that was that. Janet slid her feet into her moccasins, and groped around the corner for her bathrobe, bumping Molly, who snickered. "Should we wake Tina?" said Molly.

"She won't thank us," said Janet, who was still, unfair as she now knew it to be, as angry at Tina as she had been before she woke up.

"No, I guess not," said Molly, and pulled the door open.

They shut it carefully behind them. The long red-carpeted hall was full of shadows from the one lonely light burning in the middle of the ceiling. Their long coiling shapes looked like dragons. Janet did not mention this to Molly. She went in silence past the shadows under the telephone box and the drifts of darkness below the fire extinguisher, eased open the swinging doors with their eighteen small panes of glass, and preceded Molly down the echoing stairway.

One dim light burned above the oak desk in the entry, where once the dormitory monitor had sat to sign the girls in and out, and to corral and interrogate their visitors. The big lounge was dark, its furniture lurking in the shadows like indeterminate sleeping animals; but there was a line of light under the door to Ericson Apartment. Melinda Wolfe was up late. She was being very quiet in there.

"Do they lock the front door?" breathed Molly.

Janet made a shushing motion; she did not want Melinda Wolfe to hear them. She pushed gently on the bar of the door, and it opened without a sound. A gush of crisp and chilly air engulfed them. They stepped outside hastily and pulled the door shut. It was on a spring that made it close very slowly and then shut the final inch with a bang, so first they urged it along and then they held it back, and it closed with barely a click. Janet looked over her shoulder at Melinda Wolfe's lighted windows, and moved quickly down the limestone steps of Ericson.

The sky was patched with clouds that glowed faintly with reflected light from the campus and the town. The streetlights leered at their own reflections in the dark glass of the Music and Drama Center across the street. The dark bulk of the Chapel cut the sky behind it like the rook in a gigantic game of chess. Only the radiator skeleton of Olin was visible, like a cage from which the building had escaped. Dancing with the dragons in the Arboretum, to the music of the bagpipes, thought Janet, and blinked hard, as if that would quiet her mind.

A few more streetlights pricked the darkness that was the west side of campus, where Nick and Robin slept in Taylor above the old-soup smells of its dining hall. Janet thought she would like to go that way: tonight even Taylor might be comforting, when the familiar east side of campus was so full of odd thoughts.

But the piper was on the other side of Ericson, east toward Eliot and the Arboretum. They went around Ericson, the long way toward Mile Street, rather than the short way that passed under Melinda Wolfe's windows. The sweep of grass between Ericson and Forbes was just discernible. The light on the asphalt road made a bright circle in which a few moths fluttered. The shoe-box shape of Forbes was dark. Behind and above it the castle shape of Eliot stood dark against the cloudy sky. They stopped, facing it, and listened. The wailing drifted, waned, and steadied into a thumping march. It was either in Bell Field just beyond Eliot, or in the Upper Arb itself. Probably the field, thought Janet. Nobody was going to lug a set of bagpipes along those narrow paths in the dark. Not even dragons that had left their shadows behind.

"Bell Field," she whispered to Molly.

"I'm game," said Molly.

They took a few steps across the grass, and something flapped through the air and thumped to the ground behind them and to the left. Janet jumped; Molly stood perfectly still ahead of her, but Janet heard her take her breath in. They turned around and looked at Ericson. It was dark except for the dim small squares where the lights of the stairways shone in their little windows. Janet looked up and found the windows of their own room. The curtains blew in and out, and the stripes and shadows in the dim light made a pattern like lace. Something pale flew out of the middle window and smacked to the ground a few yards away.

"That was a book," said Janet, and thought wildly of *The Wind in the Willows*. She ran across the grass, and stumbled, before she got to the book she was aiming for, over another book. She picked it up, keeping half an eye on the windows. It was small and dark and thick. Janet opened it to the title page, and its clean paper glowed a little in the distant light from the Forbes street lamp. The dark parts of the page she looked at said, "A LEXICON abridged from Liddell and Scott's Greek-English Lexicon. Oxford, at the Clarendon Press." Janet turned a thin, crisp page, and read, "ADVERTISEMENT. THE Abridgement of Liddell and Scott's Greek-English Lexicon is intended chiefly for use in Schools. It has been reduced to its present compass by the omission . . ." Janet skimmed rapidly along, to the small type at the bottom that said, "OXFORD, *October*,

1871." She had read the right-hand page; she looked now at the left-hand one, which proclaimed, in an isolated line in its middle, "Impression of 1878."

Molly, who had gone on past her and collected the other book, walked back across the grass, loomed over Janet, and said, "I've got Matthew Arnold's *On Translating Homer* here."

"Liddell and Scott," said Janet. "Classics."

"Those came out of our windows."

"They can't have; we haven't got those books."

"You saw it too."

"Yes, I did," said Janet. She stood up, since the grass was damp. The book in her hand smelled clean and inky. She leafed through it slowly, looking at the fantastical Greek letters in boldface; all its pages felt crisp and smooth and clean. She held it out to Molly, who took it and gave her the Arnold, a tiny red-bound book. It, too, was clean and fresh. Janet found the title page. The Clarendon Press at Oxford. 1861. She looked at Molly, who was frowning at Liddell and Scott; and another book swooped out of the air and landed between them.

"Lordy!" said Molly, but bent immediately to pick it up. Janet, breathing carefully in an effort to get her heart to slow down, moved around and looked over Molly's shoulder. This one was McGuffey's *Fifth Reader*. It was more battered than the other books; on the title page Molly had turned to was a small dark thumbprint obscuring the date. Janet forgot, looking at it, the night, the piper, her heartbeat, and her wet feet, and felt as she had felt many years ago on a school trip to a museum. She had looked for fifteen minutes at a porcelain doll in a grubby white dress, and burst into tears.

Something rustled behind them. They sprang apart, dropping the book. A small person in a long white gown, her hair straying over her shoulders and her arms full of books, came pacing toward them across the dewy grass.

"It's the Fourth Ericson ghost," said Molly, as calmly as if she were identifying a starfish.

"No, it isn't," said Janet, with great relief. "It's Peg Powell."

"She may *look* like Peg Powell," said Molly. She stooped for the McGuffey and shook out a crumpled page or two.

"Should we speak to her?" said Janet. "I wonder if she's sleepwalking?"

Peg bent over and came up with the Arnold. Janet had thought she was holding that one herself, and took a firmer grip on the Liddell and Scott. Peg came closer and closer. Molly promptly stepped aside; Janet stood her ground, and just as she thought she was going to break and run whether she wanted to or not, Peg stopped. She was not exactly looking at Janet; but then, she didn't have her glasses on.

"Oh, thank you," she said, precisely as she would if you passed her the salt. She held out the hand that was not cradling a pile of books. "It's so tedious to pick them out of the wet grass."

Janet handed her the Liddell and Scott, reluctantly, and stooped for the McGuffey. "This isn't a college text, is it?" she said. She had a vague notion that one ought not to confront or challenge somnambulists.

"No, it was brought along for sentimental reasons," said Peg, tucking the Liddell into her pile and holding out her hand again for the McGuffey. "Well, good, I think that's all of them. Maybe we'll have some peace for a few nights now."

In ironic commentary, the distant bagpipes, which had been muttering in the background, wheezed into a mournful, rolling tune that would have been more at home on a church organ.

"Does this happen often?" said Janet.

"No, I wouldn't say often," said Peg, judiciously. "It does get tedious, though. I'm going to take these in now; the damp's not good for them." She gave Janet a brilliant smile and trailed away over the grass toward the side door of Ericson, her white gown floating around her.

Molly went after her, and stood at the bottom of the steps until Peg had opened the side door and disappeared inside. "I guess," she said, rejoining Janet, "if she came down, she can go up again by herself. We'd better make sure Nora knows she walks in her sleep."

"I'd think Sharon would have to know," said Janet.

"I hope she didn't, if she was letting Peg climb in and out the window their freshman year."

The bagpipes set up a vigorous hooting.

"Come on, let's go find the musician," said Janet.

"If you can call it music," said Molly, but she came along.

Past the square shape of Forbes and the battlemented bulk of Eliot they hurried, and stood at the top of the steep hill that led down to Bell Field. The moving stream slid darkly along two sides of the field with only a muted gleam or two. Behind it the trees blotted out the sky. The town was behind them now, and the scattered farms and the vast area of the game preserve sent no light to show up the clouds. How could anybody have lugged a set of bagpipes around in this dark? She and Molly were probably going to break a leg just getting down the hill unencumbered.

"I don't hear anything," said Molly.

They stood listening. A car went by on the highway, to their left, beyond Dunbar and the lilac maze. A few stubborn summer insects creaked. A pigeon in the eaves of Eliot rustled and mumbled and settled to quiet again; one querulous coo answered it. A faint music came out of Dunbar, but it was electric and rather desperate-sounding. Janet's feet were cold, and the belt of her bathrobe was slipping. She undid it and knotted it again viciously.

Somewhere in the woods across the field, the bagpipe spluttered and wheezed and played again. Tom, Tom, the piper's son, learned to play when he was young.

"Very funny," said Janet.

"Not your ordinary pennywhistle," agreed Molly, chuckling. "Shall we follow?"

"He's on the other side of the water and we haven't got a flashlight."

"A silly omission," said Molly. "Put it down on the next Jacobsen's list. Flashlight, piper hunters, for the use of."

"I think he's moving along the stream," said Janet. "Maybe he'll come to us."

"Well, let's go down to the bridge and wait, then."

They groped their way down the steep steps that descended the hill with Eliot, stepped softly along the sidewalk, under students' windows and then past the big triple windows of the dining hall. The sidewalk ended at a service door; Janet and Molly skidded on down the eroded gully to the bridge, and frightened two ducks, which floundered out onto the lake, making indignant noises that for a moment almost drowned the sound of the bagpipes.

When the lake was quiet again, the bagpipes were quite close, just the other side of the stream, and were playing a song that Janet, who had helped Danny Chin run the lights for their high school's production of *Twelfth Night*, recognized at once. When that and I was a little tiny boy, With a heigh, ho, the wind and the rain, A foolish thing was but a toy, For the rain it raineth every day. Their school edition had not footnoted that song; she still remembered Danny's astonished glee when she dragged out her father's Shakespeare and showed him what that verse meant.

"There he is," said Molly softly.

Eliot's outdoor light on this side was burned out. Across the water and up the hill, the light mounted on Dunbar's south end lit up half the sidewalk and the top of the hill and cast the bottom of it, where the piper was coming out of the woods, into deep shadow. Molly stepped onto the bridge, and Janet followed her hastily, before the prickles going up her spine could turn into cowardice. She suspected that Molly was trying to make up for having backed away from poor harmless Peg, but that was no reason to abandon her.

They stopped in the middle of the bridge, where it was highest and gave them the best view. The sound of the pipes moved on across the grass; something scraped on the concrete of the sidewalk, and the piper became visible as a black shape of horrendous appearance, to Janet's considerable relief. She had begun to be afraid that there was nobody there at all, just the sound of the bagpipes moving alone in the night.

"It's Robin," said Molly, sharply, and ran down the far side of the bridge. Janet scuffed after her, cursing the moccasins, which had stretched with age.

But it really was just Robin Armin, in his ragged jeans and white muslin shirt, all bedecked with his bizarre instrument and grinning amiably.

"You dimwit, why hasn't anybody lynched you before now?" said Molly in a heated whisper.

"Very few people actually awaken," said Robin. He was whispering, too, but a whisper so resonant that Janet cast a nervous glance up the hill at Dunbar. All its windows were still dark. "I play every term, for those who are awake still," said Robin. "What woke you, do you know?"

"You did," said Molly, with finality.

"I don't know," said Janet. "I think my mind was working something out, and when it came to a conclusion it woke me up."

"I'm sorry to rob your sleep," said Robin. "I have to go on my rounds now, but if you'll be my guests tomorrow night I'll buy you pizza that's fresh, so saving you from the Food Service's idea of Sunday supper."

"I have to have dinner with my family," said Janet. "But take Molly for pizza. I think I probably woke her up thrashing around in bed, anyway."

"Six, then," said Robin. "I'll call for you." He turned, a little ponderously, and went on up the sidewalk past Dunbar. They stood on the bridge in the chilly air, listening to the water slide underneath. A few minutes later, when he was presumably somewhere in the neighborhood of the lilac maze, the pipes began again faintly.

"Isn't he cute?" said Janet to Molly.

"Huh," said Molly. "You want another dip in the lake, just let me know."

Tina got up early, which probably wasn't her fault, and whistled, which certainly was. Even the suspicion that she was whistling Bach did not ameliorate the offense. Janet jammed her pillow over her head, which not only dulled the noise, but kept the blazing sun out of her eyes. It was supposed to rain on Sundays; couldn't the climate get anything right this year?

Tina's whistling receded, and was cut off by the quiet closing of the door. Why didn't she just bang it, as long as she was whistling anyway? The birds were whistling too, never mind that they were supposed to be going south for the winter. Janet flung the pillow to the floor and sat up crossly. It was nine o'clock, an obscene hour at which to be up on Sunday. On the other hand, if she got up and had a large breakfast, she could read until five and then go off to her family dinner with a clear conscience.

Janet put her feet into her moccasins. They were damp, and speckled with bits of grass and leaf mold. What in the world—oh, the piper. No wonder she was cranky. And no wonder Molly was still asleep.

Tina opened the door quietly and came whistling in.

"Shhhh!" said Janet as she came around the corner. "Molly's asleep."

"She was sound asleep when we came in last night," said Tina, as if that were an excuse for waking somebody. She was wearing a pink cotton dress with a voluminous skirt and a lace collar. She looked dreadfully healthy.

"We had some excitement in the night," said Janet, still quietly.

"What?" demanded Christina, crossing to her already-made bed and bouncing herself down on it.

"We heard somebody playing the bagpipes and went out to investigate."

"Well, for heaven's sake, I heard it too," said Christina. "I put the pillow over my head and went back to sleep."

"How practical of you," said Molly drowsily, from under her own pillow.

"Sorry," said Janet.

"Oh, well," said Molly, dumping the pillow on the floor and revealing a tangle of brown curls and a bleary face, "I can do my Physics now." She sat up. "The piper was Robin Armin, Tina. Just think what you missed."

"Was Nick there?"

"No," said Molly.

"Well, then," said Christina. "Do you guys want to go to breakfast?"

"Just let me wash my face," said Molly.

"No, thanks," said Janet. When they had gone to Eliot, she took her anthropology book over to Taylor and ate watery scrambled eggs and flexible toast and read about the forest people of New Guinea. The people were very interesting, but the anthropologist would have gotten a D from any decent high-school English teacher. Janet wondered if you could write a paper about the bad style of anthropologists. It was a pleasure to finish with them and turn to Aristotle, whose translations at any rate were of a perfect clarity by comparison.

At five o'clock, with only three pages of Aristotle left to read, she said good-bye to Molly, who was muttering, "Fuck Physics" under her breath about once every five minutes, got out of the basement the old green bicycle she had had since she was eight, and rode home for dinner.

She took the sidewalk to the asphalt road between Forbes

and Ericson, and the asphalt road to Mile Street, and Mile Street three blocks to Chester Avenue, and went out Chester with her hair blowing straight behind her in a most pleasing way. It was a wide street that had as yet lost none of its elms. It stretched away in a long tunnel of brilliant yellow leaves and black branches. The leaves were falling slowly. The houses on Chester were Victorian, larger and solider than the ones Janet and Molly and Peg and Tina had walked by on their way to Jacobsen's. That was Danny Chin's house, and that Professor Davison's, and that was where Lily-Milly's boyfriend lived, and over there in the red-and-yellow monstrosity lived the child who had gotten Andrew into such trouble with the wasps' nests last summer.

After eight blocks, Janet turned right, swept past her old elementary school, turned left, and pedaled past a church and a greenhouse and two long, low, modern houses of no great distinction, to her own house, on a corner lot across from an area of prairie wetland that the College and the Town had been disputing over for seven years. The house, a large and irregular stucco monster with a red tile roof and red trim, had disappointed her dreadfully when they moved into it, because she had passionately wanted a Victorian one with clapboards and gingerbread. But she was used to it by now.

Andrew's red bicycle lay halfway up the driveway; Janet swerved around it onto the grass and nearly ran over one of Lily's rag dolls. She parked her bike where it belonged, in the covered rack beside the garage, and walked back to pick up the doll.

It was an old one of her own, a vaguely Oriental-looking creature that her mother had made on demand not long after Janet met Danny Chin and his family. It had not lain there long; it was freshly washed (she could tell because it was tan and not gray) and still smelled faintly of ironing. Janet straightened with it slowly, and thought of Liddell and Scott.

Vincentio was barking madly and flinging himself against

the back door. Janet ran up the porch steps, wedged herself through the smallest possible opening, slammed the door behind her, and suffered herself to be leapt upon and licked all over. Vincentio, a ragtag mixture of rottweiler, Labrador, German shepherd, and probably Missouri hound dog, had been named for his propensity, as a puppy, to hide in corners. He had outgrown this juvenile shyness as soon as he was large enough to make his friendliness inconvenient to its objects.

Eventually he wore himself out and sat panting on the floor to recover. Janet's eye took in the new rag rug he was sitting on—Lily must finally have given up that old yellow bathrobe—and three fresh examples of finger painting on the potting table, their curling edges held down with rocks and empty pots and one brass paperweight in the shape of the Great Pyramid. She put her hand on the door to the kitchen, only to have it wrenched open. Andrew had come, now that the noise was over, to see what the dog was barking about. His grubby face lit up enormously. "Hey! Jan's back!" he shouted, and flung himself on her neck.

It was like coming home from summer camp. Her parents appeared, her mother from the basement and her father from the downstairs bathroom, and they were still exclaiming at her when Lily condescended to come downstairs, trailing rock music from her open bedroom door, and smile benignly. The kitchen smelled of roast beef and stewed apples. Janet was very pleased, but she felt overwhelmed. She had been living with strangers, who gave you a lot of room until you should choose to be friendly.

The dinnertime ritual was the same. Everybody was allowed to tell what news there might be, beginning with the youngest. Andrew had discovered a revolutionary method of fingerpainting with one's elbows, and had been taken to task by his best friend's mother for saying, "No shit!" when she told him it would use up the paint too quickly. Lily, despite having not played any of Janet's Beatles records for nine whole days, was still going to marry George Harrison when she grew up.

"And leave your kids lying all over the lawn?" said Janet. "Your Connie doll is on the back porch, guarding Andrew's paintings."

"No picking on each other until after dessert," said her father, automatically. "What else, Lily?"

"You tell 'em," said Lily, and stuffed an entire roast potato into her mouth.

"They did the music aptitude test at school and she's going to be very apt," said Andrew.

"I'm going to play the flute, stupid," said Lily, with remarkable enunciation through the potato.

Janet expressed approval of this plan. "I had a musical experience myself last night," she said, and told them about the piper. After the flurry caused by Andrew's declaration that he would get a set of bagpipes and drown out Lily's flute playing had been dealt with, their father said, "Do they still choose the piper by committee, I wonder?"

"What?" said Janet.

"It's a tradition that goes back to the founding of the college," said her father. "I was on the committee for several years. It's not exactly a faculty matter—at least, I was approached by a student, myself—but it was started by Professor Dunbar, I believe. He was a Professor of Natural Science, before they started dividing everything up, and he was a fanatical Scotsman. Who is it this year, Jan, do you know?"

Janet said, "Robin Armin. He's a Classics major—or maybe Theater."

"What else has happened, Jan?" said her mother. "Are you sorry you didn't go to Grinnell?"

"Oh, no, it's wonderful," said Janet. "King's not good for much, but everybody else is splendid. Especially Evans. Oh, Daddy—what do you know about *The Romance of the Rose*?"

"That's out of my period," said her father, automatically, "but it seems to me that it was begun by a genius, continued by an idiot, and translated into Middle English by Chaucer. It's the prime example of the medieval allegory of love."

"Where can I read about it?"

"C. S. Lewis is your best bet," said her father.

"Narnia?"

"No, child. What *do* they teach you in these schools? It's about time you realized that Lewis was a brilliant medieval and Renaissance scholar. *The Allegory of Love* is still the standard work on the subject, and he wrote it in 1936."

"Before *you* were born," said Andrew to Janet.

"What else, Janet?" said her mother.

Janet thought about Nick, but since all her public expeditions with him had not been describable as dates, and she was still angry with him anyhow, she decided against mentioning him. She told them a little about Tina and Molly; she told them about the battle for Schiller, which her father had also heard of, in somewhat distorted form, from Anne Beauvais, who was in his Romantics seminar; she told them about the peculiar influx of theatrical types.

"It's Medeous," said her father. "She has delusions of performing Greek drama in the original language."

"Oh," said Janet. "I almost forgot. We saw a manifestation of the Fourth Ericson ghost."

"Who'd she look like?" said Lily.

"We didn't see *her*," said Janet. "It was when Molly and I went to find the piper. Somebody was throwing books out of the fourth-floor windows."

"Which ones?" said her mother.

"Liddell and Scott, Matthew Arnold's *On Translating Homer*, and McGuffey's *Fifth Reader*."

"That's not what the canon says, is it?" said her mother, amused. "They should be more consistent, if they want to fool people."

"So you don't think it was the ghost really?" said Andrew.

"I don't know," said Janet. "The books were dated in the 1800's, but most of them looked awfully clean and new."

"But it was dark," said her father.

"Well, did you keep the books?" said Andrew. "You could take them to a book analyzer and he could tell you—"

"No, Peg Powell—she lives on my floor—came along and took them," said Janet. "But I could ask her to let me see them."

"She probably threw them out in the first place," said Lily. "Why else should she come along?"

"Same reason we did—she heard the piper. Anyway, I'm not sure she had time," said Janet, considering. No, Peg hadn't been breathing hard or looking disheveled; and even running for all she was worth, she couldn't have gotten down four flights of steps, out the main door, and around the far side of Ericson, past the bulge made by the Little Theater, between the time the books went out and the time she appeared.

"What about your news?" she said to her mother.

Her mother had taken Lily's Girl Scout troop canoeing on the river, and they had all been very grumpy about being made to work, believing, like all children of their generation, that all transportation was equipped with engines. She had made a new rag rug, painted the upstairs bathroom, washed the dog, and weeded the garden, though goodness knew you oughtn't to have to do that in September. She had read one of the books Janet had pressed on her before going off to college, and thought it very interesting but rather rough, which was probably Janet's father's fault, because living with an English teacher meant you couldn't pass over a single stylistic flaw, ever.

Janet's father put up a mild protest, which Janet overrode with, "Which book?"

"*Babel-17*," said her mother. "Your father really ought to read it, if only to tell me what's wrong with the lingustics; but I think he'd only throw it across the room."

"Like the ghost," said Andrew, and giggled.

"Yes, the ghost," said their father. "Jan, if you can get those books away from the mysterious and suspicious Peg, I really would like to take a look at them."

"Okay," said Janet. "I assume I could get her to lend me the Arnold or the McGuffey. I don't have any excuse to borrow the Liddell. So where is *Babel-17* rough?" she asked her mother.

"I'll show you after dessert," said her mother. "Your father hasn't told his news yet."

"One good, one bad," said her father. "The level of idiocy of our entering freshmen is *considerably* down this year—I'm much encouraged. Even the premeds seem to have some glimmerings of grammar in their fuzzy little heads."

"Thanks, Dad," said Janet.

"You're privileged; of course your level of idiocy is less than the average. Now, the bad news. Tyler's got pneumonia and is going to miss most of the term recovering from it; I have the joyful choice of taking his Modern Poetry course or taking over for Davison as chairman so *she* can take his Modern Poetry course. She says the misery of the one is about equal to the misery of the other, so I can choose."

"I think he should take the poetry course," said Janet's mother. "He's *been* chairman; let's have some different misery, at least."

"Sure, take the poetry course," said Janet. "You can have a wonderful time telling them how awful all the moderns are, and comparing them to real poets."

"That, my child, would require first that I read the moderns, second that I have a grasp of what they are attempting, and third that I be able, ideally, to demonstrate both that it is not worth doing and that they are doing it very badly."

Janet's mother began to laugh; Janet stared at her father with a sinking and peculiar feeling. "But you've got a Ph.D.," she said.

"Take it from me," said her father, "it is possible to get a Ph.D. in English while ignoring no less than three literary periods. You must have read *something* in all of them, so as to fling their names about; but you can be quite ignorant of at least three and still do very nicely."

"Which three are you ignorant of?" said Janet.

"The moderns, the whole of the twelfth century, and the Jacobeans," said her father.

"You should have waited until she went to graduate school to tell her," said Janet's mother. "Here, have some pie to soothe your disillusionment."

"I'm not disillusioned," said Janet, accepting the pie just the same, because the lemon meringue pie in the dining halls tasted like lemon Jell-O with chalk in it. "I'm just mad. I thought you knew what you were talking about."

"With regard to what?" said her father.

"Free verse."

"I took three undergraduate courses in it and gave up," said her father. "I've given it a fair try, if you like; but I'm not really qualified to teach it."

"You could tell the students that," said Janet. "Ask them to help out. Ask them to formulate a theory on the spot—well, by the end of the class, anyway."

"Dear Lord, please don't do anything of the sort," said her mother. "It's bad enough when you're suffering from students' theories about poetry you understand. Duncan," she added, very sharply. "You'll hate it."

Janet's father had a glazed look in his eye, and had not yet tasted his pie. Janet felt simultaneously guilty and triumphant. Her father was going to be difficult no matter what he was doing; he might as well spend his time redeeming his faults. She looked at him intently, and after a few moments, during which Andrew bolted his pie, clamored for more, was called a disgusting pig by Lily, stole the crust she had left behind, and, when she accused him, said the dog had taken it, their father stopped staring out the window and looked at Janet again.

"I'll make a deal with you," he said.

Janet eyed him warily.

"I'll teach Tyler's course this term if you'll take it before you graduate."

"Uh," said Janet.

"Maybe he'll die," said Lily cheerfully.

"*Lilian*," said their mother.

"It's a thought I've had myself," said their father, "but it's unworthy. He's a very nice man, Lily-Milly; his taste is warped, that's all."

"Should he take some zinc?" said Andrew.

"Not that sort of taste," said his father. "The literary equivalent of zinc supplements is a very interesting notion, though. Well, Jan, what about it?"

"Okay," said Janet, heavily, "but you have to listen to me complain every single Sunday evening."

"I thought you only wanted to come home every other Sunday," said her mother.

"For that term," said Janet, "I'll make an exception."

She and Lily cleared the table; her mother washed the dishes and Andrew and her father dried them; then she played a game of Snakes and Ladders with Andrew and read him a chapter of *Kim*. When she came out of his room, she looked across the hall to the door of her own room, which still bore in wobbly Elvish letters the adjuration, "Say 'Friend' and Enter." Janet looked at it for some time. All the rest of her books were in there, and a few garments she was inordinately fond of that she had not thought suitable for college. "Mellon," she said softly, obeying its command in Elvish, to the closed door. She had painted it pale blue three years ago, and done a good job. It looked blandly back at her, like a summer sky in the early morning. Janet shook her head at it, and marched into the bathroom instead. Lily, who suffered from nightmares and was an early riser, had gone to bed by the time she came downstairs again. It was nine-thirty.

"I think I'd probably better go now," she said. "I've still got some reading to do."

Her parents got up and accompanied her outside, examined the tires on her bicycle, made sure the light worked, hugged her, and waved her off. Back to summer camp, thought Janet.

The yellow leaves still fluttered down in the light of the street lamps. The old, sad, spicy smell of autumn was beginning to overtake late summer's baked scents. A light wind blew from the north with the promise of cold. Maybe she should have cadged another wool blanket; her bedspread wasn't very heavy, and Tina always wanted the windows open at night.

She had never asked Peg or Sharon about those bunk beds. Well, she thought, pedaling faster, i will. I'll make sure Peg and Sharon know that Peg sleepwalks, and I'll ask about the bunks, and I'll ask to borrow those books.

She wrestled her bicycle into the basement of Ericson and went slowly up all the stairs. The first floor smelled of popcorn, the second of cider, the third of some sweet and vaguely sickly thing she did not recognize, and the fourth of pizza. Janet went along to the lounge, and found Nick and Tina and Robin and Molly sitting around in a litter of soda bottles and white cardboard boxes spotted with tomato and bits of cheese. They hailed her enthusiastically and offered her the last limp slice and a bottle of orange soda. Janet accepted the soda, and watched with amusement as Tina moved to the middle of the sofa she was sharing with Nick so that Janet could sit on the end.

"So how's your family?" said Molly.

"Very much themselves," said Janet. She grinned. "My father's got to teach Modern Poetry this term, because Tyler's sick; I wish there were some way I could add it."

"I thought you hated the moderns."

"So does my father."

"What period?" said Nick, confusing Janet momentarily. Oh. He meant the time the class met. "I don't know," she said.

"I'll look into it," said Nick, "and give you a report."

"I told him about the piper," said Janet, "and he said they used to be chosen by committee."

"Oh, they still are," said Robin, "and a very select one it is, too."

Molly rolled her eyes at him; he looked first puzzled, and then a little affronted.

"That reminds me," said Janet, getting up again, "I want to ask Peg and Sharon something before they go to bed. I'll be right back."

She walked down the hall, turned into the bathroom, and rescued her lakey clothes from the sink, wringing them out and hanging them over the walls of the shower cubicle nobody liked because it had a draft. She washed her hands and went along to her own room. Tina and Molly weren't there. Janet sat down on her bed, and hoped the spread would be warm enough. She shook her head suddenly. My mind *is* going, she thought. She got up and went back down the hall. Halfway down the stairs, she thought, I forgot to take the clothes out of the bathroom, so why am I going down to the laundry room?

Or was she going to wash the bedspread?

"Hell," said Janet, setting up a mild echo, and sat down hard on a terrazzo step. She fixed her goal firmly in her mind and stood up again. With her hand on the door to the fourth floor, she stopped. She had *had* her mind on her goal before. Suppose she tried not thinking about what she was doing? Considering the peculiar physics of Aristotle, she marched along the red-carpeted hall for the third time, and stopped outside Peg and Sharon's door. She knocked, rather harder than she had intended.

Sharon, unsmiling, opened the door. She was wearing a very short red dress and a necklace of shells. Janet wondered if she were going out at this hour, or if she had come back from a date rather early. Nobody had yet set eyes on Sharon's boyfriend.

"Hi," said Janet. "Is Peg there?"

"Library," said Sharon.

"Well, maybe that's just as well. Did you know she walks in her sleep?"

"Sure," said Sharon. She looked hard at Janet. "She doing it recently?"

"Last night," said Janet. "She was wandering around outside our windows picking up books."

"Huh," said Sharon. "I thought I had that fixed. Okay, I'll take care of it."

"I also wanted to borrow one of the books," said Janet.

As before, Sharon stood aside and waved at Peg's shelves. "Take a look," she said, and sat back down at her own desk, where a fat book of dense print was open next to a notebook full of tiny, neat writing.

Janet knelt on Peg's blue-and-purple Indian bedspread and inspected the books. There was Liddell and Scott, crisp and blue and small. She opened it to the title page. Just the same. She turned to the next pages. The Advertisement was the same, too; but the copyright page said, "Impression of 1970." She looked for the Arnold and the McGuffey, but they were not there. She checked all four shelves again, running her finger along the spines of the books to prevent missing a title or two. Nothing.

"The ones I want aren't here," said Janet, climbing off the bed. "Thanks anyway, Sharon."

"Probably got them at the library," said Sharon, not looking up.

Janet went out and shut the door quietly.

CHAPTER 6

Janet slept badly, dreaming of heavenly spheres that were like sweet bells jangled, out of tune and harsh, with consequent unpleasant reverberations in the lower world. She overslept (if Tina whistled, it did not disturb her), and awoke with a tremendous start with fifteen minutes to get to her fencing class. She arrived just in time, hungry, disheveled, and reeking of deodorant, since there was some chance they might actually get some exercise this time. The students were arranged in two lines, and at the end of one line was an extra figure. Nick. Of course; she was his partner. She hurried into place just as Miss Swifte emerged from her office with the attendance sheet in her hand.

Nick, in a pair of brand-new, stiff-looking jeans and a maroon sweater that was too big for him, winked at her. He looked freshly scrubbed, and had even combed his hair. Janet scowled at him, a forgotten question making her even more irritable than she had been.

"What's the matter?" said Nick.

"What are you doing here, after that exhibition on Saturday? You don't need this class."

"Ah, but that was stage fencing," said Nick. "All style and no substance. This probably won't help you kill somebody in fair fight—but it's a little more solid than Benfield's and my little game."

"It *looked* real," said Janet.

"Well, that's its job, isn't it?"

That was a neat answer; Janet was too irate to consider its actual merits. Arguing with him was not going to accomplish anything. Maybe she could beat him in their first fencing match instead.

They spent half an hour in stretching exercises and then in practicing the lunge without the foil. Then they were taught how to hold the foil, and spent considerable time choosing grips that suited them. Miss Swifte had some undersized and some oversized grips, and a few that were exotic; Janet chose an odd but comfortable one called a Belgian, which felt as if it gave more support to the wrist. Then they practiced thrusting at the uninspiring concrete block wall; and finally, with five minutes of the class period to go, they lined up facing their partners again and learned how to parry. Janet knew perfectly well that being angry would not do her any good; nor would a burning desire to impress Nick. What was required was a burning desire to make her foil do a particular thing at a particular moment; who was standing in its way was irrelevant.

Nick didn't have much reach on her, but he was very fast. Miss Swifte came along and corrected his grip, which was a comfort; but then she corrected Janet's, which, with the Belgian sword, should have been rather more difficult to get wrong. Janet vowed to practice for an hour a day. Stage fencing, indeed.

Nick came up behind her as she was hanging up her jacket, and said, "Have you got time for lunch before your next class?"

"Sure," said Janet, rather ungraciously.

"Where should you like to go?"

"Well—I said I'd meet Peg and Molly in Taylor, but it's such a gloomy day, I'd rather eat in Eliot. They'll forgive me. We can probably sit with Nora and Sharon."

"Let's make it Dunbar," said Nick. "I'd like to eat with you without a crowd of my friends or yours; I don't know so many people in Dunbar."

That was promising; it was a pity he was being promising when she was sweaty and irritable. They walked out of the Women's Center into the misty noon. Bell Field was half-hidden; the stream was invisible, and only the tops of the trees, sickly yellow and drained red, showed above the blank wisps that twined whitely in the woods. They went down the steep steps and along the side of Eliot, down the eroded gully and across the wooden bridge, as Janet and Molly had gone Saturday night to meet the piper.

"How long has Robin Armin been playing the bagpipes?" said Janet as they walked up the hill to Dunbar.

"As long as he's known there were bagpipes to play," said Nick.

"Was he playing last night, do you know?"

"He ought not to have been," said Nick, "it wasn't the time. Why?"

"Oh, I dreamt of horrible music. It was probably just the orange soda on top of too much Aristotle."

"I should certainly hope so," said Nick. "Robin makes excellent music."

There was beginning to be a crowd in Dunbar, but it was all of strangers. They dawdled along in line, talking about what a good teacher Miss Swifte was, and whether it was possible to compare her methods to Evans's. Dunbar's food line was set up with its desserts first: today, an uninspiring collection of limp grapefruit slices, little bowls of chocolate pudding topped with whipped cream that was far too stiff to be natural, and soggy-looking squares of yellow cake with some arcane red stuff in their middles.

"Every time I actually look at the food they give us," said Nick, helping himself to three bowls of pudding and shaking a plate of cake gently, "I remember that passage in *That Hideous Strength*."

"Oh, you mean what Merlin says about the twentieth century?"

"'Your people eat dry and tasteless flesh but it is off plates as smooth as ivory and as round as the sun.'"

"Right. That cake's not very dry."

"If there's any left over it might be good tomorrow," said Nick, withdrawing his hand from the plate and taking another helping of pudding instead. Janet considered all the little bowls on his tray and suppressed a dreadful desire to ask him if he were having his period. She missed Molly suddenly, and was aware of an impatience with this acquaintance with Nick, so fraught with emotion and so imperfect she could not even make a careless remark. Well, there was no way out but through.

The room was furnished with unprepossessing chrome-and-vinyl chairs, of the stackable sort, and rectangular tables for two, which could be pushed together for people who wanted to eat in large groups. It occurred to Janet that you could not get a table for two in Eliot or Taylor. She and Nick set their trays down on the end table of a long row. Nick then picked the table up and separated it from its fellows.

"Sit down," he said, "and tell me about yourself."

"That's a very foolish request," said Janet, sitting down anyway. Nick waited until she was settled, and then fell casually into his own chair, as if he would not much have minded missing it and sitting on the floor instead. He looked a little put out; Janet went on ruthlessly. "Nobody you'd want to listen to for five minutes could possibly respond sensibly to it."

"I could," said Nick, in an injured voice.

"Tell me about yourself, then."

"I eat the air, promise-crammed," said Nick, in melancholy tones. "You cannot feed capons so."

"Who's usurped your rightful place, then?"

"You are too sharp by half," said Nick.

"Oh, come on. My father's a professor of English; of course I know *Hamlet*."

"You didn't know Milton the other day," said Nick.

"Well, but Daddy's a romantic; he loves Shakespeare, especially because Keats seems so much like him; but he can't stand Milton." Having rattled this off, she felt herself going extremely hot in the face, and rapidly dumped the bowl of tomatoes into her plate of macaroni.

Nick, however, either had not intended to embarrass her in the first place or was easily distracted. "Keats seems so much like *whom*?"

"Shakespeare."

"Keats? That querulous, agonizing little emotion-ridden pestilence-befuddled liverer's son?"

"What *have* you been reading?" said Janet, staring at him with her fork suspended.

"What do *you* fancy he was like?"

"Keats? I don't know. I meant the poetry. Daddy says he's the only poet since Shakespeare who sounds remotely like him—whose imagery is anything like as varied and as well controlled, and who can convey so many layers of emotion at one time. I haven't read everybody in between—and neither has Daddy, he missed the Jacobeans—but even I can see the resemblance."

"Say me some Keats, then."

Janet looked at him with a certain alarm. He sounded quite grim about it. His glasses had slipped down his nose, and he was looking at her half over and half through them, without seeming to notice. He had crossed his arms on his chest, and both his hands were in fists. "All right," said Janet. "All right." What in the world could she recite? He knew the sonnet on Chapman's Homer; most of the rest he would probably have labeled "querulous." Not "Ode to a Nightingale," which had illness and drugs in it; not "La Belle Dame Sans Merci," which, in Nick's mood, would probably be labeled not only querulous, but pestilence- *and* emotion-ridden. Something out of "The Eve of St. Agnes" or "Hyperion" might do the trick, but she had only recently discovered them and did not trust her memory to do them justice.

I'll give you querulous, thought Janet, and cleared her throat. "'This living hand, now warm and capable Of earnest grasping, would, if it were cold And in the icy silence of the tomb, So haunt thy days and chill thy dreaming nights That thou wouldst wish thine own heart dry of blood So in my veins red life might stream again, And thou be conscience-calmed—see here it is—I hold it towards you.'"

Nick's hands had fallen to his sides. Janet, looking straight at him now that she had done remembering, and feeling a little smug, realized with a shock that he had turned rather pale. He pushed his glasses up his nose with a hand that shook. "That's *Measure for Measure*," he said, just audibly. "Or *The Winter's Tale*? Or *Troilus and Cressida*; I always forget what gems are hidden in that dungheap. That's not Keats. Is it?"

"Yes, it is," said Janet; to her fury, she sounded apologetic.

"As you love me, don't tease me. If it's Keats, what's it from?"

"It was written in the margin of *The Cap and Bells*," said Janet; she thought the "as you love me" showed a great deal of assurance, but now was not the time to fuss at him about it; he was seriously upset. "His unfinished play. My father says—"

"I cry you mercy," said Nick, getting up, "I'm unwell. No, it's all right, don't bother. I'll call you later."

No you won't, thought Janet, watching him with a maddening mixture of worry and annoyance. He got out of the room without falling over, so he was probably all right. She went back to her own lunch, though she felt very little enthusiasm for it. She looked at Nick's abandoned tray, and suddenly giggled. In some peculiar way, he *was* having his period.

She was struggling with a desire to eat the bowl of pudding Nick had left behind when a resonant and charming voice, made more charming by its diffidence, said, "Excuse me."

Janet looked up, half smiling, and then firmly closed her mouth. It was not Kit Lane, but his abominable brother—John, they said—no doubt about to exercise upon her some of his famous sarcasm.

"Excuse me," he said again, so shyly that she was rendered speechless, "did we have a fight in the library over *The Romance of the Rose?*"

"*We?*" said Janet, rather more feebly than she had intended. He was perfectly gorgeous; it was indecent. She wondered, suddenly, what it might be like to go through life having that effect on everybody. How could you possibly live up to it? If you were homely, or merely cute, or plain but nice like Molly, or austere like Sharon or even healthy like Christina or normally pretty like Nora, you could always startle people with your eloquence or your intelligence or your athletic ability. What did you have left to startle them with if you looked like this?

"All right. You are the girl I was rude to?"

"Yes," said Janet. .Honesty and a curious feeling of pity prompted her to add, "I did bait you a little, maybe; but I just wanted some basic information, like when I could have the book."

"Oh, I've got no excuse; I was just in a foul temper. May I sit down?"

"Sure," said Janet.

The young man sat down in Nick's chair and pushed Nick's tray to one side. "I'm very sorry indeed," he said. "I wonder if you'd allow me to make it up to you?"

All these people were always offering to make something up

to you. Would this one offer pizza, too? Janet contented herself with looking inquiring, and he said, "The Old Theater is doing *Rosencrantz and Guildenstern Are Dead* in repertory with *Hamlet*; should you like to go see one of them?"

"Both," said Janet instantly; he laughed, she blushed. "But that's not fair, you weren't that rude. Make it *Hamlet*."

"No, I think I was. Both, then. Have you any Saturday classes?"

"One-B," said Janet, mournfully.

"I'll get tickets for Saturday nights, then." He got up, looking more relieved than seemed reasonable. "Oh," he said. "I'm Thomas Lane."

Janet got up, too, and held out her hand. "Janet Carter," she said.

His hand was very cool and light. He grinned. "Ought I do have offered a performance of *The Cenci* instead?"

He had recognized her name, then. Her father was the only professor who taught that play. "No, thank you," said Janet, who did not care for Shelley, "Shakespeare will do just fine."

"I'll call you, then, when I've got the tickets." He vanished into the surge of the noontime crowd.

Janet sat down again and stared at Nick's abandoned tray. She felt as if she had betrayed a child. She wondered, in parallel with feeling guilty, if it was wise to accept invitations to the theater from strangers whose only observed behavior prior to the invitation had been discourteous and odd in the extreme. Perhaps she could get Anne or Kit to tell her something about Thomas.

"Thomas," she said slowly. Thomas, the one of whom Kit had said there wasn't a chance of his behaving like that.

"Oh, *hell*," she said under her breath, stacking her own tray recklessly atop Nick's and carrying them both to the return chute. What was she going to say to Nick?

She pushed her way through the long line of students and found herself back in the first-floor corridor of Dunbar, with its brown carpet that would not show the mud. She stopped at the first telephone she saw and called Fourth Taylor. It rang thirty-four times and was finally answered by a laconic male voice that said, "City Morgue. You stab 'em, we slab 'em."

Controlling her fury at this adolescent wit, Janet said, "May I speak to Nick Tooley, please?"

"Minute," said the voice. It returned very shortly, and said, "Not here. Can I take a message?"

"No, thanks, I'll try later," said Janet politely, and slammed the receiver back onto the hook. She looked at her watch, and ran down the corridor as if the long-legged seekers of Schiller were after her. She stopped suddenly at the foot of the stairs, and then ran up them and banged on the door of 423, where Schiller had been delivered. Nick might very well have sought refuge there, if he was really sick.

Nobody answered the door. Janet ran back down the stairs and went with as much speed as she could muster back to Ericson. In the empty room, she shoved the books and notebooks for her next two classes into her knapsack, flung it onto her back, and ran back downstairs with a corner of *Modern Anthropology* digging into her shoulder blade. She tore across campus to Sterne Hall and ducked into the Health Service. Two pale girls and a boy with his arm in a sling sat rather sullenly on the benches provided. Janet approached the nurse on duty, who, clearly and infuriatingly indulging young love, checked the sign-in book and said that Nicholas Tooley had not been in today. Janet thanked her as courteously as she could manage, and darted back halfway across campus to Professor Soukup's class.

Professor Soukup was enough to take her mind off her troubles; but Professor King, in the next class, merely proceeded to tell them exactly what they had just read in their first textbook. Janet, while allowing that this might be necessary because the style of the textbook was so bad, was considerably annoyed. The information did not seem to her, in any case, to be any more than common sense might have produced; there was no need to have gone to the ends of the earth for it. Why couldn't they have a nice, intelligent discussion of fossils?

She sat making elaborate doodles in the margins of her notebook, until she noticed with alarm that she had written the dates of Keats's birth and death and was about to put down Shakespeare's, as if there were some numerological answer to her problems. She put down Shakespeare's anyway, and looked at the figures. 1795–1821; 1564–1616. No, that was of no use whatsoever. She supposed she should have checked all the bathrooms on First Dunbar, or possibly all the bathrooms in the dormitory. Or he might have gone outside and wandered about in the woods and fallen over. Idiot boy. Why should Keats make anybody ill—anybody with a reasonable romantic sensibility, anyway?

Janet sat up a little straighter and turned a page in her notebook, in case Mr. King should have noticed her mind wandering. He didn't appear to notice much beyond his difficulty with the chalk and the blackboard, but you never knew. Then she applied herself to the problem of why she was assuming it was the Keats that had gotten Nick. Far more likely it was fencing on an empty stomach; or fencing on top of one of Taylor's vile breakfasts; or fencing in a large, hot wool sweater on a mild autumn day.

What *was* she going to tell him about going to the theater with Thomas Lane?

Janet stamped back to Ericson and discovered Molly in the room, lying on the floor and muttering over her math book. "You got a call," Molly said, without looking up.

"Oh! Was it Nick?"

"Nope. Thomas Lane; he said to tell you he'd got the tickets for next Saturday and Sunday, and if that's not all right you should call him. He said he thought a week's gap would stale the comparison. Why do all your friends talk like books?"

"What book do you talk like, then?"

"I used to talk like *The Wind in the Willows*," said Molly, closing the math book and rolling over on her back, "but I'm in danger of talking like a physics text crossed with a mental health manual, if this keeps up. We *are* taking Shakespeare next term, aren't we? The thought is all that keeps me going."

"It's only the second week of classes; are you sure you want to be a Bio major?"

"I'm entirely sure I don't," said Molly. "But I do want to be a marine biologist, and this seems to be the way to do it." She sat up and snagged a scrap of paper from the corner of Janet's desk. "Uh-huh, I thought so. I forgot part of the message. Thomas Lane has four tickets to each play, and do you know anybody else who would like to go?"

"You and Nick could come with us."

"Who the hell is Thomas Lane, and where are you inviting me, and why can't we bring Robin instead?"

"He's a very rude young man."

"Robin?"

"No, Thomas."

"And that's why you're going with him somewhere that has tickets, two nights in a row."

"Exactly," said Janet, and sat down on her bed.

Molly glared malevolently, and Janet said, "He's doing it as an apology. He yelled at me in the library. We're going to see *Hamlet* and *Rosencrantz and Guildenstern Are Dead*, or maybe the other way around."

"I'll come see *Hamlet*," said Molly, "but they made me read Stoppard in eleventh grade and I hated it. Why don't Robin and I come with you to *Hamlet*, and you can take Nick and Tina along to the Stoppard?"

"Because I want all the pleasant people in one party?"

Molly leaned forward and fixed her huge eyes on Janet. "Which one of them are you mad at?"

Janet thought it over. "Both, actually."

"Well, then, you'll be putting all the nasty people in one party."

"Your logic overwhelms me," said Janet. "Did Thomas leave a phone number?"

Thomas, it appeared, lived on Second Forbes, the inhabitants of which were a little quicker to answer their telephone than those of Fourth Taylor. He was there, too. His voice was almost too much for the telephone; Janet could hold the receiver four inches from her ear and hear him perfectly. After she had expressed her approval of his plans and secured his for the additions to their party, she called Fourth Taylor again and, getting an irate female voice after forty-three rings, asked for Nick. He wasn't there. She thought of leaving a message, but they would probably tease him about it. She could talk to him after English class tomorrow.

She hung up the phone and wandered down the hall to the bathroom, where she considered her face in the mirror for some time. It was a pleasant and serviceable face, as always, and certainly all that burgeoning red hair was nice, even if it refused to be straight and sleek like the mane of a horse. But it did not look to her like the sort of face that beautiful young men would either be rude to or bother to make amends to. It did not even look much like the sort of face a theatrical and poetical type like Nick would look twice at. Well, he probably liked her for recognizing Eliot, even if she had missed on Milton. But that still left Thomas as much of a mystery as ever. A civil apology would have been enough, surely; or offering to buy her a hamburger in the Tea Room, if his conscience was really hurting him. Tickets for the Old Theater and all of two weekend evenings—not to mention the hours on the bus, one coming and one returning—seemed excessive.

She went back to the room. Molly had flung her math book against the wall and was lying on the bed laughing. When Janet asked her what in the world she was doing, she said she was placing bets with herself about how seriously she had damaged it.

"Oh, no, you don't," she added, as Janet headed for the abused book, which was lying between her desk and the wall. "You have to bet, too, if you're going to pick it up and ruin my fun."

"Okay, I bet you a dollar you cracked the spine."

"Money leaves me unmoved," said Molly.

"Okay, if I'm wrong I tell you all about Thomas."

"Done."

Janet eased the book off the floor and examined it. "You win," she said. "I'm amazed. All you did was bend the dust jacket and the first four pages."

"Put the poor thing back on my desk and tell me about Thomas."

Janet did as she was instructed, and sat down on her own bed. "He is stupefyingly gorgeous," she said.

"I bet he's not cuter than Robin."

"He's not cute at all," said Janet. "He exists in another realm entirely."

"Sounds distracting," said Molly.

"Yes, I think it probably will be." She told the entire story, which Molly met with a nice mixture of indignation and amusement. When the story was done, she asked, "What are you going to tell Nick?"

"*Et tu?*" said Janet, exasperated. "I've been wondering that all afternoon. *Your* job is to explain to me that I'm being very silly. Why should I tell him anything? Besides, you talked me into inviting him. I'll tell him he's invited."

"I did not talk—oh, never mind. Maybe Thomas and Tina will hit it off," said Molly.

"Thanks a lot."

"Well, how many of them do you want, anyway?"

"That's another thing," said Janet. "How come nobody so

much as looked at me the entire time I was in high school, and now they're swarming out of the woodwork?"

"Didn't they really?" said Molly. "You're much nicer to look at than I am, and I had six boyfriends in four years. They were jerks, though."

"All of them?"

"Well, four of them, anyway. Of course, I was a jerk too, so we got along very well."

"Do you think you're a jerk now?"

"Only when bored or hungry."

"Speaking of which, do you want to go to dinner?"

"Let's wait for Tina."

"Where is she?"

"Watching a *Star Trek* rerun. It's over at five-thirty."

"Tina watches *Star Trek*?"

"Why not?"

"Never mind," said Janet. "I think I must be being a jerk—and I'm not even bored or hungry."

"Could you hand me that math book? I might as well be both at once."

Janet gave her the book. "Speaking of which," she said, "I told my father about the books flying out the window, and he said he'd like to see them. But they're not on Peg's shelves."

"Not even the Liddell and Scott?"

"There was a modern printing, not the one we saw."

"Huh. Why does your father want to see them?"

"He collects college folklore. I think he's writing a book on it; he won't say, and he'd probably have to publish it under a pen name, or posthumously."

"After the garden loam," said Molly, and giggled. "I wish I'd known; I could've asked Peg at lunch. And speaking of *which*, where were *you*?"

"Eating with Nick in Dunbar."

"Are you planning to desert us regularly?"

"It's not you, it's Taylor. I couldn't face it in this weather."

"It has a melancholy charm," said Molly. "It prepares one for the miseries of math class. I think I chose the wrong professor. There's one who teaches with Zen proverbs, and another who corrects your spelling, according to Nora. Either one would have to be better than somebody who just tells you what you're supposed to know, once, and goes on." She sighed heavily, and opened the math book.

Janet looked longingly at her little row of unread books, and then thoughtfully at her complete Shakespeare. Then she reminded herself that while she had certainly done some reading for English 10 in the past weekend, she had not done the reading actually assigned for tomorrow's class. She pulled Volume I of the little red-and-white paperback set off her lower shelf, and settled down on the bed with the General Prologue to *The Canterbury Tales*.

After half an hour she decided she had better go read in the fourth-floor lounge. It could not be easy to study mathematics while in the background your roommate alternately chortled and read bits of verse in an incomprehensible dialect aloud to you. She was pronouncing it wrong, anyway; most of it didn't scan. Evans had promised them a lesson in Middle English phonetics tomorrow; it appeared to be his policy to let you struggle through something on your own before explaining it. Janet got up quietly and slipped out the door. Molly didn't look up.

She was well into the "Knight's Tale" when Tina came back, and it was not until she was stopped dead by a line with five footnotes to it, none of which told her what she wanted to know, that she realized there had been voices and laughter in their room for some time now. She closed the book and left the lounge. The door to their room was open. Janet, proceeding down the inner hallway still bemused by Chaucer, was in time to hear Tina say, ". . . taking me to a concert on Wednesday," in a voice of immense exhilaration; but by the time her brain had registered the words she was already around the corner, and Tina was looking triumphant and Molly guilty.

"Hi, Tina," said Janet. "Dinner?"

"If you guys don't mind Eliot. Nick said he'd probably be eating there."

"Good," said Janet, "I want to invite him to the theater." She wanted to stretch the rest out, but something in Tina's face made her say hastily, "And you, too. Do you guys want to go see *Rosencrantz and Guildenstern Are Dead* with Thomas Lane and me?"

"*Thomas Lane?*" said Tina. "The one Peg showed us in Taylor, the day we bought the curtains?"

Janet thought about it. "I guess he was one of them," she said.

"Of course he was. It was Nick and Robin and Rob and Thomas Lane and Jack Whatshisface."

"Nikopoulos," said Janet.

"Right. And Thomas was the most gorgeous of the whole bunch."

"Well," said Janet, "do you want to go?"

"What about Molly?"

"She and Robin are coming with us another night to see *Hamlet*."

"What *is* Rosencrantz Whatever?"

"It's a very funny modern play by Tom Stoppard."

"Well, okay. It sounds like Shakespeare."

"It's *Hamlet* from Rosencrantz's and Guildenstern's viewpoint. But it doesn't matter; I read it before I read *Hamlet* and I thought it was hilarious."

"Well, okay," said Christina again. "Thanks." She put the books she was holding neatly on her lower shelf, shrugged out of her pink nylon jacket and hung it over the back of her desk chair, tucked her gray Blackstock T-shirt into her pink corduroy pants, put the jacket back on, zipped it to just below the Blackstock seal on the T-shirt so that the lion seemed to be peering over the zipper pull, and said, "Let's go, before the line gets too long."

Outside was a gray evening sliding all too quickly into dark. Forbes Hall looked like a modern prison and Eliot like an ancient dungeon. Even the inside of Eliot was gloomy. The dark wood frowned at them; the lights seemed as far away as the moon.

Nick had taken a table in the farthest corner, overlooking the wooden bridge and the place where the stream came out of the lake. He was wearing a blue Blackstock T-shirt that was too big for him. Janet considered the Latin motto, which was generally translated as "Hold fast to learning and fear not," and wondered if he had put the shirt on to give him courage against whatever had ailed him this afternoon. He looked much more like himself: his color was a little high and his hair had come uncombed. He had spread the maroon sweater, a tan raincoat, and a red umbrella over the table and was glaring at all comers. His face lit up when he saw them in a way that made Janet's stomach try to fall out. "Thank God," he said. "I was afraid the footballers would get here first and throw me out the window. How are you, ladies?"

"Sick of mathematics," said Molly, slapping her tray down one chair away from him.

Janet sat between them, on Nick's right, and watched Tina take the chair on his left. He looked inquiringly at Tina, who said, "I don't think I'm supposed to be in Chem 30, even if I did get a perfect score on the AP test."

"Good Lord, I should think not," said Nick. "That's not a course for freshmen. Who's your advisor?"

"Fields," said Christina.

"Well, be round with him and get into Chem 23 where you belong," said Nick, and turned to Janet. "And how is it with you?"

"As with the indifferent children of the earth," said Janet, without thinking; then, as Nick looked wary and Tina confused, she said quickly, "Do you want to go with Thomas Lane and Tina and me to see *Rosencrantz and Guildenstern Are Dead* at the Old Theater next weekend?"

"What about Molly?" said Nick.

Janet explained, again.

"Certainly," said Nick. "Stoppard is a wicked man and I should very much like to see his play. But have an eye for Robin; he'll probably disgrace you again, if you take him to see *Hamlet*."

"No, he won't," said Molly. "I'll bring a canvas bag, and suppress him if he asks for it."

"What has Robin got against Shakespeare?" said Janet. "I thought it was just Olivier he was laughing at."

"Shakespeare said clowns should speak no more than was set down for them," said Nick.

"Well, Hamlet said so," said Janet, amused, "but—"

"Is Robin a clown?" said Molly. "He seems very sober to me."

"It's his studies," said Nick. "He's a mad rogue, really. Wait until he's got all this Greek past his gullet, and you'll see. Or wait until we produce our play this winter."

"How's that going?" said Janet.

"Nobody else wants Ericson Little Theater for anything, so we may have it. We've too many actors already, but if any of you likes to do makeup or lighting, we'd be pleased to overburden your schedules for you."

"I can do makeup," said Christina.

"I've done lights," said Janet slowly, "but we'll have to see. Next term is going to be pretty bad, I think."

"I'll sit in the front and applaud," said Molly, "math book in one hand and physics text in the other."

"What play are you doing?" said Christina.

"Probably *The Revenger's Tragedy*."

"Oh, good, I'll bring my father," said Janet.

"Why, does he like the Jacobeans?"

"No, he missed them altogether, and I thought I'd reform him."

"Tourneur's not likely to reform anybody," said Nick, "but bring him by all means; I don't imagine we'll have much of an audience."

They settled down to their food. They were joined shortly by Sharon and Nora and the short black student who dressed like Christina. He was, mercifully, not dressed like her today; he had on black jeans and a pink shirt. He turned out to be Sharon's boyfriend; his name was Kevin Lorca; and he gave Janet one bright conspiratorial glance and then ignored her. He seemed fairly morose, but Sharon was bubbly in comparison to her usual demeanor.

Nora looked tired, and, asked by Molly what was the matter, said that the freshmen had been acting like nitwits as usual. "Not you guys," she added. "But those kids in the two triples at the other end of the hall have been buying every sort of mind-altering substance the history of mankind has to offer, and giving away free samples to all and sundry. I expect them to put up a sign any day now. And I'm tempted to report them and let the College kick them out, but at least two of them are just silly children who will turn out very well if they can survive till they grow up."

"It's that Beauvais girl who's the troublemaker," said Sharon darkly.

"Who, Anne?" said Janet; next to her, Nick had moved slightly and then taken a long drink of milk.

"No, her baby sister. Anne's a swimmer, she wouldn't touch the stuff. I guess Odile needs some way to be different from Anne. She could have gone to another college and saved us all a lot of trouble." Nora sighed heavily. "I'm going to call them all in and lecture them one by one and warn them, and then we'll see. Just what I need. I've got Eco 60, isn't that enough for one term?"

"What's Eco 60?" said Janet. "It sounds like a brand of gasoline."

"Intermediate Price Theory," said Nora. "Or, How to Go Permanently Crazy in Six Easy Lessons."

"That reminds me," said Sharon, "I need twelve more credits in the social sciences. Any decent lower-level Economics courses next term?"

"You can take 10 and 11," said Nora. "They won't give you credit for 10 until you've passed 11, but it's not really hard."

"I dunno if I want *two* courses," said Sharon; "I thought I'd take some Anthro spring term."

"Don't take it from King," said Janet. "He makes you want to tell him, sit down, dear, I'll do this for you. It's awful."

"Fields is doing the anthropology of religion in the spring," said Tina. "You could get credit both for fuzzy science and for scientific fuzzies."

Nick and Molly laughed; Nora, who had probably been tired of that joke by the end of her freshman year, looked weary; Sharon nodded thoughtfully; and Janet realized that if Nick or Molly had said that, she would have laughed too. Lord, what fools these mortals be.

Nick got up, passed behind Janet rather than Tina, and went back for seconds. Well, he hadn't had any lunch to speak of. When he got back, Sharon and Nora and Kevin were standing up to leave.

"Don't mind me," said Nick.

"We'll stay and keep you company," said Tina.

"Must you?" said Molly. "I wanted to ask you about those math problems, Tina; I can't make head nor tail of them."

"Bring him along afterward," said Tina to Janet. She grinned at Nick. "We'll give you some tea."

"That will be excellent," said Nick with his mouth full.

The rest of them went out chattering. Janet fought down a desire to go find something that took a great deal of chewing. "I guess you're feeling better?" she said.

Nick was cutting up an unidentifiable meat; when she spoke, his hand jerked, and his knife clattered on the green plastic tray. He looked startled and mildly guilty, like somebody suddenly accused, several years after the event, of sneaking into the State Fair without paying. "I cry you mercy," he said; then he seemed to examine this high-flown remark and find it wanting. "I really am sorry," he said. "Let me play you a song after dinner, shall I?"

"Certainly," said Janet, as gravely as she could manage. Pizza; theater tickets; music after dinner. It was enough to make one contrive to be offended, just to see what would be offered next. Not that much contrivance seemed to be needed. Classics majors were a sensitive lot: either starting at nothing like Nick and Thomas, or hauling bagpipes about at night like Robin and then being terribly sorry he had woken anybody up. Sensitive, or senseless? thought Janet, and almost laughed. Nick was attending with great seriousness to his abominable food, and seemed to notice nothing.

After dinner they walked through the foggy air, out of which the falling leaves blew suddenly in their faces, to Nick's room instead of Janet's. Robin wasn't there. Nick shut the door, shot the bolt, sat Janet in his desk chair, offered her tea, dragged a battered black guitar case from under the bed, and proceeded to tune the guitar. He was a lot faster about it than Janet's friends who had taken guitar lessons in high school.

He sang a song she could never remember afterward, a light and clever one about autumn, rather than spring, being the proper time for lovers, because it is the nature of man to defy the elements. Janet applauded when he was done.

He laid the guitar back in its case, knelt next to Janet's chair, put his hand on the back of her neck, and kissed her. How clever of him, thought Janet, to give away the advantage of height so that she would feel matters were somehow under her control. Not long after, she decided that the person with the advantage of height got very little out of it besides a crick in the neck; and sliding out of the chair, she met Nick on his own ground.

This time nobody quoted any Milton, but Janet was brought briefly to herself by the memory of a Bill Cosby routine about kissing couples and chapped lips, and very nearly laughed again. Then she said, "We were supposed to take you back to Tina for tea."

"I know," said Nick into her shoulder. "What's to be done about Tina?"

"I think," said Janet, "that if it were made clear to her where matters stand—assuming that that can be determined—then she would give up gracefully and find somebody else to be interested in. I think she has eclectic tastes." Oh, dear, that probably wasn't at all a kind thing to say.

Nick did not seem to have noticed; he had managed, without her noticing it, to get another button on her smock undone, and was now able, because of the construction of that garment's neck, to slip it down off her shoulder. "Are we walking out together, then?" he said.

"No," said Janet, "we seem to be rolling around on the floor." She was pleased with her insouciant tone, but spoiled it on the last word with a faint gasp; Nick had kissed the hollow of her shoulder, not a spot to which she had ever thought such attention would produce such effects.

Nick, however, lifted his head and laughed. "It comes to the same thing, these days," he said.

"What it had better not come to," said Janet, doggedly, "is an uninvited third party to this enterprise."

Nick thought this over. She hoped he didn't think she was still talking about Tina. She had meant to speak more bluntly, but it was difficult enough to talk at all.

"Fair enough," said Nick. "Shall I do something about that, or will you?" He kissed the other side of her collarbone.

"I think," said Janet, "that you should do something about it while I look into the alternatives. Anything I can do requires a trip to the doctor."

"Fair enough," said Nick again. He laid his head back and grinned amiably at her, and she realized that she would have to get up first. She knelt back, buttoning her smock. Her fingers were shaking. Nick, damn him, looked as if he had been attending an interesting lecture and was a little excited by it.

They went, holding hands all the way, down the drafty stairwell of Taylor and back into a night still foggy but much colder now. The wind had died, and the leaves lay still in the gutters. Ericson was warmer than Taylor, and somebody in the basement kitchen was making chocolate-chip cookies. The door to Janet's room was ajar. A smell of Constant Comment wafted out at them. They went along the narrow passageway, and found themselves greeted by Tina's and Molly's backs, hunched over Molly's desk.

"Are you *sure* you want to major in Biology?" Tina was saying.

"Yes!" said Molly. "Biology is fine. I understand tidepools. No tidepool ever formed that had the slightest use for calculus. I think Mark Twain was wrong."

"What?"

"It's lies, damned lies, and *calculus*."

"Try Classics," said Nick. "No mathematics more advanced than Euclid."

Both of them looked around. "You go to hell," said Molly, pleasantly.

Janet looked smiling at Nick, whose hand had tightened on hers, and saw that he was looking sick again. Then she looked at Tina, who was pointedly not looking at their hands and who wore a fixed and less than persuasive smile. Janet thought Nick might well feel unhappy. She felt guilty herself. But when she tried to let go of his hand, to spare Tina's feelings, he went on clutching hers.

CHAPTER 7

The rest of the week was maniacal. Evans took the English 10 class through a collaborative analysis (i.e., he asked questions until he got either the answers he wanted or some other answer that was acceptable because he had never thought of it) of the General Prologue, "The Knight's Tale," "The Miller's Tale," "The Friar's Tale," and "The Nun's Priest's Tale," with appalling speed. (Nick said, "If you could make a spaceship drive out of that energy, the galaxy would be yours.")

Professor Soukup, who had handled Aristotle with the kind of offhand confidence used by the judges at cat shows on their subjects, was frankly (or so he said) bewildered by Plato, and appealed to his class for help. (They ought to have read Plato first, but the textbooks had been late arriving from the publisher—whether because of the general recalcitrance of publishers or because of Professor Soukup's handwriting, nobody seemed certain.) Janet began to wonder if her notion that her father could teach Modern Poetry by admitting ignorance and asking for assistance might perhaps be a little unfair to the students.

Professor King became less nervous but far more boring, and announced his intention of instituting a weekly quiz "to be certain that people understand the material." Since Janet had failed to discern what there was to understand in it, aside from a fascinating study in how anthropologists mangled their native languages after dealing in other people's, this announcement left her uneasy.

Miss Swifte decided that Janet was scoring too many hits off Nick, and gave her another partner, a young woman who was six feet two inches tall, weighed a hundred and twenty pounds (which was to say, five less than Janet, who resented it), and was composed almost entirely of arms, legs, and knee-length brown hair. She would bundle it up at the beginning of every class, but halfway through it would always tumble down and get into her eyes. This made her aim uncertain but did not dim her enthusiasm, and it was not much more pleasing to be punched by a foil in some area that did not count for a point, than to be bruised in one that did. Since Janet would have liked her opponent very much in other circumstances, and since Nick was doing brilliantly against his new antagonist, which made her suspect his incompetence against her, she was enormously annoyed in all directions.

On Saturday they were to go see *Hamlet*. Saturday morning was Evans's lecture on *The Romance of the Rose*. He spent forty of the period's seventy minutes in a leisurely examination of the history of the allegorical form, which was all very well in its way but had as its main effect the entering of a list in Janet's notebook of another seven works of literature that she really ought to read. Then he stormed through the work itself, devouring the remaining half hour like a hurricane demolishing a barrier island, and leaving Janet wondering if she had been awake.

Nick, who had borne her off for a romantic walk followed

by lunch after Tuesday's and Thursday's classes, vanished after Saturday's class while she was putting her books away in her knapsack. Janet sulked back to Ericson, laid out neatly on her desk all the things she needed to read this weekend for next week's classes, took out her complete Shakespeare, and lay on her bed to read *Hamlet*.

It seemed to her, as it always had, like an uncharted sea out of which rose from time to time the familiar rocks of the soliloquies and certain well-known lines that she had been happily chewing over since she was seven or eight years old. I could a tale unfold whose lightest word would harrow up thy soul. Oh, God, I could be bounded in a nutshell and count myself a king of infinite space, were it not that I have bad dreams. There's nothing either good or bad but thinking makes it so. Blessed are those whose blood and judgement are so well commeddled that they are not a pipe for Fortune's finger, to sound what stop she please. Lord, we know what we are, but know not what we may be. I am more an antique Roman than a Dane. This quarry cries on havoc. Such a sight as this Becomes the field, but here shows much amiss.

Having read the play, and had lunch with Molly, who was fretting over what she should wear to the theater, Janet settled dutifully to her anthropological reading. She thought of writing to the university presses involved and advising them to let their clowns speak no more than was set down for them. That was all she would have to write on her quiz paper, if she didn't pay more attention.

At four-thirty she flung the anthropology text across the room, took off her smock and her jeans, and put on a green denim skirt and a white gauze top. She was saving the velvet dress for Nick, who didn't deserve it in the least. Molly, who had read physics unmoved throughout the procedure of changing, made a strangled noise when Janet came back from the bathroom.

"I don't *own* a skirt," she said reproachfully.

"Put on that daishiki with the elephants," said Janet. "It's nice and festive. Those boys won't dress up anyway, you know."

Molly, grumbling, shed her sweatshirt, washed her face vigorously, put on a bra, made disgusted noises, took it off again, and put on the daishiki. Those boys, when they arrived at five o'clock, had left on their patched and faded jeans, but had changed sneakers for boots and put on white shirts, a plain muslin one in Robin's case and a silk one with ruffles in Thomas's. Robin swept Molly a bow and said, "Milord Hannibal, my felicitations."

"I only did it to please Janet," said Molly. "She thinks elephants are festive."

"Oh, they are," said Thomas. "More suited to some other play, maybe—but never mind."

They went across campus to the Student Union, a small, square building of yellow brick, with a clock tower to it, that contained very little of interest aside from the students' mailboxes. They settled on its steps to wait for the bus, a station that gave them an excellent view of the Chapel with the sunlight on its clean lines, and of the little red maples that surrounded the Bald Spot. Chester Hall lurked among its larches in the distance, and the Music and Drama Center swore at Olin over the heads of ten or so people and three dogs playing Frisbee. It had been a warm day, but it was getting chilly. Janet had her green jacket and Molly's sweatshirt in her knapsack, but the boys were going to get cold.

They didn't look cold. Robin was teasing Thomas about something that had happened that morning in their Aristophanes class. Professor Medeous taught that one, and apparently delighted in making her students explain, in detail, the dirty jokes in Aristophanes. Thomas was attempting to uphold the theory that she invented jokes where there were none, the ambiguous nature of the Greek language and the uncertainties of translation making this an easy task.

Robin kept saying to him, "There are more things in Heaven

and Earth, Horatio, than are dreamt of in your philosophy," which was making Thomas rather angry. The bus was late. Molly was watching the entire business with a sardonic eye. Janet finally said to Robin, "Have you been reading *Hamlet* too? I thought I'd better; sometimes it's hard to understand the lines when they're spoken."

"It certainly is," said Robin, grinning. "Speak the speech trippingly, my ass."

"The review said this bunch was doing the play in American accents," said Thomas, "except for the actor doing Polonius, who's British."

"That will help," said Robin.

The bus arrived in a cloud of exhaust, and they got on it. Janet would just as soon have sat with Molly, but Robin, laughing, drew Molly into a seat next to him. Janet and Thomas sat behind them; Janet got the window. Robin promptly turned around, rested his chin on the back of his seat, and proceeded to harangue Thomas about the production of *The Revenger's Tragedy* they would be doing with Nick winter term. Robin was worried about the lighting, apparently, while Thomas kept telling him he ought to be thinking about the wigs instead. They finally abandoned this contest and began to discuss the play itself.

After about fifteen minutes in which terms like "masque" and "satirical tragedy" and "amorous subplot" warred with long Italian names for supremacy, and nobody listened to Janet or Molly if either of them did try to speak, Molly gave Janet a wry grin over her shoulder, took Janet's copy of *A Tan and Sandy Silence* out of the front pouch of her daishiki, and settled down to read it.

Janet had Arthur Koestler's *The Watershed* (the next book for Professor Soukup's class) in her knapsack, but reading on the bus made her sick. She looked out the window in time to catch the best view of Blackstock, as the bus climbed the hill that led them out of the river valley the town was built in. The buildings between which she ran and bicycled and trudged laden down with books made one tight cluster, the chapel tower, the brick battlements of Taylor, the black glittering clock tower of the Student Union, the brick stack of the heating plant and the mellow sandstone of the Anthro building crammed in the center of a circle of trees, green and red and yellow. You could have put the whole thing in your pocket.

Janet tapped Molly on the head and pointed. Molly closed her book rather impatiently, but once she had looked, she went on looking. "It looks ready to sail away," she said. "On a sea of trees. Over the Arboretum and the game preserve to Canada and the end of the world."

"They'd have to put up the sails first," said Thomas. "I don't envy them the job. I climbed that smokestack my freshman year."

"Why on earth would you do that?" said Molly.

"A bet," said Thomas, a little grimly.

"I thought freshmen had to climb the water tower," said Janet. Blackstock's policy of having no fraternities or sororities had not prevented a certain amount of informal hazing of freshmen, especially the boys; but at least, if you had any backbone at all, you could thumb your nose at the crowd you'd gotten in with and go find some group whose initiatory rites were more to your taste—people who read science fiction, or liked to fly kites, or play Ping-Pong, or get up at five in the morning to gather mushrooms. She wondered exactly what group of young idiots had decided climbing the heating-plant stack was the only gate to the inner circle.

"I started out as a Poli Sci major," said Thomas, just as if she had spoken. "They were getting a lot of grief from the guys in the hard sciences, and decided to prove their manhood by risking their necks. I should have switched majors right then; it would have saved me a lot of time."

"You're going to want it, next year," said Robin, soberly.

"I can take Latin in the summer, I hope," said Thomas. He

looked over Janet's head, out the window. "Look how the light picks out the ridges of the stubble fields."

"Seasons of mists and mellow fruitfulness," said Janet, unthinking.

"Oh, do you know the rest?" said Thomas. "It drives me crazy that Keats died when he did; I think that Ode shows a whole new direction for him. Such a waste. Say it for us."

Janet collected herself and did so. It was not one of her favorites, being rather unlike Keats in many ways. It was probably the one she should have said for Nick, but she had not been aware until now that she knew all of it. She stumbled on the last two lines of the second verse, but Robin knew those. He declaimed them with a slightly exaggerated air that made Janet wonder if he shared Nick's prejudices, but on the whole she thought things had worked out very well.

Robin then started in declaiming the Player King's speeches from the play-within-a-play from *Hamlet*, with such unctuous exaggeration that he had all three of them laughing until they cried. Luckily there were only two other students on the bus, well toward the front; and the driver was used to far worse demonstrations.

One of their fellow passengers eventually got up and swayed carefully down the aisle toward them. It was Diane Zimmerman, in a red velvet off-the-shoulder dress and high heels. "Are you going to see *Hamlet*?" she said. "I thought I recognized that awful verse. I'm taking my brother; he thinks he doesn't want to go, but he's wrong."

"It's amazing how Blackstock captures whole families," said Molly. "Half the people I know have a brother or a sister here. My aunt went here."

"Amazing," said Thomas; Janet thought she heard a sour note in his voice, but when she looked at him he was simply gazing in admiration at Diane's beautiful shoulders; so it was probably something else she had heard.

"Why does your brother think he doesn't want to see *Hamlet?*" she asked Diane.

"Oh, he thinks all literature should be political, and he's completely certain that nobody before 1700 had a social conscience."

"But that's folly," said Robin, hotly. "Hasn't the child read anything?"

"He *stayed* a Poli-Sci major," said Thomas.

"I thought that was a good department," said Molly.

"Well, it was," Robin said, "but Goldstein went to be President of some Eastern university and Marquez went to teach somewhere—Grinnell or Colgate or one of the other ACM places, and nobody left has any sense of history. They read Aristotle so they can feel superior and then they start on Rousseau and those fellows, and the time between is as the void to them."

"My God," said Thomas, "that's my speech."

"That doesn't necessarily prevent its being true," said Robin, grinning, "though it does create a strong presumption of falsity."

Thomas looked at him hard.

"I cry you mercy," said Robin, "that word was ill-chosen. Fancifulness, may I say rather?"

"If you must," said Thomas, but he looked less disturbed.

"You *have* been reading *Hamlet*," said Diane to Robin.

"Oh. You know us theater types," said Thomas. "A head full of quotations, in no good order."

"Do you think *Hamlet*'s the best choice to show your brother he's wrong?" said Janet to Diane.

"Yes, I do. Or at least, if the reviews of this production are right, this production is the right one. The guy in the paper said that productions of *Hamlet* usually cut all the political stuff—Fortinbras, and all the speeches about usurpation and disease in Denmark; but this one leaves it all in."

"What does it leave out, then?" said Thomas.

"He said a lot of the antic disposition gets cut."

Robin uttered a dismayed cry at such a volume that the bus driver looked over his shoulder and said, "No fighting back there!"

"It's intellectual distress," called Thomas.

"Hasn't your brother got ears?" said Molly to Diane.

"He's sulking," said Diane.

"How can they cut the antic disposition?" said Robin heatedly. "Are they mad? Do they want to gut the play? Don't they know Hamlet must be his own clown?"

"Are you going to behave yourself?" said Molly.

"Let him rant now," said Thomas, "or there's not a hope he'll be quiet in the theater."

"I've got a canvas bag," said Molly. "Suppression will occur on demand. Or provocation."

"And did they also cut all the references to Hamlet's madness?" demanded Robin of Diane.

"No," said Diane, backing off a couple of steps and catching hold of the back of a seat as the bus rounded a sharp corner, "the review said that Hamlet is simply assumed to be truly mad."

"Oh, for God's sake," said Thomas, over a renewed cry from Robin. "If I'd known that I'd have gotten tickets to something else."

"There, there," said Janet. "We can have a nice malevolent discussion about it afterwards."

"The only comfort," said Thomas, gloomily, "is that companies that fuck Hamlet up invariably do an impeccable job on *Rosencrantz and Guildenstern Are Dead*."

Diane went back to her brother, Molly returned to Janet's book, Robin and Thomas began an idle discussion of exactly why a director and company that could do a superb job of Stoppard's play couldn't seem to manage *Hamlet*, and Janet looked out the window, where the mild rolling fields of corn stubble and soybean debris, dotted with barn, silo, house, and spiderlike rusted farm machinery, were being replaced by the little frame houses, used-car dealerships, and fast-food restaurants of the city's outermost suburbs. In the low light of sunset they looked like the set of a modern play in which everybody talks interminably and nothing is resolved.

Janet wondered, for the nth maddening time, where Nick had gone after English this morning. She hadn't even thought of calling him; he was never in, and nobody on Fourth Taylor liked to answer the telephone. Molly could never get Robin on the phone, either; but he would at least send her notes via Campus Mail, which was often faster than leaving a phone message and waiting for an answer to it. She could send Nick a note this evening. She had meant to ask him what he wanted to do about dinner, and tell him where to meet to catch the bus, when she saw him after English, and then he had inconsiderately taken himself off.

She wondered how he would get along with Thomas. She wondered what Tina would make of the whole enterprise. Nick and Thomas could probably talk theater until they were blue in the face, leaving Janet to either join in and abandon Tina, or make boring tennis or girl-talk with Tina and miss all the fun. She glared at Molly's curly head, and the bus pulled into the theater lot.

The Old Theater was in fact a ten-year-old building of stark appearance, made of a particularly muddy sort of yellow brick, entirely without windows, and shaped like a slightly squashed pear laid on its side. They walked up the sidewalk that made the stem, and entered through huge glass doors. The flat or squashed bottom of the pear was connected to an art museum, some of the possessions of which were generally on display in the lobby of the theater. This time, presumably in honor of *Hamlet*, there was a vast silk and canvas cloud somewhat in the shape of a camel, hanging from the ceiling, and an extensive display of sixteenth-century fans and perfume bottles in the glass cases.

Janet ruthlessly dragged Molly away from this and led her into the cramped little gift shop, where you could gape at porcelain masks of tragedy and comedy, copies of all the plays the theater had done in its history, toy copies of the Globe and the Old Theater, puppets in historical costume, paperweights with famous theatrical scenes in them, mugs written with quotations from Shakespeare and Shaw and Euripides and Ibsen, collections of critical essays, penny whistles, and little clay owls.

Molly was very satisfactorily delighted with all this, and had in fact to be prevented from spending her next term's book money on a miniature model of the Old Theater complete with the costumed cast of *The Lady's Not for Burning*.

They went to their seats about ten minutes before curtain time. Robin had refused to take a program book, because they all contained rubbish, he said; but once they had sat down, he insisted on reading Janet's over her shoulder. "Oh, Lord, they've raked up that Olivier nonsense again," he groaned. "Tragedy of a man who could not make up his mind, indeed. What poppycock. What insolent rubbish. How anyone can watch the play and say such things I do not know."

"It's these nineteenth-century poets reading it in their studies," said Thomas from Janet's other side. "Upsets the order of the incidents."

Janet, who had heard the problem of Hamlet's delay discussed since as long as she could remember, was rather taken aback, but decided to reserve judgment. She went on placidly reading her program book, which was stuffed with the pronouncements of famous actors past and present concerning the proper handling of the play and the character, and with the conflicting remarks of directors on the same subject. She was amusing herself with a reflection of how Olivier might have directed Edmund Kean when the lights dimmed. Before the audience had quite ceased its rustling, a huge and startled voice boomed, "Who's there?"

Janet almost jumped out of her skin, and had the satisfaction of feeling Thomas jerk also. An equally startled voice said roughly, "Nay, answer me; stand, and unfold yourself," and Janet, who had dutifully read the footnotes for this scene, suddenly realized what they were saying. The first voice did not unfold itself, but persisted, "Barnardo?" and Barnardo gave in and answered, "He." One of the people on the dark stage uncovered a dim light. Their voices grew hushed; and Janet forgot where she was.

She discovered at the first intermission that no such happy thing had happened to Thomas or Robin. Robin, perhaps mindful of Molly's canvas bag, had been quiet during the performance, but excused himself immediately to go outside and laugh. The other three, laboring through the crowds in search of something to drink, perched eventually on top of a radiator that had not yet been turned on for the winter, and entered into an acrimonious discussion punctuated by lemonade.

Molly, who was a realist, was perturbed by the fact that the actor playing Hamlet was Korean, while the rest of his putative family was tall and blond. "What'd they do, adopt him?" she said.

Thomas, whose opinions on this subject were remarkably similar to Nick's, dismissed her objections but launched into a tirade of his own, consisting largely of a minutely detailed list of what lines and speeches had been left out and how these omissions were warping the meaning of the play.

Janet thought he was probably right; but she was enjoying the play far too much to worry about it now. She had fallen for the Korean actor, a slight, short, mobile young man with a mane of straight dark hair that might not be Elizabethan (Thomas said Robin thought Hamlet looked like a sailor of those times, but hardly like a prince) but was certainly effective. She didn't blame him for going mad, either. Luckily, it was only a fifteen-minute intermission and they needed five of those just to get back to their seats.

The lights went down. Robin climbed over Janet's knees and sank into his seat just as the sharp, clear voice of Hamlet said, "Speak the speech, I pray you, *as* I pronounced it to you, trippingly on the tongue." Robin made an infuriating snort, but said nothing. The lights came up on the Players in their gorgeous, tawdry clothes—the only Elizabethan clothing in the entire play, everybody else being dressed like a cross between hippies and farmers, another thing that had annoyed both Thomas and Molly.

The play moved toward its high point. Thomas hissed in her ear, "They cut the dumb-show, the idiots," and Robin was heard, during the Closet Scene, to damn Sigmund Freud, Ernest Jones, and all their intellectual children; but for the most part they were quiet.

Janet found herself most interested in Ophelia and Horatio. She had always considered Ophelia a poor-spirited creature; but this one, with an inflection of her docile lines that Janet had never conceived of, and a delicate way with gesture and facial expression, delivered the impression of a spirited and sensitive young woman. She was delighted with Hamlet's bawdy remarks, and responded in kind. (Robin was delighted, too, and chortled well into the interior play, which was staged somberly and with a great deal more effect than Janet would have believed it capable of.)

As for Horatio, he did not have much to say, but if you watched him over Hamlet's shoulder, as it were, you could see that he was always alert, that nothing escaped him—as, indeed, he had promised; but he had been doing it all through the play, and only now, watching, did you call it to mind. His steady replies to Hamlet's hysteria in the interior play's aftermath, the extremely sharp eye he bent on Rosencrantz and Guildenstern when they came to tell him how angry the King was, and especially his wariness and distress when the

King exiled Hamlet to England, were like a commentary that pointed up all the important points of this part of the play. He stepped forward to go with Hamlet, Rosencrantz, and Guildenstern after the King had dismissed them, and was swiftly waved back by Hamlet. Janet felt for him very much.

Hamlet watched Fortinbras's army go by, and standing alone on a bare stage (having shooed Rosencrantz and Guildenstern into the aisles, where they fidgeted and alarmed the members of the audience closest to them and made Janet feel like a part of Fortinbras's army herself), he meditated on why he had let his capability and godlike reason to fust in him unused. Janet had always thought of this soliloquy (one of her favorites) as rising steadily in intensity; but he began rather frenziedly and got quieter and quieter. The rustling and murmur of the audience quieted with him; until into a dead silence he said, in a friendly and meditative way, as if he had decided which shirt to wear, "From this time forth, my thoughts be bloody, or be nothing worth."

He jumped off the stage, disdaining the ramp, to join Rosencrantz and Guildenstern; grinned at having made them jump; and swept them before him up Aisle 7 and so out. Janet let her breath out. There was a long silence, and then, as the lights went out and the house lights came up, a great deal of applause.

People began to get up. Molly, Robin, Janet, and Thomas sat in a row, looking straight ahead. Janet finally looked at Thomas. He turned his head and regarded her gravely. "It's all downhill from here, you know," he said. "By any normal standards. By some weird sort of tragical morality, it's all uphill. But he's such a devil, Shakespeare. He's going to give us some of the most exquisite scenes of the whole play; and for what?"

"You know," said Robin, as if in answer, "if they do not play the wrong sort of merry hell with the gravediggers, most of this production will answer very well. There's more antic disposition than I'd feared, and you see that they could not cut it all, 'tis too interwoven with the play. Clever Will, a devil indeed, but a most sweet contriver."

"Are you on terms of such familiarity with all your favorite poets?" said Molly.

Robin provided her with an open and delighted grin, and said, "No, indeed; I'd never speak of Miss Austen so, nor Dr. Johnson, nor even Master Coleridge, though he thought better of himself than he ought to have. But our Will, you see, wrote those Sonnets, and after reading of them, it's hard to be formal with him."

"I suppose it's no ruder than calling them by their last names, like the critics do," said Molly. "As if they were suspects in a murder case."

"Are you liking the play?" Janet asked her.

"Oh, yes, a lot. It's wonderful to hear Shakespeare in American accents. Polonius seems a little out of place, though, doesn't he? Like somebody imported for the occasion."

"Claudius might have, I guess," said Janet.

"You science majors are so literal," said Thomas, with a laugh. "He speaks with an English accent not because he comes from England, but because he's of the old school."

"Right," said Molly.

The lights went down abruptly, and out of the darkness the velvety voice of the actor playing Gertrude said, rather raggedly, "I will not speak with her." Horatio's light, flexible tenor, also rather uneven, answered, "She is importunate, indeed distract. Her mood will needs be pitied." Like Hamlet, thought Janet, except that Hamlet was not importunate. The Queen, in a long-suffering voice, said, "What would she have?" and the lights came up. Janet noted with interest that the quiet Horatio could say quite a lot, when he had to. And then her spirited, sensitive Ophelia whirled in upon them. Janet sat bolt upright, tears starting to her eyes; but what she thought, quite clearly, was, *Hamlet*'s not crazy. *This* is how people are crazy here.

The play tore on to its relentless and bloody conclusion; but as Robin and Thomas had said in their different ways, it stopped twice: once in the graveyard, in a scene that made Robin so happy Janet wished Molly would get out the canvas bag; and once again in the great hall, when Hamlet told Horatio what had happened on the way to England. The graveyard scene impressed Janet particularly, both because Hamlet seemed like a different person and because Horatio seemed just the same as usual, having lapsed back into his old taciturnity the moment he and Hamlet were back together. While Hamlet and the Gravedigger and Robin and indeed the rest of the audience laughed happily at the peculiar macabre jokes, Janet watched Horatio eye Hamlet as if he were a friend newly released from the hospital; Horatio looked, in fact, like a man who would be consulting his watch every ten seconds, if he had had one.

When he said, in the second quiet scene, after Hamlet had agreed to the duel with Laertes, whom the audience knew perfectly well to have intentions of not only using an unbated foil, but of poisoning it too, "If your mind mislike anything, obey it," Janet thought, he knows, somehow, that everything is about to go to hell, but his habitual relations with Hamlet won't let him say what he would need to say.

The play ended as it always ended. "You didn't tell me I should bring Kleenex," said Molly thickly to Janet.

"It's a *tragedy*," said Janet, blowing her nose on a very old wad of dusty tissue from the bottom of her knapsack. "Of course you need Kleenex."

"Lend me some of yours, then," said Molly.

"Allow me," said Robin, and handed her a huge and very clean handkerchief. Janet turned to Thomas for similar aid, and found him blowing his own nose. She was greatly taken aback, but warmed to him enormously.

"It's a happy ending, really," she said to him.

"It is not," said Thomas. "It's only the happiest one could

hope for, given the world of the play." He blew his nose again. He looked more human with it reddened and his eyes swollen. "'As this fell sergeant Death is swift in his arrest,'" he said; and suddenly seemed to notice Janet making do with her sodden bit of Kleenex. "I do beg your pardon; here you go," he said, and presented her with a second handkerchief.

"Good grief," said Janet, accepting it gratefully. "I've never in my life known a boy to have even one handkerchief."

"It's hanging around with Robin and his ilk," said Thomas. "And I suspect they only have them because they come in so handy for theatrical stunts."

"Are we in a hurry," said Molly, "or can we sit here peacefully until the crowds are gone?"

Robin looked at his watch. "We may sit," he said. "We've missed the ten-thirty bus, and will have to take the eleven-thirteen city bus down to the Greyhound station and get home again that way."

"Fine," said Molly. "Now, was that or wasn't it a splendid performance?"

"On the whole, not in the least," said Robin. "But they disgraced their calling less than they might have."

"What was wrong with it?" demanded Molly.

"Thomas?" said Robin. "You were keeping the list."

"I've kind of lost track of it," said Thomas slowly. "It did take fire after the first intermission, don't you think? That was an excellent Hamlet."

"I still say he shouldn't have been Korean," said Molly. "It distracted me. I kept making up adoption scenarios in my head."

"No, but that was one of the best parts," said Thomas, with great earnestness. "Because it's true, you know—he's not like any of them, he's completely alien to that whole bright, corrupt court. All of them are against him, even the ones who love him, and none of them can help him out of his terrible dilemma, because their minds and spirits are not like his. He is a stranger in his own country and his own family. He hasn't got anybody." Thomas looked at Janet as Hamlet had looked at Ophelia—as if he had been loosed out of Hell to speak of horrors. But when she let her startled sympathy inform her face, he turned suddenly back to Robin and demanded, "Didn't you feel that, seeing that little dark figure down there all alone among them?"

"He had Horatio," said Robin, fixing Thomas with a grave and anxious look.

"Yes, he did," said Thomas slowly, looking back at him and sounding a little apologetic. "And this was a very good Horatio, I thought. But Horatio can't do anything for him, you know. All he can do is listen. Even when he knows, knows with all his heart, that Hamlet's doom is coming, he can't persuade him of anything. Their minds don't meet, either, really—though you think, if the parts are played right, that they did meet once, when both of them were students. I've thought I'd like to write a play about what they got up to at Wittenberg. I bet they drove everybody right up the wall. But not anymore. Once Hamlet gets home, and everything has gone rotten, there's an estrangement. Did you notice that they deleted the references, except for the antique Roman line, that implied Horatio was Danish, and kept all the ones that imply he's a foreigner? Horatio is a balm to sore feelings, maybe—but he doesn't understand, either. Hamlet's all alone," he finished, with an absolute flatness that was worse to hear than the most violent feeling could have been. Janet looked at him and worried while the rest of them argued.

"I thought that might be partly Hamlet's fault," said Molly. "I've known people like that, whose intellect set them so far apart they couldn't bother to think how other people felt. And on top of that Hamlet's a prince. It must have been hard for Horatio, too."

"Tragedy of character," said Robin, staring at Thomas.

"Situation," said Thomas instantly. "He's doomed, that's all."

"Nobody's doomed," said Robin, with great scorn. "Fate awaits our doing."

"We await Fate's."

"If you do that, Fate will doom you; but it's you who will have made that doom."

"All I'm saying," said Thomas, lifting his chin, "is that some situations are hopeless. And Hamlet's was one of them. And—"

"This is an old argument," said Robin to the two girls.

"Oh, have at it," said Janet lightly; this was not the sort of argument one could stop, but one might be able to lower its emotional temperature a little.

"Yes," said Molly. "I've got the canvas bag, in case of dire need."

"You'd better put it on my head right now," said Thomas, summoning up a smile that made Janet's throat hurt. "I didn't mean to get so exercised."

Robin said gaily, "'Our indiscretion sometime serves us well when our deep plots do pall.'"

Thomas's face went from strained to wretched. "Don't," he said to Robin, "say the next line."

"Is it character or situation should prevent me?" said Robin, still gaily.

Thomas managed a better smile and answered him with spirit. Janet didn't listen to them. The next line was, "There's a divinity that shapes our ends, rough-hew them how we will." Unless Thomas were as militant an atheist as her father, it seemed an odd sentiment to object to.

CHAPTER

8

Janet had forgotten to put a note in Campus Mail for Nick when she got off the bus, but on Sunday morning the early-rising Tina found a folded paper stuck under their door, and dropped it on Janet's pillow. Janet rubbed her eyes until they stayed open, appreciated sourly the fact that Tina, who must be curious, had nevertheless gone off to take her bath, and unfolded the paper. It was written in the same peacock-blue ink, with the same fountain pen, that Nick used for his class notes. He had a peculiar hand, like that of a calligrapher suffering from some nervous disease. It looked rather tidy from a distance, and the letters were uniform; but they sprawled, especially at the bottom, and some of them were hard to make out.

"Lady," said this epistle, "if you will meet me for lunch in Dunbar at twelve-thirty, I will most humbly receive your instructions for tonight's entertainment." He had closed with something that might have been "Love," "Yours," or "Fuck you," followed by a completely indecipherable scrawl in which a very wild imagination might have found an N and a T. Janet grinned at it, and put it away in her top drawer.

It was eleven o'clock. She and Molly and Robin and Thomas had stayed up until almost three, talking about *Hamlet*; and then she had dreamed of the fencing bout (which she understood a great deal better after listening to Robin and Thomas arguing over it), in the middle of which the participants had flung off their masks and revealed themselves as Nick and Thomas rather than Hamlet and Laertes. She thought Nick might fancy himself as Hamlet, but the notion of any rivalry between them was not welcome. Thomas had been lovely company, but he had not acted like a man smitten or about to be. She wondered if one's time at college might be better served with friends like Thomas than with lovers like Nick; but it was rather late to back out, and besides she was curious.

"Tomorrow morning," said Molly's drowsy voice from under her pillow with its yellow-and-white-striped case, "*I* am going to get up at the crack of dawn, pile millions of scraps of paper on Tina's pillow, and go out, shutting the door without a sound."

"Where are you going to get millions of scraps of paper?"

Molly pushed the pillow to the floor. "Have you looked in the wastebasket? Between my math homework and your paper for Evans, we're halfway there already. Tina can contribute the rest with that letter she keeps writing and tearing up."

"Who's she writing to?"

"I suspect it's her high-school boyfriend," said Molly, "but she won't really say. Be nice to her, anyway; she's suffering from something." She sat up and fixed Janet with a fierce, if sleepy, blue eye, and Janet did not list for her exactly the faults Tina was suffering from.

When Tina came back, Molly had returned to bed with Fourth Ericson's copy of the Sunday paper, and Janet was sitting propped up with pillows like an invalid, reading Plato.

The translation was lumpy and difficult. Perhaps she should learn Greek.

"How was the play?" said Tina, appearing suddenly in her pink bathrobe and fuzzy slippers, all scrubbed and healthy-looking with her wet hair pinned neatly on top of her head.

"Depends who you ask," said Molly. "I thought it was wonderful. Thomas thought the second half was wonderful. Robin thought it was much flawed." She looked at Janet.

"I loved it," said Janet. "They didn't cut any of my favorite speeches, but I guess they got a lot of Thomas's. And it *was* awfully Freudian."

"Well, why *is* he so interested in his mother's sex life?" demanded Molly.

"Because it reflects on Denmark—and it reflects on him. That's why he thinks his flesh is sullied; because his own mother could do such an awful thing."

"What awful thing?" said Tina, picking clothing out of her drawers. Janet and Molly always rummaged, but whatever Tina wanted seemed always to be meekly on top, and folded, too.

"Married her dead husband's brother."

"What's awful about that?"

"They thought it was incest, just like marrying your own brother would be."

"That's silly," said Tina. "Any geneticist could tell you that."

"Well, that's what they thought."

"I doubt they cared much about genetics, as such," said Molly. "You're right, though. All that talk about harlots and blood and bastardy. As if they thought you inherited moral, not physical, traits."

"Well, schizophrenia's inherited, isn't it, and a lot of mental problems that make people do things the Elizabethans would think were immoral?"

They wrangled amiably until Nick arrived, explaining that he had been seized with a fear that his note would not be delivered in time. Molly and Janet had to grab their clothes, run to the bathroom, wash and dress hurriedly, and run back again. Nick had sat down on Janet's unmade bed with her copy of *The Daughter of Time*, which he was reading in bits whenever he came over. He refused to borrow it because he had no time for extracurricular reading. Tina was sitting on the end of Janet's bed, smiling and talking in her pleasant voice about the antics of her Bio 10 teacher. Nick looked a little harried; he had closed the book over his finger but seemed to wish he could get back to it. Serve you right for not just meeting me the way you suggested, thought Janet.

It was a sunny day with a brisk wind, and while there was very little green left on the trees, the grass, as Nick remarked, was the color of Ireland.

"Have you ever been there?" said Tina, as they crossed the wooden bridge to Dunbar. The lake was bright and ruffled. The ducks were nowhere to be seen.

"Once," said Nick. "When I was just a baby. My family used to tell stories about it—how I, a mere babe in arms, grabbed for my father's glass of ale just as if I knew what it was, and the like. I don't remember any of that—but ever since then I've had the same dream, and in it the greenest land you've ever seen. I thought of it when I read Frodo's dream," he said to Janet. "I wonder if Tolkien was thinking of Ireland."

"What's the rest of *your* dream?" said Tina, clearly impatient with Frodo.

"It varies," said Nick. "Depending on what I've been reading, you know. But the land is always the same."

"I've got a dream like that," said Molly. "About a house. In the dream, I think it's the house I grew up in. But it's a lot larger, and the wrong color, and hasn't got any neighboring houses. The only thing about it that's really like our house is the mulberry tree in the back yard. But I know it's ours."

"Give to airy nothing a local habitation and a name," said Nick. "Are you a lunatic, a lover, or a poet?"

"Lunatic," said Molly. "Coming soon to a dormitory near

you. Just as soon as we do this next chapter in math, I'm done for."

"I'll be the lover," said Tina, holding the door of Dunbar open for them.

"That leaves you as the poet," said Nick to Janet.

"And what about you?"

"The dreamer," said Nick. "Just the dreamer."

They filed into Dunbar dining hall, made their choices among grilled-cheese sandwiches, eggplant parmesan that looked like a collection of stepping stones in some alien red swamp, or chicken pot pie. The latter was a thing Janet had never seen in a Blackstock dining hall, and she asked the student server about it.

"It was supposed to be fried," said the boy, "but the apples for the pies were bad and we got too many carrots. I think they're Taylor's carrots, but Dunbar hates Taylor, so Taylor's out of luck. Anyway, put it all together and you get pot pie."

"Is it *very* glutinous?" said Molly.

"Shouldn't be. Somebody else got our cornstarch."

They moved on, and eventually stood in an inconvenient crowd by the milk dispensers, looking for enough empty tables in proximity. Janet became aware, over the sea of heads, of a sturdy dark arm waving vigorously.

"There's Sharon," she said.

Sharon and Nora had one table for two with a vacant one next to it; and by dint of some shoving and squeezing and stealing two chairs from a stack just inside the door of the steamy kitchen, they fitted everybody around these two.

"Cheer her up," said Sharon generally. "I can't do a thing with her."

"What's the matter?" said Tina.

"Your goddamn classmates," said Nora, as if it were their fault. Her round face was flushed, and she looked as if she had not washed her hair in a week. Her white blouse was clean but unironed, and her jeans had a sort of gray sheen on them. "I have *never* seen such idiot freshmen. I am going to have to report them to the Dean of Residential Life, and *he* is probably going to have them arrested. *Stupid*. They think because they've got coed dormitories and independent studies in the social effects of television and an administration that turns a blind eye to people living with their lovers in dorm rooms, they can suck up any fucking illegal substance they want to, carouse around all day and all night, throw books out the windows, keep their whole end of the floor awake all night, make three National Merit Scholars fail their physics exams—I'd like to kill them."

"Jen and Barbara down on Third smoke dope all the time," said Sharon mildly.

"And you smoke it with them. So what? Who cares? You're *quiet* about it—and you don't fail quizzes, either, right?"

"I did freshman year."

"But you didn't make other people fail theirs."

"Not that I recollect."

"They can do any damn thing they can think up if they don't bother anybody else and their work doesn't suffer," said Nora. "*I* don't care. *College* doesn't care either. But we can't put up with this. Jesus Christ, apart from anything else, one of them's going to go out a window some fine night."

"Good riddance," said Tina.

"You can say that, you're not responsible for them. I am."

Nick said reflectively, "'I would there were no age between sixteen and three-and-twenty, or that youth would sleep out the rest: for there is nothing in the between but getting wenches with child, wronging the ancientry, stealing, fighting.'"

"Huh!" said Nora. "I wish that was all. I wish we *had* any ancientry."

"Can't you talk to Melinda Wolfe?" said Janet.

There was a silence: Nora looked at Sharon and then away,

Sharon looked at her plate, and Nick stared over Janet's head as if she had not spoken.

"That *is* what she's for, isn't it?" said Tina.

"She can't threaten them with anything I haven't threatened them with already," said Nora.

"But maybe she can think of some other approach," said Molly.

"Maybe," said Nora. "Anyway, never mind the young idiots. Are you guys okay? I haven't given half a thought to anybody who was behaving. Is the course load too much? Are you getting enough sleep? Any petty squabbles you want settled?"

Make my roommate stop making eyes at my boyfriend, thought Janet. Molly said, "The course load is too much, but not too much too much. Everybody seems to be suffering about the same, so you assume it's normal. And it's really amazing what people will put up with if they do think it's normal. Maybe I'll switch to Psychology."

"Not around here," said Nora. "It's a bad department since Jensen left."

"Thomas was saying that about Poli Sci," said Janet.

"What, that it was a bad department since Jensen left?" said Nick.

Janet thumped him on the head with her soup spoon. "Goldstein, I think he said," she continued. "Are we losing a lot of good professors lately?"

"Just got two more good ones in Geo," said Sharon.

"I think a couple of departments are just in a slump right now," said Nora. "It happens." She rose, picked up a tray that still contained most of the food she had put on it, and said, "I have to study. See you later."

They watched her go out the door. Sharon said to Janet, "Kevin tells me you do a mean fifty-yard dash."

"Fat lot of good he was to me at the time," said Janet, over Molly's, "What?"

"We'll tell you later," said Janet. "If we may," she added to Nick.

"Do, do," said Nick irritably. "Only not in the public hall, for God's sake."

"Bound to get out eventually," said Sharon. "Part of the game. Homecoming's coming up, you know."

"Well, I'd at least like to keep it until then," said Nick, still irritably.

"Your brother kept it longer than anybody, didn't he?" said Tina.

Janet thought Tina looked irate, too—presumably in sympathy, but her remark made Nick even grumpier. He mumbled something and took a devastating bite of his sandwich. Then he caught Janet looking at him, and grinned. "What bits of your lunch are you going to make an unnatural combination out of today?" he said with his mouth full; and Janet felt so fond of him that she was obliged to hit him with her spoon again. She understood for the first time the behavior of much younger children toward the objects of their romantic attachment.

Sharon went off to the library to work on a term paper. Molly tried to persuade Tina to come help her with her math, but Tina sat obdurately eating fruit cocktail until Nick suggested that they they all go for a walk. "You, too," he said to Molly. "You can do your perishing mathematics while the rest of us are carousing in the city."

He then took a firm hold of Janet's hand and kept it through an extensive ramble into the Lower Arboretum, past Janet's favorite island, away from the river and any paths she knew, through drifts of last year's brown leaves, through yellowing ferns and bright yellow black-eyed Susans and the pale gray-blue asters, through the constant flutter of the red and yellow and brown leaves, falling and falling in the sunlit air.

"I love autumn," said Molly, scuffing along in the crispest leaves with her hands in the pockets of her denim jacket and her bell-bottoms—not a style she usually favored—dragging behind her and adding to the enormous noise she was making. "It's sad."

"It always reminds me of *Fahrenheit 451*," said Janet. "Everything burning to death, all the metaphors and all the uses for fire."

"Play the man, Master Ridley," said Nick, very softly.

Janet could feel Christina about to ask what the hell they were blathering about. She looked at her quickly. Tina's eyes were on Nick's downbent face. After a moment she shook her head, bounded ahead of the other three, and returned with a handful of horse chestnuts. "Let's throw them in the river," she said.

They did this, and when that palled they spent half an hour finding the right flat stones, and had skipping contests. Molly lost cheerfully; Nick got very grim about it, finally beating Tina, who gave up with perfect good humor, and then tying with Janet, who did not really want to be beaten, and especially did not want to be in the position of somebody who let her lover win. She meant to win—but the last rock she chose sank like the rock it was the first time it hit the water, while Nick's skipped three times, hit a log with a hollow thunk, and slid quietly under. Janet looked at her hand accusingly, and then held it out to Nick. "Congratulations."

Nick had the grace to look embarrassed; he drew her hand through his arm and said, "It's getting cold; we should turn back now."

"God, yes," said Tina, "I've got to read a chapter of biology and take a shower and get dressed for the theater."

They trudged back in silence. Janet took a shower while Tina read her biology, and sat around in her bathrobe reading Plato, which for some reason felt extremely decadent. Tina's dressing took forty-five minutes, to Molly's vocal admiration and Janet's silent scorn. She ended up looking as if she had just pulled her gray-and-pink-striped shirt dress over her head; and given that she had a marvelously clear skin to start with and was endowed with nice pink cheeks, Janet failed to see why she had spent half an hour on her makeup.

Janet herself put on the green velvet dress at a quarter to six, asked Molly to pin on the lace collar for her, brushed out her red hair, and was absurdly gratified when Molly exclaimed over her too. "I wish I had a camera," said Molly, sitting on her bed in her most ragged pair of jeans and the University of Pennsylvania sweatshirt and a very old pair of blue slippers with chewed white fur around the edges. "I feel like a proud mother sending my daughters off to the prom. Don't get pregnant, now."

Janet laughed at her and picked up her knapsack; Tina, astonishingly, blushed.

"Don't break the spine of that math book," said Janet to Molly, and followed Tina out the door.

It was colder than it had been last night. The sunlight made everything look warm, but the sky was a brittle and comfortless blue. Tina had snagged a huge gray shawl from her closet as she went out, and when they stepped out of the shelter of Ericson into the blasting wind, she wrapped it around her head and tucked her hands into it. Janet glanced sideways as they labored past the Music and Drama Center, and burst out laughing. "We look like a peasant woman and her daughter going to market."

"I really hate to trade you for a cow, dearie," said Tina, in a cracked voice, "but there's no help for it."

"I keep telling you," said Janet petulantly, "you'd do far better to get a batch of chickens."

"Too noisy," said Tina, shaking her head in the heavy shawl. "Always cackling; my poor head couldn't stand it, not for a moment."

"Pigs," said Janet.

"I can't get pigs for you, dearie; not enough flesh on you."

"You're not selling me to be *eaten*!" said Janet. "After what you've fed me this summer? They'll take one bite and come lynch you. Tell them I can work."

"But you can't, dearie. Head always in a book, the dust could be over our heads before you'd notice."

They went past the chapel, with the yellow leaves whirling around its tower and the pigeons starting from its roof; and the force of the wind blowing across the open ground beyond it made speech impossible. Janet looked sideways at Tina. Did she know what she was saying? Tina's wind-pink face, in the depths of the shawl, looked half-pleased and half-desperate, as if she were finding her own game too much. She needed encouragement if she were being fanciful; she needed squashing if she were being malicious. Which?

Ahead of them, Nick jumped up from the steps of the Student Union and began waving.

"There's Nick," said Janet, and walked faster.

As they crossed the asphalt road, Thomas came out the scuffed red doors of the Student Union and walked down the steps to stand by Nick. He was a foot taller. He wore a red shirt rather than a white one, but otherwise was dressed as he had been yesterday evening. The wind blew his curling pale hair straight back from his thin face and swirled leaves around him like a magician's scarves.

Nick had put on a dark blue suit and a sedate tie, but he was wearing that same maroon sweater under the suit jacket. His hair looked like a squirrel's nest. Janet walked right up to him and kissed him on the nose. He dug his fingers into her hair and rubbed the back of her neck. "You look splendid," he said. "Like a Victorian storybook illustration. Tina, how elegant you are under all that wool. I hope you'll take it off in the theater?"

"If it's warm in the theater," said Tina, beaming.

"I didn't know you owned a suit," said Janet.

"It's Rob's," said Nick. "Hence the sweater. He's bigger in the shoulders than I am."

"Thomas, aren't you cold?" said Tina.

"Nope," said Thomas. "This is just about how I like it." He shook out the silk folds of one sleeve, and grinned. "Besides, the color of my shirt keeps me warm. Look, here comes the bus."

They got on, and sat down on the proper side to get the good view of Blackstock, Janet with Nick, and Tina with Thomas in front of him. They shared the bus with a noisy group of music students and Professor Rivers, going up to hear a concert at Orchestra Hall; and with a morose-looking couple on their way to an assigned production of Anouilh's *Antigone*, which they did not seem to expect to enjoy.

The bus ground up a hill and rounded the curve, and Janet tugged at Nick's arm and leaned across him to look out the window. Thomas had made Tina look. The still small clump that was Blackstock smiled at them in the late evening sunlight. The air was clearer tonight, so that the buildings seemed better rooted. Janet smiled back at them. She had been craning her neck at this view since she could barely see over the lower edge of the car window. First it had been where Daddy worked, and then it had been where she would go to college; and now, suddenly, it was home. Four years, thought Janet, with a quite inexpressible pleasure. She looked at Nick's blunt, interested profile. He was only a freshman himself. They would have a great deal of time.

Right on this thought, Tina's voice was raised in mingled delight and dismay. "You're a *junior*?" she said to Thomas.

"Cheer up," said Nick. "He came so late to his major he's going to have to take an extra year."

"Not if I have anything to say about it," said Thomas.

"Don't you like it here?" said Tina.

"I love it here," said Thomas, flatly, as if he were asserting the year in which Elizabeth ascended the throne. "But I have other things to do."

"And miles to go, before you sleep," said Nick.

"My high-school English teacher," said Tina over the back of her seat, "said that line was about death. I never really believed it."

"You can't ask Robert Frost," said Nick, reflectively. "He's dead."

"What did you think it meant, Tina?" said Thomas, a little hollowly.

"I thought it meant he had miles to go before he slept," said Tina. "He's driving a horse through a snowstorm after dark and he's a long way from home. That's what it says. It doesn't say a single thing about death."

Nick and Janet looked at each other. After a moment Nick said, "While there is a great deal to be said, in the abstract, for that view of poetical criticism, I think it does miss a something in this poem. Did you like it?"

"Yes," said Tina.

"Why?"

"I liked the way it sounded and the way it described the snow. Snow does that."

"The pleasure of recognition," said Nick.

"What?"

"Aristotle validates your reaction."

"Be quiet," said Thomas, "leave the girl alone. I don't mind talking about poetry, but I'm damned if I'll talk about critics."

"And you so eager to get on to graduate school, where they do nothing else," said Nick.

Oh, dear, thought Janet, looking at the back of Thomas's head and the stiff set of his shoulders, this will never do. "Tell us about what you're going to do with *The Revenger's Tragedy*," she said.

This occupied them thoroughly, if not altogether happily, for the remainder of the journey. Nick disapproved of something Thomas wanted to do with the costumes. They argued about the Duke and Vindice and Castiza and a whole horde of other Italians, until the bus pulled into the parking lot of the theater.

Having arrived early, they waited together in the theater's lobby. The conversation was not lively, and Janet had an uneasy feeling that this was simply one of those groups that would not coalesce into a decent conversation. It was lacking a particular flexible type of personality. She had had two of them around last night; she would have to remember this when putting together expeditions in the future.

For the present, she asked Tina to help her, when they got to the gift shop, to pick out a birthday present for Molly.

"What, the stage for *The Lady's Not for Burning*?" said Thomas. "It would be hard to get it home on the bus. Maybe they could ship it."

"We can't afford that," said Janet. "I was thinking of—"

"I'll go in with you," said Thomas. "Molly's the only person I've ever met who could stifle Robin for a moment."

Nick looked at him with both eyebrows raised and what might have been a smile. "Count me in," he said.

"I suppose you know a dozen," said Thomas; he sounded more resigned than angry.

"Not that many," said Nick.

"How long have you known Robin?" said Janet. Something vaguely trapped in Nick's face made her add, "Maybe Molly can apply to you for advice on how to woo him."

"She's welcome," said Nick. "We are old friends. We met young."

"Embryonic, in fact," said Thomas.

"Only twins do that," said Nick, mildly; Janet thought that Thomas had tried to provoke him, but apparently what he had said made no more sense to Nick than it did to her.

Janet gave up on both of them. Tina must have felt the quality of the silence too. She said, "Thomas, you're a junior, so tell us, how early in the term is it reasonable to be behind on all your classwork?"

"Early in the term is fine," said Thomas. "It's late in the term that you have to worry about. How far behind are you?"

"Two chapters in Chemistry and a problem set in Bio."

"Didn't you get your chem class changed?" demanded Nick.

"Yes, I did, that's why I'm two chapters behind."

"And what's the excuse for the Bio?" said Thomas.

Tina smiled at him. "I'm going to a play."

Nick and Janet looked at each other; Janet thought of the long, wasted afternoon by the river, Tina's refusal to go and help Molly with her math problems. Besides, it didn't make sense; Tina didn't have bio class until Tuesday. If it were a problem set from her previous class, then some event previous to the class it was due in must be responsible for her not having done it.

None of this was worth saying, of course—or indeed worth figuring out in the first place. It was a shame that Thomas might take up with somebody willing to be, even in minor matters, underhanded; but if she exposed Tina's foolery, she would look a great deal worse than Tina and Thomas would pay no attention anyway. Besides, he was a junior, and could presumably look out for himself.

Janet steered them over to the model Molly had wanted. She was mildly annoyed at having her present turned into a group project; but Molly certainly wanted the model more than she wanted anything Janet could afford on her own.

"We should ask Robin if he wants to come in on this," she said.

"Don't push him," said Nick. "He's skittish. We can manage, I think, if the shipping is not too dear."

He went up to the desk to inquire about this, and Janet went on poking about in the prints and calendars and greeting cards, looking for a birthday one to go with the model. Thomas and Tina had drifted over to examine the puppets; Thomas said something, and Tina laughed.

None of the cards was at all right for Molly. Janet left them and flipped through the calendars. Cats; Sierra Club; British castles; German mountains; *Hamlet*. Janet cast a glance at Thomas, who was giggling with Tina, and stealthily eased the calendar out of its envelope. It began with a woodcut of the Globe Theater, skidded through a few sketches of later theaters and their actors, and round about April settled down to a gorgeous series of photographs from famous productions of *Hamlet*.

Janet tucked the calendar under her arm, snatched one of the cat calendars as camouflage, and sneaked up to the desk. In the arithmetical flurry that followed Nick's report of the cost of the model, nobody bothered to ask her what she had bought. Divided by four, the cost of the model and the shipping was a lot of money, but not too frightening an amount. They arranged matters with the clerk, telling him to send the model to Janet's parents to avoid discovery, and went to find their seats.

Thomas had gotten the same ones for both nights. This time nobody looked over Janet's shoulder and maligned the program book, though it was chock-full of peculiar existentialist pronouncements. Janet began reading them aloud not because of their sense or lack of it but because their phrasing was so funny. She had just found one that made all three of her companions laugh when the lights went down.

The whole audience was roaring inside five minutes. Janet had not paid much attention to Rosencrantz and Guildenstern the night before, but there was clearly more to them than had met the eye. She glanced sideways a few times; to her relief, Tina was laughing as much as anybody. She was also holding Thomas's hand and leaning her head exhaustedly on his shoulder whenever she could stop chortling long enough to manage it; but that was no business of Janet's.

The *Hamlet* scenes, when they got around to them, were played exactly as they had been the night before. This was jarring at first, but became progressively less so as the play sobered itself up, until by the end the scenes with Hamlet in them were funnier than those with Rosencrantz and Guildenstern. Janet began to feel afflicted with mental double vision. Last night, you were made to feel, all this hilarity, spotted with philosophy and twisting itself around to despair, had been going on somewhere backstage; now you were backstage, and on the other side the tragedy of Hamlet, Prince of Denmark, was taking its accustomed course.

When the applause had died down and people were starting to leave, Nick and Tina went off to their respective restrooms. Janet turned and said to Thomas, "I like Hamlet's universe better."

"I don't know," said Thomas. He pinched up a fold of his red silk sleeve and said it again, more slowly. "I don't know. Would you rather be innocent or guilty?"

"I'd rather be guilty and punished than innocent and punished."

"Would you?" said Thomas, with half a smile. He offered it to the stage; he had not looked at her since the lights came up. "There are great pleasures in the latter."

Janet considered this. "It depends on the punishment," she said. "If it's death, I'd rather deserve it."

"Ah, but which sort of death?"

"Hamlet's, of course," said Janet, trying to sound light. "With the flights of angels to sing him to his rest and make sure what dreams don't come."

Thomas turned his head and did look at her; his face was expressionless, but his eyes were a little large. "I never connected those images," he said. "To die, to sleep, no more—what dreams may come—I have bad dreams—and flights of angels sing thee to thy rest. I would have thought it was ironic, though. My God, you could write a good paper on that, I'd bet. I wonder if the Christian imagery takes over so that by the end of the play it's *not* ironic? There's the talk with the Gravedigger, and all that stuff about Christian burial."

"Well, are you taking Shakespeare next term?"

"No, I can't possibly, I'm twelve credits short in Latin and my Greek is lopsided, no tragedy. And it's Aeschylus next time—just my rotten luck. He's impenetrable and his grammar's like a nest of snakes."

"Major in English," said Janet, with considerable joy in doing to a Classics major what Classics majors kept doing to her.

"I can't, it'd take another three years—oh. Ha, ha, ha. Very good. Is our timing really that bad?"

"Invariably," said Janet.

Thomas and Tina spent the bus trip back kissing one another. Nick was violently amused by this, and finally persuaded Janet up to the front of the bus with him so he could laugh quietly.

"It's not a completely worthless idea," said Janet. "You could kiss me."

"Once, if you like," said Nick, "but there is nothing romantic or stirring about this bus. A dormitory room is bad enough, God knows."

"Some people take blankets to the Arboretum."

"In the spring, maybe," said Nick.

Because they took the commercial bus rather than the college shuttle, and saw Nick to the doors of Taylor, the remaining three ended up walking along the south edge of campus and then taking the asphalt road between Forbes and Ericson. Tina said good-bye lingeringly to Thomas. Janet thought of sneaking quietly away, but she was afraid Thomas might apologize to her. She and Tina finally turned toward Ericson and went in its side entrance. The first-floor landing smelled of ironing, the second of coffee, the third of that same sweet peculiar stuff Janet had noticed once before, and the fourth, stiflingly, of the same.

"Is that marijuana?" said Janet to Tina, as they gained their own landing.

"Is what marijuana?"

"That smell like somebody burning a rope covered with brown sugar."

"I don't know," said Tina.

They pushed open the double doors at the end of their corridor, and the smell hit them like warm water. Of course. It was at this end of the corridor that the freshmen lived who were causing Nora such worry. They must have joined forces with the more sensible pot-smokers on Third. Janet's eyes were beginning to water, and she wanted to get a look at Anne Beauvais's little sister.

"Let's ask them to open their windows," she said, and knocked on the left-hand door.

"I'm going to bed," said Tina, mildly, and went off down the hall.

Nobody answered that door. Janet turned across the hall and tried the other one, loudly. Somebody opened the door at once. They had put a couple of green towels—which they had certainly not gotten from the college laundry service—over their desk lamps and turned out the overhead. The resulting light was pleasant over the upper part of the room, but clashed viciously with the red carpet.

The student who opened the door was very like Anne. Her yellow hair was short and curly, and she seemed if anything even taller—her head brushed the top of the doorway—but those were the only differences. She was barefoot and bare-legged, wearing a large muslin shirt with an embroidered hem. "Hello?" she said.

Janet introduced herself and suggested that a little ventilation was in order.

"Well, I don't know," said Odile, in the mellow voice she also shared with Anne. "It's not my smoke." She turned back into the room and called, "Jen, Barbara, come here a moment."

She stood aside as she spoke. Janet stared into the smoky

green light of the room. It was like a dusty forest clearing at sunset. The shrouded lamps cast meaningless shadows and warped all the familiar college furniture. There were two other tall slender figures, one in green draperies and the other in nothing whatever, standing talking against the dark windows; and a third one, in white gauze, lying on the floor with a candle in a Food Service saucer balanced on her chest. The Food Service saucer was the only thing in the room that looked like itself. Janet's head hurt. She did not, really, want to speak to any of these people, and started to say so.

Then two more figures rose from the floor behind one of the beds, stepped over the person on the floor, and came up behind Odile. They were both brown-haired and ordinary-looking; much shorter and solider than Odile, and wearing jeans and sweaters. One of them had wire-rimmed glasses, the other horn-rimmed ones. Both of them looked as if they were suffering from sleep deprivation and pink-eye simultaneously; Janet could have hugged them anyway.

Odile said to them, "Janet here thinks we must open some windows."

"We paid a lot for that smoke," said the girl with glasses, as if she had had to think hard to figure this out, "and we're not done with it yet."

"You're losing it just the same," said Janet, "it's going down the stairway and all along the hall. I live in four-oh-four," she added, with perfect truth but lying intent. She wanted very much to ask why they didn't just drink themselves into whatever state they were all in and stop polluting their immediate environment; but it would be impolitic. And rather silly—they probably weren't old enough to drink, so it would be just as illegal, and just as bad for their college work, and they might even deck the room out like this to do it in, too. But unless they got sick in the hall, she would at least be able to walk past their door in blissful ignorance.

"You can come in too," said the other brown-haired girl. "The night is young. Odile has stuff she hasn't distributed yet."

"Thank you," said Janet, "I've been to a Stoppard play, and that's enough for one night."

Odile smiled distantly.

The two with glasses looked wide-eyed at each other.

"Are you a butterfly dreaming it's a Chinese philosopher?" said the girl with the wire-rimmed glasses, looked again at her companion as if for corroboration, and giggled contentedly.

"No," said Janet, wearily. She felt a hundred years old. The shadows in the room wavered like water. The light in the corridor was beginning to hurt her eyes. The sickly smoke rasped in her throat like the taste of Tabasco sauce. She thought of Nora, shouldering her senior year as an Economics major and having to listen to nonsense from these creatures, people most other RA's would either have let go to hell or reported long ago. "I'm a Puritan masquerading as a college student. And I advise you to open those windows, because I'm going to talk to Melinda Wolfe."

They looked at her blankly.

"Never mind," said Odile. She put a hand on each of their backs and pushed. "You go down to bed now; we'll manage."

They walked at Janet as if she weren't there; she dodged hastily, and they went past her, through the stairway doors and, from the sounds, down the steps without any mishap.

"Now," said Odile. "Do you know Melinda Wolfe?"

"She's my advisor," said Janet.

Odile opened her eyes in an expression just slightly exaggerated—theater types, thought Janet—and ducking her head she stepped outside into the hall and shut the door behind her. "What is your major?"

"English," said Janet, taking a step backwards so she could hold Odile's eye without hurting her own neck. Odile smelled of violets, and the embroidery of her shirt was columbines. Her skin was like honey.

"Ah," said Odile. "You had not thought of Classics?"

Janet stared at her, and stopped an impatient answer just in time. She had heard the question too often. It made no sense, but it meant something. "I haven't decided for certain," she said. "I'm only a freshman."

"Ah," said Odile again. "Well, attend for a moment, then. You see that the more foolish children are asleep across the hall and that I have sent the less foolish children downstairs to bed also. With what remains you have nothing to do."

"I have to breathe it," said Janet, so as to have said something. "And you're fretting Nora terribly."

"We do not fret Nora," said Odile. "The children we may leave out of account from this day forward."

That was what Nora had called them, children. Odile was a freshman herself. Janet suppressed, again, the urge to argue; this was not what was important. She wished she knew what she was bargaining with. She said, "If Nora thinks things are under control, I do too."

"So," said Odile. She smiled suddenly, and Janet smiled back completely without meaning to. Odile said, "This is not your atmosphere, I think? But Classics has room for Puritans also. We need you; we are the leaven, but you are the loaf. Do you remember that, when you think on which major you will choose."

Her tone was kind and friendly, and Janet's skin prickled all over. "I'll remember," she said. While memory holds a seat in this distracted globe; you bet. "But the smoke?"

"I think one puts a towel along the crack under the door, that keeps the smoke from leaving. We will do so. Good night." She slipped back into her room and shut the door.

I wish I knew what just happened, thought Janet. She went quickly down the hall and into her own room as if she were heading for home in a game of hide-and-seek. It smelled comfortingly of the Russian tea Tina made. Janet opened all the windows anyway, and made Molly and Tina wrap themselves up in their bedspreads while they drank the tea. It took the burned-rope-and-sugar taste out of her throat, but eventually she was obliged to go take a shower to get the smell out of her hair. It was almost as bad as the lake water.

CHAPTER 9

September ran out in a late and freakish thunderstorm, and October breezed in, golden and smiling. Daily life, which had been full of starts and uncertainties, settled into a routine. Tina and Thomas became a model couple, making sheep's eyes at one another and explaining one another's views whenever one of them was absent. Molly and Robin pursued an erratic and puzzling course. You could not make any assumptions about whether Robin would be present, whether for dinner or lunch or an afternoon walk or the Wednesday night foreign films or the Friday and Saturday night popular ones. He always sat by Molly, or on her bed if she wasn't there when he dropped by, which was fairly often, since he never seemed to take the trouble to learn her schedule. But he never touched her. It was true that Molly was so scornful of people who snuggled in public that you would not expect her to do it herself. She and Tina did take the bus up to Planned Parenthood early one Saturday while Janet was struggling in Professor Evans's class with his comparison of *Volpone* with *Peter Rabbit*. But Janet was half convinced that Molly had gone only to get better help for her cramps.

They both came back looking a little white and subdued. It was like an assembly line at a factory, Molly said; she supposed they couldn't help it, but it made you want to go find a nice nunnery in Spain and spend your time writing steamy poetry in cipher. Janet looked at her anxiously; Tina, for once, sat down on her bed and whooped with laughter. It was uncertain which reaction Molly wanted. She and Tina showed Janet their birth-control pills, in clear plastic boxes, thick round things the size of a hamburger bun, with the days of the week written around the edge; they looked like some aberrant perpetual calendar.

Neither of them was at all good at remembering to take the things. Janet ascribed this to the fact that both of them, having meekly taken the first pill after dinner as recommended, spent the entire night in the bathroom, being sick, and walked around hollow-eyed from lack of sleep all next day, refusing to walk in the woods in the most beautiful weather imaginable.

Molly was sick the first three nights and then felt fine; Tina was sick every night for the whole month of October, and refused to stop taking the pills. She also refused to go to the college Health Service, which, given that the doctor in charge had persistently declined even to do pregnancy tests, let alone any gynecological work, was perhaps not completely unreasonable. Tina lost ten pounds and took to having an afternoon nap; Janet and Molly nagged at her and got nowhere. Molly gained ten pounds, all around the waist, and grumblingly offered to trade metabolisms with Tina. Tina just smiled. She was still a nice pink, except that on her thinner face the color looked more hectic than healthy.

Janet finally lay in wait in the lobby for Thomas one late-October evening before dinner, and asked him if sex, however wonderful, could possibly be worth all this. "Do you realize Tina's throwing up every night? It's not good for her."

"*I* didn't make her do this," said Thomas, scowling. "She can stop for all of me. And she has to take the bloody things for a month before we can have sex, wonderful or not—and as you may possibly have noticed, there is no privacy in this damned college anyway."

He stamped up the stairs. It was the first time he had showed his temper since she had met him in the library—even in the face of chronic provocation from Nick. Janet sat down in the lounge, where a mixed group of students was watching the news on television, and wrestled her own temper back where it belonged. She had in fact noticed. Whatever provisions Nick had or had not made against the intrusion of a third party into their proceedings, there had been no occasion on which it was necessary to inquire, except in a purely academic sense.

The problem was not really privacy, it was time. Janet was carrying a normal term's load, three ten-week courses with their accompanying reading and writing. Nick was contemplating a double major in English and Classics, and was accordingly taking an extra course—and it was beginning Latin with Medeous, who was extremely demanding. He also kept thinking of dropping either the English or the Classics, depending on which was giving him more trouble, in favor of a Music major, and was taking piano lessons, as well as singing with a group of people who had not been able to get into the Chamber Music class this term. And he had his own projects: arguing with Robin and Thomas over *The Revenger's Tragedy* they would produce winter term, setting poetry to music, writing an opera of *Cyrano de Bergerac*, writing a sonnet a day "to keep his hand in." Janet had not written a line of poetry or a word in her journal since she got here; she suspected him of never sleeping.

As far as she could tell, studying at Blackstock was a full-time job, and nourishing a beginning love affair was a job and a half. And yet it would be quite impossible to disentangle oneself. Staring at black-and-white images of the carnage of the war in

Viet Nam and listening to the unimpassioned voice of the television announcer recite horrible statistics, Janet found herself thinking of Claudius's words near the end of *Hamlet*. "It is the poisoned cup; it is too late." The audience, for some inexplicable reason, had laughed at the line. Thomas said they always did, people in theaters thought death was funny, probably because they had seen too many movies. Even in the midst of that laughter, Janet had felt cold, clear through, at that line. It seemed to describe not the complex and foolish and only half-believable situation the supposedly canny Claudius had gotten himself into, but the sum of wrong choices and irrevocable actions. Nick was not a wrong choice; but associating with him seemed to have been an irrevocable action. Four years, Janet told herself again. You have four years. There will be lighter terms, Thanksgiving vacation, summer, something.

Was it possible that when people objected to coeducational colleges, it was this sort of problem, and not an impertinent and disgusting desire to police other people's morals, that really moved them? No, probably not. Morals had very little to do with this, not the kind of morals that people who wanted to police other people's were most concerned with, anyway. Whether this affair was ever consummated or not, it required patience, attention, energy, wit, and generosity.

The source of these requirements banged through the front door of Ericson, whistling "Sweet Baby James." Janet ran out of the lounge and intercepted him. Since Molly wasn't around to complain, she kissed him. The kiss became complex. Somebody came in the front door, and they let go of each other.

"What's up?" said Nick. "Has something happened that you're lying in wait for me?"

"I was lying in wait for Thomas, actually, but he's in a terrible mood."

"Don't tease him; they just told him he couldn't graduate this year."

"Tina will be delighted. Between bouts of nausea. I'm *not* sure I think much of a method of birth control that mimics pregnancy."

"I've got something better than that," said Nick. "It just came in today." He dug in all the pockets of his shabby brown jacket, finally emerging with a little white box stuck shut with a blob of red wax. "An old herbal remedy."

"Are you sure it works?"

"If it doesn't, I will pay the fee."

"What does *that* mean?"

"You decide."

Janet weighed the box in her hand. "Does it have side effects?"

"My sister said it made her ears itch."

"Does it really work?"

"Word of honor."

All right, thought Janet, let's find out just what that means. "When?" she said.

Nick sighed. "I think it must be after the end of the term. Robin is going home, but I'm not; I'm going to paint Ericson Little Theater for the College, and they're going to let me stay in my own room during vacation."

"Why aren't you going home for Christmas?"

"My family's in England."

"They've got lousy timing. You can have Christmas dinner with us."

Robin came in the front door then, and the three of them went upstairs to collect the other three. They had an engagement to go see Zeffirelli's *Romeo and Juliet*, this weekend's offering by the college. Janet was afraid Robin would laugh at it, but he was very quiet. He did abuse the music afterwards.

As October disappeared in piles of leaves, Janet felt her classes drift out of sync with her preoccupations. Fencing was all right; but the philosophical problems in classical science became foggier every class, and Anthropology was only a little better. English class had by slow degrees attained the sixteenth century, marched with wary smiles through *Volpone*, gazed with horror and guilty laughter upon *The Duchess of Malfi*, and run aground on the enormous rock of *King Lear*. There was love poetry behind and before them, but *Lear* blocked their path like a broken statue in a narrow pass of the mountains. Evans had cheerfully explained to them that *Lear* was for mature tastes and they were reading it for his pleasure, not for theirs.

Janet read the loveless squabble of Regan and Goneril for the favors of Edmund, and felt distinctly sick. The main movement of the play seemed to her completely chaotic; her only comfort was that Evans would probably not compare it to *Squirrel Nutkin* or *The Story of a Fierce Bad Rabbit*.

She sat in class the Thursday before Hallowe'en, listening to a discussion of Albany's inability to move quickly and its effect on the play from Act III onward, and contemplated with pleasure the beginning of Fall Term Recess at five o'clock this afternoon. Friday and Saturday were free of classes. She wondered what anybody would be doing for Hallowe'en. Nobody had so much as mentioned it, though carved pumpkins had appeared in some of the lounges. Her habit had been to go trick or treating with Danny Chin, who had finally written her a postcard informing her that his Christmas vacation began on December 20th. Janet thought she would see what Nick and her roommates had in mind.

Nick, asked after class, said, "Lock my door and cower under the bed." Janet poked him and he kissed her and that was the end of the discussion. They went off to Eliot and settled at their corner table with Molly and Robin and Peg. Janet had made sure to get a seat facing the windows. It was a cloudy day. The gray lake was dotted with mats of yellow leaves. Every little bare maple along the stream had a circle of red leaves on the ground beneath it, as if it had gotten undressed and left its clothes on the floor.

"What is anybody doing about Hallowe'en?" said Janet generally.

Robin said, "Lock my door and cower—"

"Under the bed," said Molly, not patiently. "You can't get under your bed, you dodo, it's packed full of boxes."

"Lots of room under mine," said Nick with his mouth full.

"I thought we could have a party," said Janet to Molly. "Hot cider. Cookies. Pumpkin bread."

"Invite Nora," said Peg. "She's working too hard."

"And Sharon," said Janet. "Maybe she could bring Kevin."

Peg shook her head. "Kevin's family lives in the city; he's going home." Nobody asked the obvious question; Peg smiled at them and added, "They don't get along with Sharon."

"There's a fine recipe for disaster," said Nick. Janet wondered if she should be glad or sorry that his family was in England.

"You know who else we should ask," said Molly. "Those two kids in the triple at the end of the hall—the ones Nora calls the foolish children. Their freaked-out roommate's moved across the hall with Odile and her cronies, and I think they feel kind of lost and abandoned. That was their whole social group, along with Barbara and Jen from Third."

"What are their names?" said Janet. "They never come to floor meetings."

"Neither do you," said Molly.

Peg said, "Rebecca and Susan."

"Could you ask them, then?" said Janet.

"Sure," said Peg. "What time?"

"Afternoon or evening?" said Janet, mostly to Nick.

"We should make sure it's okay with Tina," said Molly.

"True," said Janet guiltily.

The conversation turned to other matters: the obligatory appearance of Schiller at Homecoming, which none of them had witnessed, Homecoming at Blackstock being a thing that "nobody went to," which, as Molly remarked, meant that there were a great many nobodies at Blackstock. They then considered a rumor, proffered by Peg and heatedly denied by Nick and Robin, that Professor Medeous was getting married; and concocted theories of how the Food Service got its broccoli to behave as it did.

When Molly ran off to her biology lab session and Robin went away to wrestle with Aristophanes and Peg departed to commune with Homer, Janet and Nick held hands under the table and talked about *The Duchess of Malfi*. Janet was indignant about it—by Aristotle's standards, which she had first encountered in high school and read again in Professor Soukup's class, it was not a tragedy of any good sort.

Professor Evans had told the class to beware of Aristotle because they weren't ready for him yet, and referred darkly to "students who have had their minds permanently injured by too early an exposure to thought." Janet had scrupulously kept Aristotle out of her paper on *The Duchess of Malfi*, but Evans had evidently discerned some injury in her mind just the same, and scribbled scathing comments all over the margins. The fact that he had then given her a B+ had not soothed her in the slightest.

Nick, who had gotten an A and the single remark, "I will suffer a great deal from someone who presents me with original and rational ideas—but tame your semicolons," was, Janet thought, much too full of himself. She had presented the play as a failed tragedy; Nick thought it was a black comedy, and kept reciting speeches he thought were funny. He held that the only rebuttal would be the recitation of the same passages in such a way that they were *not* funny, which was perfectly impossible, especially for somebody who had never been trained for the theater and whose main dramatic accomplishment as a child had been the lugubrious recitation of "The Raven" to the accompaniment of her sister on the bongos. Janet explained this to Nick, and had to be content with the minor triumph of making him laugh too much to continue the discussion.

Nick had an afternoon class, and Janet walked him to it and then wandered aimlessly back across the campus. The grass was still green, but that would not last much longer. Now that most of the leaves were gone, the shapes of the buildings were clearer. Chester Hall really did sneer at you. It was the same red brick with limestone windowsills and limestone toothing stones that comprised Masters and the old Chemistry Hall, not to mention Ericson. But while Masters seemed to peer anxiously out from behind its four white pillars, Chester looked at you with its twelve-paned windows in their lancet arches as if you were a blot on the earth. Janet chose to pass it on its chapel side, and proceeded absently over the brick crazy quilt of the Music and Drama Center's plaza, and so to Ericson.

There were no classes tomorrow, and none Saturday. When Evans's class met again Tuesday morning, it would be to discuss *Paradise Lost*. There was reading to be done for Monday, too, but Janet pulled the red Dover edition of the poem off her shelf and lay down on her bed with it.

She rapidly made the discovery that Milton's notion of an English sentence was as erratic as those held by the authors of her most obtuse anthropology texts.

The infernal Serpent; he it was whose guile,
Stirred up with envy and revenge, deceived
The mother of mankind, what time his pride
Had cast him out of Heaven, with all his host
Of rebel Angels, by whose aid, aspiring
To set himself in glory above his peers,
He trusted to have equalled the Most High,
If he opposed, and, with ambitious aim
Against the throne and monarchy of God,
Raised impious war in Heaven and battle proud,
With vain attempt.

Structure a sentence in an English paper like that and they'd write three times as much taking it apart for you. Or this, for pity's sake:

> *All is not lost—the unconquerable will,*
> *And study of revenge, immortal hate,*
> *And courage never to submit or yield:*
> *And what is else not to be overcome.*

You couldn't parse that; it would fall apart in your hands. And yet he could get away with it. He had you cheering him on, whereas the anthropologists imbued you with fury and a desire to stone them to death with copies of *The Harbrace College Handbook* and *The Elements of Style.*

She was far past the lines assigned for Tuesday when Molly and Tina came back. Tina had immediately acquiesced to the party, and they were deep in plans.

"Do you think Rob Benfield would like to come?" Janet said. "Nobody ever sees him except Nick."

"Thomas says he hangs around with the Classics professors mostly," said Tina. "He had to stay on for a fifth year to finish his major, so most of his friends have graduated."

"Poor creature," said Janet, and added his name to the list. "We can tell Nora to ask her boyfriend. I want to get a look at him."

"You'd think we would have," said Molly. "She's got a single."

"Well, he might have one, too, and you know she knows we're dying to see what he's like. The people on his floor are probably less nosy."

"They couldn't possibly be more nosy," said Tina, much more grumpily than she usually said anything. "Every time I run into Odile in the bathroom she asks me personal questions about Thomas. In that fake French accent."

"What makes you think it's fake?" said Molly.

"Her sister hasn't got one," said Janet, thoughtfully. She had last seen Odile's sister draped over Robin, and never had discovered the extent of their acquaintance.

Thomas arriving just then, they asked him to the party, and he said gravely that he would be delighted to spend so terrible a night in such splendid company. Janet had fully expected him to say he was going to cower under his bed, having formed the theory that the boys were planning to attend some private party where they could behave disgustingly without incurring the censure of their girlfriends.

Nick and Robin's arrival was presaged by their singing an Elizabethan round in the staircase. Janet went out into the hall to hear them better. The husky tenor and the clear one twined around one another like the roses they sang of. "'The roses die, the grass doth fade, and thou dost walk an ice-pure maid.'" They became entangled suddenly, and broke up in laughter. Robin began again alone. "'Roses, their sharp spines being gone, not royal in their smells alone . . .'"

"Not that one!" said Nick, quite close; they must be on the third-floor landing.

"This, then," said Robin, in the light voice that meant he was in a mood. "'She that could think and ne'er disclose her mind; Sees suiters following, and not look behind; She was a white—'"

"Fuck you too, Armin," said Nick, not amiably.

"Whenever you like," said Robin in the most careless voice he owned. "But it won't help you a jot."

Janet melted back along the corridor, unwilling to be caught eavesdropping, and was able to meet them at the door to the room. Nick gave her a fierce hug, as if he had not seen her for months. Over his shoulder, she saw Robin close his eyes, not in disdain or impatience or even common politeness, but simply as if he were tired to death. She and Nick preceded him into the room, and she tried to give Molly an eloquent look.

Molly raised both eyebrows—any such attempt at signaling made her impatient—but when she saw Robin behind them she sprang up, scattering lists, and held out her hands to him, quite against her habit. Robin smiled at her.

"You did it, didn't you?" she said. "We didn't hear you."

"You weren't meant to," said Robin, dropping her hands.

"Have you been playing the bagpipes again?" demanded Christina.

"Midterms," said Robin.

"Oh," said Tina.

Friday morning, Tina and Molly dragged Janet away from *Paradise Lost*, despite her assurances that it was a fantasy novel and she needed to finish it so Molly could read it and they could perfectly well buy refreshments without her. They took their bicycles, because they could fit more in the baskets than they could carry, walking; and they sailed down Main Street in a welter of brown leaves. The storefronts bristled with black cats and pumpkins and witches' hats.

"Should this be a costume party?" asked Tina as they parked the bicycles in front of the grocery store.

"Costumes optional, I think," said Molly. "It's short notice, and everybody's been studying for midterms."

"I didn't have any," said Janet. "All my teachers seem happy to rely on a final exam."

"Yeah, but you have to write a paper a week for Evans," said Tina. "I'd rather take a midterm."

"That's why I'm in English and you're in Biology."

"While I," said Molly, flinging a bag of candy pumpkins into their cart, "am neither fish, flesh, nor fowl."

"I think Nick feels like that," said Janet.

"Why should he?" retorted Tina. Janet deduced that Nick was getting on Thomas's nerves. "English, Classics, what's the difference? It's all just grammar and literature."

"It's a very different atmosphere," said Molly, piling molasses, cinnamon, and ginger into the cart. "Those Classics people are creepy; I think Nick should stick to English."

"Thomas isn't creepy!" cried Tina.

"No, and he's only been a Classics major for a year, too. Poli Sci, Chemistry, Art History, Astronomy. I didn't know they *let* you change your mind that often."

Tina chuckled. "There isn't much they can do about your mind, is there?" she said, thereby revealing, Janet thought, an interesting idea of the purposes and effects of education. "It depends on your advisor and the department heads how often you can change your major."

"And who," said Janet, a little hollowly, "is Thomas's advisor?"

"Melinda Wolfe," said Tina. She looked thoughtful for a moment, performed a double take and gazed at Molly wide-eyed. "*Robin* is a Classics major," she said.

"He is not creepy," said Molly patiently, "but he is extremely strange. The same may be said for Rob and Jack. And all the other Classics majors they hang around with are creepy. Anne Beauvais always smiles at me as if she were going to eat me for supper."

Janet knew what Tina meant by creepy. She meant that the people in question were creeps—that they did not conform to whatever arbitrary standards their particular peer groups had decided on, and possibly but not necessarily failed to conform to more general societal standards, like washing and making sure their shirts were buttoned straight and not bringing up awkward subjects in conversation.

She thought she knew what Molly meant, too; but what Molly meant had more to do with Anne Beauvais hanging on Robin like a creeping vine, or Odile standing in the doorway of that stifling, shadowy room, smiling and patient and uncomprehending. And yet Tina and Molly were perfectly amiable together. It was a wonder anybody ever talked to anybody else.

They spent Friday writing invitations and dropping them outside people's doors, and Saturday peacefully baking. Janet called her mother three times to get recipes she did not have in her head after all. Nick made them stop and come with him to eat lunch, conveying Robin and Thomas's regrets—they were engaged, with their fellow students of Aristophanes, in a detailed postmortem on the midterm examination in that class, which everybody had flunked.

"I thought Peg said Robin already took Aristophanes," said Janet.

"Oh, he did," said Nick, "from Ferris. But the play they read in the original in that class was *The Frogs*. They're doing the *Thesmophoriazusae* this time, so he took it again."

"The what?" said Tina; the only reason Janet had not said it was that she knew Tina would.

"It means the women going to the Thesmophoria," said Nick. He made a pause long enough to be irritating and not long enough to deserve being hit for, and added, "It's a festival sacred to Demeter and Persephone, that's all. It's a slight thing, that play, full of parodies of Euripides and a lot of low comedy to do with men disguised as women. Robin likes that kind of thing."

"Don't you?" said Janet.

"It's all very well in its way," said Nick, "but it gets wearing. So does Robin." He hesitated, tilted his head at Molly, and said, a little lamely, "Don't mind him."

"I don't," said Molly. "Not in the least. That way lies madness. Good God, what is in this soup?"

"Canned okra, I think," said Tina. "All I can say is, they had better be done with their postmortem by the time the party starts."

"Thomas said to tell you specially that he was coming," said Nick.

Something in the way he said it made Janet look at him. He

was buttering a large baking-powder biscuit; then he spooned honey onto it; then he rushed it into his mouth before the honey could run down his wrist. Then, of course, he had his mouth full; and by the time he had swallowed, Molly was asking him which plays of Euripides were parodied in the *Thesmophoriazusae*, which necessitated an explanation of which of those were extant and who had done good translations of them. Tina then demanded what "extant" meant, and had to have the entire history of lost classical manuscripts explained to her.

Janet considered interrupting, but what she thought of as the fatal flaw of the novel-reader prevented her. She had meant to ask Nick if he and Robin were coming to the party, since neither of them had actually expressed any intention of doing so. But the flaw of the novel-reader is to want to know what will happen if a situation is allowed to develop unmolested. So she let them talk, and ate her canned okra and tomato soup, and wondered if they should move any of the furniture in their room to make more space for the party.

After lunch Nick went off to practice with his chamber group. Molly and Tina and Janet cleared off their desks and bureau tops, lugged miscellaneous cushions out of closets and suitcases, vacuumed the floor, strung up black and orange crepe paper, put a dozen orange candles in Food Service glasses borrowed for the occasion, and started a gallon of spiced cider steeping, in a pan cadged from the dormitory kitchen, over Molly's illegal hot plate.

"Should Nora have to see that?" Janet asked her.

"She's got one herself," said Molly. "It's only the ones without asbestos pads under them that she gets frantic about."

"Remind me not to volunteer to be an RA," said Janet.

"That reminds *me*," said Molly, "what happened with those weirdos at the other end of the hall?"

"I think," said Janet slowly, "that Odile stopped inviting the two Nora was worried about after I threatened to tell Melinda Wolfe on them."

"I can still smell the stuff sometimes when I come up the side stairs," said Molly, "but not as much." She was making her bed—not a thing anybody except Tina normally managed to do—and she added to the pillow she was shaking, "Would you really have told Wolfe about them?"

"You bet," said Janet. "Better for her to deal with it than for the whole college to get wind of it. The College tries to stay out of people's private lives; but you've no idea what they're like once they're roused. They'd love an excuse to reinstitute dorm monitors and visiting hours and room searches, and those girls were going to give them one."

"Are you sure? Sounds like a lot of trouble to me."

"Not as much as parents screaming at them about corrupting their precious babies."

"I guess." Molly twitched her bedspread straight and sat down on the floor. "Do parents ever scream at your father?"

"Only when he teaches *The Cenci*."

"What's that?"

"Shelley's play about incest."

Tina came back into the room with a bowl of apples and put it down in the middle of Janet's desk. "What are we wearing?" she said.

"I thought I'd come as a radical college student," said Molly.

"You need an army jacket and bigger bell-bottoms," said Tina, with complete solemnity. Janet suspected her of joking, but it was not easy to tell with Tina. Her sense of humor ran in different channels than Janet's or Molly's, and if Nora was right, Tina had been made to doubt that she had any sense of humor at all in the first weeks of their acquaintance. Tina was not, Janet would bet, accustomed to lacking confidence; it made her unpredictable.

"Huh," said Molly. "I've got a copy of *The Prophet*; that's worth ten army jackets."

"Bleah!" said Janet, involuntarily.

"You be quiet. Nobody who reads Hermann Hesse has any right to sneer at *The Prophet*."

"Hesse may be boring, but he's not stupid."

Tina cleared her throat. "Is anybody dressing up or not? We've only got half an hour."

"I'm going to put on a clean shirt," said Janet, hauling her green wool sweater, her gray Blackstock T-shirt, and her cotton undershirt over her head in one wad and shoving them under the bed. She did it mostly to see Tina wince, and was immediately ashamed of herself.

"I," said Tina, "am going to put on a dress."

"Thomas will be delighted," said Janet. "Did you guys take your pills yet?"

"I'm going to take it late," said Molly. "I prefer to feel nauseous at noon the day after a party, thank you."

"Nauseated," said Janet. "Nauseous means to afflict, not to be afflicted."

"Ah," said Molly. "I get it. I am nauseated, you are nauseous."

"She, he, it is nauseized," said Janet, diverted.

Tina opened her top bureau drawer, took out the dispenser, and clicked a pill into her hand. "Hey," she said, "four more days, a week off for my period, and then—"

"Good-bye unicorns," said Janet.

"Only you," said Tina with mild exasperation, "would think of it like that. *I*'ve never seen a unicorn—"

"I never hope to see one," offered Molly.

"Well, I do," said Janet, nettled.

"Have you explained this to Nick?" said Molly.

"Not yet. I've got till the end of the term."

"Oho," said Molly. "I see that there are advantages to living in town."

"A few," said Janet. "A few." She went around the corner to her closet and pulled out the white muslin shirt her grandmother had made, with green leaves and vines embroidered on all the hems, and three tiny roses that it was a game to find. Tina came past her, rummaged in her own closet, took out something black, and left the room.

"Are you going to dress up?" said Janet to Molly. "Nobody will mind if you don't."

"What a gorgeous shirt," said Molly. "It doesn't go with jeans, though, somehow."

"It probably wants a skirt," said Janet, "but I haven't got anything but jean skirts."

"Oh well," said Molly. "I don't want to be called Hannibal again." She propped her chin in her hands, scowling, and then brightened suddenly. "*I* know!" she said, and bolted out of the room.

When she came back, she was wearing a very large and shabby army shirt over the blue long underwear and the red-and-blue flannel shirt she had already had on. "There!" she said. "Nora let me raid the lost-and-found. So here I am, radical college student, scoffers, for the use of." She climbed up on her desk and reached her copy of *The Prophet* off the topmost shelf, which it shared with *The Wind in the Willows*, the complete works of Ezra Pound, and a battered copy of *Three Men in a Boat*. She called it her security shelf, and Janet knew she had not touched one of those volumes since she got here.

Tina came back into the room in a soft black dress with a scooped neck and a short skirt. She had belted it with a pink scarf. She looked, for once, a great deal more elegant than healthy. Molly whistled at her.

"What a wonderful dress," said Janet. "You look like Mata Hari."

Tina dimpled and blushed at them, and the first knock came at the door. It was Peg Powell in her best Victorian nightgown ("I even ironed it," she said) and Sharon in a tight one-piece trousered garment of a peculiar color between ginger and mustard. It went gloriously with her skin, but suggested that she had been rather thinner when she bought it. "Wouldn't dare wear this in public," she said, "but I thought you guys'd appreciate it."

Somebody else knocked, and Janet let in Nora, looking extremely tall in a narrow orange dress and orange tights with black cats on them; Diane Zimmerman, dressed like the Tenniel Alice in Wonderland; and the two foolish children from the end of the hall. The one with the horn-rimmed glasses had come as the Patchwork Girl of Oz; her roommate with the wire frames was wearing jeans and a flannel shirt, and said sheepishly that she had been obliged by a term-paper deadline to come as she was. Janet got Nora aside and ascertained that the Patchwork Girl was Rebecca and the other one was Susan.

The hot cider went around, in borrowed Food Service cups; Janet opened the box of gingerbread and the box of pumpkin cookies; people shuffled around and sat down shyly. Susan perched on the end of Molly's bed, and Molly greeted her with enthusiasm. "Perfect," she said, "I am a radical college student and you are a conservative one."

"Oh, nonsense," said Diane. "A conservative one would wear a wool kilt and a white blouse and a sweater."

"Not here she wouldn't."

"And a radical one," said Diane ruthlessly, "would have—"

"My costume," proclaimed Molly, "is perfect. *I* have a copy of *The Prophet*." She waved it.

"What's radical about *The Prophet*?" demanded Diane.

"I never said it wasn't radical," said Janet hastily. "I said it was stupid. It's bland and badly written."

"Read us something better, then," said Molly.

Janet looked at her. No, she wasn't angry. She wanted to know what Janet thought was better. Janet got up and pulled the volume of Keats from her bottom shelf. It fell open in her hands. "La Belle Dame Sans Merci." Yes, that would do nicely. It was Hallowe'en, after all. She sat down on her desk and began to read.

> *"O what can ail thee, Knight at arms,*
> *Alone and palely loitering?*
> *The sedge has withered from the lake,*
> *And no birds sing."*

"What's sedge?" said Tina.

Janet dropped her eyes to the footnotes. "Sweet flag or yellow iris," she said peacefully; and went on reading.

> *"O what can ail thee, Knight at arms,*
> *So haggard and so woebegone?*
> *The squirrel's granary is full,*
> *And the harvest's done."*

Only a faint cry from Tina of "Foul! No repetition" marred that verse. Janet read on.

> *"I see a lily on thy brow,*
> *With anguish moist and fever dew,*
> *And on thy cheeks a fading rose*
> *Fast withereth too."*

This produced a prolonged wrangle on its exact meaning; Diane Zimmerman finally overrode everybody and parsed the sentence for them. "His brow is moist with anguish and with the dew of fever," she said. Somebody made a rude pun about excrement, and Janet hurried to the next verse. To the Knight's meeting with the Lady in the Meads, his setting her on his pacing steed, her finding him roots of relish sweet and honey wild and manna dew, her taking him to her elfin grot, where he shut her wild, wild eyes with kisses four, her audience returned only a few mild giggles.

> *"And there she lulled me asleep,*
> *And there I dreamed, Ah Woe betide!*
> *The latest dream I ever dreamt*
> *On the cold hill side."*

Nobody said a word.

> *"I saw pale Kings, and Princes too,*
> *Pale Warriors, death-pale were they all;*
> *They cried, 'La belle dame sans merci*
> *Thee hath in thrall!' "*

Nobody breathed.

> *"I saw their starved lips in the gloam*
> *With horrid warning gaped wide,*
> *And I awoke, and found me here,*
> *On the cold hill's side.*
>
> *"And this is why I sojourn here,*
> *Alone and palely loitering,*
> *Though the sedge is withered from the lake,*
> *And no birds sing."*

Janet closed the book and looked at all the upturned faces, variously solemn, pleased, thrilled, or bemused. Molly was grinning. "That's lovely," said she, "but what does it mean?"

"It's about love," said Janet, holding Molly's wide blue stare with her own eyes, "and what do we know about that?"

Somebody knocked on the door. Rebecca, who had not yet progressed beyond the end of the room's little corridor, as if she wanted to make sure an escape route was handy, opened the door. It was Thomas, resplendent in his red silk shirt and black pants and boots. Janet felt the room, all full of women, go quiet with attention. She smiled down the corridor at Thomas, who was looking dubiously at Rebecca, whom he did not know. "Come on in," she said. "Tina, it's Thomas."

Tina made room for Thomas on her bed, and he sat down with an arm around her waist. He looked a little nervous. Janet introduced him to everybody; Susan said timidly, "You're in my history class, I think—Europe in the Age of the Reformation, with Larkin?"

"Yes, of course," said Thomas, smiling kindly into her earnest brown eyes. "You always sit in the back. What did you think of Thursday's lecture?"

Susan, though she looked alarmed, managed to say she thought Larkin had contradicted himself; Thomas pressed her for details; Nora, who had taken the same course two years ago, joined in; and Janet felt she could safely tend to replenishing the supply of cider.

Everything went swimmingly. The history discussion drifted sideways and divided into three or four, one economical, one concerned with costume, one with literature, and one with Reformation gossip. The literary discussion became musical; it developed that Rebecca played the banjo, and she was sent to fetch hers. She played a selection of folk songs, union songs, and contemporary ballads, after which Molly got out the Grateful Dead albums and made everybody sing "Box of Rain." Thomas appeared to have resigned himself to being the only male present, and made a neat and unobtrusive circle around the room, flirting or confiding or teasing or just conversing as the various guests seemed to demand. He got to Janet last, on his way back to Tina, and seemed to realize that she had been noticing him.

"I like your friends," he said peaceably. "Very soothing, after a bunch of bickering classicists."

"Where are they?" said Janet, who had promised herself not to ask him.

He did not pretend that her question was too ambiguous for him. "Did they say they were coming?"

"No, and they didn't say they weren't."

"Well, they aren't," said Thomas. "Medeous has a Hallowe'en party every year."

"And they didn't want to bring us?" said Janet, equal parts of hurt and anger warring in her stomach.

"They couldn't bring you, you're not Classics majors."

"Neither is Nick, at least not yet."

"No, but he's taking Latin."

"Why aren't you there?" said Janet.

She expected him to say something about Tina. He looked at her out of his pure gray eyes, the only eyes of that color she had ever seen, with the pale lashes longer than Tina's, and he said, quietly, as if he were entrusting her with some great secret, "I am become weary of that crew."

You're talking like them all right, thought Janet. She felt herself beginning to frame a sentence that was in effect an apology for Nick's behavior, and made herself stop. If he baited Thomas incessantly, he must have a reason. Thomas could surely take care of himself—as he had in fact done by coming here tonight; or if he couldn't, he had Robin, quick and sharp as a rapier. "What's wrong with them?" she said, trying to make it a request for information rather than a challenge.

Thomas drew in his breath, and let it out again audibly. "I can't explain."

"Robin does get wearing," said Janet, offering Molly's suitor in place of her own.

"Does he?" said Thomas, as if she had proposed some resplendent new literary theory. "Well, then, if I tell you that, when that lot is all together, he is the best of the lot, you may understand why sometimes I choose other company."

"Are Anne and Odile Beauvais part of that crew?"

"Oh, yes."

"Do they do drugs when Medeous is around?"

Thomas made an abrupt noise that might have been a laugh. "What would stop them?"

"Common sense?" If Medeous was winking at illegal drugs, Janet didn't want to know about it. Her reputation did not hint at it: quite the contrary; but one could, presumably, be a demon in the classroom and as mild as milk in a social setting.

Thomas simply shook his head. "They haven't got any," he said. He went on looking at her. "If you stay with Nick," he said, "and you ought to—if you do, it's going to be like this. Either you are excluded, or you join them. And you oughtn't to join them."

"Can I beat them?" said Janet, more or less automatically.

"It's worth a try," said Thomas. He put a hand on her shoulder. Through the stiff muslin, his fingers were cold. "But you mustn't seem jealous, ever. If—"

At this point Nora suggested that they turn out the lights and light all the candles and tell ghost stories.

"Later," said Thomas, and went to sit by Tina.

Janet joined Molly and Susan on Molly's bed, and listened to Nora tell a comic story, Peg a creepy but predictable one, and Sharon a perfectly terrifying tale that she said was Spanish. In the silence that followed it, through the open window came the complaint of the bagpipes.

"Oh, *Robin*," said Molly with a kind of loving exasperation.

"Let's go catch him," said Sharon, scrambling to her feet and turning Tina's desk lamp on. "I've heard about this fellow for three years and never seen him."

This seemed to please the entire party; in a gabble of agreement, they streamed out the door. Molly snatched her jacket out of her closet and bolted after them. Janet looked at Thomas and Tina.

"I wouldn't," said Thomas.

"It's only Robin," said Tina, considering him with some confusion.

"What she said," Janet said to Thomas, snatched her own jacket from the floor of her closet, and ran after the others.

She caught up with them on the wooden bridge between Eliot and Dunbar; they had stopped to listen for the elusive sound of the pipes. For a group of young, festive women, they were very quiet. Janet made her feet scuff on the dust of the path, and Molly said quietly, "Here's Janet."

"Shhhh," said everybody.

Janet joined them on the bridge and stood looking out over the lake. It was as clear, flat, and dark as the starry sky, except where a lone street lamp set by the bridge at its other end sent a line of wavery yellow across it. The night was cold; only a clean, weedy smell came from the lake. From Eliot on her left and Dunbar on her right came muffled sounds of merriment. Beyond them, after a few minutes, the sound of the pipes skulked again. It was somewhere beyond Dunbar.

They went up the hill, past the long bulk of that building, and stopped to listen again. At the hill's crest, past the parking lot, in the lilac maze, perhaps. When they got to the edge of the maze, the sound was definitely coming from the fields beyond; and when they got to those, it was clearly somewhere across the highway, in the Lower Arboretum. They tumbled down the long slope to the highway and darted across its empty asphalt to the gravel space on the other side. The woods were dark, dryly rustling. The stream made a tiny sound; it was rather low just now. The pipes were silent.

Nora and Molly, in the lead, started down the path to the wooden bridge; and Janet hissed, "Wait."

They stopped obediently. Janet edged through the crowd of girls to Molly. "Horses," she whispered.

They all stood still. And under the rustle of dry leaves in the light wind, the sounds came clearer now: not only the sedate thud of hoofs and the creak of leather, but a dim jingling that, as it grew louder, made a music purer than the bagpipes. Janet opened her eyes wide, staring into the mottled darkness; next to her, Peg pushed her glasses up her nose and said, "I see lights."

Janet saw them too. They looked like fireflies, and then perhaps like lanterns; and then they were just an enormous greeny-gold glow that showed up the trunks and branches of the trees, the dead dry stalks of weed and a few late-blooming flowers, like things in a pencil sketch. The broad path on the other side of the bridge lit up, every stone and stick on it like a jewel; the light touched the rough wooden bridge and made it dazzling; and then they could see the riders.

Janet murmured, "Get back," to Peg, and pushed Sharon and Molly into the bushes. Peg turned and did the same for Susan and Rebecca. Nobody protested. The first riders came, sedately walking, down the broad path to the bridge. The horses were black as coal. Their manes and tails were braided and strung with beads and ribbons that did not sparkle, but glowed, with a light that showed the riders but cast no shadow. The riders were strung with beads and ribbons, too, covered with flowing clothes of no familiar pattern. Their faces were pale and solemn. Their yellow hair blew behind them, though they went slowly and there was little wind.

These were the first three, who might have been men or women. The fourth was a woman in artful tatters of red and green. If you had seen a picture of her, or tried to describe her, you would have had to say she was in rags. But in motion her dress was complete and perfect. She had red hair, not like Janet's or Melinda Wolfe's, but like black wood with a red grain in it. Her face was high and pale like the others', and her hair sprang from a peak at her forehead and waved back at her temples in the same way as theirs.

The three riders and the woman on the black horses passed by, stirring up the gravel, and swung onto the highway. Behind them were smaller horses, brown, homely-looking ones that might have come from the farm attached to Blackstock. They, too, were alight with beads and ribbons. On them were men and women exceedingly beautiful, but looking, after the four who had just passed, as homely as the horses. Janet thought she saw Anne and Odile, but they all looked so much the same, she was not certain. She did see Melinda Wolfe, in a dress that looked sometimes green and sometimes gray, and knew her by her red hair and the tilt of her head. With her was a young man who might have been the newest instructor in Classics, or might not; and behind them an older man with dark hair and an angelic face, who was definitely Professor Ferris of Classics.

They went by, too; and behind them on white horses came people Janet knew. The nice thick boy with the southern accent, with whom she had talked about squirrels. Kit Lane, like a dark copy of Thomas. Somebody who looked so much like them both that he must be the mysterious Johnny. Robert Benfield. Jack Nikopoulos. And Nicholas Tooley. His curly head, his blunt profile, the faint slouch of his shoulders, were unmistakable. And in that crowd of stern or smiling faces, only his was scowling. He was having to manage not only his own horse, but another white horse with an empty saddle. Robin's, Janet supposed; you could hardly play the bagpipes on horseback.

They all went by, looking straight ahead; and when they were all gathered on the highway, somebody let out an unholy whoop, and the entire troupe of them went pounding up the empty road, striking sparks from it and making it look, in the moment of their passing, like a river of gold. They went up the hill in a flurry of light, and turned the corner at the top, and were gone. A last sound of bells drifted down.

Nobody said anything. The night was silent. In the woods beyond the stream, the pipes began again.

Molly stirred herself at Janet's side, marched out of the bushes, and stamped down the dirt path and across the wooden bridge. The piping stopped in mid-squall. It was so quiet you could hear Molly's bell-bottoms dragging in the dirt. Janet went after her, as she had gone over the other wooden bridge the last time they met Robin and his pipes, because she felt some obscure twinge of danger. But it was, once again, only and really Robin. He was not in his old patched jeans and T-shirt, but in something velvet, dark blue or deep green or maybe black, with a coat to it, and high boots; and his coat's small carved buttons, like the jewels of the riders, made a light of their own. In it his neat-boned face with its tidy beard looked wary and affronted.

Molly was afronted too. "Cowering under the bed," she said flatly.

"It was good advice," said Robin, in a mild tone.

Janet, fighting a desire to inform Robin that it had not been phrased as advice, thought she had better fade over the bridge and take the rest of the interested audience back to interrupt Thomas and Tina and finish the last of the cider. But as she took her first step backward, silently, Robin addressed her over Molly's shoulder. "Janet Carter," he said. "Where's Thomas?"

Stifling an indignant and irrelevant "How should I know," Janet said temperately, "He's in our room with Tina."

"Good place for him," said Robin.

"Are you tired of that crew, too?" said Janet.

"Are you tired of the wet rain, and the cold snow, and the way the wind moves the air around?" said Robin.

A whole cloudy discussion of weather, and human and poetic reaction to it, rose up in Janet's brain. She scowled at Robin, and said, "I'm tired of not being told anything."

Molly, who still had her back to Janet and the rest of the guests, made an impatient movement.

"If you'll see her home, Robin, we'll be going," said Janet.

"For Christ's sake," said Molly, with the first real anger Janet had seen in her since they met. "I can see myself home."

And you'll probably have to, thought Janet. She turned and

walked back to the goggling crowd. "Come on, you guys," she said. "There's a whole loaf of pumpkin bread waiting."

They came with her obediently, chattering all the while about the horses. A few awed references to the light cast by the company of riders were scornfully laid to rest by Peg, who told them to for pity's sake go read "The Hound of the Baskervilles" if they thought such effects were so hard to come by, and to remember that there are Chemistry majors in the world. While Susan and Sharon were attempting rejoinders to this, probably more out of pique than conviction, Nora said quietly to Janet, "Are we about to have an upheaval?"

"I haven't the faintest idea," said Janet. "I don't think you have to worry. Molly's method of coping with a broken heart is probably to memorize her math book."

"Thank God," said Nora. "Now that the idiots at the end of the hall are settled, I thought I might have some chance of passing my courses and graduating. Try not to have any upheavals."

"If we do," said Janet, as they topped the rise where the lilac maze crouched in the dark like a giant unkempt sheep, "I'm sure Melinda Wolfe would advise us."

Nora laughed, not very pleasantly. "Do everybody a favor," she said. "If you want to go that route, tell me and I'll introduce you to somebody harmless."

"Thanks, I think I've got one of those," said Janet. "But I'll let Molly know."

"You mean Nick?" said Nora, and laughed again. "Nick Tooley harmless? He rides with Medeous. She's not interested in harmless people."

"Well," said Janet, "I'm not sure I am either. At least, if I weren't trying to go to college I wouldn't be."

"But you are trying to go to college," said Nora. Her voice was a little breathless, though they had been going downhill, and were now abreast of Dunbar again. "What's *your* remedy for a broken heart?"

They filed over the wooden bridge and trudged up the eroded gully between Forbes and Eliot. The sounds of merriment had mostly died down. Somewhere at the top of Forbes, a large group was singing "Amazing Grace" with agonizing slowness in several warring keys. Janet's party had fallen silent, as if they wanted nothing better than to know her remedy for a broken heart.

"Writing poetry, I expect," said Janet, carelessly. "What's yours?"

"Ice cream," said Nora.

"I cut my hair off," said Susan. "It made me feel like somebody else. It was down to my knees. I estimate I won't be the girl who was heartbroken again for another two years."

She was greeted with a chorus of giggles and a flurry of other suggested remedies. Last of all, when everybody else had had her say and they were climbing the steps to Fourth Ericson, Sharon asked Peg, who had not spoken, what her remedy would be.

"I'd imitate the Lady of Shallott," said Peg.

The Lady of Shallott had killed herself for love of Lancelot, and floated down the river to Camelot in a boat. Janet opened her mouth to contest so extreme a solution, looked at Peg's quiet face, and closed it again.

Molly came back at six o'clock in the morning, waking Janet, who had had a series of incoherent and disturbing dreams involving horses, bagpipes, the river, rapiers, and the bust of Schiller. "Take your pill," she hissed at Molly.

"Oh, God, two in one day will probably bring on the effects again," said Molly; but she rummaged in her drawer for the dispenser, and did as she was told.

"Where were you?"

"Tell you later," said Molly, rolled, army jacket, shoes, and all, onto her bed, and put the pillow over her head.

She was still there when Janet got up at eleven. Tina was

already gone. Janet took a shower, and as she was coming back down the hall, in her bathrobe, with a towel around her wet head, she heard a melodious whistling in the staircase; not Tina, but Nick, working absently, and with variations, on one of the songs from *Cyrano*. "Night making all things dimly beautiful, one veil over us all, you are all light, I am all shadow." He burst through the double doors, and, seeing Janet, let fall his armful of notebooks and hugged her vigorously. He was not in fact quite all bones, but had a good thin layer of muscle over any part of him Janet had had the opportunity to investigate; his hugs were irresistible.

Janet squeezed him firmly and dropped her arms. He stepped back, his hands on her waist below the belt of the bathrobe, and looked wary and a little affronted, very much as Robin had last night. The end of the term seemed very far off.

"Have you talked to Robin today?" Janet said.

"No; why?"

"We heard the pipes last night," said Janet, "during the party you didn't bother to tell us you weren't coming to." He raised his eyebrows but said nothing. Janet went on, "We saw you ride past. You weren't cowering under your bed. Would it really be too much to ask to request that you tell me you had another party to go to?"

"I'd hoped to get out of it," said Nick, briefly.

"Well, why couldn't you have said that?"

Nick now looked completely confused, like an actor being given the wrong cue. Janet could see, on his expressive Irish face, the precise moment when he flung caution to the winds. "I thought you'd want to go," he said.

"All I want," said Janet, "is a little basic communication. You don't have to go sneaking off to Classics Department parties without me; all you have to do is to tell me that's where you're going if you think I expect you somewhere else."

"There aren't so many of them," said Nick, rather vaguely.

"You can have them every Saturday night if you want to!" said Janet. "Just *tell* me."

"I'm not much used to that," said Nick.

A number of unwise answers rose to Janet's lips. She rejected them. It was difficult to explain what was the clearest thing in the world to you, the basis of your assumptions and the thought behind your actions. She finally said, less temperately than she wanted to, "Can you manage to tell me if you won't be appearing?"

"I don't expect to not be appearing at all often."

"That'll just make it worse."

"Will it?" said Nick, as if this were some brand-new psychological theory of great appeal but little likelihood. He pushed his glasses back up his nose and kissed her on the right eye. "That would be a pity."

Is that a capitulation or a threat? thought Janet. She felt obscurely in the wrong, as if these things ought to be managed on some level other than that of speech. Which way, she was fairly sure, lay madness, or at least a great deal of trouble. "I wanted to ask you," she said, pursuing this thought rather than the actual discussion, "about your herbal remedy."

"What about it?"

"Where do you get it? Could we persuade Tina to try it instead of those damn pills?"

"It's rather a complex formula," said Nick, slowly, "made me by a friend, as a favor. Thomas would have to ask him. And you know, Tina is a biologist and a materialist; I doubt if she wouldn't be suspicious."

"What is there to be suspicious *of*, for heaven's sake?"

"Not a thing, bless you. But she'd want to know what was in it; and I couldn't tell her, not for my life."

It was true that Tina had read the entire text of the package insert for her pills on the bus coming home, according to Molly, and also that she had pestered the doctor at Planned Parenthood with a lot of questions. Janet would have pestered the doctor, too, had she been reduced to going to one. Having seen what the pills did to Molly and Tina, she preferred Nick's remedies. She wondered what the package insert on the box said. She had put it away and almost forgotten it. If the instructions were too vague or disquieting, she should find out in time to arrange an alternative.

"So, then," said Nick. "Molly wants to teach Robin to play Scrabble. Shall we watch the carnage?"

CHAPTER 10

The package insert, when Janet got around to examining it, was handwritten in flowing characters, like the lists of ingredients on the baked goods from natural-food stores. It said, "For the preventing of conception in the young and healthy; they are hot and dry in the third degree, provoke hunger, and wholesome for the stomach, stay vomiting, stop the terms, help sore heads in children and the studious."

A much better list of effects than that of the pill, thought Janet. The instructions for taking it were complex, but seemed to say it should be made into a strong tea and drunk at noon every day during the time the patient was ovulating; if this could not be determined, the insert said gravely, the patient might drink the tea every day she was not undergoing her courses. Janet thought at first that this had something to do with sore heads in the studious; but a little application to the *Oxford English Dictionary* showed that it meant she should not take the medicine during her period.

The ingredients were listed by their Latin names. Janet made a note to ask Nick—or Robin, maybe, or Thomas; or better yet, Peg—to translate them for her.

November rains stripped all the trees except for the stubborn and covetous oaks. It was unseasonably warm, bare ground and bare trees luxuriating in the springlike air. The lovely shapes of the undressed elms stood up against all the red sunsets like the leading of a stained-glass window, and all the wide lawns of Blackstock were still green for Thanksgiving.

Halfway through November, some of the crocuses planted around Ericson put up questing shoots; Janet and Molly, along with a collection of seniors from First, Anne and Odile Beauvais, and Susan and Rebecca, helped Melinda Wolfe rake leaves over them and anchor the mulch with evergreen branches. Wolfe herded them all into Ericson's main lounge afterward, where she had had the Food Service set up urns of tea and coffee and a few trays of cookies. She left them pulling grass and pine needles out of one another's hair, and filling the thick Food Service cups; and returned balancing two huge silver platters covered with confections too beautiful to eat.

In the hubbub of exclamation, Janet and Molly looked at one another, and back at the trays. There were petits fours in their pale colors, with frosting flowers—no, preserved flowers, roses and violets and marigolds and nasturtiums; there were perfect miniature fruits, each with the color and bloom proper to its skin: apples, peaches, pears, plums, oranges, none bigger than a large marble—marzipan, those must be; there were rolled-up lacy cookies dipped half in chocolate and filled with cream; there were candied orange slices and ginger chunks and whole red strawberries all sparkling with sugar; there were slabs of shortbread pricked with a fork in patterns of flowers; there were small cakes like chrysanthemums; there were piles and drifts of the glistening red seeds of the pomegranate; there were, in fact, exactly as Keats had said in "The Eve of St. Agnes," candied apple, quince, and plum, and gourd (by which he meant melon, and Melinda Wolfe provided cantaloupe);

jellies soother than the creamy curd, and lucent syrups, tinct with cinnamon, all right, Janet could smell it from where she stood; and dates, too—all of which Porphyro had brought to seduce Madeline.

"No?" said Melinda Wolfe, as if she had heard Janet thinking; but she was talking to Rebecca. "I'll eat the first one myself, then, and destroy the symmetry." She put her long fingers into the midst of the marzipan fruit, plucked out a peach that was golden on its smooth side and dusky red on the side with the seam in it, and put it into her mouth.

"Somebody ruin the other tray, then," said Rebecca, rather breathlessly, "and then we can all eat."

Anne Beauvais put out her honey-colored hand to the other tray and took one of the lace cookies. It crumbled, of course, as soon as she bit it; and she caught the crumbs of chocolate with her tongue and licked the cream off her fingers with a kind of delicate exaggeration that mesmerized Janet for several frozen moments and then made her want to laugh. Anne had not only been watching too many old movies, she was wasting her talents on the desert air by displaying her charms in a girls' dormitory.

Or was she?

Molly came to stand beside her, the freckles showing more than usual. Her eyes were enormous. "What was that a rehearsal of, do you suppose?" she said softly.

"I think it's Anne's natural style."

"She was looking at Wolfe the whole time."

Tina's rumor; Nora's remarks on the way back to the Hallowe'en party. "Well," said Janet, "it's none of our business."

"Yes, it is. Anne tries to make our business hers, quizzing Tina in the bathroom about Thomas. And she followed me into the Bio Library and told me Nick was a wild one. And she keeps acting coy and knowledgeable with Robin. She looks at him from under her eyelashes."

"What does Robin say?"

Molly sighed. "He asks me why I would be a breeder of sinners. Then he says that without women like Anne, Hell would be like a lord's great kitchen without fire in it. In't, I should say. And then, when I am about to murder him, he says Anne has been angling for him for years and I must protect him."

"May I lend you my horse and armor?"

"I wish you could," said Molly.

"Shall we go and eat some of the artwork?"

"So you think it's safe?"

Molly hadn't even read "The Eve of St. Agnes."

Janet said, "With Anne around, what would she want with us?"

"It's the pomegranate seeds that worry me," said Molly. "Blackstock isn't really my idea of Hell, but its physics program is a pretty good imitation."

Janet patted her on the shoulder. "We'll confine ourselves to the marzipan, then; there can't be anything sinister about marzipan."

They stepped up to the table and almost ran into Melinda Wolfe, who smiled at them. "I forgot Susan's a diabetic and Odile is on a diet," she said. "I see you're hesitating as well. Is there something I can fetch for either of you?"

"Oh, no," said Molly, "what's here is fine. We were merely reminding one another to be moderate at dinner."

"Given dinner," said Janet, "that shouldn't be much of a problem. But you shouldn't have gone to all this trouble."

Melinda Wolfe laughed, and moved back toward the table of delicacies. She passed through a broad beam of sunlight and her hair took on sparks as if it were full of glitter dust, the kind they let you put on valentines in the second grade. Her blue jeans glowed like velvet; inside the thin white shirt, the sun made her skin glow gold. Molly and Janet moved after her, slowly.

"It's a small repayment for all your work," said Melinda

Wolfe, turning on them suddenly. "On behalf of the crocuses, I thank you. Go on, eat; I have to get some real fruit for the handicapped."

She slid through the crowd of girls and out.

"If I were Susan or Odile," said Molly, "I don't think I'd like that."

In Professor Soukup's class, they examined from each of its many sides the gap between philosophy and modern science. In Professor King's, they were still plodding through the minute details of Malinowsky, who had further delighted Janet by disproving the universality of the Oedipus complex, thus lending a certain tardy credence to Robin's comments on *Hamlet*. In Professor Swifte's class, they were learning the difference between rapier and saber techniques; and in Professor Evans's, having been wafted through Milton's grand epic like thistledown, disputing bitterly whether Milton had been of the Devil's party without knowing it, they were now traveling the heavenly circles of John Donne's poetry, which by sheer audacity of metaphor seemed to be trying to mend the rift between philosophy and science.

The week before Thanksgiving, Janet carried her winter-term schedule card to Melinda Wolfe for approval.

She had allowed ample time to find again that buried office. The spaces between the temporary buildings were silted full of brown leaves. The ivy was red as blood. Melinda Wolfe had hung a different wreath of dried plants on her door: huge orange and yellow marigolds, round purple chive flowers, the blue sprigs of rosemary with their stiff gray-green needles, two flat-topped bunches of white elder flowers, and a scattering of yellow yarrow, the ferny leaves of which formed the base of the wreath. It smelled sharp and medicinal in the mellow air. Janet knocked on the door, and was told to come in.

Melinda Wolfe's office looked as if she, like everybody else, was falling behind in her work. Papers and folders were piled four feet tall on her desk and on the floor around it. She herself was sitting in the desk chair, which she had wheeled around to the front of the desk. She wore a blue sweater, probably cashmere, and a plaid skirt in blue and yellow and green. She was not falling behind in personal grooming.

She smiled at Janet and gestured her to the other chair. "I found your file," she said. "Almost a miracle. It was still in the drawer. What have you thought of for winter?"

No ceremonies, thought Janet. All right. She proffered the card. She had put down Swimming, Shakespeare, Astronomy, and Greek Literature in Translation. "You do know that the Astronomy Department consists of one professor who still holds to the fifty-five-minute class period?" said Melinda Wolfe, groping along the edge of her desk.

"But he can show me how to use the telescope?"

"Oh, yes, he can do that," said Melinda Wolfe, and, having found a pen in the pile she was investigating, removed it. "All right. It's good to get the Phys Ed out of the way; and Anne Beauvais is helping to teach swimming next term."

"Is she a student of yours?"

"Yes; specializing in Neander's account of the travels of Alexander." Melinda Wolfe signed the card and handed it back. "She tells me you threatened her sister."

This was not how one's advisor was supposed to go on—especially after feeding one with the delights of Paradise and telling dirty jokes like a teenager. "Did she say what I threatened her sister with?" said Janet.

"Yes. I do," said Melinda Wolfe, "keep my fingers on the pulse of Ericson, no matter how unruly it may seem to you."

"They were putting an unconscionable burden on Nora," said Janet, too angry to be afraid, "and I don't think I should have to wear a gas mask to walk down the hall." Faced with Melinda Wolfe's unblinking scrutiny, she found herself quoting, with considerable vigor, one of Dorothy Sayers's characters. "*Some* consideration for others is necessary in community life."

Her advisor, mercifully, began to laugh. "Never mind," she said. "But do think, how much of the burden did they bind on Nora, and how much of it did she take herself?" She handed the pink card back to Janet. "See you next term," she said. "Good luck on your finals."

Janet thanked her with restraint, and emerged with profound relief into the narrow alley. She shut the door with more force than necessary, and one of the brittle flowers of yarrow bounced off the wreath and landed on the sleeve of her jacket. Janet thought of tucking it back into the wreath, but the entire structure looked far too dry and fragile to be messed with. She slid the flower into her pocket and left in a hurry.

Back in her room, she found Molly and Robin in the throes of an argument. She had left them peacefully intending to sing "Box of Rain" in two-part harmony. Robin was asserting that the reason this was impossible was that the original perpetrators were so very bad at singing. Since he had already, in previous sessions, asserted that Stephen Stills could not sing without whining and Bob Dylan brayed like an ass (which last, Janet thought, was more or less true), Molly was less tolerant than she had been. She had, it appeared, just given up arguing in the abstract, and was about to start insulting him personally.

Janet snatched her English textbook and retired to the lounge with John Donne, Thomas Campion, and Thomas Wyatt. Their subject matter did not help her forget Molly and Robin. That relationship seemed to her utterly mad—but it endured, and Molly even seemed happy. What they had said to one another the night they walked in the woods till dawn, Molly had never told her in detail, despite a great deal of nagging.

Promptly at dinnertime, Nick's violent whistle ascended the staircase ahead of him. It was his own setting for Wallace Stevens's "The Emperor of Ice Cream," which Janet was firmly persuaded nobody else in the universe would think of putting to music. She put down her book and crept down the hall to meet him. The quarreling voices in her room had not abated a whit.

"Shhhh," she said as Nick came through the swinging doors. "They're fighting again."

"That's not fighting," said Nick. "That is just getting acquainted. Come into the lounge, then; I have something to show you."

He shut the door behind them, and sat next to Janet on the orange couch. The room was scattered with last Sunday's newspaper, which was always left until its successor came, to give harried students more time to read it. The battered college-issue sofas and chairs and tables were littered with soda cans, pens, somebody's tennis racket, several people's geology books, a number of Styrofoam cups half full of cold coffee, a large stuffed tiger belonging to Nora that she had donated for the desperate who wanted to hug something at four in the morning, one hundred and sixty-four crayons, all out of their box, the box itself, and a great many sheets of drawing paper, most of which contained either abortive maps or drawings of geological strata. Janet had turned on one table lamp to read by; the rest of the room was dim except where a single band of red sunlight edged through the window and striped the far wall.

Nick took a wad of white tissue out of his jacket pocket and unwrapped it. In the dim light of that untidy institutional room its contents struck the eyes like a sheet of lightning. Janet opened her mouth, and said nothing. It was a necklace made of thin linked rose leaves and stems and thorns, with a rose and a bud as the pendant. It looked like ruddy gold, which might have been an effect of the light.

"I didn't make it myself," said Nick, a little anxiously. "I drew up the design, and got Robin to make it. And then I couldn't wait until Christmas to give it to you."

She couldn't take it. For more reasons than her muddled mind could marshal, she knew she could not. But it was very hard to say so, especially without hurting his feelings, especially since this was a relationship whose emotional boundaries she, not he, had tried to enlarge.

"It's all right, really," said Nick. "Robin is making another one for Molly. He'll have it by her birthday. But your birthday is no use; it's in August."

"Is hers just the same?"

"Certainly not. Hers has French lilies."

Janet picked up the delicate thing. It was almost weightless in her palm, but the thorns pricked faintly.

"Here," said Nick, and gathered the rebellious mass of her hair in his two fists and held it out of the way while she put the necklace on and fastened the clasp. It was briefly cold, and then seemed not to be there at all. The thorns did not prick her neck.

"I don't know how to thank you," said Janet; and bit her lip at the extremely unfortunate nature of this common remark.

"Your eyes will do it nicely," said Nick, and kissed her hand.

It was the curious custom of Blackstock College to hold classes on the Friday and Saturday after Thanksgiving, so that nobody could go home for a four-day weekend. Janet, having ascertained that her father had invited only two of his own students to Thanksgiving dinner, proposed to bring along Tina, Thomas, Molly, Robin, and Nick; and was given permission.

The two students he had invited were Diane Zimmerman, who was in his Rhetoric class, and Peg Powell, who was not in any of his classes, but to whom he had garnered an introduction through Professor Medeous so he could pick Peg's brain about the Fourth Ericson ghost.

Nick had already been to dinner three times, and had been an enormous hit with everybody except Janet's mother. He had not given up trying to charm her; but he sensibly refrained this time. Given the way her mother was eyeing the necklace of roses, Janet was grateful for his restraint.

Diane seemed to find Andrew delightful. Peg sat in a corner, smiling. Janet came to keep her company, and watched with amusement as Lily took immediately to Tina and her father to Robin and Molly and her mother and Vincentio to Thomas, while Andrew, having exhausted the charms of Diane's storytelling and the contents of her knapsack, gamboled among the rest of them but seemed most pleased with Nick, who had let him play the flute to accompany the guitar. He let him do it again, too, after dinner. He played some of his own songs, the ones to do with autumn and winter and Greek heroes and the profoundly silly one about elephants that he had written to Molly's daishiki, which she was wearing. He did not play any of his own love songs, but he and Robin did sing a number of their Elizabethan rounds, making everybody else learn the words too.

At some point during this exercise, Janet's father brought his folding chair over to where Janet and Peg were sitting. "I understand," he said to Peg, offering her a plate of cranberry bread, "that you pick up after the Fourth Ericson ghost."

Peg looked at him warily from behind her glasses.

"Does she always throw the same books?"

"Well," said Peg, "yes—but that's not to say the same three or four. There are about a hundred and fifty of them."

"What do you do with them after you pick them up?"

Peg gave him the kind of look a timid and dutiful student gives to a teacher who is being an idiot. "I put them back in the library," she said.

"Why does—oh," said Professor Carter. "She throws the Thompson Collection."

"Well, that's who she *was*," said Peg, irately.

"How do you know?"

"Because those are her books; and because she talked to me once."

"What did she say?"

"She said that her name was Victoria Thompson and she was homesick. She came from North Dakota. She thought Minnesota was too hilly, and everybody talked strange."

Janet's father then put a series of questions about which books the ghost threw how often, for all the world as if he were examining Peg for her comprehensives preparatory to graduating her. Janet sat watching the flames of the disregarded candles on the dinner table reflected in Peg's glasses, and feeling as Horatio must have when Marcellus and Barnardo told him the ghost of King Hamlet was stalking around the battlements.

In the house she had grown up in, surrounded by the smells of turkey and bayberry and chocolate sauce, with Vincentio ranging around the table hopefully, she dragged into the light of normality the night she and Molly had first gone out to find the piper, and been pelted with books from the windows of their own room. How strange that they had not thought it stranger. It had in fact been altogether peculiar, even if you recalled that they never locked their door, and that Tina was a heavy sleeper.

Janet got up and went into the kitchen, where her mother was scraping the dishes, helped predictably by Diane and Molly, and astonishingly by Thomas. "Can I spend the night?" she said.

"I thought you might like to," said her mother, "for post-Thanksgiving breakfast. I'm sorry I can't put up the whole lot of you, but you can all come back for buckwheat pancakes if you like."

"I've got a nine-thirty class," said Janet tardily.

"So has your father. I don't know what's the matter with Blackstock," said her mother, as she had said every Thanksgiving for fifteen years. "Why can't they do away with their precious midterm break and give you a couple of days off for Thanksgiving?"

"The latest theory," said Diane, who had somehow received the job of stripping the turkey carcass and was up to her elbows in grease and bits of stuffing, "is that it would be too hard on the kids who can't afford to go home. Midterm break isn't over a holiday, so they don't mind so much. Theoretically."

"The kids who can afford to go home usually do it anyway," said Janet.

"Yeah, but they're not supposed to," said Diane. "It permits a glow of righteousness to emanate from the rest of us."

"Blackstock students have one of those anyway," said Janet's mother.

Janet walked her friends to the end of the block, kissed Nick, and trudged back slowly under the high frosty stars. All the puddles in the road were rimmed with white ice. She could see her breath, and tried, as always, and failed, as always, to blow rings of it. Smoke, of course, was denser; but that was not enough reason to take up smoking.

She read Andrew a chapter of *The Wind in the Willows*, which he was hating violently but insisted on finishing just the same. Then she went to bed. Her bed felt too soft, and the quiet in the room was amazing. She lay staring into the dark and assembling the forces of her intellect. There was something at Blackstock that deadened thought. No, not all thought—she had not had the slightest difficulty in absorbing Milton, Aristotle, Malinowsky, or anybody else who could write English or be translated felicitously into it. She had written critical papers that had not been utterly scorned; she had learned the rules of fencing, past and present; she had passed quizzes on philosophy and anthropology and, when Evans became impatient with the quality of class discussion, on the progression of metaphor in "A Valediction: Forbidding Mourning."

There was something at Blackstock that made it difficult to think about particular topics. The Fourth Ericson ghost and anything connected with her—including, for some odd reason,

Peg's remark about having bunk beds in her room when she hadn't. Assuming there was a ghost, why would she exert this influence when, apparently, she had told Peg all about herself anyway? If she were hiding, why throw books out the window? She seemed rather flexible for a ghost; most of the ones Janet had read about had been confined to appearing at a particular time in a particular place to perform particular actions, whether washing blood out of a garment, weeping hysterically, or putting down milk for a cat whose ghost did not, after the manner of cats, oblige by appearing also. This seemed like a cross between a ghost and a poltergeist. Well, there were certainly enough upset adolescents, the generally assigned cause for poltergeists, whether supernatural or natural, around Ericson.

What else? She revolved the incidents of her first weeks at Blackstock through her mind. It suddenly struck her as odd that everybody should be so averse to using Melinda Wolfe as Melinda Wolfe's position required, as an advisor and mediator, the last resort before making an official report that the College would have to take notice of, with unpleasant effects. Unless, of course, Melinda Wolfe had explained to all the RA's that she did keep her finger on the pulse of Ericson and the RA's were to stay quiet and let her work in her own way.

What an aversion to asking Melinda Wolfe for help might have in common with the ghost of Victoria Thompson, aside from the fact that Janet had found them difficult to think about at Blackstock, was another question entirely. Janet turned on the bedside lamp, dragged notebook and pen out from under the bed, and wrote down everything she had thought of. She sat up a while longer, considering Tina's weird mixture of denseness and perspicacity; Robin's peculiar way of conducting a romance; Molly's rare detachment from herself and her preoccupations; Nick's inability to say he would not be somewhere; Thomas's transformation from a raging maniac to a soft-spoken charmer; Peg's sleepwalking; Nora's conscience;

Sharon's speech patterns. They were too familiar to her now; she could not reconstruct how she had seen them when they first met, except for Thomas, and he had never behaved like that again. It was as if she had met another person entirely in the library.

Nothing at Blackstock—except the pressures of work—was keeping her from thinking about any of those things. It was the ghost and Melinda Wolfe off whose oddities thought seemed to slide like rain down a window. Janet was getting sleepy. I wonder, she thought, turning off the lamp and sliding back under the patchwork quilt her grandmother had made, if I should sleep at home once a month, just to clear my mind.

A week later, on the eve of final exams, Janet and Tina had a birthday party for Molly. They had found a local bakery, tolerant of college students, that would make a three-layer chocolate cake and write on the top, in red icing, "If it doesn't work, it's Physics." Molly was, in fact, scowling over her physics book when they marched in, singing, with the cake. Thomas and Nick came behind them with the toy theater, which they were to quietly insinuate into Janet's closet until it was wanted. She had had to clean up the closet floor for this purpose, greatly astonishing Molly. "I can see rereading *The Lord of the Rings* instead of studying for finals," she had said, "but why clean your closet?"

Now she lifted her head with great deliberation from her book and surveyed them all, Tina and Janet and Robin and Thomas and Nick, with as forbidding an expression as freckles and large blue eyes would allow. Janet had a sudden awful feeling that Molly did not like surprises. Then Molly grinned. "Lucky for you idiots I didn't decide to study in the library," she said; and flinging the despised physics book in the general direction of the sink, she bounced off the bed and blew out the candles on her cake.

Robin had already given her the necklace that morning; she

was wearing it now, with a Grateful Dead T-shirt, having remarked in passing that it was a pity the Dead had not chosen lilies as their flower, since Janet's necklace would have been more becoming to the shirt as it was. She clearly had no expectation of any presents aside from the cake. Tina and Janet had left it to Thomas to decide when to bring the thing out of the closet, and he seemed in no hurry about it.

Tina handed Molly a long knife abstracted from the Food Service by Thomas, who was on financial aid and worked in Taylor, poor creature, five mornings a week. Molly used the point of the knife to pry off all the sugar roses, which she then distributed at mathematically exact locations around the cake. Everybody got one and a half of them. They all ate their cake, and sat around drinking Tina's Russian tea. Thomas had scrunched up Tina's bed pillows to lean against, as he always did; Tina would complain bitterly about it later, but now she lay with her head in his lap and her pink-stockinged feet on her desk and looked blissful. Nick sat at Janet's feet and let her rub his head. Robin and Molly sat at the extreme ends of Molly's bed and conducted a vehement argument about the costuming of *The Revenger's Tragedy,* diverging into the finances of the College, the intention of the playwright, how hot it was likely to be in Ericson Little Theater in the middle of January, and whether it was difficult to sew velvet.

Janet found in her mind the words of some of Tolkien's people, discussing the story they were in and how they might end it. Bilbo had thought of, "And they all lived happily ever after until they died. It is a good ending," he had said, "and none the worse for having been used before." "Ah!" said Sam, "but where will they live? That's what I often wonder." Janet wondered, too. For four years they would live here. After that, unless somebody made a prodigious and possibly miraculous effort, they would scatter to the four corners of the world, their fellowship broken, and do what all of them had done to be here in this room now: find new friends. It seemed wasteful. Perhaps they could buy an island somewhere.

Janet looked around the room again, trying to imprint it in her memory, sight and sound and sense: the steamy warmth of the radiator, the worn path in the carpet before the chipped sink, the smell of tea and chocolate, and sage from Nick, and Tina's wearisome white lilac perfume, and a background of dust because nobody had had time to clean the room since the Hallowe'en party. Molly in her Blackstock sweatshirt, with chocolate on her nose; Robin in a red velvet shirt with huge puffed sleeves and tight cuffs, tugging it out of the waistband of his jeans and turning its hem up to show Molly its construction. Tina's long, beautiful legs in those silly pink stockings, her smiling face upturned to Thomas and her yellow hair spread over his lap. Thomas, who caught Janet's eyes and said, "In such a night Medea gathered the enchanted herbs That did renew old Aeson."

"What?" said Tina, dreamily, not at all in the sharp tone with which she usually speared you if you said something she did not understand.

"In such a night," said Janet, backing up, "Stood Dido with a willow in her hand Upon the wild sea banks, and waft her love To come again to Carthage."

"In such a night as this," said Nick, in his theater voice, "When the sweet wind did gently kiss the trees, And they did make no noise, Troilus methinks mounted the Troyan walls, And sighed his soul toward the Grecian tents, Where Cressid lay that night."

"In such a night," said Robin, so softly that after his last loud words to Molly you could scarcely hear him, "Did Thisbe fearfully o'ertrip the dew, And saw the lion's shadow ere himself, And ran dismayed away. There's an end of your romance, Thomas; what a play to choose."

"After we take Shakespeare next term," said Molly to Janet, "will I be able to do that?"

"I think it requires a misspent youth," said Janet, "but a good memory might get you through." She was still looking at Thomas. "I know what you meant," she said.

"Do you so?" said Robin. "Then say it another way."

Janet considered, and while she was considering, Nick said, "'True happiness is of a retired nature, and an enemy to pomp and noise; it arises, in the first place, from the enjoyment of one's self; and, in the next, from the friendship and conversation of a few select companions.'"

"What?" said Janet.

"Addison," said Nick, tilting his head back and grinning at her.

"And was that what Thomas meant?" said Robin.

"Part of it," said Janet, looking back at Thomas.

"I hope so," said Robin. "That's a poor thin sort of happiness."

"That's the eighteenth century," said Nick. "But I thought, we were all pleased to be here so comfortably, each with his mate, and the wind howling outside. All it wants is a fireplace."

"They have them in Sterne Hall," said Tina, without opening her eyes. "If we get good numbers in Room Draw, you guys, maybe we could get a triple there next year."

Janet removed her gaze from Thomas in a hurry, and looked at Molly. It was nice that Tina wanted to live with them again next year; it meant they had been succeeding in treating her kindly. But what did they want? And why, after all, if a sixsome with Tina was pleasant, should a threesome be less desirable? People were very strange, oneself most emphatically included. But the mood was broken now, the moment she had wanted to capture whole was past. She raised her eyebrows at Thomas, and Thomas bent his head so that his pale hair mingled with Tina's richer tresses, and kissed her forehead and said something to her softly.

Tina got up, pulling him by the hand, and preceded him into the little hallway. They came out again carrying the toy stage, and set it on Molly's bed between Molly and Robin.

Molly's whole face went round with astonishment and then with delight. "Far *out*!" she said. "Janet, you fiend, you were watching me every minute. *Look* at this!" She lifted out the figure of a woman in a red dress, and another, with yellow hair, in a blue one.

"She knows how to take a gift," said Nick to Janet.

"I suppose I'll have to read the play now," said Molly. "Who wrote it?"

"Christopher Fry," said Thomas. "If you haven't read it, what did you want the stage for?"

"Because it's miniature," said Molly, still delving among the actors, "and infinitely more interesting than a dollhouse. What's the play about?"

Thomas looked at Nick, who shrugged; and at Robin, who said, "I cannot read Fry, more's the pity."

"It's about two people who save each other," said Thomas. He was looking at Tina. She was finding out how many of the doors of the set would open and close—all of them, it appeared—but after a moment she seemed to feel his gaze, and looked over Robin's head at him. They really were a most gorgeous couple.

"From what?" said Tina.

"Death, and life," said Thomas.

"I'll get it out of the library tomorrow," said Molly.

"You'll do no such thing," said Janet. "This is for you to play with during your vacation, not during your finals."

"All right, all right," said Molly. "Now. Where shall we put it? I don't suppose there's such a thing as an extra desk down in the basement?"

There were in fact several, in the dimly lit cavern, next to the laundry room, where you could store your belongings over the summer. Molly and Tina argued over which they should take. Janet wandered back into the depths of the room, past derelict gooseneck lamps with their necks twisted unpleasantly sideways, and chairs missing their seats, and chairs missing their legs, and chairs reduced to piles of polished sticks, and rolled-up lumpy mattresses and discarded springs. Against the back wall were stacked pieces of bunk beds; most of them were the familiar iron pieces, but in one corner there was a vast heavy pile of beautiful maple pieces carved with vines and fruit, on one headboard of which some vandal had smeared ERICSON 410 in black paint.

It's Peg's bunk bed, thought Janet. She was inordinately pleased for a moment, until she realized that this solved nothing. Four-ten had once had a bunk bed in it, that was all. She ran her finger along the headboard's carving, and came away with a black smear of dust.

It was cold in the room, and the voices of the others had gone. Janet turned to go find them, and was met by Robin coming cautiously down the narrow aisle made by bunk-bed parts on one side and discarded drawers sans their chests on the other. He grinned at her and laid one dusty hand on the nearest maple slat.

"What," he said, "thinking of bed still?"

His tone was friendly, but there was something intolerable in it—knowledge, conspiracy, invitation—something. Was this what happened when you were walking out with somebody?

"Go away," said Janet, scowling at him.

"Molly wondered where you were," said Robin, unsmiling. He turned and went back the way he had come.

Janet let her breath out and wondered if she had made Thomas this mad by asking him if sex with Tina was worth the effects of the pill. It's only Robin, she told herself, and followed him.

When she got upstairs, the rest of them had just set the new desk up in the narrow hallway with the closets, so that Tina could squeeze past it every day of their stay in Ericson, and complain about it, too. Janet helped them set the theater on the desk. Robin observed that it was very dark in the hallway and went back to the basement to get one of the gooseneck lamps. Robin behaved exactly as if nothing had happened, and Janet decided she would do the same.

Thomas tinkered with the lamp for half an hour, with tools borrowed from Sharon, and finally achieved a strong yellow light, which he trained on the theater.

Molly refused to turn it off that night. Janet woke two or three times, and saw, over the hump that was Molly with her pillow over her head, the round bright light shining on the little arrangement of house and garden and cellar and street, where two people were saving each other from death, and life. She might check the play out of the library tomorrow herself.

CHAPTER 11

Christmas break began on December 11. Janet spent the first ten days of it with Nick, though she told her parents she was getting a start on her next term's reading. She had no intention of keeping her excursions into adulthood a secret from them forever, but she thought she would like to read a few more chapters, so to speak, before venturing a book report.

On the evening of the twenty-first, drinking tea in Nick and Robin's dim, dusty room in Taylor, she found herself dismissed until Christmas so that he could paint Ericson Little Theater in peace. He refused her offers to help, with a faint surprise that somehow made it impossible to insist. Janet went home at four o'clock in the winter twilight, trying not to feel sulky. She remembered what Thomas had said to her at the Hallowe'en party. It had not occurred to her that the things she might be excluded from would include such homely and eminently sharable tasks as painting a goddamned theater, nor that the company Nick preferred to hers would be his own.

The house smelled of tomato sauce and brownies. Janet

skulked up the stairs to her room and sat down heavily at her desk. She could make good some of the lies she had been telling her parents by actually doing some of next term's reading, she supposed. She had her complete Shakespeare already, though it would really make more sense to get rid of some of the less exciting stuff, like the astronomy or the introductory essays that came with the Greek literature. She rummaged through the desk to find her list of textbooks, some of which she knew her father owned, and came across Danny Chin's postcard, with its Hertzsprung-Russell diagram on one side and its terse announcement on the other. He had gotten home yesterday. He had not called; and neither had she.

Janet got up before she could start thinking, and going into her parents' bedroom, she sat on the bed in the dark and dialed Danny's number. His mother answered by reciting the phone number; Janet identified herself, and, having inquired for Mrs. Chin's health and submitted to having her first term's progress at college investigated, asked for Danny; there was the customary delay, because he always had to be rooted out of somewhere, even if it was only a book. Mrs. Chin accomplished this by sending one sibling after another around to find Danny and get his attention. It took only three of them this time, but Janet was relieved when Danny's light voice said, "Hello?" She was beginning to remember that stupid kiss in agonizing detail, and had to suppress a strong desire to hang up the telephone and dive under the bed.

As usual, the name of the person calling had not survived the chain of children conveying messages. "It's Janet."

"Hi," said Danny unhelpfully.

"I got your postcard."

Since this information required no particular answer, she got none. Rolling her eyes at the ceiling, Janet said, "Do you want to go ice-skating or something?"

"That would be okay," said Danny, in the judicious tone he

used about any suggestion until he was used to it, "but I'd rather go eat onion rings at Sheila's, if you don't mind. Dartmouth only has the stringy ones."

"Skate first, then eat?"

"Okay."

They worked out the details. Janet considered asking after Dartmouth, but they had never used the telephone for extended conversation, and there seemed no real reason to begin now.

He came by to collect her at ten the next morning. Lily, unfortunately, let him in, and bringing him into the kitchen where Janet was brushing Vincentio, she remarked, "Did you have a fight with Nick?" and then ran up the stairs laughing maniacally.

"Who's Nick?" said Danny, in the resigned tone he always used of Lily. Vincentio skidded across the floor and tried to knock him down, but he countered this move absently. He looked just the same: short, sturdy, brown, with a head of silky black hair that seemed not to belong to him. He had gotten new glasses since she saw him last; she wasn't at all sure that gold wire-frames suited him.

"Somebody I'm going out with," she said. "Another English major."

"Good." Vincentio sat on the floor and panted; Danny rubbed his ears. "You never did get me to read Jane Austen."

"Are you going out with anybody?"

"I never really saw the point of it," said Danny.

Janet, who had spent the past ten days learning the point of it, looked at him carefully and saw that he meant it. She considered and rejected a number of commonplace remarks, most of which sounded as if they ought to be addressed to a child of ten, not to any of one's peers—let alone the one who had been, until she went to college, the only really perceptive and intelligent friend she had. "Well," she said, "that'll save you a lot of time."

Danny laughed. "That's the only nice thing anybody's said to me on the subject since I left."

"You're just backward," said Janet, "are you gay, you don't know what you're missing, I can introduce you to somebody."

"Yep. Let's go. The onion rings are calling me."

The onion rings were greasier than Janet remembered them, but served well enough after skating in the icy wind. Over them, she and Danny discussed what college was like. Danny would have liked Dartmouth well enough had there been no other freshmen there; his classmates, or at least all the ones in his dormitory and classes, appeared to have been raised in such strict households that they used the freedom of college to get drunk every night, play poker all afternoon, and hang around with whatever sorts of members of the opposite sex their parents had most resolutely forbidden them. Janet suspected that it was these circumstances rather than any really strong character trait that had made him say he didn't see the point of going out with anybody.

She commiserated with him, which was easy enough to do when the worst trial in her immediate circle was Tina.

"Oh, well," said Danny, finally looking rather embarrassed, exactly as he had long ago when she asked him how his broken arm felt. "Maybe they'll grow up by the end of the year. Or I'll meet some upperclassmen; or some of the ones I know will realize I'm not bad for a fresher. How's Blackstock now that you're just one of the peons?"

Janet told him, in considerable enthusiastic detail, until she saw how forlorn he was looking. She had, their entire senior year in high school, alternately begged, cajoled, and ordered him to come to Blackstock. She swallowed an I-told-you-so. "There are some bad things," she said. "Well, some strange ones." In the brightly lit restaurant, with its worn red tabletops and red vinyl seats patched with duct tape, where the two of them had sat every Saturday noon since they were nine years old and if they ate all they wanted it would cost their combined allowances, the events at Blackstock seemed both remote and improbable. She told him about Peg and the bunk beds, Thomas and *The Romance of the Rose*, the abduction of Schiller and the ominous behavior of the chase in the twilight, the horses at Hallowe'en, and the books coming out the windows—her windows—of Fourth Ericson.

Danny's family were Baptists, of a fairly narrow-minded sort, which was probably why he had gone away to college, since he himself was a profound skeptic. Janet's philosophical upbringing, with its huge doses of Bertrand Russell and *The Skeptical Inquirer*, had taken with him far more thoroughly than with her. He sat listening to her with a patient expression on his brown face, but his forehead gradually creased as his eyebrows rose.

"You been reading too much poetry?" he said. "I knew being an English major would be bad for you."

"Huh," said Janet, throwing her straw wrapper at him. "My English professor this term was twice the fanatic for evidence the Philo teacher was and ten times as fanatical as the Anthro professor."

"Evans, right? Sure, he won't let you do criticism without backing it up. But what's in the poetry, Jan? That's what worries me."

"You think I can't tell fiction from reality?"

"I think you confuse feeling with fact. Look. Remember when I broke my arm in Chester?"

Janet nodded.

"Right when I felt the bone go, I thought the building was laughing at me; I felt like it had *gotten* me for daring to sneak in there. Well, it wasn't. I felt that way because I was hurt and I felt stupid because I wouldn't have been hurt if I wasn't clumsy. So you thought all those people were menacing because it was dark in there and it's a big echoey place and then they were chasing you. That's one of the things kids have nightmares about; it's probably hard-wired right into the human brain."

"What about the books?"

"Is Tina a heavy sleeper?"

"Yes."

"So Peg sleepwalked into your room and threw the books out the window and then came down to get them."

"And the bunk beds?"

"Maybe you heard her wrong. Maybe she's playing some sort of funny game; she sounds weird to me. If she is playing some funny game, maybe she wasn't sleepwalking at all. Some student acting strange is a lot more likely than a ghost throwing books out a window and impersonating said student, or whatever you think happened."

"I don't know what I think happened; I just know that all those things felt really peculiar to me and I had a hell of a time making myself think about them."

"You were never scatterbrained in your life before, of course," said Danny.

It was annoying to be facing somebody who had known you since you were six and remembered every stupid thing you ever did. She thought of trying to tell him about Anne and Odile and Melinda Wolfe. She knew already that he would simply accuse her of being afraid of, prejudiced against, fascinated by, the suspicion—because he couldn't for a moment think it was a fact, not with the little she could tell him—that they were all lesbians. She didn't think she was any of those things; but the problem with Danny was that he felt the entire human race was so peculiar that no single peculiarity, unless it was harmful, made any more impression on him than any other. He knew, mostly from painful experience, that other people had different reactions, and he could make you feel like a creep and a bigot in ten seconds.

Janet wasn't up to it. "It felt different from just being scatterbrained."

"Feelings don't—"

"I know, I know, I know, I know, I know. I was just trying to explain that *my* mental state is not the very best it's ever been either. I think all freshman years are stressful. Remember ninth grade?"

"Oh, God, Billy Gerstein."

"And Stephanie Smith."

"I never thought she was so bad."

"All right then, Debbie Nottingham."

"I'd forgotten her. Was she the one who forged the love letters—"

"No, that was Janie Whatsherface—because she got to grade the spelling papers and she's the one who got a good look at everybody's handwriting. Debbie called me Horsecart and you—"

"Okay, all right, I remember."

Janet felt a mean satisfaction warring with guilt, and asked him if he'd read any good science fiction since he left.

They went sledding two days later, and up to the city to browse in the used-book stores the day after that. Christmas Eve and Christmas Day were family days for both of them, although Nick did come for Christmas dinner, liberally bedotted with dark green and off-white paint and looking unnaturally scrubbed in all the places between. He behaved himself very well—still not endearing himself to Janet's mother, though Janet hoped he didn't notice—but then squandered all his credit by telling Janet, when they were alone in the living room after dinner, that he was going off with Professor Ferris for a week and would see her at the beginning of term. Janet recalled, strenuously, Thomas's advice; unlike painting the theater, this was just the sort of Classics-related clannishness he had warned her to be tolerant of.

Danny came over to dinner a few days later, and was treated to the sight of Lily being kindly, whether because she liked him better than Nick or because she felt sorry for him at having been deprived of a relationship he had no wish for, Janet was not sure and was careful not to find out. They met a few times more before the Blackstock term began again, doing the things they had always done; but Janet was half-relieved when she had to go back to college. Her mind was playing a number of nasty tricks on her: it kept looking at Danny and reflecting that now it knew what he was for—or at least something else he was for that it hadn't known before. She did not, on sober reflection, want to go to bed with Danny; but her mind kept presenting her with pictures of what would happen if she did.

Neither of them suggested that he come visit her at Blackstock, even though Janet wanted him to meet Molly. She felt obscurely that Danny had had his chance and refused it; or maybe she just didn't want to see her past colliding with her future.

Her relief was short-lived; her mind behaved even more badly once she was back in school. It must be a mistake, if you were going to college, to schedule your introduction to the delights of physical passion for Christmas recess. Janet had been prepared for a great deal of unpleasantness: blood, pain, *and* embarrassment; and during finals, when one's emotional resistance was low and cynicism and panic would come calling together like sisters, she had found herself thinking of the ordeal as a test of Nick, whether he would stay for her sake until things got better, or go find somebody more experienced. But it was not an ordeal; it was about the furthest thing from one that she had ever engaged in. Nick's only offense had been to behave as if nothing had changed.

Molly's experience with Robin had been the same. ("I know we just say, well, you know, *theater* people," Molly said, "but I don't see how you can pick this sort of thing up in the theater.") But Robin, too, she said, behaved exactly as if nothing had happened.

Tina, on the other hand, had had a sufficiently bad time that she required three or four sessions with Nora and several boxes of Kleenex to get over it; but Thomas was still around. Tina could not be gotten to say how he was behaving, but from all appearances (which were much more abundant with him than with the other two) he had not changed, either.

Janet found herself wishing, as the sparkling winter of 1972 settled down on all the buildings of Blackstock, that *she* had had a bad enough time to make her devote herself to a celibate life. It was maddening to be sitting in the vast auditorium devoted to Greek Literature in Translation, watching Professor Ferris with his young angelic face and his straight dark hair, more unruly than Nick's, as he told you in his deep swift voice about the glory that was Greece, and suddenly find yourself back in your bed in Ericson, a week before Christmas, with every tactile memory utterly intact. It was infuriating to be sitting in the equally vast science laboratory given over to the introductory Shakespeare course, looking at little Professor Davison, her undistinguished face and childish voice transformed by her love for what she was telling you, discourse on the genius and humanity of Shakespeare, and suddenly find oneself reliving a particular incident of the sort Shakespeare would always treat as either howlingly funny or bitterly obscene. It was disgusting to be learning to focus the telescope and find one's hand trembling. And it was hideous that the act of taking a shower and putting on one's swimming suit should create a wish to go find Nick, right now, and put all the foregoing recollections and imaginations into instant practice.

Molly did not suffer from these difficulties; neither did Tina. Janet, venting a furious indignation at the notion of being at the mercy of chemicals, for God's sake, was simply ganged up on by those two damnable biologists and explained to that she had been at the mercy of chemicals all her life, and these were just a little more potent at the moment. Before she either killed them or said something unforgivable, however, they sprang on her a scheme whereby each of them could have the room for three hours once a week. It was clear that they had been working on this plan for some time, everybody's schedules being what they were. Janet decided they were in straits every bit as desperate as hers, and just refused to admit it. In any case, having Thursday afternoon from one to four to concentrate on made it easier to shove aside the delectable concoctions of her treacherous imagination, and concentrate on what she was, after all, here for.

What she was here for immediately, in the usual manner of the universe, tried to divide itself like an amoeba and swim off in several directions. Greek Literature in Translation was every bit as seductive and insidious as its reputation. Janet became aware, in the fourth week of the term, that she had decided to take Greek 1 next term, if somebody decent was teaching it. She pinned the decision to their reading of Euripides' *The Bacchae*. Ferris had showered them with photocopies of six different translations of the most important chorus; and then, to show the futility of all of them, had read to them from the original. She could hear his beautiful voice in her mind weeks later, rolling the gorgeous polysyllables with their intricate repeating rhythms and buried rhymes out over the class like cloud shadows and sun crossing a meadow.

Nick and Robin and Anne Beauvais had put together a musical group: guitar, recorder, three voices, to do Nick's songs, and some Dylan and some Simon and Garfunkel and some Grateful Dead (not, however, "Box of Rain") and a few of the Elizabethan rounds. They did not seem to spend much time practicing, which was more a relief to Janet than otherwise; but they did play from time to time in the Cave, a dark room under the Eliot dining hall, where you could get three-two beer if you were old enough, and flat reconstituted cheeseburgers and frozen French fries and an assortment of packaged cookies and actual fresh fruit regardless of your age.

They played one Saturday night in the sixth week of term, and Janet went to hear them. Molly and Tina, who shared a biology class this time around, were greatly agitated over the next day's assignment; Peg had been walking in her sleep again and was being kept in bed and fed herb tea by Sharon; Nora was out with her mysterious boyfriend; and Diane Zimmerman disliked music played at less than ear-shattering volume. Janet thought of Susan and Rebecca at the last moment, but they were not in their room when she called on them.

So she went by herself, and sat with a glass of orange soda and a bag of potato chips. The songs were all very familiar to her by now, but she could have watched the faces forever. Anne was so beautiful that you could almost forgive her her sister; she had moreover a wholly remarkable voice with a range that was almost the despair of the Music Department. She was not animated; it might have been a statue singing; but she made her defects virtues. By her very stillness she made the songs live, as if she were only the window one saw them through.

Nick and Robin, as always, were having the time of their lives. Janet had never figured out their musical jokes, which seemed to be two parts telepathy and one part knowledge so esoteric that it, too, was probably the despair of the Music Department; but she could by now tell when they were making one. Nick had a flick of the eyebrow and Robin a quirk of the mouth that spoke volumes. Janet remembered Thomas's sour remark that they had known one another before they were born. It did look like that.

Despite the dark and the uncomfortable chairs and the bad food, the Cave always had trouble clearing its customers out by one A.M. At twelve-thirty, Robin went into the back room and returned with his pipes. The audience, which was fairly large for this late in the term, made a noise divided about equally between dismay and anticipation. Ten or twelve people did leave. Janet looked at the door, and then got up and went to the very back of the room, disposing of her trash along the way. There was a cushioned bench along the cold outside wall, and she sat down on it, hoping this was far enough away. At least she could tell Diane what she had missed.

Robin made a couple of gusty, querulous hoots, and then, with an expression of diabolical glee visible even in the dim lighting, launched into the most awful noise she had ever heard him make. It had no pattern that she could distinguish; it simply wandered among the nine notes available to a player of bagpipes in a manner so random it had to be deliberate. Every time she thought it might be settling to a tune, or even repeating its last series of random notes, it did something vile. It was like music turned inside-out.

The audience, which had suffered here, in its time at Blackstock, more threats than Darius hurled at Alexander, rose up and fled. Some of them were laughing; the rest, Janet was sorry to see, wore the expressions of people plotting revenge. Robin would be lucky not to find all his belongings taken out and installed charmingly in one of the bathrooms; or that stuff that exploded when you stepped on it scattered all over his floor; or the door to his room removed and the opening plastered and painted over.

Robin divested himself of his hellish instrument and came wandering among the tables to make sure everybody was gone. Janet, being an attachment of one of the musicians, was allowed to stay so long as she did not clamor for beer, which she had no intention of doing. She grinned at him as he came by her bench. "What on earth was that?" she said.

He smiled back. He had dimples just above the line of his beard; they were shallow, and visible only in odd light like this. They were probably the reason Molly put up with him. He said, "That is the Ceol Mohr, that the MacCrimmons invented for the pipers. That other music you've heard me play, they play for common folk, and this is noble; but the Ceol Mohr, they play for themselves."

"Why do you say they, and not we?"

"For fear of my immortal soul," said Robin, smiling again. "I'm not a Scotsman." He glanced to his left, and said, "Nick and Anne and I will be some little time; there was something amiss with 'All Along the Watchtower.' Do you go and cheer up Thomas, who's trying to get drunk on this goose-piss, the pitiful soul."

He went away. Janet found Thomas in a dark corner, with five large, empty, clear plastic cups in front of him. "What on earth's the matter?" she said.

"Hello, Jenny," said Thomas with great gravity. "It's this beer. It runs out as fast as you put it in, and leaves nothing of itself in the passing."

"It does too," said Janet, sitting down resignedly. "You're talking like Robin. And my name's not Jenny."

"It was the piping put me in mind of it," said Thomas. "That's the Scottish nickname. Is there Scots blood in you?"

"Scots-Irish, I think," said Janet. "The most disreputable kind. Why are you drinking this stuff; what's the matter?"

"I don't know what to do about Tina," said Thomas. "How do you and Molly manage?"

"Molly manages," said Janet. "I behave myself so she won't murder me. But look, nobody made you take up with Tina. What's the matter with her?"

"I'm not sure," said Thomas. "She isn't stupid, and she isn't insensitive, and she's very obliging. She's *lovely* in bed," he added with the utmost gloom.

Just like Tina, thought Janet, not to tell them that things had gotten better. She supposed one could have deduced it from Tina's willingness to take her three hours of privacy a week.

Thomas sighed heavily. "But she doesn't—she hasn't—she

doesn't read. Well, she will, if I ask her to; but it doesn't take, somehow. She hasn't any imaginative life."

"Sure she does," Janet said. "It's just not literary."

"Well, what is it, then?"

"Either musical or scientific, I guess. I'd bet on musical."

"I wouldn't," said Thomas. "She likes music; she knows a hell of a lot more about it than I do. But she doesn't love it. She's just dutiful. She gets a mild pleasure out of it, that's all."

"Well, science, then. Psychology, maybe; that's the only thing I've found her reading for the fun of it."

"Oh, God," said Thomas. "While it would reassure me for Tina's sake, it wouldn't help my case much." He dropped his face into his hands, knocking two of the empty cups to the floor. When Janet emerged from under the table with them, he was staring at her with an expression of consternation. "I do beg your pardon," he said. "It was unconscionable to talk to you like that about a friend of yours—especially somebody you've got to live with. I'm not going to break up with her, don't worry about it. I just have a difficulty, that's all."

"Well," said Janet, abandoning caution, "I have exactly the same difficulty. Only I'm not sleeping with her. Why don't you talk to Molly? She truly appreciates Tina; she really likes her without having to work at it. You ask her what to do."

"She's so damned romantic," said Thomas.

"Molly?"

"No, idiot—Tina. Romantic in the most prosaic way imaginable. I don't know what to make of it."

"Talk to Molly," said Janet firmly. "Here. They're coming to throw us out. Put your coat on. Haven't you got a hat, for pity's sake? It's ten below out there."

"What a nice motherly type you are," said Thomas, vaguely.

"A lot you know," said Janet, but she said it under her breath. She turned him over to Anne and Robin with considerable relief, and let Nick walk her back to Ericson. They discoursed amiably of winter-inspired poetry, and said nothing of Thomas or Tina, or of romance at all. The whole business was far, far easier when Nick was present: the person who lived in that body was of far more account than the body was, and required a more concentrated and diligent attention, leaving much less room for mere mortal longings.

CHAPTER 12

Janet wrote her first poem at Blackstock in the sixth week of the term, which fell in the middle of February. She had assumed that if she ever got around to writing it at all, this poem would be for Nick. But it was not, probably because his own poems were so much better.

It was the February thaw that inspired her, if indeed you could call such a mood inspiration. This was a time of year that she usually looked forward to, mostly because it was an almost annual occurrence and so allowed recollection of other Februaries, including those few when no thaw came; and partly because it was reassuring to see that the ground was still there, pleasant to run from one class to another sans hat and gloves but without risk of frostbite, and comforting to consider that the hounds of spring were as usual on winter's traces.

But this year it depressed her unutterably. The sky grew warm but stayed cloudy. The snow did not melt altogether, but shrank back in filthy ridges of gray and black, from which protruded lost mittens, paper cups, cigarette butts, and leaves neither raked up by human agency nor decently decayed by nature. The trees, which in November had seemed merely free of mortal trappings, were now indubitably dead. In the warm spots where the snow did melt all the way, it revealed merely a waste of black mud and brown grass.

Most maddening of all, this bleak landscape conspired with some mental difficulties of her own and produced a crisis. The mental difficulties arose from the fact that no good teacher would let you read all the way through Milton and Chaucer without making certain you had a clear idea of how they viewed the world; and in Evans's case, without making very certain that you understood their stories in their own terms before you were allowed to apply your own. Janet's father was an atheist and her mother a lapsed Catholic turned Unitarian, which meant that she knew a lot of Christmas carols in Latin and refused to let her husband make fun of religion no matter how silly it sounded.

But Milton and Chaucer were Christians, there was no denying it. And while the early Greeks mercifully were not, they were most certainly not atheists either; even Euripides, deny them how he might, could not keep the gods out of his plays. The whole of theater was religious in its origin—rotten at its core, her father said gloomily, which was why he preferred the Romantic period, when nothing of the slightest interest was done in English drama. But Janet had been reading the medieval and Renaissance poets, and then Milton. It was not their arguments that oppressed her, on the rare occasions when they troubled to make any. It was the sense of that whole intricate, solid philosophy, stretching for centuries in both directions, infusing life like a strong light, taken for granted and used in a hundred ways for symbolism and imagery and situation, as clear and real as Tolkien or Eddison's worlds, that weighed her down with a sense of indefinable doom. Evans had made it clear to anybody who would pay attention that Milton had not been of the Devil's party.

On a particularly dreary Wednesday afternoon, Janet flung her astronomy text to the floor, dug her journal out of the bottom drawer of her desk, and sloshed over to the library, where she found a deserted padded room at the bottom and resigned herself to her fate.

This winter shrills its dirge self-satisfied,
And all is black, or gray, or ragged brown,
And all the world in rags its bread has cried,
And begged the gates of that unheeding town
Men once called heaven.

That made no literal sense whatsoever, but it had caught in a net of words at least half her feeling about this weather, interior and exterior. She bit vigorously on the cap of her pen, and went on.

Such a time as this
Must make our reasoned doubt a certainty:
We see the universe just as it is,
Unveiled by miracle of bud or tree.

She wanted to put "miracle" in quotation marks, or scar it somehow with sarcasm; but if the poem itself didn't do that, she had failed anyway. She read the lines over several times, biting her lip instead of the pen. Oh, the loveliness of the sonnet. Just where she wanted it, the turn came in the very form of the poem. The next word was But.

But even while I watch the senseless sky
Cracked hideous in the water at my feet

Janet sighed heavily. This was where she always ran into trouble. The puddles of the February thaw, reflecting black branches and the usual patched blue and gray of the late winter sky, were among the first things she ever remembered noticing, before the cherry blossoms or the blooming crocus or the startling red of an autumn maple. They had held for her, all her life, the fascination of things seen in a mirror, the intimacy of things seen through a telescope, the curious charm of a dollhouse or of Molly's toy theater. And this year they made her think the sky had fallen and broken on the pavement. That might make another poem, but it certainly could not at this point be crammed into this one. And the poem did not care, anyway, how she felt now or had felt then, unless that served the movement that the poem had gathered before this "But."

She left the lines alone, and went on.

Dread rumors crowd me, dark forebodings: I
Remember, as improbable as spring

The last line of the poem was breathing down her neck. Janet left a blank line and wrote it alone by itself at the bottom.

The star, the cup, the cross: that tale's ending.

Was that what you wanted, she asked the poem. Thanks a lot. How am I supposed to get there? What a rotten rhyme. I wanted a couplet at the end, anyway; what is this? The poem looked at her blandly and kept its own counsel. It was done; she had to patch up the rest as best she might. What a stupid tangle she had got herself into with the rhyme scheme. She needed a rhyme for "feet," to end a line that made some sense of the foolish phrase, "as improbable as spring." She scribbled and crossed out and erased and threw her pen around a bit, but in the end there was nothing for it. She had been reading too much Greek literature.

But even as I watch the senseless sky
Cracked hideous in the water at my feet,
Dread rumors crowd me, dark forebodings: I

Remember, as improbable as spring
To this abyss where Night and Chaos meet,
The star, the cup, the cross: that tale's ending.

There was something there; it was maddeningly far from perfect, but there was something. Janet briefly damned Keats for inventing alternate forms of the sonnet to plague her; scrawled "The Atheist in Doubt" across the top of the page, thought despairingly of what Danny would say about the entire endeavor, and went back to Ericson.

Molly was lying on her bed completely surrounded by sheets and wads of yellow paper, much scribbled upon. She was writing up her lab report. She glanced up as Janet came in, and then sat bolt upright. "What in the world have you been up to?"

"I wrote a poem," said Janet, startled. "That's all."

"Far out. Can I read it?"

"It's awfully rough, but sure. Here. It's pretty legible; this line finishes up around here and this one actually comes before that one."

Molly took the notebook and read. "I like the title. You read about Christians in doubt until you want to throttle them all, but you never hear about atheists in doubt."

"Are you an atheist?"

"Nope," said Molly, not looking up. "I believe in an order for good in the universe. You can't look at a tidepool and not believe that." She grinned suddenly, and raised her head. "Of course," she observed, "people do it every day. I can't, though. But I won't put up with this nonsense of organized religion. I'm a scientist and I will rely on my experience, thank you."

Janet decided not to argue with her; not when the basis of her own problem was not one whit less woolly. Molly looked back at the paper. "It *is* like that out there, isn't it?" she said. "But I don't get this part. How can a miracle unveil the atheist's universe; and you haven't got buds and trees in winter anyway."

Janet looked over her shoulder, scowling; and then laughed. "Oops," she said. "That was dumb. Here. 'Not veiled by miracle.' How's that? It scans the same, and it's what I actually meant."

"Oh, all right." She read the rest of it through without a word, her face perfectly solemn; and then she dropped the notebook on top of her own notes and said, "Brrrr."

"What?"

"I never thought religion was scary before. I thought it was either stupid or comforting." She picked up the notebook again. "There's something about this last rhyme."

"It's awful," said Janet. "But that's the way it wanted to go. I might be able to fix it later."

"I had no idea you could do this."

"It really isn't very good, but I'm glad you like it."

"What a thing to say!" said Molly. "How does that reflect on my taste, I'd like to know? No, I really like it; it made me think differently. So what if it's not perfect?"

"It's a sonnet," said Janet. "They're supposed to be."

"Have you been looking at tidepools?"

"No, it's Chaucer and Milton and Euripides."

"Oh my," said Molly, absently.

"Doesn't scan."

"Say Ferris, then; Euripides is his fault."

Janet burst out laughing.

"Well?" said Molly.

"You might as well say, genetics is Mendel's fault."

"You might just as well say, I breathe when I sleep is the same thing as I sleep when I breathe."

"It *is* the same thing with you!" said Janet, and they collapsed laughing on one another's shoulders.

"Whew," said Molly, wiping her eyes. "They always said too much study makes women hysterical. Don't tell anybody. Are you and Nick all right? It seems weird to me that Chaucer and Milton make you write poetry but Nick doesn't."

"It seems weird to me, too," said Janet. "He writes me poetry. But I think he's a lot more used to this than I am."

"He can't be much more used to it, can he?"

"He's mentioned at least two previous girlfriends," said Janet. "And I see Anne Beauvais looking at him sometimes."

"That girl certainly gets around," said Molly. "She's always slinking at Thomas; Tina's going to bop her with a spare ski if she doesn't watch out." She drew a breath; then she picked up her notebook and pen and began to write.

Janet sat on the carpet until Molly let the breath out again, and then got up quietly and retrieved her astronomy book. It was usually a mistake to push Molly, and it was always bad manners to interrupt anybody's studying. Did Molly know something about Robin and Anne, or, like Janet, did she merely wonder?

In the eighth week of the term, Nick and Robin's production of *The Revenger's Tragedy* began its five-night run. Janet had not gotten around to reading it. She had gathered from all the discussion that it was Jacobean rather than Elizabethan: complex, bloody, grotesque, with a bitter and maniacal humor. Nick and Robin usually spoke deprecatingly of the verse. She had never gotten them to say why they wanted to produce it; it seemed to have been an idea they had had always.

She and Molly and Tina, neither of whom had read the play either, or helped with the production, college being what it was, arrived early on the first night, and sat in the front row. Ericson Little Theater was a high, narrow room with twelve rows of four dusty red velvet seats in the center, and varying numbers and sizes of rows tucked into its sides. The stage was tiny, but Robin had pronounced it large enough for a sword fight, though, he said, you would not wish to try to produce something like *Henry V* on it, or anything whatsoever by Shaw. It had a bit of carved and gilded woodwork adorning its ceiling and door frames, mostly figures abstracted from the convoluted arms of the college and presented in unaccustomed isolation: the lion looked startled, the dove embarrassed, and the snake extremely smug.

Tina and Molly were arguing about invertebrate biology. Janet rested her chin on the back of her seat and watched people come in. Professor Evans and his wife, looking resigned; Professor Davison and her husband, looking amused; Odile Beauvais and her roommates, looking svelte; a scattering of other English professors and a few from Music and Modern Languages and History. A sprinkling of curious students. Diane Zimmerman, without her sulky brother but with Miss Andrews and Mr. Hecht from English 10 last term. Peg and Sharon and Kevin and Nora—and good heavens, that must be Nora's boyfriend, never glimpsed till this minute, a lanky young man with long dark hair. Janet started to nudge Molly, and stopped, gaping.

Melinda Wolfe, in a long black velvet skirt and a white blouse, had come in, followed by a whole line of pale, stern people variously dressed, and in the midst of them Professor Medeous in a brisk green linen suit with all her mad-colored hair streaming down her back in a most unbusinesslike manner. She was the woman who had worn red and green tatters and ridden a black horse on Hallowe'en. Janet had not recognized her; but that was Medeous, and that was the same woman.

She and her entourage filled two rows in the middle of the room. Behind them again came a group of eight or nine Classics majors; none of the ones Janet knew well, though, because all of those were in the play. When they had all sat down, the room, from being half-empty, became almost full. And just in time, too; even as Janet caught Melinda Wolfe's eye and boldly grinned at her, the lights went halfway down and the curtain came up.

They had certainly worked hard on the set. The stage floor was a smooth reflective black—marine paint, Janet remembered, very difficult to get off the hands. The walls were draped with green and red—glowering green, smoldery red, like colors full of gray, or obscured by smoke. Spaced between the hangings were enormous reproductions of woodcuts Janet recognized from the medieval part of English 10: devils stamping naked souls into a boiling caldron; the bony arms and legs and grinning skull of Death showing through a rich robe and a smiling youthful mask; another bony Death, in cap and bells, leading a reluctant Queen away from her palace and out of the clutching arms of her King and her ladies; a brawny fellow in a fig leaf vainly hiding behind a tree from the sun, the all-seeing eye of God; a serpent lurking among the innocent leaves of a stylized strawberry plant; and one of those peculiar medieval lions, like a large dog with a mane, its paw on the neck of a meek but much more realistic boar, while on a branch above their heads a shabby vulture watched.

Since the play's beginning seemed to be delayed, she turned around and surveyed the audience again, and was in time to see her parents, harassed, enter with Lily-Milly, rebellious. She had probably nagged them into saying she could come to the play and then decided she didn't want to, and they had—unwisely, in Janet's opinion, but thank God Lily wasn't her kid—determined to keep her to her word. They sat down just behind Medeous and her group of long-limbed, long-haired, long-faced cohorts; and Janet's father waved to her and then leaned forward to speak to Medeous. She listened to him with a cool and remote expression, and then smiled briefly, shaking her head.

The lights went down the rest of the way, and Janet turned back to the stage. A procession of indistinct figures marched across it by the light of two rather dim torches, from left to right. About halfway across they got a light on the face of the procession's leader. It was Jack Nikopoulos, his dark face made darker by a gray wig and beard. He wore green, inappropriately enough; it was the same vivid summer green as Professor Medeous's suit.

"Duke," said Thomas's resonant voice from somewhere near

the front, stage right, in a friendly tone that made the hairs on Janet's neck stand up, "royal lecher: go, gray haired Adultery And thou his son, as impious-steeped as he." At this point, by accident or design Janet never did determine, they got a light on him, too.

Janet heard Molly take her breath in. She was staring herself. Thomas was holding a skull; but that was not why. Thomas was beautiful; everybody agreed with that. But he did occasionally, in his usual dress, look a little pale and washed-out, like a bad print of himself. He was wearing black, doublet and hose and cloak and hat with feather, with just a little lace showing at the cuffs and neck. He made every view of him Janet had ever seen seem like a bad print of this one. She hoped none of the more impressionable girls in the audience would swoon or shriek. Really, you would think a voice like that was blessing enough for any one person.

The voice like that had been going on, serenely, with its speech; it had just addressed the skull when Janet gathered herself to pay attention. "Thou sallow picture," said Thomas, uncannily, "of my poisoned love." I'd hate that if I were Tina, thought Janet. She didn't like it much herself. Even less did she like the lascivious telling-over of the charms of the character's poisoned love: to say that one's beloved could make a moral man sin eight times a day instead of seven, and could make a usurer's son give up all his inheritance for a kiss, and then to rant because the Duke, reacting in exactly the same way, had poisoned the woman for refusing him, seemed to Janet to be a peculiar sort of love and perhaps to miss the point.

It was a crazy play; that was evident in no time. Thomas abjured the skull to be merry, merry, because murder never did go unavenged. Then Nick came in, wearing green velvet and looking wonderfully rakish, and said, in a resigned tone that raised a chorus of laughter from the audience, "Still sighing o'er Death's vizard?"

Nick, it appeared, was Thomas's brother (Janet wished for a

program book). His news was that the Duke's son had asked him to hire a pandar. If Thomas cared to come disguised to court and apply for the position, he would then be in a position to exact his revenge.

This determined, Odile and Anne Beauvais came drifting onto the stage, trailing clouds and green gauze and wearing dreamy expressions that just escaped the foolish. The audience made a few titters, uncertainly. Odile and Anne were, respectively, Nick and Thomas's mother and their sister. They asked for news, and were regaled with court gossip, which dealt with the Duke's son being on trial for the rape of one Lord Antonio's wife. It also came out that the whole family felt that the Duke had killed Nick and Thomas's father indirectly, by making him die of "discontent, the nobleman's consumption." The audience, being democratic in nature, thought this was fairly funny. They hissed at Thomas, however, when he made the aside, "Wives are but made to go to bed and feed." Janet noted that his character was excessively given to aphorism.

The next scene was the trial of the Duke's son for rape. The Duchess and the prisoner's two older brothers pleaded for mercy. Another son, apparently a bastard of the Duke's, made a number of highly amusing asides expressing his hope that the rogue would hang as he deserved; he said, in fact, that he wished the entire court would become a corpse. He was played by the southern boy who thought one should make stew of the squirrels. He still had his accent; it worked surprisingly well, perhaps because it marked him apart from the others.

The youngest brother, whom Janet did not recognize, did not appear to be suffering from remorse, and made a number of jokes that might have been funnier to an audience with fewer feminists in it. Janet did hear Professor Evans's unregenerate laugh, and deduced that Junior Brother was probably going to come to a bad end.

The judges sounded in a hanging mood. The Duke suddenly broke off the proceedings. The Duchess was angry because her husband had not simply refused to let the law touch his child at all. She decided to seduce the bastard son in revenge; the bastard son was not at all averse to this, saying that since adultery begot him, it was only reasonable that he in his turn should commit it.

The audience was amused. It was even more so when Nick reappeared, followed by a Thomas now garbed in dull brown and wearing an unreal wig of black hair streaked with red. When Thomas said, "What, brother, am I far enough from myself?" the entire room erupted in laughter, and there was a scattering of applause. When Nick tugged the wig into place and buttoned Thomas's coat for him before answering, again resignedly, "As if another man had been sent whole Into the world and none wist how he came," there was another wave of laughter. Janet was glad they were getting this reaction, but she was not exactly amused herself.

But Robin came in as the Duke's eldest son, who had not attended the trial. He was dressed in red, and professed himself delighted to employ Thomas. They engaged one another in a series of bawdy puns and remarks that had two meanings if you knew who Thomas was, and Janet did laugh. So did Molly. When it turned out that the virgin whom Robin had his eye on was Thomas's own sister, Janet laughed until she cried.

She stopped, though Molly didn't, when Robin suggested that Thomas might approach the girl through her—and Thomas's—mother. She did admire, in Thomas's following soliloquy, the deft transition from shock, outrage, and horror to the thoughtful mischief with which he pronounced his decision to go disguised to his mother and try her standards.

In the next scene Rob Benfield came on as Antonio, the lord whose wife had been raped by the Duke's youngest son. The wife was now dead, having preferred death to dishonor. Janet was once again rather disconcerted to hear the wife's virtues praised: though she excited lust, she "ever lived As cold in lust as she is now in death." Nick, whose name, it transpired, was

Hippolito, swore on his sword—"thou bribeless officer"—to avenge the lady's death, since everybody assumed the Duke would contrive to get his son cleared of the charges. Antonio then made the extraordinary statement that his greatest joy was that it should be called a miracle that he, being an old man, had yet a wife so chaste; and they all trooped out.

Anne Beauvais drifted back on and pronounced a short, touching meditation on the difficulty of being a maid with no fortune but her honor. Janet found it very difficult to keep a straight face, but somehow nudging Molly in the ribs did not seem like a reasonable action.

To Anne entered Professor Ferris with his round angelic face, and proceeded to enact a clown. He brought on the disguised Thomas, whom Anne dealt with briskly by smacking him in the face. Janet glanced covertly at Molly—after all, here was Robin pining after Anne Beauvais, who wouldn't have him, and Thomas pretending to act on Robin's behalf while secretly hoping that Anne would continue to refuse. Molly looked perfectly serene.

After this things got wilder and wilder, and in fact funnier and funnier, except that everybody, and especially Thomas, kept saying things like, "Without gold and women there would be no damnation; Hell would look like a lord's great kitchen without fire in't." And women were either chaste—which meant you not only behaved yourself, but didn't wish to do otherwise—or utterly wanton; there was no middle ground. Janet began to wonder if the author had done all this on purpose; it seemed that every time the play warmed and grew funny, somebody would say something like that.

The disguised Thomas had no luck persuading his sister to the Duke's bed, but he did succeed, to his mingled chagrin and delight, in bribing his mother to force the girl to give up her chastity. Janet had no tender feelings for chastity at the moment, but the disguised Thomas and the greedy mother made her skin creep. She was relieved when the intermission came.

"Whew!" said Molly.

Tina said, "I don't know whether to laugh or go under the seat."

Janet had expected a querulous demand to have the entire plot explained, and was much cheered by this response. "I don't either," she said.

Molly got up and fetched a program book from a stack that had appeared near the main door. "This says," she said, strolling back to her roommates and sitting down, "that the play is a satirical tragedy."

"What does that mean?" said Tina.

"I'm not sure," said Janet. "People die, but you don't care?"

"*Women* die," said Molly savagely.

"You noticed that, too? I thought maybe it was just me."

"What I want to know," said Molly, "is whether those boys are emphasizing that element on purpose. They're so good, it's hard to tell. What do you think of your Thomas, Tina?"

"I think he's awfully good," said Tina. "They all are. You know—maybe it's just me, but you know I had trouble understanding the Old English in that play we went to?" Janet groaned inwardly; as far as Tina was concerned, there was modern English and Old English and that was it. "Well," said Tina, "Robin and Nick and Thomas are doing this whole play in Old English, and it's a lot easier to understand them than it was to understand those professional actors."

"That's not Old English," said Molly, whose Shakespeare studies were going to her head. "It's Elizabethan English. We wouldn't understand Old English no matter how good the actors were. But you're right. They're easier to understand than most of the actors we saw in *Hamlet,* too."

"Part of it's gestures and stage business," said Janet. "And I guess the rest is just not going too fast."

"But they're not boring, either," said Molly, paging through the program book. "Good grief, look at this. All the characters' names mean something in Italian. Vindice, that's Thomas—Vengeance. The mother is Gratiana, Grace, and the sister is Castiza, Chastity." She let out a hoot of laughter. "Robin's Lussurioso—Lust."

"Is it an allegory?" said Janet.

"It doesn't say."

"That would explain how shallow it feels, somehow, and how it keeps jumping between comedy and tragedy. If these aren't really exactly characters, but just attributes."

"Huh," said Molly. "I didn't come to watch a bunch of attributes, thank you."

"You can watch Robin's, can't you?" said Tina wickedly.

The curtain rose again on the Duchess's two older sons. They were plotting to get their brother executed before somebody pardoned him. But which brother, thought Janet. Robin-Lussurioso was in prison for trying to kill his father the Duke. And Junior Brother was still in prison for rape.

The officers of the prison thought it was the younger brother they were supposed to be dispatching. Junior Brother, on finding that he was going to die almost immediately, waxed extremely witty. Janet realized that, under a blond wig and some rather clever makeup, she was looking at Professor Ferris; that voice was hard to disguise. He was apparently going to play all the clowns in this production.

Vindice-Thomas then returned, in a high and unhealthy state of excitement. He explained to an uneasy Hippolito that, acting his part as a pandar, he had promised to bring a lady to meet the Duke here. He went away, and returned supporting a heavily veiled and draped female figure, babbling frenziedly to it as if it were in fact a hired courtesan. He then pulled back its veil to show his ever-present companion, the skull, thickly painted with makeup. The audience made a gasp compounded about equally of amusement and shock. Hippolito leapt back two steps, took a shaky step forward again, and said, "Why brother, brother," in a shaky tone that seemed to be trying to sound pleased.

Vindice ranted on a little about how well he had fitted out the skull, and then slid into a few remarks about the vanity of earthly wishes, to which Hippolito was able to reply more calmly, "Brother, y'ave spoke *that* aright. Is this the form that, living, shone so bright?"

At those words, spoken in Nick's voice to Thomas, Janet felt a shiver overtake her. Vindice, meanwhile, had taken Hippolito's theme up eagerly, and went on for some time in this vein, "Does the silkworm expend her yellow labors for thee? For thee does she undo herself?" He ended with the usual sort of abominable remark, "Here might a scornful and ambitious woman Look through and through herself; see, ladies, with false forms, You deceive men but cannot deceive worms." It was enough to make anybody take to makeup. He then finally got around to explaining that he had poisoned the mouth of the skull. Hippolito-Nick said, in very doubtful tones, "Brother, I do applaud thy constant vengeance, The quaintness of thy malice, above thought."

There was a brief chuckle from the audience at the pun in "quaintness," but Janet shivered again. She felt that Nick was not playing his part quite as he ought. She thought Nick was trying to say something to Thomas. Thomas, or Vindice, however, went obsessively along with his plot. And perhaps, after all, it was reasonable for the one brother to have doubts. The entire scheme was preposterous, and so very disrespectful to the murdered woman. Vindice was not entirely sane.

The doomed Duke, his mad-colored hair released from its ribbon and streaming down his red-clad back, came in, affable and grateful. He and Vindice looked oddly alike—it was the wigs, of course. Thomas-Vindice told the Duke that the woman in question was a country lady who would be bashful until the first kiss, and that she had somewhat of a grave look about her. The audience laughed; Janet heard Tina chortle; but

Janet looked at Molly, who mouthed, "Shakespeare did it better."

There followed an entirely horrible scene (though half the audience thought it was hilarious) in which the Duke kissed the skull, fell down writhing, and kindly if improbably kept his murderer apprised of the progress of the poison and, like Desdemona only even less plausibly, kept talking long after he should have been utterly unable to do so. They finally put their daggers over his tongue and his heart to keep him quiet. His wife and son entered. They had a brief discussion of whether anything was sweet that was not sinful, expressed their extremely low opinions of the Duke, and departed amorously. The Duke said, "I cannot brook," and they killed him. The pool of blood that oozed from his wounds crept silently across the stage. Janet swallowed.

Hippolito and Vindice dragged out the mercifully silent Duke, and the two elder brothers returned, gloating over their brother's execution. They immediately fell to quarreling over whose idea it had all been, and were interrupted by an officer carrying a grotesque and lifelike bleeding head. They pretended to weep ("Think on some dame," said one to the other, to help him be properly sad) and were interrupted again by their older brother, Robin as Lussurioso.

There followed a flurry of exclamations and recriminations, which, since none of the characters was worth an ounce of sympathy, was in fact very funny. The wrong brother, of course, had been executed: the younger brother, whose claim to the dukedom did not have precedence over Supervacuo and Ambitioso. These two swore revenge for their younger brother's death.

Robin-Lussurioso now sought out Hippolito and began berating him for recommending Vindice in the first place. Nick-Hippolito apologized humbly with a swift glance at the audience that made them roar; and then Vindice came in. Lussurioso yelled at him, Thomas-Vindice was impudent,

Lussurioso proceeded to threats, and Vindice ran away. Once again, Janet had the impression that Robin was trying to tell Thomas something. She was beginning to feel very uneasy.

Hippolito apologized for recommending Vindice. Lussurioso-Robin said he could make amends by bringing his brother to court. Either the author was crazy—entirely possible—or else Lussurioso knew perfectly well who Vindice really was, in which case Hippolito was awfully stupid for agreeing. Janet was actually grateful for this apparent blunder; otherwise she would have felt cold and apprehensive indeed. There was, after all, no reason to assume that Vindice was going to get away with all this murder. And what was Thomas trying to get away with?

Hippolito-Nick and Thomas—no, Vindice as they had first seen him, without the wig—began discussing what Lussurioso might want with Vindice. Vindice still seemed vaguely excited, and addressed the absent Lussurioso in paradoxical terms. Hippolito—and Nick, Janet was sure of it—took him up rather sharply and advised him to consider how he would change his voice so that Lussurioso should not recognize it. Vindice said he would bear in him some strain of melancholy, and on the word began a lugubrious, slow speech that made most people in the audience laugh but drove Janet to distraction.

Lussurioso, arriving, interviewed Vindice. Janet noticed that Thomas's lines were all in prose now, in addition to being in the melancholy voice. Lussurioso explained to Vindice what Vindice-disguised had done to Vindice's mother and sister, and suggested that Vindice should therefore wish to kill his own disguised self in revenge. Vindice gloomily agreed, in verse again, and Lussurioso left. The two brothers considered their problems for a while, and decided they would dress up the body of the already-dead Duke in the brown suit and wig used by Vindice when he impersonated a pandar; then everybody would deduce that the pandar had killed the Duke and made off with the Duke's clothing.

"Say *what?*" whispered Molly. "Nobody thinks like that."

Janet shrugged. Tourneur had. And she believed that these lunatics would. Revenge was apparently bad for the brain.

Vindice and Hippolito entered, dragging their mother Odile-Gratiana between them. There followed a tedious and emotional scene wherein, after they threatened her like two Hamlets against one Gertrude, she repented of trying to persuade her daughter to sleep with Robin-Lussurioso. They all made a lot of sententious remarks, and the brothers left.

Then Anne-Castiza came drifting in and there was another tedious emotional scene. Anne explained that she was now content to do as her mother wished and sleep with Robin; after she had flung all her mother's arguments back in her face and reduced her to hysteria, she confessed that she had done this only to try her. The mother said, "Be thou a glass for maids, and I for mothers," with which ambiguous remark, the two Beauvais sisters swept out in a cloud of green gauze. Janet wondered why the scene had not been more moving. Was it its predictability, or something in the way the Beauvais sisters played their parts?

Thomas-Vindice and Nick-Hippolito came in with the Duke's corpse, which they had dressed in Thomas's brown suit and the wig of black hair streaked with red. After some discussion of how Vindice would be killing himself in stabbing the disguised corpse, and considerable impatience on the part of Hippolito, they arranged the body, and just in time, for Lussurioso-Robin came on.

Being informed that the pandar he sought was asleep, and drunk, under a tree, he told Vindice to stab him. Vindice stabbed the body of the Duke dressed in Vindice's clothes, and Janet almost jumped out of her seat.

Lussurioso, after identifying the body as the pandar's and rejoicing, suddenly noticed that it was in fact his father, and deduced that his father had been dead already, and that the pandar must have killed him. After a great flurry, Lussurioso was proclaimed Duke, and promptly arranged for some revels.

Vindice and Hippolito then decided that they would disguise themselves as the maskers ordered for the feast, and so kill anybody they still needed to kill. They got themselves up in green, with wigs of long yellow hair. They killed Lussurioso-Robin; a moment later, four more maskers, in red, all with wigs of black hair streaked with red, danced in, swords out, and paused in confusion. They were Lussurioso's brothers Ambitioso, Supervacuo, Spurio, and one of their minions, also in search of Lussurioso to kill him.

There was also confusion in the audience. Janet saw all the players looking over her head, and turned around. Somebody had trained a dim silvery light on Professor Medeous and her companions. They had all stood up, including Melinda Wolfe, who looked extremely grim. Medeous stood up last, the tallest of them all, with the black hair, streaked with red, falling around her fine-boned face, and looked at the stage for several long moments, like a teacher who has just received an answer so stupid and wrongheaded that no commentary is possible. Then she turned, and the rest of her row turned too, and they all marched out the main entrance, with the light following them and all but drowning out the red of the EXIT sign.

From the stage, Thomas called with extraordinary clarity, "The King rises. Give o'er the play. Lights, lights, lights, lights." And the curtain clapped down like a snapped neck, and all the lights came up.

Janet and Molly blinked at one another.

"What in the world was that all about?" said Molly.

"*Miching mallecho*," said Janet, in a shaking voice; quoting, as Thomas had, from *Hamlet*. "It means mischief."

"Is that the end of the play?" said Tina.

"No," said Molly. "Professor Medeous was affronted. So they quit."

"But they're not supposed to pay any attention to that sort of thing, actors aren't."

"No," said Molly, "they aren't."

"The show must go on. Right. Nick didn't want him to do it," said Janet. "Didn't you think so?"

"I did wonder," said Molly. "When he was showing his brother the painted skull? If that was the way they'd rehearsed it? Yes. I think you're right."

"What are you talking about?" said Tina.

"I'm not sure," said Molly.

"You *sound* like you're sure."

"It's the hair," said Molly. "The Duke had hair like Professor Medeous's—and how does she get it like that, I wonder—when he was killed—"

"But not at the beginning," said Janet. "It was gray. 'Gray-haired adultery.'"

"And all the bad-guy revengers had hair like that."

"Did he want to insult her?" said Tina, bewildered. "I mean, I know he was thinking of changing his major since he can't graduate anyway, but—"

"That's a very strange way to state one's intention," agreed Janet.

"And what did it *mean*?" said Tina. "She can't be an adulterer; she's not married."

Janet's parents and sister appeared before them. "Do you have to go congratulate your swains," said her father, "or would you like to come over and have cocoa and talk over the play?"

"Do you think they did that on purpose?" said Janet.

"The costuming, yes. Having Professor Medeous walk out, I've no idea."

"They must have planned it," said Molly, "because of the light."

"Unless some enterprising soul was improvising," said Janet's mother.

"What I want to know," said Janet's father, "is whose conscience young Thomas wanted to catch."

"'The play's the thing,'" agreed Janet, quoting *Hamlet* yet again, "'wherein I'll catch the conscience of the King.'"

"There is no King," said Molly. "We'll have to ask them."

"I don't think they want to talk to us right now," said Janet. "Let's go drink cocoa."

"I have to talk to Thomas," said Tina, leaping out of her seat.

But the door of the little Green Room was locked and no sound or light came from behind it. They went to Janet's house and drank cocoa and ate spice cookies. They did not talk about the play, but about Molly and Tina's struggles with invertebrate biology and Janet's progress with the small telescope. Tina was fidgety and received the eventual suggestion that they go home with great alacrity. They got back rather late, and found no telephone messages awaiting them.

Janet dug her overdue library copy of the play out from under her bed, and read the ending. Vindice confessed to Antonio, whose wife had suffered from the court's corruption at the play's beginning, that Vindice and Hippolito had killed the Duke and a selection of his sons. Antonio promptly arrested and executed them. Hippolito did not have much to say. Janet felt rather sorry for him; Vindice was the trouble-maker, really.

Vindice explained to him that "'Tis time to die when we ourselves our foes,'" went on for a little about how his alter ego the pandar had predicted all this, and ended, "I'faith we're well—our mother turned, our sister true, We die after a nest of dukes! Adieu."

Which made precisely no sense to Janet. No wonder her father had skipped the Jacobeans.

CHAPTER 13

The next day was Thursday, which meant Tina and Thomas would have lunch by themselves, Robin and Molly and Janet and Nick would eat with whomever else they could encounter, and Nick and Janet would have the room in Ericson to themselves for three hours after lunch. Janet and Molly pelted Nick and Robin, when they turned up meekly on schedule, with every question they could think of; and Robin and Nick said they would explain everything at lunch. The four of them had barely sat down, alone for once at a small corner table in Eliot, when Tina flung herself into the empty chair and burst into tears.

"Thomas hasn't turned up," said Molly, patting her on the back and giving Janet the sort of meaningful look she usually despised.

Tina, as usual, was commanding at least as much irritation as sympathy. Janet accordingly left the cooing to Molly, and fixed Nick and Robin with as forbidding a stare as she could manage. "Do you know anything about this?"

Nick put his head in his hands. Robin said blandly, "He is fighting for his life, Christina; if you must cry, do it for that."

"What the hell does that mean?" said Molly; Tina just went on crying into the sleeve of her pink cashmere sweater.

"Academically," said Nick, popping his head up suddenly. "He's having to explain to the head of the Classics Department why he should be allowed to continue at Blackstock."

"Begin at the beginning," said Janet, between her teeth, "go on until you get to the end, and then stop."

Nick and Robin looked at each other; Robin shrugged.

"Robin and I had a scheme," said Nick, "to perform a *Revenger's Tragedy* that would show, subtly, to the initiated, that Medeous runs that department as the Duke ran his court. She would have known, and the Classics majors; but nobody else would. They might think the play treated women shabbily—which it does, really—but that was all.

"Now Thomas wanted more than that. He's going to switch to English, you know—if he survives—but there is something about Medeous. He couldn't just walk in and tell her so. He had to make a grand and irrevocable gesture. And he was responsible for the costuming, and he held it up so late we could not get replacements. But we could stage the play without the wigs, at least; and we thought, Robin and I, that everyone had agreed to that. You remember, Jack came on, at the beginning, with his gray wig? But Thomas was at them every moment he was backstage; and he must have persuaded them."

"Jack our Duke is graduating this spring," said Robin. "And Ambitioso and Supervacuo are in Modern Languages and Chemistry; she can't touch them. They thought it was a lark."

"What about Rob Benfield, though?" said Janet.

"He said," said Robin, "that Thomas had pointed out how silly the revengers would look if three of them had on those wigs and the fourth did not. Rob hates to make a play look silly; and he hates like poison to look silly himself. His first love is theater; if she won't let him graduate, he'll go off whistling."

Tina, hiccuping, had sat up and was rubbing her blotched face. Nick pulled a large blue handkerchief out of his jacket pocket and handed it across the table to her. She mumbled something, smiling grotesquely, and buried her face in the cotton.

"So hark, Tina," said Robin. "Thomas isn't angry, he is merely occupied. You had better pull yourself together. He's going to be in need of twice as much comforting as you think you are; he doesn't need you weeping all over him."

"He could have called me," said Tina thickly.

"He was probably rather distracted," said Nick.

"What do you know?" said Tina, still from behind the handkerchief, but with somewhat more clarity and vigor. "You never call anybody."

Janet thought it was ungrateful of her to attack the person whose handkerchief she was using, but she looked at Nick to see what he made of the accusation. He was smiling. "So, then," he said, "I must know very well the reasons a man doesn't call, mustn't I?"

"You are certainly perpetually distracted," said Robin. "You got that speech wrong again in Act III. You said, 'those who are known by both their names and prices,' when it is, 'both by.'"

"It scans better that way," said Nick, unperturbed. "Tourneur hadn't much of an ear."

"He had sometimes," said Janet. "'A lord's great kitchen without fire in't'?"

Tina flung the handkerchief down on the table. "How can you talk about poetry!"

"I thought," said Janet, losing her temper, "that we were tactfully giving you time to collect yourself."

Tina jumped up and ran out of the dining hall. Molly got up. "Oh, don't," said Janet. "Don't spoil her. Why should she get sympathy for making a public scene? Eat your lunch."

"She wants somebody to go after her," said Molly.

"I don't care. She's being childish and manipulative."

"It's rather odd," said Robin. "You'd expect her to sit here suffering in quiet where we could all see her."

"For God's sake!" said Molly, who had started to sit down but now thrust her chair so violently under the table that she splintered the table's edge.

"I am a player," said Robin. "I know how these things are done. She's miserable, yes; but she does with her misery what she thinks will give her the most attention from the audience."

"You are a bunch of cold-blooded bastards," said Molly distinctly; and she left too, though with dignity; she even picked up her tray and deposited it on the conveyor belt before stalking out the door.

Janet felt tears in her own eyes. She had never cared what Tina thought, but to be condemned by Molly was unbearable. She took a huge swallow of milk and eyed her fellow criminals. Nick looked stunned, as well he might. Robin, damn him, was amused.

"Who would like to walk out next?" said Janet.

They looked at her.

"Which reminds me," said Janet, struggling a little. "Why did Medeous walk out? A lot fewer people would have made any connection if she'd just sat there and gritted her teeth."

"She got her revenge," said Robin, in mildly astonished tones. "By ruining the end of the play."

"And I thought Tina was childish. Good grief, isn't life too short for that kind of petty behavior?" She had meant this question to be rhetorical, and in fact nobody answered it. But there was a moment of curious stillness, during which Nick stopped cutting up his hamburger (he never ate the buns) and Robin went on pouring milk into his coffee cup until it almost overflowed. He put the milk glass down smoothly, and Nick squished off a bite of hamburger and put it in his mouth.

Robin said, "It may be that they have similar temperaments. But Medeous has power too, and power can make men petty."

"And women too?" said Janet, rather more sharply than she meant to. The casual denigration of the play was still with her.

Robin looked rather blank.

Nick said, "He thinks 'men' means 'people.' Don't scold him. He doesn't agree with Tourneur, you know."

"Tourneur doesn't agree with me, either," said Robin. "Did you note what they call the image clusters in that play? Money and food and law. That's all."

"And lust," said Janet.

"The word, yes, over and over. But not images of lust. The play's curiously dry in that way. There's a great deal of greasy punning, but they seldom describe the deed. Not like *Lear*, or *Hamlet*."

"Did you ever play in *Lear*, Robin?"

"I was the Fool," said Robin.

"Can you tell me what it means? We read it in English 10 and it made no sense to me at all. We're about to read it again in 13. I guess Davison might explain it better than Evans, but I doubt it."

Nick looked thoughtful, and Robin erupted in laughter. He almost upset his coffee cup. When Nick righted it for him, he leaned his chair back and whooped. Long after Janet and Nick had given up making sardonic remarks, he was still wheezing. "Dear, dear, dear, dear," he said finally, wiping his eyes with his napkin. "Explain *King Lear*? Nobody can explain *King Lear*, that's the beauty of it. *Will Shakespeare* couldn't explain it. He wrote what he wrote; that's all."

"It's a good thing you don't teach English," said Janet, irately.

Robin snorted feebly. Nick said, "As I was about to say when I was so rudely interrupted, you might think of it as being about authority and the neglect of authority and the abuse of authority. It's a great deal more than that of course—it's about love and hatred, too. But abuse of authority is where it all starts. That may help center your thoughts." He grinned at her.

"I was in the same production Robin was in," he said. "I played Kent."

"How could you perform a play if you didn't know what the playwright meant by it?"

Robin said sententiously, "A poem should not mean, but be."

"Oh, go on. If anybody else said that, you'd call it modern nonsense."

"You needn't know what the playwright meant," said Nick hastily. "You need to have some reasonable unity in your mind, that's all."

"Huh," said Janet, unconvinced, but aware that it was almost one o'clock.

"Go along, children," said Robin. "If you see Tina, try and salve her affront."

"Huh," said Nick, with more emphasis than Janet had used.

They went hurriedly out of the dining hall and through the wordy tunnels. Somebody had added a verse of a Rod McKuen song, which had already garnered seven rude comments. A little beyond it Tennyson and Robert Blake were warring for space. A few political slogans, predictable and unpoetic, marred what little remaining empty space there was; somebody had then come along and filled in the huge black letters with lines from Thomas Nashe's "A Litany in Time of Plague," written very small in red ink. Janet looked at them thoughtfully as she walked by. Horrible things were happening in the world outside the college, said the political slogans; and they always had, said the interlocutory verse. "This world uncertain is." She took Nick's hand, quickly. When I graduate, she thought, then I'll think about these things. When I know something.

They went up the steps and down the red-carpeted hall, their fingers entwined, smiling secret smiles at each other. And stopped with a certain shock outside the open door of Janet's room. Nick shrugged and gestured Janet in.

Molly, in her air force parka and her red cap and mittens, a pile of notebooks beside her, sat on her bed.

"Where's Tina?" said Janet, cautiously.

"Wallowing all over Nora," said Molly. "It's Nora's job. I'm sorry I called you names. She really is completely self-centered; I don't blame you for being sick of it."

"Well, I'm sorry I wasn't more civilized."

"I tried to be, and all it got me was idiocy. She *likes* making the worst of things. She wouldn't listen to any sense or advice; she just wanted to lie around wailing." Molly stood up. "I'm off to lab. I made Tina take her coat with her, so you can go ahead and lock the door. See you at dinner." She stumped out in her heavy boots and shut the door behind her.

"Well, that's better," said Janet, filling her blue enamel kettle at the sink and plunking it down on Molly's illegal hot plate. She crawled under Molly's desk to plug in the hot plate, which was a primitive device without an on-off switch.

"It's not better for Tina," said Nick.

"Fuck Tina," said Janet, without thinking.

"I've considered it," said Nick.

Janet remembered not to bump her head on the underside of the desk. She backed out carefully and sat back on her heels. "Very funny."

"You two aren't just to her."

Janet stood up, carefully. He looked a little troubled; he did not have the look that meant he wanted to be annoying. She said, "If you think you're going to make me more just by telling me you want to go to bed with her, you've fried your brains studying."

"Don't you want to go to bed with Robin?"

Janet sat down on her bed and gaped at him. "*Robin?* Are you kidding? Robin is an alien. If he treated me the way he treats Molly I'd kill him. I don't even want to go for a walk with Robin without you or Molly as an interpreter."

Nick snagged the hairbrush off her bureau, sat down behind her, and began spreading her hair out on her back preparatory to brushing it. "I did not ask, do you want to marry Robin; I did not ask, did you wish to be a friend of Robin's; I did not ask, did you wish to go for a walk with Robin. I asked, did you not wish to go to bed with him?"

"I can't isolate it like that," said Janet. The kettle was boiling. She made herself a cup of contraceptive tea—it tasted like mint that had begun to go rotten—and Nick a cup of Constant Comment, to which he was addicted. They drank in silence, and Janet sat down where she had been.

"I forget how young you are," said Nick, beginning to brush her hair.

"You, of course, are as old as Methuselah."

"Not quite."

"Come on, you're a freshman too."

"I took a long time to get through high school."

"How come?"

"That," said Nick, "is a very good question. Let us answer it together."

They both fell asleep afterward, sleep being in as short supply as free time at this point in the term. Janet woke up first. Luckily Nick was not sleeping on her watch arm. She looked at the watch; it was three-fifteen. Nick could have another half hour or so.

She lay staring at the ceiling, blue and gray with snow light, and found her brain picking over the day's conversations as if they were a poem. A clichéd question about the shortness of life had been greeted oddly; Nick had said she was young, as if he were not; and there were other remarks, Thomas's about how long Nick and Robin had known one another; the large number of plays they seemed to have been in together. She had called Robin an alien; what if that were true? On the other hand, Nick, for all his affected speech and peculiar notions, was as human as he could be; and Robin, however maddening, was not nearly as weird as people could get. Anyway, why in the world should old aliens attend a liberal-arts college in Minnesota? If they could get here without being noticed, they must have better sources of information than this. It was a nice plot for a science-fiction novel, but it really made about as much sense as *The Revenger's Tragedy.*

"Insufficient data," muttered Janet, and went back to sleep herself.

Tina was intolerable for two weeks. Janet and Molly finally got together and made a schedule, based on the difficulty and urgency of their classes on a given day, of which of them was required to be nice to her and which could retreat to the library or be monosyllabic. Molly ended up with a heavier burden, since she and Tina shared a class and a lab period, but she professed not to mind.

Tina spent so much time listening for the telephone and flying out to answer it that Nick suggested she take her mattress out into the hall and camp out under the phone cabinet; it would just fit, he said, between Nora's door and the bathroom. This piece of wit caused Tina to flee wailing. If it had not been Molly's day to be kind to her, Janet might have come to blows with Nick. As it was, she lacked the energy.

On the eve of finals, Thomas called Thursday afternoon at three-thirty. Peg answered the phone, and banged on the door. Janet was dressing; she buttoned her shirt in a hurry and went barefoot to answer it. "It's Thomas for Tina," said Peg.

"I'll take it," said Janet, and marched grimly out into the hallway.

"This is Janet. Tina's got lab, you know that."

"How is she?" said Thomas's resonant voice.

Janet was strongly tempted to tell him she was happy and singing and going out with one of the football players in Dunbar. "How the hell do you think she is, you dimwit?"

"Bad, huh?"

"As bad as you can imagine, and add seventy-five percent."

"Well, shit. Will she speak to me?"

"I'm sure she will. I don't know what exactly she'll say,

though. If you have something fireproof and waterproof, I suggest you put it on. She won't know whether to sear you to a crisp and serve you up in Taylor, or weep all over you."

"I couldn't help it."

"Don't practice your excuses on me." There was a silence at the other end; Janet suddenly remembered that Thomas had been through an ordeal that was probably worse than Tina's, even if equally self-inflicted. "Are you staying?"

"Yes. I am now a proud member of the English Department."

"Congratulations, I think."

"We'll see. Will you ask Tina to call me?"

"Don't be so stupid! Get over here with a dozen roses and look as sorrowful as you can."

"That won't be hard," said Thomas. "I'll see you this evening."

"You will not. Molly and I are going to be absent. Don't you have any idea how to conduct an apology in a romance?"

"Apparently not," said Thomas, and hung up.

Janet slammed the receiver down and stamped back to her room, full of the particular anger that meant she was ashamed of herself. What was the point of snapping at Thomas? And why encourage him to make things up with the detestable Christina? The first sign of trouble and she turned into a whining brat. On the other hand, Thomas had no business breaking up with her by disappearing for two weeks and then not apologizing properly. She rounded the corner from the little hallway into the room proper. Nick was sitting up in her bed, dressed but very tousled.

"That was Thomas," said Janet. "I yelled at him."

"I heard you," said Nick. "Anybody would think Tina was worth defending."

That was a Robin remark, and Janet had no intention of responding to it. "Let's put our shoes on and make the bed," she said. "Molly gets so embarrassed if she sees any signs of what she knows perfectly well goes on in here."

Janet and an unembarrassed Molly dragged Nick and Robin

off across the frozen lake for an early dinner in Dunbar. Normally one did not eat in Dunbar in the winter; it was glass on three sides, pleasant in spring, summer, and fall, but chilly and depressing with frost crawling up the outside of the glass and condensation running down the inside. The lighting was bad, too; they relied on nature to supplement it, and during a Minnesota March nature was not cooperative.

Robin and Nick took the news that Thomas had managed the switch to the English Department, apparently without being expelled, in the same irritating way they took so much other information. They looked at one another with eyebrows raised; then Nick shrugged and Robin rolled his eyes at the ceiling.

"He's sticking with Tina, still?" said Robin.

"If she'll let him," said Janet.

"She'll let him," said Molly. "If he gives her a good dramatic scene first."

"Oho," said Robin. "Disillusionment comes to the tolerant."

"That sounds like the title of another goddamned Jacobean play," said Molly.

"It sounds like a Greek comedy, really," said Nick. "But Robin, my lad, if disillusionment really ever does come to the tolerant, you are going to be in a great deal of trouble."

"How is it," said Janet hastily, "that we know more about Thomas than you do?"

"There's departmental gossip," said Nick, "which is how we know these things, but it hasn't caught up with events yet. You, I presume, have talked to Thomas directly—an unconscionable shortcut, which we will now put to its proper use by going about the Classics majors and telling them all about it, with distortions."

"Rumor," said Robin, "all stuck about with tongues."

"Painted full of tongues," Molly corrected him instantly. The few stage directions in Shakespeare had fascinated her, and she was particularly fond of this one.

Nick burst out laughing in a manner more like Robin's than his own; Robin merely smiled. "I cry you mercy," he said.

"That's okay," said Molly kindly. "You're only a Classics major, after all."

Nick got up and left the room, hooting.

"And he might as well be one also," said Robin, "the way he acts."

"Everybody gets weird before exams," said Molly.

Janet, watching the dining-hall doors swing in Nick's wake, thought resignedly that at least this was better than turning pale and wan at a recitation of Keats.

After dinner Janet and Molly found themselves a corner of the library—you could not expect a whole padded room to yourself on the eve of exams—and studied diligently for several hours. At nine-thirty Janet looked over at Molly, who seemed wholly absorbed in her despised physics book, and decided to get her something to drink without bothering to ask. They could always take it back to the room and freeze it on the windowsill.

The soda machine on their level was empty. Janet went down a flight of steps. The machine there was still stocked, but there were six people waiting to use it, and the one presently in possession had been reduced to hitting the side of the machine with her fist and threatening it in Spanish. She was a typical Minnesota Swede, but had obviously been studying Spanish for some time. Janet was stiff from sitting so long; she decided to take a turn through the third-floor stacks and see how matters stood when she got back.

It was not really possible to take a turn around the third floor. The warm room, bright with fluorescent lighting and smelling of library bindings and stale coffee, was full of people. Every carrel was occupied, and if you walked by them half the people hunched their shoulders in unconscious irritation and a few actually glared at you. The long oak tables under the western windows were full, mostly of desperate researchers who should have done their term papers a month ago. Every aisle between stacks had at least two people in it, their heads tilted sideways like parakeets.

Janet gave up and wandered out of the stacks and down a short corridor that contained offices and a few classrooms. There might be another Coke machine down here, or at least a drinking fountain. But there wasn't, just the bare concrete emergency staircase with its red EXIT sign glaring. Janet turned around and walked back up the hallway, and then down it again, reading the signs on the doors. LIBRARY 304; LIBRARY 306; LIBRARY 308—RARE BOOK ROOM, OPEN M–F 9:00–1:00, 2:00–8:00, SAT 12:00–4:00; LIBRARY 310—MRS. KNUDSON; LIBRARY 312—THOMPSON COLLECTION. Janet stopped. No hours were listed. She pressed her nose against the frosted glass of the door, but the room was dark. She put her hand on the knob and turned, and the door opened without a sound.

Janet felt for a light switch, found it to the left of the door, and pushed both switches up. One of them, it appeared, controlled the fluorescent light in the ceiling, which, after the manner of its kind, flickered and hesitated before blinding you. The other controlled incandescent lighting in three glass cases in the middle of the room. Well, all right. She had been meaning to visit this room since Thanksgiving, but not unnaturally had not gotten around to it. Molly would be fathoms deep in her physics for hours, and they had agreed to stay until the library closed.

Janet walked forward. The books of the collection were on shelves around the edges of the room. In the usual cockeyed manner of Blackstock, you could check them out. She found, widely scattered, the Liddell and Scott, McGuffey's *Fifth Eclectic Reader,* with its four sister volumes, and the Matthew Arnold essay. Newton's *De Rerum Natura,* in Latin; yellowing nineteenth-century texts in astronomy and mathematics; more Greek, Homer and Herodotus and Xenophon and Sophocles. The poetry of Wordsworth and Keats and Shelley; no Byron.

A multivolume set of Shakespeare bound in green and gold. Pope and Dryden, Addison and Steele, Elizabeth Barrett Browning but not her husband, Dickens but not Hardy.

Janet considered the glass cases. Victoria Thompson, who had died in 1897, had owned an ivory comb and an ivory-backed mirror carved with a dolphin, and a couple of scrimshaw hair combs. She had owned a ruby bracelet and several rings, opal and amethyst and garnet; and she had been fond of red dresses. There were a velvet one and a red-and-blue calico and a red silk. She had also had a great deal of embroidered underwear that anybody today might be happy to wear as a dress or a pantsuit. Janet moved on around the cases, reading the typed cards interspersed with the exhibits. One of them referred to Miss Thompson, as Peg or somebody had indeed done on Janet's first day here, as a member of the class of 1899.

Janet felt as if she had been hit in the stomach. Yes, of course she must have died here, or why would her ghost run about tossing her college books out the window? But the thought of her dying as a sophomore at college made the entire display suddenly obscene. Good God, thought Janet, are they going to collect the underwear belonging to that girl who killed herself a couple of years ago and put it in a glass case with her favorite record albums and her high-school class ring and her goddamned Poli-Sci books?

Maybe they would at that. Janet had been going at the display backward, and now came to the long typed scroll that introduced it. The books comprising the Thompson Collection had been given to the College at Victoria's death by her parents, and had been housed in the college library since about 1925. But the other articles were displayed as a result of the efforts of the Women's Caucus, because Victoria Thompson had not died by accident. She had thrown all her books out the window and taken laudanum—and where had she gotten it, for heaven's sake—because she was pregnant. "In 1897?" said Janet hollowly.

She turned off the lights, shut the door, and went back to

Molly, passing the soda machine with only a momentary twinge. Their padded room had cleared out; now there was only a thin dark-brown boy writing feverishly on a yellow legal pad, and Molly, who was making origami cranes out of the scratch paper from her calculations. She took one look at Janet and got up off her pillow in a hurry. "What's the matter?"

"Let's go, I'll tell you on the way home."

They climbed the stairs to the top of the library, took off their slippers and stuffed them into their knapsacks, struggled into their heavy boots and put on coats and hats and mittens, and went through the glass doors into the freezing night. There were seventeen inches of snow on the ground, the top two soft, fresh, and still clean. The sky was clear, the stars impossibly distant, and the air like thin ice. Because there was no wind, it was pleasant.

"So what's wrong?" said Molly. They passed Masters Hall, its columns luminous like the snow, and turned right to pass Chester, which was only a dark block behind its larches.

"The Women's Caucus has a special display in the Thompson Collection."

"That's right, I read about it in the newsletter."

A lump of snow fell out of a larch onto the swept sidewalk in front of them.

"It says Victoria Thompson killed herself because she was pregnant."

"In 1897?"

Another lump fell behind them. Janet walked faster. Chester Hall's blind dark windows were like openings into a whole lot of very unpleasant alternate dimensions. The architect must have gotten the proportions wrong or something. She said, "That's exactly what I thought."

"I didn't know you could *get* pregnant in a girls' college in 1897."

The larches rustled, and something crackled. Another lump

of snow landed behind them, and a dusting of it went down Janet's neck where she had tied the wool scarf too loosely.

"Hey!" shouted Molly. "Quit throwing snow, goddamn it! Stupid jerks." She walked faster too. Janet was relieved; Molly was more likely to throw snow back, and with people in the kind of mood they got into during exam week, a snow fight could get nasty.

"It wasn't a girls' college," said Janet. "It's been coeducational since the day it opened. They were very strict about everything, though. But I guess there have always been ways to manage these things."

"I didn't know good girls did manage them in those days."

"All the worse when they did, then. If she felt she had to kill herself—"

"Right."

"Do you think there really is a ghost?"

"I don't know," said Molly. "I have to admit," she said, as they turned left between the Music and Drama Center and the ghostly skeleton of Olin, "I thought Tina might be doing it for the attention. But she's not getting any attention out of it—and after this last exhibition over Thomas, I'm certain it's not Tina's style to mystify everybody and chuckle quietly over it."

"The display says that before she killed herself she threw all her books out the window."

"And how do they know?"

They climbed the snowy steps to Ericson. The College was good about keeping snow shoveled, but the wind was better at spreading it out again.

"Good question," said Janet, yanking open the heavy door. The foyer smelled overwhelmingly of coffee. Janet saw in a moment that this was because there was an urn of it on a table in the lounge, surrounded by the ruins of sandwiches and cookies. Nine or ten girls were seated and sprawled in the room. The television set was off and they were all reading or scribbling. Two of them scowled automatically at Janet and

Molly, who ducked quickly up the stairs. "That's a very good question," said Janet "Any good scholar asks about sources. We can go back tomorrow and check."

"I have a physics test tomorrow," said Molly. "Maybe in the afternoon."

Tina was not in the room, but her bed was rumpled and on her desk was a green glass vase full of tiny red roses, huge white carnations streaked with red, and a few drooping clumps of greeny-yellow flowers. The sweet scent of the roses and carnations was underlaid by an odd bitter smell.

"My God!" said Molly. "I guess Thomas was repentant all right. What are those ugly little green flowers?"

Janet, whose mother grew herbs, sniffed at the maligned blooms and laughed. "I think it's rue," she said. "Do you suppose Tina will get it?"

"Where did *Thomas* get it this time of year?" said Molly. "You can't tell me florists sell something that looks and smells like that."

"Health-food store, maybe," said Janet. "I think you can use it to make tea. It must be good medicine if it tastes like it smells. It's better in the summer in the garden."

"I don't suppose we could get rid of it? Just the rue?"

"Tina would kill us. We can open the window if you want."

At four o'clock that morning, four hours from the time of Molly's physics test, while Janet was awake listening for the sound of bagpipes, Tina came along the hallway whistling Mozart, put her key into the lock so quietly that Janet did not hear it, and managed to squeeze past Molly's toy theater without making anything rattle or swearing under her breath. She closed the window over her bed, undressed, and went to bed as quietly as a ghost, and Janet did not hear Molly stir or turn over. But she was annoyed just the same.

They ascertained the next afternoon that the room housing the Thompson Collection contained no sources for its allegations. Molly dragged Janet, protesting, to the little cubicle given by the College to the Women's Caucus, and they talked to the student in charge, a tall, thin young woman with long black hair and a great deal of eye makeup. She was rather abrupt in her manner, but readily fished out for them photocopies of Victoria Thompson's diary and two letters written by her mother to her aunt afterwards. The mother's letters employed a lot of circumlocution—which was just as well, thought Janet, because if one could not be amused and indignant about that, there would be no barrier between oneself and the awfulness of Victoria's story. In conjunction with the diary it was clear that the exhibit's summary of events had been accurate. The diary made Victoria's lover sound rather like Kit Lane; but of course Kit's was a type much in vogue at the time. Victoria's family had wanted very much to know who the young man in the case was—so they could horsewhip him, or what? said Molly—but possessed no clue at all.

"It's not Tina's style to fake a ghost," said Janet to Molly as they went down the steps of the Student Union afterwards, "but is it Peg's?"

"I don't think so."

Despite all the upheaval, nobody failed any courses. Tina got straight A's. So did Molly, but that was forgivable. Janet got a B in astronomy, her theory being sound but her mathematics rather uncertain.

So they began Spring Term. Janet was back with Professor Evans for English 11, at the civilized hour of eleven-fifteen in the morning; she was taking History 12, required for graduation, to get it out of the way; and after very little conscious thought but a great deal of consideration in the back of her head, she was taking Greek 1 from Professor Medeous. She had meant to take it the following fall from the exacting but kindly Ferris, whose fault it was anyway that she was interested. But next fall contained two vital and daunting English courses and next spring a rare offering of Greek Lyric Poetry, which, if she took Greek 1 and 2 and Homer, she would be allowed to register for. So she gritted her teeth and wrote down Medeous's name on her form.

Melinda Wolfe had not said a word about it; she had smiled pleasantly and signed the sheet and asked if Janet wanted a Phys Ed course this spring. Janet had not: she figured, though she didn't say so to her advisor, that walks with Nick would probably fill the bill very well, even if they could not be credited toward graduation.

Spring Term began on March 27, and was distinguished by five inches of snow. People who had gone home to balmier places for spring vacation, including Molly and Tina, grumbled a great deal; Janet thought they were crazy. Nick and Robin, who had both stayed at Blackstock helping Medeous with a computerized concordance to Euripides, grumbled also. Thomas thought they were crazy. As a result of the final conversation on this subject, Janet found herself engaged to go traying with him down the hill to Bell Field one more time before the thaw came.

It was already rather warm, and the snow was soft; but a previous party had packed a couple of paths down already. Janet had invited Nick to come along, but he was going to a small party that Professor Ferris had arranged for the members of his forthcoming Aeschylus class. So she and Thomas met at the top of the hill with their trays under their arms. Janet had abstracted a red one at lunch, red being the easiest color to find should the tray escape and go shooting across the frozen field. Thomas had a blue one, and also one of the triple-sized, scarred brown trays on which the bowls of toppings were set out every Sunday for people to concoct their own desserts with. He was wearing one of those huge thick sweaters in incomprehensible Irish stitches, and no hat. He had had the wit to put some gloves on.

"I'm amazed you have any ears left," Janet greeted him.

"There's a hood on my winter jacket," said Thomas, dropping

his trays in the trampled snow. "But I'm not wearing my winter jacket in March. It just encourages them."

"Encourages whom?"

"The sprites of the weather. How do you want to do this? Some solo trips first to get the feel of it, and then try the big tray? I've never used one of these before. I hope we don't break it. You go first so I can push you; you've got less mass than I have."

Janet sat down on her tray, tucked up her feet, and said, "Ready."

Thomas gave her a huge shove. The tray slithered down a few yards, hesitated at a spot where they hadn't gotten the path smoothed down to start with, fell six inches with an ungodly bump, and flung itself down the hill fast enough to bring tears to her eyes.

They had made the bottom of the slide properly: instead of stopping abruptly in the hollow made by everybody's stamping feet, the tray skimmed halfway across the huge expanse of Bell Field, slowed, and slowed, and stopped somewhere past the middle. The setting sun lined the bare branches of the trees across the stream with gold, but down here there was a blue and gray twilight. The sky had already lost the profound and chilly color it got in winter.

Janet got up and picked up her tray just as Thomas came hurtling past her, whooping. He got more distance than she had, jumped up at once, and came trudging back through the clinging snow, beaming. "My goal is to crash right through those bushes and end up in the stream," he informed her.

They climbed gasping to the top of the hill, and this time elected to make a race of it. Janet won the first time, but never again, though they kept at it for more than a dozen tries, filling the air with snow dust, covering themselves with snow, and attracting a small audience comprised of people on their way to dinner in Eliot. The spectators drifted off soon, complaining about the cold.

"Let's try the big tray," said Thomas. "You can beat me another time."

"What other time? It's going to be fifty tomorrow."

"Next winter, then," said Thomas, rather gloomily. "I'll be here, imitating a freshman in the English Department. Is it a date?"

"Sure," said Janet.

They climbed the hill, stacked their trays on the sidewalk, and considered the large brown one.

"You'd better take the front, I think," said Thomas, "to give me a little more room for my legs. Sit down where it's comfortable, and we'll work from there. Can you scoot forward about six inches? Yes, I know we'll resemble a pretzel, but there's no help for it." He sat down behind her, enveloped her knees in his long legs, and wound his arms around her shoulders. Janet thought suddenly of her mother's herb garden in the blazing middle of July, with the slabs of red paving overgrown with thyme, and the sundial in the middle, counting only sunny hours. Thomas smelled of rue.

"Let's go," said Thomas; they made a concerted convulsive movement, and the tray went walloping down the hill as if it were on runners. It bounded off the path they had made about halfway down, turned sideways, and ran them with terrible speed parallel to Eliot, alight high on its hill, and tossed them out under one of the little maples at the edge of the stream.

"Jesus," said Thomas, picking himself up, "are you all right?"

"Sure," said Janet, taking his offered hand and hauling herself to her feet. One elbow and her tailbone felt sore, but she would have done it again in a moment. "You weren't scared, were you?"

"Yes, I was—for two of us, since you haven't any sense." He picked up the tray. "It's dark. We'd better stop."

"Molly said she'd make us cocoa."

They floundered slowly through the snow, which down here was still knee-deep, with treacherous mattings of bent grass and drifts of leaves underneath. Janet became aware, for the first time since they began this encounter, of a certain constraint in the atmosphere. Seizing on the first topic of mutual interest that came to mind, she remarked, "I'm taking Greek 1 from Medeous starting tomorrow."

"What the hell for?" demanded Thomas, stopping and staring at her. "Take it from Ferris in the fall, for God's sake."

"I can't, I've got Eighteenth-Century Literature with Evans and the horrible Modern Poetry class."

"Well, you can't take it from Medeous."

"Why not?"

"She's very jealous."

"Of me? She doesn't know me from Adam."

"Well, she will, won't she, once you take a class from her?"

"What has she got to be jealous *about*?"

"You are the *dimmest* intelligent woman I have ever met in my life," Thomas said, flung both his trays down in the snow, and took off at a great speed on his long legs.

Janet snatched up a wad of snow, compressed it briefly, and hit him square in the middle of the back with it. He didn't turn. Janet picked up the trays and turned in the other direction, over the icy wooden bridge and up the hill to eat in solitary splendor at Dunbar. Let Thomas explain to the rest of them, if he dared.

After she had eaten, she stopped by Nick and Rob's room in Taylor; neither of them was there, so she left Nick a friendly note and went to the library, where she spent the rest of the evening very happily reading an edition of Keats's letters. When she got home, Tina and Molly were in bed, drinking tea. "I wish you wouldn't fight with Thomas," said Tina reproachfully.

"I don't fight with Thomas. Thomas fights with me."

Tina rolled her eyes at Molly, who had the good sense not to respond. Janet went away, fuming, and brushed her teeth.

* * *

Greek 1 met in a small and oddly shaped room on the first floor of Appleton, the building devoted to the Department of Fine Arts. The building itself was an uninspiring twin to the library, redeemed only by the possession of a rather pleasant fountain with an abstract sculpture in the middle. Nobody had been so optimistic as to turn on the fountain yet, but its bowl was full of melted snow and the gray metal sculpture looked well in a halo of icicles. The room's windows looked out on the fountain; the room itself might once have been somebody's office. A long table with a lectern and eight desks had been crammed into it, but there turned out to be only six students. One of them was Odile; another, to Janet's considerable astonishment, was Thomas. He came in last, and gave her a sheepish grin. Before she could decide how to respond, Professor Medeous came in.

Janet had not realized before how tall she was. She must be well over six feet. Her hair fell to her knees. She was wearing a skirt and blouse in the red-and-green plaid of the Erskine tartan, to which Janet doubted she was entitled. She carried a pile of books and papers under one arm, and swept the class with a grave impersonal gaze that widened suddenly, on Thomas. She seemed as surprised to see him as Janet had been. She put the books and papers down on the table, still looking at Thomas; and he stood up and gave her a Drop-Add slip. She went on looking at him, and he took a pen from his pocket and gave that to her. She went on looking.

"Double major," said Thomas to her, exactly as if there were nobody else present.

"For a seven-year stay, that will do well," she said, and signed the form.

Odile giggled. Medeous gave her a quelling look, and Odile swallowed hard and sat up very straight. Janet looked at Thomas, but he was still holding out his hand to Medeous for his green slip, and when he had gotten it back and turned to face the class, he looked perfectly blank. He sat down behind Janet, which annoyed her; and the class began.

Medeous taught them the Greek alphabet, which was entertaining; and the maddening and erratic system of accents, which was not. Thomas, of course, knew the Greek alphabet perfectly and had also mastered the accents. His gorgeous voice, too large for the little room, made music of the nonsense syllables the rest of them were stumbling over. What the hell was he doing here?

Medeous was pleasant and patient, but not at all comfortable to deal with. Janet could not believe that this was the woman who had been suspected of making up dirty jokes for her class in Aristophanes. The rest of the class, especially Odile, seemed willing to laugh at their own mistakes in pronunciation; but nobody tried it twice. A profound lack—indeed a positive denial—of humor seemed to be Medeous's primary characteristic, if you left out her mere physical presence. She made the little room seem crowded. Janet found herself tucking her feet far back under her desk, in case Medeous should trip over them. And yet there was really plenty of room. It was enough to make you go get a ruler and measure the distance between your desk and the teacher's table.

Medeous dismissed them a little early, with instructions to do the exercises in Chase and Phillips associated with the alphabet and the accent system, and to glance at Lesson 3, which had alarmingly to do with something called the First Declension.

Janet left in a hurry, but Thomas caught up with her beside the fountain.

"Look, I know you hate my guts," he said, "but just don't act like it in there, all right?"

"I thought Medeous was a jealous god?"

"I want her to be jealous about the wrong thing."

"What's the right thing, for God's sake?"

"Nick, you idiot."

"You've got to be kidding."

"Nope."

"And look. Could she really get you expelled just for mocking her in a play?"

"Not exactly. Not through normal college channels, no, so you don't need to give me that lecture you're contemplating about the Student Council and the Grievance Committee and all that. Look, Tina's got a class; are you meeting anybody, or do you want to have lunch?"

"I'm meeting Peg and Diane in Dunbar, so we can watch the lake melt. Come on, if you want."

"Peg gives me the creeps."

"What?"

"She's so quiet."

"That's just because she doesn't know you very well. Come on. Tina will like it if I take care of you."

"I'll be sure and praise you to the skies. Are you three rooming together next year?"

"I don't know," said Janet.

CHAPTER 14

At Blackstock, the spring of 1972 was a miracle. You could not say of it, as one commonly said of spring in Minnesota, "If it falls on a weekend, let's have a picnic," or "I missed it this year, I was in the shower." It began in a leisurely manner in early April, and hindered only by a few sodden snowfalls that had vanished before sunset next day, it opened itself out slowly like a gigantic paper fan, and bestowed its gifts one at a time, instead of dumping them wholesale on your unsuspecting head and vanishing with a nasty chuckle into the wilting heat of summer.

There was an entire week in which nothing bloomed but snowdrops and bloodroot and the rue anemone, which Janet refrained from picking and giving to Thomas. The willows turned a brilliant yellow-green all along their drooping boughs. Nick and Janet, crossing the wooden bridge to Dunbar in order to wander happily among the trees on that side of the stream, found a mass of writhing garter snakes, brown and yellow with here and there a bit of black. A nest of vipers. I die after a nest of Dukes, thought Janet, adieu. She liked snakes; but looking at these squirming on the sunny bank, she shivered.

Her classes were splendid—rather a waste, when one could have ignored them altogether in favor of the weather. Medeous always made your heart jump when she walked into the room, but she was a very patient and careful teacher who could always find some inspired way to explain something somebody was stuck over. She needed this talent, since two of the members of the class were no good at languages. Why they had chosen a knotty and practically useless one like Classical Greek, Janet could not imagine; it transpired that one of them wanted to enter seminary and the other had a Greek grandmother. The one drawback of the class would probably have been advertised as an advantage: there were so few students, you could not hide if you were having an off day. Especially with the two linguistic dimwits fumbling all the questions, almost everything would come around to everybody. But learning Greek was, on the whole, satisfactory. And Medeous had more humor than one might suppose. The first sentence she gave them contained a pun. It translated as "The evil women in the tent are hitting the road," where the Greek meant only, "striking the thoroughfare," and not "embarking on a journey." Janet wrote it up in nice big letters and posted it over her bed, where it made an odd contrast to the colorful signs saying, "TAKE PILL!" that Molly and Tina had been obliged to tape up over their own pillows.

English 11 was such a wild delight that she could hardly bear it. She had not expected this reaction to the authors with whom the course began: Pope, Swift, Johnson. But they inhabited the period of Evans's expertise, and his enthusiasm for them was so great and the clarity of his understanding so compelling that Janet found herself reading them as she might read a particularly misty far-future work of science fiction. She was by nature and training an adherent of the Romantic school; but she was at the moment a little frightened of it and all its works. It produced a bewildering and infinite universe devoid of answers. The Augustans, with every bit as keen a feeling for those aspects of existence, had chosen to deal with them very differently. And when you were in love with someone who perplexed you, and friends with people you could hardly stand half the time and didn't understand even when you could, there was a great deal more comfort in the Augustans than in the Romantics. She remembered the moment in which Nick had quoted Addison on happiness, and thought she knew why he had chosen so moderate an author.

History 12, which was parceled out by the department for its own convenience, so that all you registered for was a class period, turned out to concern the French Restoration, and to be taught by Mr. Wallace, a chunky, bearded young man who was rumored to be a Marxist. He certainly had a very startling classroom manner; it involved a great deal of shouting and thumping of his fist on the table. He never shouted at or about the students, no matter how stupid they were being; what incensed him appeared to be the idiot fluctuations of history and the imbecility of humanity in general. Janet found him amusing but not very comprehensible; but it didn't matter. You were allowed to go pretty much your own way in this class, and what Janet found herself doing was reading the complete works of Honore de Balzac (in translation, in old editions out of the college library whose yellowing pages had never been cut). And this was another form of science fiction, an alien culture faithfully described, complex, alive, and fascinating.

She was able to express all this, at considerable length, to Molly, who had been greatly taken with their Shakespeare course, and mourned continually that one was not required to read poetry in order to become a marine biologist.

It was a blissfully quiet term. Nobody had any upheavals.

Thomas did not show any temper. Nick, thank goodness, had stopped making digs at Thomas, and Robin unbent enough to play tennis with Tina. She said he had a very peculiar notion of the rules, but at least he never got tired before she did.

Nick and Robin pulled their exasperating mysterious act only once, at lunch in Eliot on a glorious day at the end of April. Janet was complaining bitterly about a class of Greek verbs that upset all she had learned previously. Just as she got her feet on the ground, this new set of endings leapt up to confound her.

"Well, learn them if you know what's good for you," said Nick, scraping the pineapple filling out of the middle of his cake and giving it to Tina, who was going to make a sandwich out of it. "Medeous won't hear anything against the language."

"I don't know," said Thomas. "She's been uncommonly patient this term. I can't help thinking she's pulled off some coup, somehow, somewhere; she's as smug as a cat in a dairy."

Nick and Robin looked at him, both their heads cocked at the same angle and each with the left eyebrow raised. Tweedledum and Tweedledee, thought Janet, grinning.

Thomas found them less appealing, apparently; he scowled and said sharply, "And she hasn't once sworn at the two dunces in our class."

"And I have," said Janet. "We play this awful game where one student has to ask another a grammatical question—and you've got to know the answer, when you're asking, in case your victim doesn't. And I took pity on one of the dunces—Mr. Caspar, wasn't it, Thomas? I asked him for the future subjunctive of the verb *blapto*. It means to hit or harm; but that doesn't matter."

Robin and Nick burst out laughing; Tina and Molly looked patient. "So he made it up," said Janet, "properly, I guess; he stuck the sigma between the root and the first-person singular subjunctive ending."

"And Janet," said Thomas, also laughing, "said, 'no, no, no, there *is* no fucking future subjunctive!'"

"What did Medeous say to that?" said Nick, looking suddenly sober.

"She made me figure out what part of speech 'fucking' was in that sentence," said Janet. "And then she made me translate it."

Nick looked at Thomas, who nodded. Nick looked at Robin. Robin made a wry mouth, as if he had eaten something sour. They went on staring at one another. Thomas grimaced at them and began to eat his dessert. "Did she finally wrench Chester Hall away from the Music Department?" said Nick to Robin.

"No," said Robin, "and she won't, either. They haven't anywhere to move those pianos, since the practice rooms in the M&D Center all leak."

"This bodes some strange eruption to our state," said Nick.

"You just hope that's all," said Robin.

"What are you talking about?" said Tina.

"Departmental politics," said Thomas, soothingly, and hit her in the forehead with a grape.

The ensuing food fight involved two other tables and took them all out onto the balcony.

May ninth was Thomas's birthday. Tina was taking him out to dinner at the only fancy restaurant the town afforded, and had been dampening about suggestions for a cake or a surprise party or an expected party. Janet decided she would have to give him the Hamlet calendar before or after Greek class. She had found some wrapping paper in the college bookstore with Greek letters on it in green and red and yellow, which was satisfying. Molly, seeing her wrapping the calendar that morning, said, "Is that for Thomas? Are you going to see him in class? Can you give him my present?"

"Sure," said Janet, and Molly fetched a box containing three jars of orange marmalade, one with whiskey in it, one bitter, and one sweet, and proceeded to wrap it in some silver paper she had been hoarding for months. "Since Tina is being selfish," she said.

Janet was startled. "They don't get to see much of each other; why shouldn't they spend Thomas's birthday on their own?"

"It's not that," said Molly. "It's the way she scotched all the suggestions for a party later, or earlier. We could all use some diversion. Sharon's crabby, and Peg looks like a ghost, and Nora's fretting over her comps. And I think Thomas would have liked it. He doesn't seem like he's used to having a fuss made about him."

"Well, I'll do the best I can in the time I have. Do you want to come to lunch with us—I thought I'd do it then, instead of handing the stuff to him on the sidewalk."

"Can't—bio class."

"Can't you skip it for once?"

"I could if it was for once. I skipped it last time to go for a walk with Robin."

Something in her voice made Janet look at her. She was sitting cross-legged on the floor, her hair falling in twists across her face, making the blue ribbon of the package into a coil of little fringes. Janet said, "Does Robin need diversion too?"

"Mmmm," said Molly.

"Is there anything good at the theater? We haven't been to a play since last fall."

"Diane says they're doing something odd—*Godspell*, I think."

"Sounds more religious than diverting."

"It's a musical version of the Gospel According to St. Matthew," said Molly, snipping off her extra ribbon and handing the package up to Janet.

"I guess Nick might like it," said Janet, dubiously.

"Nobody really has time, is the problem."

"Well, what's the senior play this year? At least there's no commuting time for that."

"Something awfully modern with a long title." Molly got up and rummaged in her desk. "Here. *The Persecution and Assassination of Jean-Paul Marat as Performed by the Inmates of the Asylum of Charenton under the Direction of the Marquis de Sade.* Yuck," said Molly, emphatically.

"Well, let's go anyway; we can always leave."

"Okay; I'll talk to Robin. Oh, Lord, I'm going to be late. Say happy birthday to Thomas."

Janet, with less distance to travel, since Appleton was just up the road, made a more leisurely departure. Greek was especially trying that day, and Medeous seemed a little out of temper by the end of class. Janet escaped with relief, and waited for Thomas outside.

The silly metal fountain was spurting merrily, and people had as usual been throwing pennies into it. They gazed up at her like dozens of eyes. An oriole was singing madly somewhere in the larches. She was craning her neck after it when somebody bumped solidly into her. It was Thomas. Janet staggered a little and sat down on the wet rim of the fountain.

"Oh, hell!" said Thomas. "What are you doing here?"

"Waiting for you to come to lunch, as I have done every Tuesday, Thursday, *and* Saturday afternoon for the last six weeks."

"Well, I can't come to lunch."

If she had not had presents for him, she would have let him go; if she had not had Molly's package too, she would have hurled her own at him and departed. But she did have Molly's package, and the ground was wet from an early-morning shower.

"Happy birthday, Thomas," she said.

"Oh, Christ," said Thomas. He put both long hands over his eyes. Janet looked at him with a certain alarm, but before she could think what to say, he took his hands down again. "I beg your pardon," he said. "Let's go to lunch."

"You needn't come to lunch if you don't want to; just don't snap at me like that. What's the matter?"

"Just fighting with Medeous. She originally said I'd have to retake Greek 1 if I wanted to take Aeschylus, and now she says I don't have to—after wasting six weeks when I could have been filling out my distribution or something."

"Well, at least you won't be wasting four more."

"But that makes this a twelve-credit term; I'll never graduate at this rate."

"Don't you want to wait for Tina?"

Thomas was silent. They were walking down the hill amid the larches where Janet had hidden Schiller last fall. The gloom made his expression hard to read, and when he noticed she was peering at him he shook his hair over his eyes.

"Is that still bothering you?" said Janet.

"It's still bothering you, isn't it?"

"Well, Tina's still Tina. Molly says she's growing up nicely, but all it looks like to me is that nobody's thwarted her recently."

"I can't figure it out," said Thomas. "Is there really nothing there, or are we all just going the wrong way about it? We've made her think she's stupid, which I can assure you had never entered her head until she got here; and that does alter people's behavior for the worst."

"Nobody who gets straight A's in Blackstock's premed program can possibly be stupid. It's not her intellect, Thomas, it's her taste, or something. She's awfully ordinary and conventional for somebody that bright."

"Thanks a lot," said Thomas.

Oops. "If I've insulted anybody," said Janet, "it's Tina. I was thinking she loved you for your looks."

Thomas stopped dead just outside the door of Dunbar. "I don't think I want any lunch after all," he said.

Something in his face made Janet swallow her fury. "Here,"

she said. "Coals of fire. See you later." She piled the two packages on his armload of books and went in a hurry up the stairs and into Dunbar. Peg and Diane waved at her from a table overlooking the lake. By the time she had gotten her food and greeted them, Thomas had disappeared.

During the last week of classes, they got their Room Draw numbers through campus mail. Janet and Nick had gone to check their boxes after English 11. Neither of them got mail very often, since Janet's family lived in town and Nick's neglected him. They met in the middle of the basement room where the mailboxes were, unfolding the little blue squares. "Huzzah," said Nick, mildly. "I can have a single, if I want one."

Janet only half heard him. Her number was alarmingly low. "I hope Molly's got a phenomenal one," she said. "Otherwise it's the Morgue for us." The Morgue was actually Murchison Hall, the ugliest of the modern dormitories, and the most ill-designed. It was also inconveniently situated on the far west side of campus, close only to Taylor's dining hall, and not connected to the steam tunnels that linked the older inner buildings.

When they met Molly at lunch, Molly looked glum, too; and a glance at one another's numbers showed that they were definitely in trouble. "It's Murchison for us," said Molly.

"It's worse than that, I bet," said Janet. "This looks to me like we fall off the bottom of the list and end up in some off-campus house that wasn't one last year and hasn't got any lounge furniture or bookshelves or locks on the doors."

"What's Tina got?" said Nick.

"It's Wednesday; we don't see her till nine o'clock tonight," said Molly. "She's got that physics seminar."

"Well, you'd better make up your minds, hadn't you?"

"Triples aren't very popular," said Janet, "and there aren't any in most of the rotten dorms. Except Taylor."

"We could ask for Ericson again," said Molly. "Single-sex housing isn't very popular either."

"The question is, can we stand Tina?"

"I can," said Molly. "I know you can't believe this, but I like Tina. She's an awful nuisance when she's upset—but you haven't seen what I get like, and I haven't seen what you get like, come to that. And it's nice to have somebody to study bio with and help me with the goddamned math courses. But you don't get anything out of rooming with her."

"I'd get a nicer room," said Janet, ruthlessly. "I don't hate her or anything, but it seems like she's either being dim or dramatic and I can't stand either of them."

"She's not smart in any field you respect," said Molly.

"I respect biology!" said Janet, indignantly.

"Oh, all right—but you don't know anything about it, you just have to take it on faith. You like me because I read poetry and science fiction and kids' books."

"I like you because you're a decent human being who knows what civilized behavior is, and you have a splendid sense of humor and a very sweet temper," said Janet, more indignantly.

"Well, all right," said Molly, turning pink, "that too. But—"

"Tina has a sweet temper," observed Nick. "You don't give her a chance to display it, Jenny my lass. You don't give her a chance to do anything. You just back away when she does something you don't like, and the rest of the time you try to pretend she's not there."

Janet looked at him. Molly said, "You don't know what you're talking about. You haven't seen her struggle."

"Yes, I have," said Nick, "and so has Tina. Tina isn't stupid, you know"—Janet rolled her eyes; if one more person said that to her, she would scream—"and she can tell perfectly well," said Nick, "when you are being tolerant. Nobody who notices it likes to be tolerated."

"I take it you think Robin doesn't notice," said Molly.

Nick grinned at her.

"Nobody who notices it," said Janet, in as icy a tone as hurt feelings would allow, "likes to be lectured, either. Will you kindly stop speaking in vague generalities and explain just what I ought to be doing differently?"

"It's not doing," said Nick, "it's feeling."

"Custom," said Janet, very coldly, "can almost change the stamp of nature. Suppose I wish to be what I would seem to be; how should I begin?"

"Don't mix Shakespeare and Socrates," said Nick, rather shortly. "They don't blend well. Think of Tina as a real person, that's all, not just a collection of annoying habits."

"Quit bullying her," said Molly, switching sides abruptly. "Never mind, Jan. We could ask Diane to get a triple with us, maybe—she's always complaining about her roommate."

"I know, but she wants a single if she can manage it." Janet took a deep breath. "No—if you want to, let's just ask Tina." She found herself grinning. "She's probably got plans to get a double with somebody we've never heard of."

"I don't think so," said Molly, quite seriously. "I don't think she has many real friends."

Janet stuffed a roll into her mouth before she could say something regrettable.

Tina had a number so high people had been telling her that she should try for a single—a very uncommon thing for a sophomore. The notion seemed to frighten her, and she received Molly's offer of trying for a triple in Ericson with almost hysterical relief.

"I was so afraid you'd want to go off without me," she said, and embarrassed Janet enormously by flinging her arms around her. She smelled of tea-rose soap. Janet patted her on the back; then Tina hugged Molly, which made a great deal more sense, if she had only known it. Janet would rather have liked to hug Molly herself, but there seemed no real excuse for it. So they added their numbers together, and instead of studying for the exams that loomed a week away, they went on a tour of the triples available in Eliot, Forbes, Taylor, and (forlorn hope) Sterne, with its boxcar suites and fireplaces and unscarred woodwork.

Room Draw was a prolonged and uncomfortable procedure, like a combination of sitting in the dentist's waiting room and getting your SAT scores back in the mail. The College did its best by assigning time periods to ranges of numbers; but if you came at the bottom of a range, you still had a weary wait of several hours. Tina and Molly and Janet sat in the old boys' gymnasium, now reduced to Registration, Room Draw, and an occasional amateur theatrical event too large for Ericson Little Theater, and watched rooms melt away like toffee.

There were plans of all the dormitories tacked up on the wall, and a host of harried student helpers crossing rooms off as they were assigned. Holmes, a coveted residence since it was the only new dormitory with any satisfactory features, was all crossed out when they got there on their assigned afternoon; Dunbar, in which they had no interest since it was devoid of triples, went black in the first ten minutes. Ericson was half full, and so was Eliot. Forbes began emptier than those two, but filled faster; there must be a clump of people who preferred an ugly new dormitory to any of the old ones.

Sterne filled up. Taylor filled up; many people preferred to be on the west side of the campus, where the ducks were less obtrusive and you could not smell the lake on warm days. Ericson went. Forbes and Eliot were filling fast. Finally it was time to get in line; and when they stepped up to the desk and spoke to the harassed minions of the Office of Residential Life, it was to secure to themselves the last triple in Eliot, on the third floor of Column A. It would get the morning light even earlier than their present room, which was probably why it was still available. Never mind, thought Janet, there are such things as room-darkening shades, after all.

They saw their names written down on the master sheet,

and the room number on three little blue cards, one for each of them. They lingered to watch the room crossed off by a tall, thin boy on a ladder. Then they burst outside into the balmy air and gave three cheers to the startled crows. Tina hugged Janet, who hardly minded; and then Tina hugged Molly; and then Janet hugged Molly, who smelled of formaldehyde.

They went over to see their room, but its occupants were all out and the door was locked. Janet found the expedition comforting just the same. Eliot smelled very like Ericson, and was of the same vintage; it was odd that they had arranged it in vertical columns instead of horizontal floors like any normal dormitory, but maybe it cut down on the noise. And the dining hall would be right below them, a useful thing in the dead of winter.

"Oh, well," said Molly, "another time." She hugged herself, grinning hugely. "I feel the way I did when I passed Invertebrates. Come on—let's go out to lunch and eat stuff that's horrible for us and miss all our afternoon classes."

They accordingly got on their bicycles and rode through the lovely air and across the brimming river to Sheila's. Here they peacefully consumed huge sandwiches that fell apart when you picked them up; piles of Danny Chin's beloved onion rings, oily and heavily battered as ever; and enormous milkshakes. Janet formed a theory that Tina was a lot better when she thought you liked her—only reasonable, but she had not thought her own dislike so obvious. The theory would want testing when she was not dazed from overeating and exhilarated by the possession of a very good room for sophomore year.

Molly might almost have made her three-thirty class if they hurried, so they got back on their bikes and, looking over their shoulders as if Professor Olsen might come marching down Main Street and collar Molly, they fled through the center of town, rode in a muddled sort of way around its outskirts, and finally fetched up coming down the highway on the far side of

Dunbar. They parked their bicycles in the gravel patch, walked onto the wooden bridge, and, in stark contradiction of their expressed intention to take a long walk, stood pitching sticks into the eddying water and talking about boys.

Molly and Tina did most of the talking; they had had boyfriends in high school, while Janet had had Danny Chin, a very satisfactory friend who happened to be male. She was certain now that that kiss had been a mistake: why grab the boy, after all, just because he *was* a boy; it was just the way women were always complaining about being treated by men. She stood half listening to Molly's entertaining tales of the Four Jerks and the Two Nice Ones. Tina had one Jerk (the one she had been tearing up letters to in fall term, apparently) and one Nice One, about whom she still sounded a little wistful.

"Well," said Molly, "he can't have been as gorgeous as Thomas."

"No," said Tina consideringly, "but he was more comfortable. Thomas is exciting."

Janet felt a little smug. Nick was both comfortable and exciting, though he was certainly not gorgeous. On the other hand, she distrusted gorgeousness. It warped the judgment of the beholder for sure; it might also warp that of the possessor. It occurred to her that it had been unkind to tell Thomas she thought Tina loved him for his looks. She had been so conscious of not saying what she thought to Tina, that she had been saying it to all sorts of innocent people without reflecting on the consequences.

The term ended in a very satisfactory manner. Janet had applied herself to her vocabulary lists, and found herself, on the final exam in Greek, happily translating an entire passage of Herodotus with only a brief struggle with the genitive absolute, and a prolonged one with one word she could not for the life of her recognize that turned out to be glossed for her in a footnote on the next page of the exam.

In English 11, they had read Jane Austen's *Emma* with enormous glee and admiration. Evans had asked them to read the first chapter and write down what they thought would happen at the end—strictly for their own use. Janet had no idea; neither did Molly; but Tina consented to read the chapter and said, immediately, "Emma marries Mr. Knightley, of course." She was right, too. After that, they leapt what Professor Evans called "the romantic chasm" and landed breathless in the wild forests of Wordsworth, whence they journeyed very far afield with Coleridge, muddled around in lovely language but confused ideas with Shelley, alternately smirked and sighed with Byron, and fetched up in the clear-eyed, sensuous, tragic world of Keats.

Janet found the Augustans more of a struggle in the exam than in the original reading, but she thought she had retained enough of that bustling, rigorous place to make Professor Evans happy.

For History 12, she happily reread all the Balzac and wrote a paper on his treatment of the conflict between sexual and creative energy: he thought they had the same source, and if you expended what vital force you had in one activity, you would find the other closed to you. Janet wondered if this was true, and was at the root of her inability to write Nick any poetry. But Nick was writing quite a lot, and nobody could say he wasn't expending sexual energy, either. She also thought long and hard over the choice: it didn't matter now, college left time for very little poetry writing anyway. But if she had to make the choice, which road would she travel?

Commencement came and went. Rob Benfield, who was graduating on schedule despite his part in *The Revenger's Tragedy*, carried the battered bust of Schiller under his arm when he went up to get his diploma, and President Phelps, who still held the record for longest possession of Schiller from his own days as a Blackstock undergraduate, gravely produced a cap for the bust's head. Rob consigned the bust to Nick once he got off the platform, and Nick narrowly escaped having it wrenched from him by a mixed group of History and Fine Arts majors who lived on his floor. Janet, Tina, Molly, and Robin were instrumental in thwarting this plot; Thomas had already gone home for the summer.

Janet had attended the ceremony mostly on Schiller's account, but she stayed to see Nora graduate, which Nora did magna cum laude. Janet wondered if it might have been summa cum laude without the effect of Odile and her roommates. Nora, approached with this theory, laughed and said it had a great deal more to do with almost failing all her French courses. She hugged Janet good-bye, said she would certainly write, climbed into her family's old Buick, and was driven away.

Janet was suddenly unutterably depressed, though she was luckier than most students. She lived in town and could visit the campus whenever she liked; and Nick was staying there for the summer and helping Professor Medeous catalog the Classics Library. There had apparently been a great argument over whether it should remain the Classics Library or be subsumed by the Main Library; and Medeous had won. Nick said this victory probably accounted for her unusual good nature this term.

In any case, Nick would be around all summer; and Janet, half of whose college fees were waived because her father taught there, had secured a part-time job at Griegs's Greenhouse that would take care of her financial needs for the next year and give her plenty of time to catch up on her sleep and her extracurricular reading, as well as to see Nick.

June was in fact quite pleasing. The weather continued to behave in an astonishing, Camelot-like fashion; working in a greenhouse afforded a lot of unexpected insight into a number of poets, especially the minor Elizabethans; and she and Nick, released from the constraints of college and the Minnesota winter, had time to do ordinary things like picnicking, learning to play tennis, attending movies, eating in restaurants, going up to the city to hear the Minnesota Orchestra, and bicycling to neighboring towns to rifle their used-book stores.

Janet still felt that something was wrong. She put it down to a natural fear that nothing this good could possibly last; but what finally made her stop and examine the situation carefully was her reading, at long last, of Christopher Fry's *The Lady's Not for Burning*. She picked it up one afternoon at the end of June. Nick was working all afternoon and evening; she was done with her work at the greenhouse until the day after tomorrow; and she had just today during her lunch break polished off the last of the new science-fiction novels that had been piling up while she was reading dead authors instead. She had a letter from Molly to answer, and thought it would be nice to be able to tell her that she had read *The Lady's Not for Burning*. She began on it after supper, and put it down very soberly at eleven-thirty.

Everybody had gone to bed, though a tinny sound as of music played far too loudly through headphones could be discerned from Lily's room. It was a fine mellow night with a light breeze, and the cicadas were singing like crazy. Janet rubbed her fingers over the library markings on the spine of the book. This pleasant and convoluted work contained two sets of lovers. If you were eighteen and had never been in love before, you could be excused for not saying or thinking or feeling the sorts of things that Thomas Mendip and Jennet Jourdemayne said and thought and felt: Thomas and Jennet were entirely grown-up and had, so far as Janet could see, been through two separate versions of hell; no comfortable eighteen-year-old could expect to be as they were when they fell in love.

But the young lovers, Richard and Alizon, so silly and inexperienced that even Janet could smile at them and feel mildly superior—they, too, seemed to inhabit a country she had never visited. "Whenever my thoughts are cold and I lay them against Richard's name, They seem to rest On the warm ground where summer sits, As golden as a humblebee." When

Janet's thoughts were cold, they stayed so. Nick was bright, but he wasn't warm.

Good grief, she thought, falling back against her wadded pillows and gaping at the cracked, familiar ceiling. Neither of us has ever even said I love you. What *are* we doing? The lady is for burning, she thought, and swallowed a half-hysterical giggle. She turned off the lamp and watched the shadows of the leaves move in a mingling of moon- and street-light also familiar to her from childhood. I'm sleeping with a friend of mine, she decided. That's all right, no doubt; but you'd think, if it wasn't love, it wouldn't take such a lot of time and thought. Maybe it is love. How would I know? What does Christopher Fry know, anyway?

No, that wasn't the way to go about it. Christopher Fry knew a great deal besides how to write poetry. Janet sat up suddenly, turned the light back on, opened the book, and looked at the date. Then she read the back flap. Christopher Fry wasn't dead. Christopher Fry was a modern poet. "Well, I will be go to hell," said Janet; thought that over, and decided it was not so pleasing an expression as she had thought when she heard Professor Wallace say it.

She pulled her journal out from under the bed and wrote a long letter to Molly.

She did not discuss the matter with Nick, though they did talk about the play quite a lot. It occurred to her that the whole atmosphere of their times together was unfriendly to personal conversation. She spent a few disconcerting afternoons and evenings with Nick trying to watch herself and him as through a plate-glass window, and succeeded only in losing two arguments about Keats and one about how exactly you were supposed to scan the verse of Fry's plays. It was like trying to think about the Fourth Ericson ghost while you were in Ericson, or about Melinda Wolfe when you were anywhere at Blackstock.

She devoted a little time to discussing the ghost with Nick, who seemed taken aback that she should question for a moment the existence of spirits. She tried to discuss Melinda Wolfe with him, but he simply launched into a rambling story of how Wolfe had taught Herodotus when Nick's brother was at Blackstock. He was conveniently interrupted by a thunderstorm, and they had to pack up their belongings in a hurry and flee from the Arboretum to Taylor, where there were better things to do than talk about Blackstock's instructors in the Classics.

When she got home that night, Janet thought of introducing Nick to Danny Chin and letting them argue matters out. So far as she could tell, the main difference in her intellect produced by one quarter of a liberal-arts education was the eruption of a mad ability to see several sides to every question. Nick and Danny were both quite sure of their opinions, and were on opposite sides of this one. She sat in her hot bedroom, waiting for the storm-cooled air to make its way through the open windows, and tried to imagine their meeting. She had in her time been able to imagine in vivid color and detail, complete with dialogue, a variety of far less likely events, including, to pick several of the more embarrassing, that she had managed to finish Keats's *Hyperion* to universal critical and popular acclaim, or that Robert Frost had praised her poetry and invited her to tea. But Nick and Danny, though an infinitely more probable combination than Janet Carter and Robert Frost, would not fit into the same scene in her mind. It was like writing a really bad poem, one whose central metaphor was flawed or whose basic emotion shallow. You could struggle all you liked; you could put down a lot of lines on paper; but you could not force these dried-up bulbs to blossom.

She did call Danny the next day. He had managed, through one of his older brothers, to get a construction job with the state, and was spending twelve or more hours a day doing strenuous things with bridges and ditches in the blazing sun.

The money was very good. He said he wished there were a locker he could check his brain into, since it wouldn't work for him anyway, and he was afraid the heat would ruin it forever. Janet told him that any brain capable of coming up with that metaphor might be delirious, but was not dull, and asked when they might meet. Danny said he had a week off at the end of August, and if he remembered to call her they would know his brain had suffered no permanent damage.

Molly's letter answering hers was a long time coming. Tina, on the other hand, wrote every week, scented letters on pink stationery with pictures of teddy bears. She wrote straightforwardly of her job as a secretary for a small firm that sold large cardboard barrels, mournfully of the fact that she and her high-school friends seemed to be drifting apart, and rather frantically of her inability to respond to Thomas's long and poetic letters in the manner she felt they deserved. Janet answered in terms as reassuring as she could manage. She suggested that if Tina just wrote to Thomas about what really interested her, Thomas would be bound to catch the interest and be pleased with her letters.

Molly wrote less regularly, but very long and entertaining letters. She was washing glassware and taking apart dogfish sharks for a laboratory on an island off the coast of Maine. Maine was a childhood love of hers, and she was wildly happy to be back there, except for missing Robin, who apparently wrote short, opaque letters and an occasional sonnet, but would not give her the kind of detail about his daily life that would have made her happy. Janet tried to find out if he wrote to Nick; he apparently sent a postcard now and again about something that amused him, but that was all.

Molly's letter on being in love, when it finally arrived, comprised eight lined sheets of yellow legal paper, written small on both sides, and was not of a sort to reassure Janet at all. Molly was having precisely the same problem with her relations to Robin—exacerbated by Robin's secretive and undemonstrative nature. She had thought she was in love with him, having felt far more strongly about him than about any of the people she had gone out with in high school. But one of them was also working at the lab, and she was feeling about him quite as she had felt about Robin, if not more so, since he was willing to talk about himself and was not always falling into silly moods and having to be chaffed out of them.

"So I don't know," she concluded, "if I should just become abandoned and have a good time, or reconsider that Spanish convent. Or I could set up some new experiments to discover what being in love really does feel like—except they're all irreproducible, of course. What do you suppose Robin would say if I went to bed with somebody else? I think he'd shrug and say it was time to go to lunch. But what if I'm wrong?"

Janet wrote back urging caution. It was with the greatest of difficulty that she refrained from asking Nick what *he* thought Robin would do if Molly went to bed with somebody else. She did pass on Molly's complaints about the paucity of communication from Robin, who was doing community theater in Omaha, Nebraska, and ought to have enough time to write. She was still intermittently tempted to burst out with the real question.

Mercifully, Molly wrote back in a few weeks to say she had thought better of it, having finally received a ten-page letter from Robin in which he explained in considerable detail what a difficult person he was, and thanked Molly for putting up with him. At around the same time Janet got a despondent letter from Tina saying that when she was interested in something, she just did it, what was the use of talking about it, and all the letters she had tried to write Thomas about her interests had sounded so stupid she had torn them up. Janet tried to find out if Nick knew anything of Thomas's state of mind, but it seemed that the two of them did not correspond. Janet finally, near the end of a clear, dry, warm July utterly at odds with the normal habits of Minnesota summers, wrote to

Thomas herself, in fairly general terms. If he answered civilly, she might bring up the matter of Tina.

He did not, however, answer at all; and as August sulked in in a halo of thunderstorms and danced out in a blaze of sunshine, and September came on as hot as summer, Janet relegated all these problems to the time when school should start again, and gave herself up meantime to enjoying the last of her vacation.

It turned out that she would have to enjoy the final week of it without Nick. Professor Medeous was taking a little group of her students to a cabin in Wisconsin for a week before classes began. Janet was unable to determine, from the various things Nick said, if this was a tutoring session for people who were behind in their work, an advanced class for those who were ahead, or just a sort of prolonged party for favorites of either persuasion.

Nick came over for dinner the night before he was to leave, and departed rather early, since he had to pack. He did not invite Janet back to Taylor to help him, which didn't disturb her particularly but did seem to affront her mother.

"You just don't like him," said Janet. "Why?"

"He's very charming," said her mother, reflectively. "I just wonder if he's reliable."

"What do you mean?"

"I wonder what he'd do if you got pregnant." She shot Janet a sort of look that Janet had been more accustomed to receiving when she was ten, and said, "You are on the pill, aren't you?"

"No," said Janet, staggered into the truth; and seeing how very alarmed her mother looked, she added hastily, "I'm using a more old-fashioned method, but it's quite reliable."

"None of them are a hundred percent reliable," said her mother, darkly.

Janet had often wondered if Andrew was an accident, but she would not have asked it for the world. "Nick is a gentleman," she said, a little hotly. "I'm sure he'd be honorable."

"Even if he would," said her mother, "you might not like it very much, if you want to go on to graduate school."

"I'm being as careful as I can."

"Well, I suppose one can't ask for more," said her mother. "I hope you're right about your swain, that's all."

"I wouldn't sleep with somebody I didn't trust," said Janet; and though she had spoken with perfect sincerity, she immediately wondered if it was true.

They went on rocking—they were sitting in the porch swing—and presently Janet's mother asked her what her hours were at the greenhouse next day, and they passed on to harmless topics.

Danny called her the next evening and, after he had been congratulated for retaining the use of his brain, asked if he could have three days to sleep and then bicycle with her to the Dundas Book Fair. He said he hadn't read a book all summer and was worried that he had forgotten how.

It was all very well for him: he had been sweating in the sun for three months, while Janet had been doing light work in a greenhouse, going for twilight walks, and lurking inside the rest of the time. It was a cloudless and ferociously hot day and the secondary roads they bicycled along were a welter of dust, which combined with the sweat to make a salty mud. Janet got mad at Danny for getting so far ahead of her and madder when he stopped to wait.

The book fair was held in and around a disused barn. The sun and the dust were about the same as on the road. The books were, as always, varied, fascinating, and very cheap. But in the first fifteen minutes Danny beat her to a complete set of the D'Artagnan romances, a huge volume of sixteenth-century maps, *Lord Hornblower* in hardcover, and six of the Rick Brant books. She did find two minor works of Dorothy Sayers in hardcover, and four Nancy Drews, the old ones where Nancy drove a roadster and there were words longer than two syllables. But it seemed a poor compensation.

They settled with their booty and paper cups of fruit punch in the shade of a huge maple. Danny's sun-dark, sweaty face was blissful. He looked like a statue of an especially smug Buddha that its caretakers had neglected to clean recently. All he needed was some bird droppings. No birds obliged. Janet finished her punch and began to be ashamed of her temper. It was Danny's youngest sister's birthday and he had to be home for dinner, so if she wanted to talk to him this was the only time to do it.

Danny was gloating over his book of maps. Janet paused to gather her thoughts. But like Danny and Nick, they would not come together in the same place. What she had was not a series of events connected by necessity and probability, as both Aristotle and Danny would require; not tangible proof of strange goings-on; not reasonable suspicions backed by evidence. She felt what confounded her as she had felt the weight of Christianity on English literature. Something pervasive and all-embracing manifested itself from time to time, in books thrown out of windows, in Nick and Robin's conspiratorial glances, in Thomas's costuming of the Classics Department, in Melinda Wolfe's gorgeous refreshments and Professor Medeous's grave demeanor.

"So," said Danny, closing the book carefully, "seen any ghosts lately?"

Tina was returning a day before Molly, which made Janet a little uneasy. She dutifully met Tina at the bus station, however, and helped her carry her suitcases up the hill, past the Morgue, past Taylor and the chapel and the tilting M&D Center and the narrow ends of Ericson and Forbes, and up all the stairs to their new room at the top of Eliot. Then they carried all their own boxes and as many of Molly's as they could find up from the basement of Eliot, where they had been deposited last June.

Molly's toy theater they made a special effort to find; setting it up for Molly had been a brainwave of Janet's, mostly so they would have some common goal to talk about. They found a stray lounge table from the previous (and rather sturdier) issue of college furniture, and lugged it cursing up the steps. Janet expended a few longing thoughts on the boring new dormitories, which had elevators in them. But after all, one had to carry only twice a year; one had to live with the walls and woodwork and the proportions of the windows and the height of the ceilings day in and day out.

Their room was furnished with three single beds, which was a blessing. The furniture in Eliot was like that in Ericson, though, like the rest of the building, a little shabbier. They had a green carpet instead of a red one. They put the old striped curtains up anyway, to see if they would get along with the carpet or not. They spent several hours moving furniture, so as to make a place for the toy theater where nobody would bump into it.

Tina was very easy to work with; she was strong and coordinated and didn't complain about being tired or about pounding her thumb with the hammer when they put the hardware for the curtains up. It occurred to Janet that she would probably make a very good sister; she would be easy to live with if there were no expectation of strenuous friendship. Maybe they could manage this. They went down to dinner at six in a very amiable spirit, and found Diane Zimmerman and Sharon Washington at the table Sharon and Nora used to occupy.

Diane had been working for a children's puppet theater, and Sharon had been doing all the dirty work for a couple of geologists in Arizona. They were both very pleased with themselves and their summers. Janet had a sudden shamed feeling that, despite a fair amount of work in the greenhouse, surely a worthy institution, she had squandered her own vacation on self-indulgence.

Tina too looked depressed, and confessed to Janet later, when they were completing the unpacking and trying to decide where to hang some botanical prints Tina had brought back with her, that she was mostly downcast because her own job and summer had been so ordinary. Janet, standing on a desk chair and adjusting a lovely curlicued drawing of wild hyacinth, looked at her uneasily. If Tina really was ordinary, then making her unhappy about it would serve no purpose whatsoever. She could not think how to ask if Thomas had been putting ideas into Tina's head.

She finally tried, "Well, Thomas had a very ordinary summer, didn't he?"

"No," said Tina, with the utmost gloom, "he was collating two manuscripts of Euripides for Professor Medeous. He just went home to do it because he doesn't like this place in the summer."

"Well," said Janet, "I had an ordinary summer myself."

"It didn't sound ordinary."

"That's style, not substance. I made it sound interesting, that's all."

"I don't see how you did it."

Janet began to recommend the works of some eminent and fascinating diarists, but Tina interrupted her. "No, that's no good—because I wouldn't be able to see that what they were talking about had ever been ordinary, if they wrote it up so well."

Janet was becoming exasperated, but she reminded herself that they had nine months in one another's company to come, and that Molly liked Tina. "Okay, look," she said, after some thought accomplished while they put their respective books on their shelves. "I've been meaning to start keeping my diary again. I'll write up some of the things you're around for—

dinners in Eliot, and walks in the Arb, and a party if we have one—and I'll type it up for you, without the private parts, and you can read it, and compare it to what happened, and then maybe you'll see."

Tina looked so radiant that Janet felt both oppressed and guilty. But she was committed now.

CHAPTER 15

Molly came back; Nick came back; Robin and Thomas and Peg came back. Molly had a new daishiki with blue tigers on it, and said cheerfully that she had six million new freckles; but she looked just the same to Janet. Peg was pale, thin, and abstracted; questioned, she squinted through her glasses and said that working as a bookkeeper for a children's clinic had been lucrative but not restful.

"You should have come to Wisconsin," said Nick.

They were sitting in Janet and Molly and Tina's room after supper, drinking mint tea provided by Peg and eating cinnamon cookies provided by the RA, who had turned out to be Kit Lane. He had left a little packet of them inside everybody's door and then vanished. Janet was reserving judgment on whether this was a good way to handle one's responsibilities. There was no need to reserve judgment on his baking. The cookies were as good as Melinda Wolfe's, if not so pretty.

Peg put hers down untouched on the pink paper napkin

provided by Tina and gave Nick an oblique look. "I thought it would be better to get away."

"You can't get away from Blackstock, not really," said Nick. He had traded in his unruly mop of hair for a neat cap of curls, turned almost as brown as Danny, and gotten the earpiece of his glasses mended. He looked as if he had managed to get very far away indeed from anything that troubled him.

"*I* felt so far away I thought I'd never get back," said Tina gloomily.

Thomas smoothed her hair back from her forehead, and she smiled at him. Thomas too was brown and serene, with his hair bleached almost white and his gray eyes startling pools in all that tan. Janet looked at Robin, who was perched on Molly's dresser surveying the rest of them, on the floor, like a supercilious vulture. He was still his pale self, but his hair and beard were sleek as the pelt of an otter.

"What in the world did you guys do in Wisconsin?" she said.

"Meditation," said Nick.

"Nothing too much," said Robin, gravely. "Know thyself. We thought on hubris, and were translated."

"Somebody needs to translate *that*," said Molly, tossing Tina's teddy bear at him.

"O Robin," said Janet, without thinking, "how thou art translated."

Nick laughed; so, after a moment, did Molly. Tina looked puzzled. Thomas had withdrawn himself from the entire conversation and was staring out the window at the red-streaked evening sky.

Robin sat perfectly still, holding the teddy bear on one knee. Then he smiled slightly. "Robin is he who translates, not he who is translated," he said.

"Were you ever in *A Midsummer Night's Dream?*" said Janet. She had just called him an ass. But you could almost always placate Robin by asking about acting.

"A time or two," said Robin.

Like Professor Ferris in *The Revenger's Tragedy*, Robin seemed always to play the Fool. So, for this play—"Puck?" said Janet.

"And made an ass of Nicholas there," said Robin.

"Now somebody say, 'That's not hard to do,'" said Nick, "and we can all laugh."

Peg said, "Is that the play where they say the course of true love never did run smooth?"

"Yes," said Thomas, turning his head suddenly. "It's a comfort to them—they're having trouble, true love always has trouble, therefore theirs is true love."

"Shakespeare's *always* like that!" said Peg. "When you find out where the quotations came from, they always seem to mean something else."

"That's what happens when you're all things to all men," said Nick.

Peg frowned; Thomas looked at him and said, "And has he saved some?"

"New Testament!" said Peg triumphantly. "St. Paul. I am made all things to all men . . ."

". . . That I might by all means save some," said Kit Lane from the doorway. "What are you playing here?"

"Eating all the RA's cookies up without him," said Molly. "Thank you very much, and do come in."

Kit came in like the cat they called him, his long black hair floating around his rosy-dark, fine-boned face. If the room had been dimmer, he would have given off light like the trappings of the horse he had ridden on Hallowe'en. He must have been in Wisconsin too. Or maybe it wasn't Wisconsin at all; Janet remembered the day a year ago that Peg pointed out the clump of boys in Taylor's dining hall. Maybe she had just gotten used to them over the school year, and a summer's absence had shown her the quality they had always.

"Were you in Wisconsin, Kit?" she said. "With all these maniacs?"

"Oh, yes," said Kit.

"Like calls to like," said Nick.

"And where were you, Peg?" said Kit, folding himself to the carpet beside her.

"Earning my living," said Peg, with no expression. She was looking not at him but at the patched left thigh of her blue jeans.

"We missed you," said Kit, in a cajoling tone that no other voice in the world—except possibly Thomas's—could have made better than laughable.

"Professor Medeous didn't," said Peg, still to the patch.

She said the title as if it were an insult. Kit tugged gently at the fat braid that hung down her back. "You'd be surprised," he said. "And she's not the sole member of the department."

Peg looked straight at him and said, "I'm going to go find out if Sharon's back. I'll see you later." She stood up and shook out the ruffles of her shirt. "Thank you for the tea, Molly."

"You brought it," said Molly; but Peg was already shutting the door behind her.

"Sharon got back yesterday," said Janet.

Kit tapped his temple with a forefinger.

"No more than the rest of us," said Thomas, sharply.

"The rest of us do what we're told," said his brother.

"The more fools we," said Robin.

"What are you all blathering about?" said Molly. "At least Vindice did something, even if he never once shut his mouth while he was doing it.

All the Classics majors looked at her consideringly, as if she were a semilegible manuscript. Thomas's mouth was tight; everybody else just looked interested.

"Don't you complain about the Bio Department?" said Kit, after a moment.

"Oh, well," said Molly. "We do, don't we, Tina?"

"Bio Department never takes us to Wisconsin, either," said Tina.

"Poor babies," said Nick. "Only to Bermuda, and California, and Alaska."

* * *

September cooled its mild, sunny way into October, and the asters blazed along the banks of the stream. Janet's Modern Poetry class was less trouble than she had expected. Most of the poems were ugly and incomprehensible, or beautiful and incomprehensible, or so stark straightforward you wondered why anybody would bother to write them down at all. But Mr. Tyler had readily consented to her doing her term paper on Christopher Fry (she had asked for Bob Dylan just to see the effect—but Jack Nikopoulos, of all the unlikely people, had beaten her to it), and it was possible to skip classes, or dream through them, or pretend to be a spy from an alien planet trying to figure out American culture.

Greek 2, under Medeous's imperturbable guidance, was fussy and demanding. People who could read Herodotus handily might still gape stupidly at Euripides or trip over Homer, excerpts from both of whom appeared with increasing frequency in the homework assignments. The two dunces were still with them; Thomas was gone, which made the class feel rather flat. Odile was still there, giving a perfect example to everyone and causing the rest of the class to draw together in dislike. Janet, who was accustomed to either being or admiring and envying the best student in the class, hoped her own attitude had never been so smug.

Eighteenth-Century Literature was an unexpected amount of trouble. It appeared to Janet that she had read already, in English 11, every bearable piece of work any of the Augustans had done, and now wandered bewildered in a world that was artificially pastoral, unaffectedly nasty, and never, never said what it meant. She still loved Evans's lectures, but it was as if he were discussing some other literature altogether; she could never connect what he said with what she was reading on any except the most intellectual level—and while intellect was certainly necessary to an understanding of these writers, it was not sufficient. It all made her think of Tina's problem with writing interesting letters.

The journal was giving her less trouble than she had feared. The brilliant weather, the familiar but still, in many ways, mysterious company, their varying degrees of wit, loquacity, and patience, were a pleasure to record; it was like taking snapshots, only a great deal more rewarding, because the technical aspects of the matter were far more under one's control.

Tina was less pleased; Tina was, in fact, in despair. Half of what Janet saw going on she never noticed, and half of what remained she simply found boring. They had a number of frustrating and inconclusive conversations about it; the upshot of the whole thing was that Janet came back from an unsatisfactory session with Pope's "Pastorals," flung her books and notebook on the bed ("Hunting," remarked the notebook under today's date, "is the moral equivalent of war—young men will shoot something"), and called up Thomas on the telephone. He was living in Dunbar with Sharon's boyfriend Kevin, who as a Physics major was, perhaps, as far from anybody in Classics as Thomas could conceive of getting.

The telephone rang thirty-two times; a young woman with a slight Chinese accent answered, sounding resigned; and finally Thomas's reverberating voice said, "Hello?" in highly impatient tones.

"It's Janet," said Janet.

"Oh, sorry; I thought it was that moron who thinks Kev and I have got Schiller. What's up?"

"Have you been telling Tina she's ordinary?"

"What would be the good of that?"

"Well, that's what I thought; but she's all worked up about it, and you know everything just gets worse when she's worked up. Are you guys doing all right?"

"Oh, I don't know," said Thomas, discontentedly. "It's all very pleasant, but it's not going anywhere. And Tina wants it to, you know; she's got an amazingly puritanical conscience for somebody of her—well, anyway, I think she thinks the only justification for premarital sex is to get married when you can." He paused. "It's a very old idea, come to that," he said.

"This doesn't sound very healthy."

"Well, breaking up wouldn't be very healthy, either. I should have done it last summer, if I was going to do it; it has such an awful effect on people's studying, and it's bad enough to break the girl's heart without worrying if I'm going to keep her out of medical school too."

"She's only a sophomore."

"She needs four years of straight A's to—"

"Okay, all right, I don't know why I'm arguing with you anyway—*I* don't want you to break up with Tina. But she needs a new social group or something. We make her feel inferior."

"Well—"

"I've got an idea."

"Splendid."

"Why don't you take Tina folk dancing? They meet every Wednesday, and you know perfectly well she doesn't really want to come with the rest of us and watch arty foreign films."

"Sounds like you're the one who doesn't—"

"Oh, I hate 'em, but I like seeing what makes Robin laugh." There was a pause while Janet considered the implications of this and Thomas said nothing. She said, "Well, why don't you take Tina folk—"

"Because I've got two left feet."

"All the better."

There was another pause.

"I suppose it can't hurt to try," said Thomas.

Janet felt obscurely guilty. "You're being very lamblike about this," she said.

"You have a talent for nonoffensive interference," said Thomas, politely, and hung up.

The folk dancing was a great success. Tina talked about it

endlessly, checked out records of the music from the library, and began getting together with two other girls from the dancing group, including Susan from last year's Fourth Ericson, to sew her own costumes. She was no more tedious than anybody else going on and on about an obsession; and she was far, far easier to live with. And in the middle of November, the day before Winter Term Registration, she broke up with Thomas.

Janet found out about it not from Tina, who had (as Tina explained later with a certain pride) accomplished the breakup in the interval between Introduction to International Relations and an appointment to sew skirts with Susan, but rather from the spurned Thomas, who was disposed to blame Janet. It was almost the first gray day of that autumn. Janet was sitting at her desk, looking out over Bell Field instead of reading Pope's "Epistle to Dr. Arbuthnot." The rich colors of grass and yellow willow and red maple lay under the dark sky like some unreadable illuminated capital.

Janet had just turned back to the beginning of the poem, and was reading with a certain sympathy the exhortation, "Shut, shut the door, good *John*! fatigu'd I said, Tye up the knocker, say I'm sick, I'm dead," when there came a tremendous pounding on the door, followed by Thomas.

Janet twisted around in her desk chair and stared at him.

"Thanks a lot," he said bitterly.

"Shut the door if you're going to yell. What did I do?"

Thomas sat down on Tina's bed, as he always did; then he shook himself and got up in a hurry and sat on the edge of Janet's desk. "Tina just broke up with me."

"Well?"

"Because I can't partake of her interests—which means solely that I am not completely absorbed in folk dances."

"And that was my idea. Are you really upset?"

Thomas glowered at her. He had let his hair grow all summer and all fall, and seemed to have no idea what to do with it. He looked a great deal like Janet's idea of an angel, except for the scowl, and the fact that he bit his fingernails.

"I wouldn't put it past you to do it on purpose," said Thomas.

"Thank you so much. Why the hell should I? You think I want a repetition of last year's behavior, when you disappeared for two weeks? No thanks."

"She's not unhappy, she's as pleased with herself as she can be."

"Well, what's the problem, then? You didn't break up with her because you didn't want to ruin her grade-point average. So now you're free, and you still won't ruin her grade-point average. What is the matter?"

"I need to find somebody else—oh, hell," said Thomas, and grinned at her. Janet received the uneasy impression that, rather than suddenly seeing that he was being absurd, he was simply sitting on his anger. "I just wonder who I'll have lunch with on Mondays. Silly of me."

You can eat with us," said Janet, "Peg and Nick and me, I mean—but I do know what you mean. You feel kind of cast adrift." She had meditated on breaking up with Nick, more as an exercise in imagination than out of any major dissatisfaction, and had experienced a remarkably strong disorientation and panic at the mere notion.

"I certainly do," said Thomas. He pushed his long hands through his bright hair, and jumped off the desk. "Sorry to barge in on you like this. I guess I'll see you Monday—where?"

"Dunbar—look, we're used to having you around, you know—are you going to disappear on Molly and me?"

"I don't know. I don't know how awkward it's going to be. I did yell at Tina; she probably doesn't want to see my face for a while. Let me get used to being a bachelor, all right?"

"Well, call if you need anything."

"A good dose of self-esteem, that's all—no, don't look so alarmed, I was just joking. See you later." He went out, banging the door.

Janet sat on her desk and looked straight down at the sidewalk, and in a few moments Thomas came trudging along it, his hands in the pockets of his denim jacket and his head bent—probably against the wind, Janet thought, but he looked dejected. She got up and went from the eastern window to the northern, and watched him slither down the eroded gully below Eliot, walk onto the wooden bridge, and pause in the middle to lean on the rail and throw bits of something brown, probably bread, onto the water. A collection of ducks gathered out of nowhere, clucking and wanking at him. He went on leaning on the rail long after he had run out of bread and the ducks had drifted away complaining. Janet leaned also, on Molly's desk, and watched the wind whip his hair over his face. Finally he turned and went, very briskly, across the bridge, up the hill, and in the nearest door Dunbar afforded. Janet straightened up, and discovered that her wrist was numb and the edge of the desk had made a white mark on her palm. She had wasted twenty minutes.

She sat down to Pope again. She had just got into a mood where she could admire his very great technical skill and be mildly entertained by the paragraph beginning, "Why did I write? what sin to me unknown Dipt me in ink, my Parents' or my own?" when there was another knock. This was a nervous brushing of knuckles across the door panels, rather than Thomas's pounding; but like Thomas, the caller then opened the door—so violently that it crashed into the stop provided against just such hasty treatment—and skittered into the room.

It was Robin. Janet's first thought was that he was coming down with the flu. He was as pale as paste and his eyes looked feverish. He came straight up to her where she sat gaping, twisted sideways in her desk chair. "Tina's jilted Thomas," he announced in the tone of a man delivering the news that the besiegers have breached the walls and there is nothing to do but die bravely.

"Yes, I know," said Janet, "he was just here. Don't you have a class?"

"I met Thomas just before; he told me, but he would not stop. You must talk to Tina."

"What's the matter with you people? What have I got to do with it? I can understand Thomas coming to talk to me—but if you think Tina should reconsider, you tell her so."

"What makes you think she'd listen for a minute? It's you she listens to. You need but mention there is such a thing as a folk dance," he said the phrase scornfully, as Janet's father was accustomed to say bits of critical jargon he despised, "and she's consumed with it on the moment."

"Don't be ridiculous," said Janet. "Besides," she added, putting aside her indignation and getting to the really puzzling matter, "what's so bad about Tina's breaking up with Thomas? He's done nothing but agonize about how to break up with her since they met. Why should everybody mind so much that she did his dirty work for him?"

Robin stared down at her for an instant, his lips parted; then, as was his irritating habit, he burst out laughing, slapped his forehead, and reeled over to Janet's bed, where he crouched, making wheezing and choking noises and snorting repulsively. Janet tossed him her box of Kleenex. She thought of going on with her reading, but it would hardly be fair to Pope, for whom she was conceiving a tardy sympathy.

Robin eventually blew his nose, smoothed down his disordered brown hair, and gave Janet a winning look. She hoped he didn't know just how winning it was. "I cry you mercy," he said, predictably. Janet wished Shakespeare had never invented the phrase. "Thomas mopes when he is without a lover. After a week or a month of it, you'll be pleading with Tina, I warrant you."

"After a month of it," said Janet, coldly, "I'll be taking my examination in Eighteenth-Century Literature and considering switching to Classics. I shall be far too busy to—"

"Don't do that!" exclaimed Robin, sitting straight up and giving her a nakedly earnest look that made it seem likely he did know how winning the other one was.

"Why the hell not? You've all been after me to for a year."

"It's too late for that."

"Will you talk sense for once!" said Janet, losing all patience.

"Sir," said Robin, in uncanny imitation of the Korean actor who had played *Hamlet* a year ago, "I cannot. Cannot what, my lord?" he apostrophized himself sharply, as Rosencrantz had spoken to Hamlet. "Make you a wholesome answer," he said mournfully, as Hamlet. "My wit's diseased." He reverted to his own expression, and looked hopefully at Janet.

"Oh, go away!" said Janet. "You're enough to try the patience of a saint. Leave me alone. I'll see you at supper. *Don't say it!*" she added furiously, as Robin seemed about to add some of Hamlet's observations about Polonius and the worms, which would, to a grasshopper mind like his, have been amply suggested by the word "supper."

"I shan't say it," said Robin, getting up off the bed and bowing to her. "Nobody is dead yet." He turned with considerable aplomb and shut the door with a dignified click that spoke volumes more than Thomas's slam.

"We're all mad here," said Janet after a moment, and turned resolutely back to Pope.

He was a great relief after Robin. He was organized; he was methodical; no matter how angry he got—and he was very angry in this poem—he turned his phrases as precisely as a woodworker with a good lathe; and instead of bursting the bounds of his own chosen form of poetry—which even Shakespeare did and which Professor Tyler was always lauding those few modern poets who had a form in the first place for doing—instead of letting the poetry go all to hell the moment he felt any strong emotion coming on, Pope simply made that miraculous container of his, the closed couplet, that much tighter. Janet was entranced. Besides, Pope had been unfairly persecuted—always supposing you could believe him, but that was a problem for later; and even if the actual author hadn't, the person he was playing in this poem had, so what did the history matter—and after this afternoon Janet could feel for him.

At a quarter to six, a disembodied whistling of "How Should I Your True Love Know" ascended the stairs, followed shortly by Nick. He seemed perfectly cheerful; but after he had kissed her and they had inquired after each other's day, he sat down at the end of her bed and looked sober. "Have you heard about Thomas?"

"What, has he drowned himself?"

Nick tilted his head and considered her for a moment; it was a maneuver that usually preceded some devastating remark in an argument, and it was with relief that she heard him say merely, "Robin's been here, hasn't he?"

"I thought he was sick," said Janet. "Why in the world should Thomas's love life exercise him like that?"

"Classics majors have to look out for one another," said Nick, rather sententiously.

"Why they, more than another?" said Janet, echoing Hamlet's words to the Gravedigger and silently cursing Robin and Shakespeare too.

"Can you ask, after that play?"

"That play" meant *The Revenger's Tragedy*; as if they had invented some latter-day superstition, none of them called it by name anymore. "Just what," said Janet, "do you think that play conveyed, for pity's sake?"

Nick looked at her, still soberly, with the dim light of Janet's desk lamp sharpening his blunt nose and chin and making his eyes look an almost luminous blue.

"Oh, come on. Is the department really like that Duke's court? Adultery, incest, rape, nepotism, misogyny, sleazy intrigue?"

"The misogyny was ours," said Nick, "and I should have to

deny the rape, I think. Seduction, now. You might very well say seduction. And for all the rest, certainly."

"Would you say the same thing if a man were running that department, or is it just—"

"I did say the same thing when a man was running the department," said Nick.

"You mean, in the play?"

Nick nodded.

"She doesn't look like a seductress. Whom has she seduced?"

"Pick a name."

"You?"

"Not recently," said Nick.

Janet abruptly lost all relish for the conversation. "Well, look, can't you report her?"

"I don't think so. The department is divided, you see; and she is a brilliant scholar and a most excellent teacher—you've seen that yourself, already. And she knows everybody. I don't think it would come to much. And what is her job anyway—to make us all happy and virtuous, or to turn out good scholars?"

"She doesn't have to go out of her way to make you unhappy and wicked, does she?"

"She doesn't," said Nick, gloomily. "It's just her nature."

"I really can't believe we're talking about the same woman—the one who's so patient with Charlie Caspar, when I'd have murdered him in the first week of classes. And she never flirts with any of the boys—"

"Or the girls?"

Janet raised her eyebrows and looked at him. He nodded. "Well, she doesn't flirt with the girls, either. She's perfectly impersonal, except that every now and then she makes a very dry sort of joke."

"You don't belong to her, that's why. People in Greek 1 and 2 haven't declared their majors yet."

"So you don't belong to her either, yet."

"There are ways and ways of belonging."

"Are you in love with her?" demanded Janet. She was sorry the moment she had said it.

Nick, however, simply said, "No."

"Is Robin?"

"Very like, very like."

Janet almost said, "Poor Molly," but was prevented by the arrival of Molly herself, looking brisk and red-cheeked and cheerful. "Hello, children," she said, "why so glum?"

"Have you talked to Tina?"

"Not on Tuesday—she's got eight-thirty Chemistry and then I've got two classes in a row and she's got lab and I've got Bio. Why?"

"She broke up with Thomas."

Molly dropped her red hat and stood staring. "I don't know what to say," she remarked. She picked up the hat. "I never would have expected it. Oh, God, is she going to wallow again?"

"I haven't seen her," said Janet. "Thomas and Robin and Nick have all been to tell me about it, but I haven't seen Tina."

"No, you wouldn't—she's sewing with Susan and then they're going to meet Sharon and Kevin and go see *Woodstock* at the Palace."

"Kevin asked if we'd like to go," said Nick to Janet, "but I didn't feel I could take it just now, not with Kevin playing Those Who Gather No Moss over and over and over again."

"It's okay; I think you had to be there. I might go as an anthropologist, but not as a music lover."

"*Anyway*," said Molly, "if she's going to wallow, I quit."

"Have you had a bad day?"

"She isn't going to wallow," said Nick. "Thomas says she's terribly pleased with herself."

"So long as she doesn't have a reaction," said Molly, dolefully. "Well, I think it's a shame. I always did like Thomas. What do you think she'll bring home now?"

"There's nothing wrong with her taste," said Nick, in rather stifled tones.

"What's the matter?" said Janet to Molly.

Molly took off her jacket, hurled it onto Tina's desk, looked at it for a moment, and hung it up in the closet. "I had a fight with my advisor, that's all," she said from the depths. She emerged. "I wanted to take English 52—Shakespeare I, Histories and Comedies—because we had such a good time last winter. And he was giving me a lot of nonsense about how many distribution requirements I was missing, and trying to foist off a lot of goddamned psychology and sociology and religion courses on me."

"Who's your advisor?" said Nick.

"Ferris," said Molly. "He's been an utter doll up till now. I don't know what's got into him. He thought the last Shakespeare course was a wonderful idea. Dimwit."

"Who won?" said Nick.

"I did. But he looked so disappointed. It wasn't really a fight, you know—Ferris would never fight. He just looked all reproachful. People shouldn't be allowed to have eyes like that. He's worse than Robin."

"I'll take it with you," said Nick. "I'd thought of the Victorians, but I'm really not sure I could bear Charles Dickens in the wintertime."

"How about you?" said Molly to Janet. "Shall we make it three and wreak dreadful havoc?"

"Well," said Janet, "I'd thought of Victorians, too—but if I wait till next year I can take it from Evans, which is probably better than Tyler. I don't see how a man who likes Robert Bly could do justice to Dickens."

Melinda Wolfe, whose office Janet could find very reliably by now, had another wreath of dried flowers up on her door. It was mostly of rosemary, both leaves and purple flowers; but it had a few sprigs of thyme and five or six enormous lavender passionflowers. Janet looked at these with interest; her mother had tried to grow them, but they did not thrive so far north.

She knocked on the door, and Melinda Wolfe's mellow voice called, "Come in!"

She had added another file cabinet to her furniture, which reduced the piles of paper but also diminished the floor space. Janet squeezed through to the chair provided for her, said hello, and pushed her schedule sheet across the desk.

"Let's see," said Melinda Wolfe. "Chaucer; Homer: *The Iliad*; Shakespeare I: Histories and Comedies." She frowned. "How are you doing on your distribution?"

"Um," said Janet. "Done with Group Four." That was History, Philosophy, and Religion, and required two courses, which she had already taken. "And Group One isn't any problem because of all the English courses—not to mention the Greek. I guess I need two more in soft sciences and three in hard science and math."

"Wouldn't you do better to take a science or math course instead of one of these English courses?"

"English is my *major*," said Janet, irritated. "Why not tell me to drop the Homer course?"

Melinda Wolfe looked at her across the cluttered desk, her green eyes intent, and it was all Janet could do not to drop her own gaze. "Because," said Melinda Wolfe, "Ben Ferris inspired you to take that course and nothing I can say is going to prevent you. Besides, you could still change your mind and major in Classics; I wouldn't want to get in the way of that."

"I don't think I can stand any math or science in the winter," said Janet. "Maybe in the spring."

Melinda Wolfe got out the 1972–73 catalog and leafed through it. "All right, that should do," she said. "There are two Math 10 sections in the spring, and Biology for the Humanist, if you don't care to cut up frogs." She looked at the sheet again. "No gym? Anne Beauvais was telling me how very well you did in Swimming; she thought you might like to take the advanced course."

Janet had been considering it, but immediately dropped the notion. "I thought I'd take Outdoor Fitness in the spring," she said. "There's some very heavy reading in this schedule; I think what I've got is enough."

Melinda Wolfe signed the schedule sheet but did not push it back across the desk. "I'm not sure what you need an advisor for," she said consideringly.

Janet collected herself and offered, "To remind me to take math or science in the spring."

"You're determined to major in English?"

"I don't know; probably. Could I do a double major, do you suppose?"

"I'd endorse the request, but you should consider it carefully. It's a lot of work; you'd have to do some twenty-four-credit terms. And you'd better start Latin in the spring if you think you might want a double."

Janet grimaced. "I'll think about it," she said; and Melinda Wolfe gave her the schedule back.

She finally saw Tina that evening. Molly had reported that Tina was having her dinners with Susan and Rebecca, who lived in Taylor; presumably Tina was doing this so that Thomas could still dine with the other four if he wanted to. Sharon, however, reported that Kevin said Thomas wasn't bothering with meals much, unless you counted one processed hamburger and five cups of Cave beer as a meal. Janet kept meaning to do something about this alarming news, but Pope had become exciting; Tyler had just added Wallace Stevens, whose work was impenetrable, to his syllabus; and Greek 2 was now being presented with large chunks of Xenophon, which were straightforward but tiring, and small pieces of Plato, which seemed, grammatically, straightforward, but were contextually exhausting.

Janet was wrestling with one of these, and had just discovered with disgust that her translation from Philosophy 12 was not at all literal, when Tina came home. She looked pleased but nervous, rather as Janet had felt in junior high school when she had found another of the forbidden James Bond ("the sex is silly and the violence will give you nightmares") books at the library sale.

Molly stopped mumbling over her Morphology book and said sensibly, "Are you all right?"

Tina, fluffing her hair back up from its confinement under a stocking cap, looked shocked. "Somebody told you."

"Everybody has told us," said Janet. "Sometimes twice."

"Pigs," said Tina, reflectively.

"Well, it was Thomas's news too, you know," said Janet.

"I know," said Tina, "but he doesn't care."

"I think he might," said Janet.

"It's only vanity, then," said Tina. She sat on her bed and kicked her boots off. She always put on winter clothes a month before they were appropriate. "He's mad because I beat him to it."

"So he beat you to telling your roommates," said Molly. "He wasn't very forthcoming with the details, was he, Jan? So go ahead." She closed the heavy book and sat up.

Tina's account seemed to please and amuse Molly, but it left Janet depressed. Tina's reasons for breaking with Thomas were exactly the same doubts Janet had been having about Nick since June, and Tina hadn't even read Fry. The only difference was that Tina was persuaded Thomas condescended to her all the time, thought she was stupid, and wished he had never started the affair. There was a part of Nick he would not let Janet see—maybe connected with Medeous—but he did not condescend, he never (unlike Thomas, come to think of it) called her stupid, and he seemed perfectly satisfied with the situation.

The discussion degenerated into a rambling argument over

where Tina ought to go on having dinner. Janet brooded. Tina went off to brush her teeth.

"Molly!" said Janet. "We forgot Hallowe'en!"

"It didn't fall inside Fall Term Recess this year," said Molly into the Morphology book. "We could have a party the night before Dead Day,' if you wanted."

Janet grinned. Dead Day was the College's term for the free day that fell between the end of classes and the beginning of exams; having a belated Hallowe'en party on it would be appropriate, though probably not productive. She said, "I meant to watch and see if they all went riding with Medeous again—and I meant to check out the Fourth Ericson ghost."

"She wasn't throwing books around last Hallowe'en."

"How would we know? We were off following bagpipes. Did Robin play them this year?"

"Probably. He had that look."

"I really think my mind's going sometimes," said Janet.

"Well," said Molly, looking up and grinning, "if you insist on filling it up with Plato and Pope and Fry—"

"Oh my."

"Then you have to expect little things like chasing ghosts to fall out the bottom."

"You make me sound like a leaky sieve."

"Isn't that an oxymoron?"

"Oh, and now you're calling me stupid."

Molly threw a pillow at her.

CHAPTER 16

Over Christmas vacation, Janet consulted her father about the reported habits of the Fourth Ericson ghost. She had meant to consult Peg first, but Peg was involved in a common form of senior-year panic that caused its victims to exhibit permanent distraction and to take up residence in the library. Janet thought she might be able to corner Peg in the flurry of returning from vacation, before classes started. In the meantime, she interrogated her father over dinner, obstructed by Andrew, who wanted to tell his own ghost stories, and interrupted by Lily, who had become a raving skeptic. ("It could have been astrology," said their mother when Janet complained about it; "be thankful.")

They finally fled downstairs to her father's basement study, and he got out his notebooks on the subject. He had in fact written five or six chapters of his book, which in the usual way of scholarly works set out all the available information, neatly parceled up into categories. He seemed to have gotten bogged down in what to make of the parcels once he had them. He shook dust from the three-ring binder in which he kept the carbon of his chapters.

"Let's see," said her father, turning the typewritten pages. "You know how this kind of thing works. Once anybody reports seeing a ghost, people will see it all over the place. And all the stories get warped and embellished. It's the folk process and the evolution of literature all in miniature. Now. Here are the first three accounts, which are remarkably consistent with one another. The man who wrote them down didn't check for collusion among his sources, but as far as I've been able to discover it wasn't very likely. And here are accounts of all the later sightings that are consistent with the first few. These here are the obviously crazy inventions, and these might or might not be actual sightings. I don't know if you want to bother with them or not. I'm going to grade these hell-begotten freshman essays—speak up if you have any questions."

With which typical professorial instruction, he turned to his desk.

Janet sat in his old green armchair with the broken spring and read. Her father wrote an easy and unassuming prose when he felt like it, though he was capable of startling flights of jargon in the literary essays he published.

Victoria Thompson had killed herself on Hallowe'en, at about nine o'clock in the evening, in the year of grace 1897. Somebody or something had first hurled books out the windows of her room in Ericson in the fall of 1904. This apparently began a twenty-year tradition of throwing books out the windows on the evening of Dead Day every term; it was therefore difficult to determine which of these had been thrown by fleshly and which by ghostly students. People were not very good at noting which volumes were flung, though the housemother who reported the first defenestration had mentioned both Liddell and Scott and the *Fifth Reader*. It was this that had caused one Dr. Bishop, Professor of Victorian and Early Modern Literature and the first person to bother cataloguing the Thompson Collection, to propose that it had been the ghost of Victoria Thompson who threw books in the first instance. Somebody had in fact tossed eight books out of Ericson onto Dr. Bishop's head in the fall of 1925, but since one of those was a collection of his own essays on Hardy, Housman, and Shaw, he was inclined to blame an earthly instigator.

Janet had rather taken to Dr. Bishop, and was disappointed when his account was succeeded by others. She went on reading. The books that might most plausibly have been thrown by Victoria Thompson (always supposing it was reasonable that her ghost should be able to throw only the books it had owned in life) had always been thrown in the fall; where the date was noted more precisely, it was always October and often Hallowe'en. She seemed particularly fond of—or was it displeased with—Liddell and Scott. *The Scarlet Letter* came in second for frequency of flinging. ("Dad," said Janet, "isn't this alliteration a little frivolous?" "It's my way of amusing myself," said her father. "I might cut it before submission.") A little green book called, grandly, *The Legendary Ballads of England and Scotland*, compiled by one John S. Roberts, was next, and after that the *Fifth Reader*. The other books thrown varied quite a lot.

"Dad?" said Janet. "Has anybody ever seen poor old Victoria, or is it just books flying around?"

"People *say* they've seen her," said her father, "but the only consistency in the descriptions seems to have arisen from word of mouth—we don't have any independent descriptions that tally. And the independent ones vary so wildly, and they don't settle down into any time or place the way the book flinging does. Just beer and moonlight and mental overexertion, I think. You can read about them if you want; it's Chapter 5-A."

Janet read about them. Victoria Thompson had been reported in a variety of dresses, but not in any of those actually in the Thompson Collection. She had also been reported in a long white gown; in a riding habit, with whip and, twice, with horse also; and in nothing at all. Since Blackstock's tradition of streaking—running through some public event in the dead of winter clad in nothing but shoes and a ski mask—was of considerably more recent vintage, she suspected that they had made it all up.

"Thanks," she said at last. "I think you should finish this. It's very good."

"Bless you, my child," said her father, laying down his red pencil and rubbing his eyes. "But I've started feeling a little guilty about it. Here's this poor girl who got herself pregnant and felt she had to commit suicide, and I'm callously collecting data on her alleged posthumous appearances. I ought to write her biography, don't you think—to even the score?"

"Well, you could do that afterward."

"I guess it's having a daughter her age," said her father, still ruminating on his revulsion of feeling. "And another one coming up on it—and, oh, God, Lily's going to be trouble like nothing on this earth."

He put his glasses on and stared through them at her. "Look," he said. The mere tone of voice made Janet want to squirm, but she sat firmly. If you snubbed them they just got more upset. "Look," said her father again. "I know your mother's talked to you about this already—but you do know we'll take care of you even if there are suddenly two of you—don't you?"

Janet grinned; she couldn't help it. "You mean I can bring Nick to stay?"

Her father hit himself in the forehead with the heel of his hand, and Janet took pity on him. "I won't take the modern equivalent of laudanum, I promise," she said. "I'll come straight home and tell you. Really. And you'll wish I hadn't."

"No, I won't," said her father. "It would be better than having you throwing contraceptives out the windows—I know you wouldn't throw a book—for all time. Think of how our reputation would suffer."

"Think what a book you could write about it."

"I'll forgo the pleasure," said her father. He was looking anxious again, as if he thought his being flippant about it would convince her he didn't mean what he said.

"I'll tell you before I do anything," said Janet. "Honest."

"Well, shake on it, then," said her father; and they did.

The day before winter-term classes began, Blackstock College and its immediate environs received fifteen inches of snow in nine hours. It made all the old brick dormitories and lecture halls into suitable subjects for postcards; rendered the chapel suddenly grim and gloomy, like the one remaining tower of a castle; softened the horrible contours of Forbes and Dunbar and even Murchison; and lay upon the irregular red surfaces of the Music and Drama Center like icing on a very botched cake.

It was all still there next day, under a dark gray sky promising more of the same, when Janet and Molly wallowed their way to Shakespeare. The east side of campus was all plowed and shoveled, but the Shakespeare class was in Masters Hall, and the sidewalk between Chester and Masters was still untouched. Somebody had swept the steps of Masters, and when they emerged, snowy to the eyebrows, they found Nick stamping snow off himself and undoing half the sweeping. He helped brush them off; then they went inside, took off their coats, and shook snow all over the pristine stone floor. They went upstairs to the third floor, hung their coats on the usually neglected hooks so they could drip all over the scuffed hardwood floor up here, and found their classroom. It was large enough for twenty or so students, but the three of them only made the number up to eight.

Professor Davison was sitting on the long table provided for the teacher, swinging her feet in a pair of gaudy pink ski boots. The painter's overalls and bulky blue sweater that comprised the rest of her outfit made her look like a rather young freshman. She looked surprised as the three of them tumbled into the room. "Well!" she said. "This is better than I'd expected. I'm sorry we began without you. Come and get your syllabuses, and sit where you like."

They did as they were told, and sat in a row behind the other five, with Janet happily in the middle. "Now," said Davison, consulting her class book, "you are Molly Dubois and Janet Carter from English 13; and you, sir, are—?"

"Nick Tooley."

"Thank you—there you are." She marked them all present and then looked intently at Nick. "Mr. Tooley, do you mean to specialize in Shakespeare studies?"

"No, ma'am, I'm a Classics major."

"It's probably just as well," she said. She looked as if she were trying to share a joke with him, but Nick had put on the blankest expression he owned.

Davison had been at the performance of *The Revenger's Tragedy*; might that have something to do with it? Janet could hardly ask why if Nick wouldn't, so she settled herself to attend to the lecture.

This began with the usual lightning summary of Shakespeare's life and times, followed by a pause for questions.

Nick raised his hand and said, "What about the theory that Francis Bacon wrote the works of Shakespeare?"

Janet turned her head and stared at him. His expression was one of hopeful inquiry, just as if Tina had not asked him the same question when Janet and Molly were taking English 13, and had her head bitten off at the very notion.

Davison looked as if she would have liked to bite Nick's head off, too; her jaw set and she looked rather pink. Then she let out the breath she had taken, and settled her shoulders under the blue sweater. "You may research the subject scrupulously, Mr. Tooley," she said, "and report to us just after midterms. See me after class, if you like, for a partial bibliography. The rest of you, please annotate your syllabuses to show an oral report from Mr. Tooley for February seventh. We'll probably be able to pick up a day before then, with such a motivated class; or we can do without *Measure for Measure*, which is really a problem play rather than a comedy."

Janet soberly entered these comments on her syllabus, quivering with interior mirth that must on no account escape. Hoist with his own petard, she thought, oh 'tis most sweet, when in one line two crafts directly meet. Miss Davison might look as if she would forget her own name if you asked her roughly, but she was a match for Nick.

Miss Davison, looking not in the least smug, talked to them for a little about Elizabethan views of history, the sources for his histories, the sorts of alterations he made to the facts, and how the histories prefigured both the later comedies and the tragedies. Then she took up a battered Riverside Shakespeare and read to them from it for half an hour.

"Well," said Molly, as they emerged into a steady fall of large snowflakes. "That was very promising."

"Yes," said Janet, "it was. I've been reading the tragedies and romances since I was eight, but I never could get through the histories. But the way she read that passage from *Richard the Second*—"

"And the way she read Falstaff!"

"Much too refined," said Nick suddenly. "A little bit of a woman like that hasn't got the lungs for Falstaff."

"Yes, Nicholas, I know," said Molly patiently, "but she put the right emphasis on the words, which is more than I've ever managed."

"She made Olivia too vivacious, too," said Nick.

"What's the matter?" said Janet.

Molly looked at him, too, and suddenly hooted. "You're just mad at her because she said it was just as well you weren't going to specialize in Shakespeare. Is that why you asked about Bacon?"

"What did she mean, anyway?" said Janet.

"Some esoteric scholarly joke, I suppose," said Nick.

He darted suddenly forward, made a huge sloppy snowball from a pile on Chester Hall's bicycle stand, and hit Molly smack in the chest with it. Then he ran. Molly dropped her books on the frozen pavement and took off after him. When Janet, lugging her books and Molly's too, and further encumbered with Nick's dropped scarf, caught up with them between Chester and the M&D Center, Molly had Nick down in the snow and was insisting that he say Uncle. He finally consented to say, "Aunt," allowed Molly to make him say it with a midwestern broad "A" sound, and was permitted to get up. They went to lunch and talked about the new songs he and Robin and Anne had learned over vacation.

Janet had gotten a B in Eighteenth-Century Literature and an A in Modern Poetry, which upset her considerably. She had hoped that she would be better served by her tardy appreciation of Pope's *Dunciad*, wherein he laid into all the critics who offended him much as Janet would have liked to lay into the anthropologist who couldn't write, only he did it with infinite grace and elegance in a form crammed with classical in-jokes. She would have felt much happier being the sort of person who could understand Swift, Pope, and Johnson but floundered hapless among the moderns than the other way around.

And she had the feeling it was worse than that. Her grade in Mr. Tyler's class had been based primarily on the term paper, and all the term paper showed was that she had a good grasp of the way in which Christopher Fry treated romantic love. She had neglected all the religious issues of his plays and failed to read one or two of them altogether. She also felt obscurely that she had wronged Professor Tyler. He had been generous and tolerant to her, letting her hare off and read Fry; but she had doodled and fidgeted her way through all his lectures and, except for a grudging admiration of Wallace Stevens, had emerged untouched. It wasn't fair. She reread the Fry paper, dwelling gloomily on all Tyler's laudatory remarks, and felt even worse. She was rather taken with the Fry concept of romantic love, and none of its varied forms was anything like what she and Nick were engaged in.

She put the paper away, sighing, and tried to sit down and translate the first thirty lines of *The Iliad*. Mr. Ferris had read them aloud to give everybody confidence and inspiration, but these emotions did not survive the peculiar Homeric constructions of the first five lines. Janet stared at the angular Greek letters and brooded. Nick was awfully testy this term. She compared her state to that of Tina, who seemed content to hang around with the folk dancers in a large amorphous group, going to movies and dances with whoever was handy; and then with that of Molly, who had discovered a whole new field for argument with Robin. Molly was entirely entranced with Professor Davison and all her literary theories. Robin thought Professor Davison, who had been his freshman advisor, was a nice girl, but too serious, and he thought her literary theories were nonsense. This subject could keep Molly and Robin happy for hours. Nick, rather oddly given that his main attitude towards Davison was not benign, nevertheless agreed with Molly about the literary theories. But when he joined the argument things were apt to get less happy.

Janet went back to the Greek, absently looked the particle *te* up in Liddell and Scott, realized with irritation that it was the first one she had learned in Greek 1 and that, further, she had neglected to translate its invariable companion *kai*—no, she hadn't, there was no kai up there. She shut up *The Iliad* and picked up the fat blue Robinson edition of Chaucer. But the General Prologue to *The Canterbury Tales*, which she had in any case read already in English 10, begins in April; reading it in a snowstorm was just too much. Janet shut up the Chaucer, too, and gazed out across the clean white expanse of Bell Field, set about with bare black trees and crowned with the icy stream.

Then she got up and ran down to the second floor, where the telephone for Column A was kept, and she called Thomas.

The phone was answered on the second ring by a woeful

male voice that said it would fetch Thomas if she wouldn't talk to him for very long. Janet promised, and in a moment Thomas said dully, "Hello."

"It's Janet; what's the matter?"

"Winter. What's up?"

"Would you like your revenge?"

"I beg your pardon?"

"I want to complain to you about my love life. Then you can make a suggestion that will result in a breakup, and we'll be even."

"What seems to be the problem?"

"Do you have to talk like a doctor? I told that boy who answered the phone that I wouldn't talk long."

"Oh, Juan. Yes, he's waiting for a call from his girlfriend—except I don't think he'll get it. But okay, sure, where do you want to go?"

"Why don't I meet you on the bridge and we can go over to the TR? I could use some nice greasy French fries."

"See you in ten minutes," said Thomas, and hung up.

It was three o'clock in the afternoon, very cold and windy, and getting on for dark. The lake was frozen solid; on the other side of the bridge, there was a small pool of open water where the effluent from Eliot came down. Two disconsolate ducks revolved slowly around it. Janet found a stale bun in her pocket and had just finished feeding it to them when Thomas came walking hollowly over the bridge. The ducks took off, squawking; Janet jumped and then smiled at Thomas. He was well wrapped in a scarf, but his head was bare. Janet didn't say anything, but fell into step beside him.

They climbed the trodden snow between Forbes and Eliot, passed Ericson, and without consultation kept to the southern side of the Music and Drama Center, even though it meant a longer walk. Olin, Chester, the M&D Center, and the chapel among them channeled the wind beautifully, though you would have thought they were too far apart to do it; it was better to walk along the edge of campus and duck sideways only when you had to. They did this in silence; they trudged past the charming sandstone castle that had been the original library, and past the vast brooding front of Taylor, and past the Student Union with its clock tower, and came finally into the steamy warmth of the Tea Room.

A number of people appeared to share Janet's craving for greasy fries; there was a short line at the counter. Janet and Thomas went and stood at the end of it. Janet looked at Thomas, in the good light, without the encumbrance of her hat or his scarf, and was shocked. Where his face had been nicely hollow, it was gaunt. She saw a lily on his brow, though it was not moist with anguish or anything else. He needed a shave, and he had not washed his hair in too long. Such symptoms were fairly common at the end of the term, but not in the first week.

"You look awful," said Janet. "Maybe you should be pouring out your sorrows to me instead."

"Thank you very much," said Thomas, without much heat. "It wouldn't help. Allow me to feel useful and intelligent by telling me your troubles; that's the best thing to do."

They ordered their food and stood looking at the grease-spattered menu and the bunch of marigolds on the countertop. When the food came, Thomas paid for it over Janet's protest and carried the tray to a remote corner of the room. At least it had enough food for two on it; he didn't look as if he'd been eating. She should have asked Kevin about him more often, last term.

"Now," said Thomas, taking a gulp of his coffee, "what seems to be the problem?"

Janet told him, in as much detail as she could muster, and doing her best to keep Christopher Fry out of it. She felt she was not being very coherent; but Thomas sat nodding at her, absorbing food and information in the same deliberate way.

When he had finished, he swallowed the last of his coffee and said, "I think you expect too much."

Janet took a deep breath, and Thomas said, "Not of love; not in the long run. I think you expect too much from the time you've had. It's only been a year; and only three months of it had any leisure at all in them. And people don't really discover everything about one another in the first months of acquaintance. They think they do, but they don't. They just like fooling themselves. And you're not very good at that, I don't think."

Janet had always feared that she was very good at it; perhaps that was just the exception that proved the rule, if she could fool herself into thinking she was good at fooling herself. She shook off this impending tangle and said, "All right. That takes care of my attitude. But what about Nick? He seems all friendly and open and cheerful, and he seems to talk about himself a lot; but he really doesn't say much. He's met my family dozens of times. All I know about his family is that they're in England and he doesn't go see them during vacations. And he makes inexplicable remarks. And he and Robin are just maddening. I'm sure Robin knows all this stuff."

"You planning to marry him tomorrow?" said Thomas.

"Robin?"

"No, you dimwit, Nick. What's your hurry? He's met your family because you love them and are proud of them. What if he doesn't love his and is ashamed of it? Do you think there are no parts of you that won't stand the light of day? Just you take a good look at them, before you go accusing Nick of being secretive and refusing true intimacy, or whatever exactly it is you're upset about." He stopped suddenly and ran a hand through his lank hair. "I'm sorry. But I meant it. Give the lad some time. These extroverted people are often the most insecure of all, you know."

"But—"

"What's the matter, do you see some better prospect wasting away for lack of attention?"

"I don't see people as prospects," said Janet furiously, "and that has nothing to do with it."

"Of course it has."

"You are the most unromantic person I've ever met."

"Thank you," said Thomas, with every evidence of sincerity.

Janet sighed. "Have *you* got any prospects?"

He shook his head. "It's so difficult to know how to go about it."

Janet stared, openmouthed; she had just started to close her mouth and school her expression when he glanced up and caught it. "Well, Tina was awfully lonely, you know," he said, "and she had a sort of theory that one must have a boyfriend in college or one is a failure; and it hurt her feelings very much that Nick preferred you. But you see how that all worked out." He shrugged.

Janet clamped her teeth together over a strong desire to explain to him that if he would just look at them as he was looking at her—possibly stopping first to wash his hair and put on a less grubby sweater, but possibly not—women would fall into his arms in droves. They would only fall out again, presumably; and maybe he didn't want that sort of woman, anyway. "What sort of person are you looking for?" she said, a little breathlessly.

Thomas's whole face hardened, as if he were about to say something unforgivable. Oh, great, here we go again, thought Janet. But then he shrugged again, and looking over her right shoulder he said, "A motherly sort."

"I'm not sure I know any."

"They're in remarkably short supply these days," said Thomas, with an extreme grimness that surprised her.

"Well, look, give us some time. You don't expect people our age to have quite gotten the knack of it, do you? We're still half children ourselves."

"Mmmm," said Thomas. "Well, maybe." He seemed to gather himself together, and looked at his watch. "Well. Are you willing to give Nick a little time?"

"I notice you don't say effort."

"I don't think it would work with Nick."

"Mmmm," said Janet, in her turn. "Why don't you come and sit with us at dinner? It's been ages."

"I notice you don't say, eat dinner with us."

"After all this?"

Thomas laughed, and got up. "All right," he said. "If I'm very good, do you think Robin and Molly will argue?"

"I guarantee it," said Janet, getting up too. "They hold completely irreconcilable notions about *Henry V*."

"Do you ever get tired of Shakespeare?"

"The woman who is tired of Shakespeare," said Janet, in her best tone of exaggerated sententiousness, "is tired of literature, for there is in literature all that Shakespeare can afford."

"Mmmm," said Thomas.

CHAPTER 17

Winter term passed peacefully. Janet did realize, round about the fifth week, that among Homer, Chaucer, and Shakespeare, she was bereft of her native language, and had to read straight through all the novels of Raymond Chandler to restore a sense of proportion and keep all her translations of *The Iliad* from coming out in blank verse.

She discovered that Nick had not read any Chandler, and once she had persuaded him to do so, they had the food for many a discussion. Thomas, it transpired, was passionately fond of Chandler. His own favorites were the same as hers, *The Long Goodbye* and *The Little Sister*, whereas Nick insisted on regarding such inferior efforts as *The Lady in the Lake* and *The High Window* as Chandler's best, which gave them food for more discussion than any of them would live to finish. Tina read one or two of the novels and settled on *The Big Sleep* to defend. Molly refused to have anything to do with Chandler, saying that the amount of violence in Shakespeare's history plays was more than enough for one term.

Tina went out with Jack Nikopoulos four times, which made Janet and Molly hopeful. But she came home from the last of these dates, at eleven o'clock of an arctic February evening, and demanded that Molly and Janet put on their boots and come with her to the little stream in the Lower Arb. She wanted to toss her brand-new three months' prescription of birth-control pills into the water and wash her hands of romance altogether.

They had a prolonged argument, dealing jointly and severally with whether Tina might not want the pills later, what she might do if suddenly thrust into a tempting situation, how the vile drugs and the indestructible plastic case might affect the wildlife, and why it couldn't wait until tomorrow. But Tina was immovable. They could stay up here if they wanted to—she was going down to the Arboretum this minute and get rid of these goddamned drugs. Janet looked at Molly and nodded. Molly shrugged crossly, got out of bed, and began to put her boots on.

"Oh, thank you," said Tina, and hugged Janet hugely.

"What are roommates for, if not to be foolish together?"

"Am I being foolish?"

"You're right to get rid of those blasted pills. Giving up on romance seems a little hasty."

"Well, it's not like I'm entering a convent. I just feel happier if I don't worry about it. Theoretical biology is bad enough, right now."

"You may have something there," said Molly, less crossly.

They went as softly as they could, in heavy boots on an uncarpeted and creaky floor, and left Eliot by the side door. The moon was full; another new fall of snow blurred all the corners of the world. Their breaths made great blue clouds in the fierce dry air. The temperature was somewhere on the wrong side of zero. They got thoroughly covered with snow just scrambling down the hill to the bridge to Dunbar. Janet hoped they would not get lost in the Arboretum and die of exposure.

"There's open water right here, Tina," she said, "and with all the soapsuds from Eliot, what are a few artificial hormones here and there?"

"I want it to be carried far away," said Tina. "It'll just bob up and down there till spring and annoy the ducks. And it's got my name on it."

"Well take it off, then," said Molly.

"No, that's cheating. Come on. I want the other stream. It's hardly ever frozen."

They trudged up the hill to Dunbar and down its other side. Half Dunbar's windows were still lighted; Janet saw that Nick and Robin's was dark and Thomas and Kevin's, next to them, was dimly lit, as with one desk lamp rather than all the overheads. Go to sleep, dummy, thought Janet.

Up the snow-caked asphalt road, past the playing fields and the ruined bones of the lilac maze, down the hill to the highway, a black ribbon in all this blue and white. No traffic. They ran across the highway—one always ran, for some reason—and slogged through the snow. Past the stone wall, a mere lumpy drift of snow, down the narrow path, which you could tell from the buried underbrush only because it didn't crackle under your weight, and so to the little humped bridge, also half hidden in whiteness.

They plunged to the middle of the bridge, pushed the snow off its railing, and leaned on it. The stream was a sunken wriggle of white in a white field. Even the trees hardly showed; they were either white with snow, or as black as the dark between them.

"It's no go, Tina," said Molly. "It's frozen."

"Listen a minute," said Janet, who knew this stream.

They were quiet. The fog of their breath billowed out over the silent snow. No, not quite silent. A remote trickle, as of a faucet dripping in a distant room, rewarded Janet's attentive ear. She listened closer, and could hear the faint rush of the water, going about its business under the stifling cloak of winter. "Hear that?" she said.

"That's all very well," said Molly, "but it's frozen up here just the same."

"We could jump on the ice," said Tina.

"You certainly could not," said Janet. "We could find a rock, though. Isn't there a pile of them just the other side of the bridge?"

"We forgot our flashlights," said Molly.

"Well, they're for finding pipers, you know. Come on, let's just scrabble a little."

Molly did this with a will, and while Janet was still entangled in a dead branch, she came up with three round, heavy stones. Janet flung the branch from her and followed Molly back to the center of the bridge.

"One rock each," said Molly. "All together, or one at a time?"

"All together," said Tina, picking up a rock. "Ready, set, go."

They lifted the rocks over their heads and hurled them onto the ice. Molly's bounced harmlessly under the bridge; Tina's produced a lovely spiderweb of black cracks and a glorious splintering noise; and Janet's, hitting this a little off-center, made a hollow crunch followed by a jagged black hole.

"Go for it, Tina," cried Molly.

Tina dug in her pocket and extracted her round box of pills. She leaned alarmingly far over the railing and shied it at the hole. It slid neatly across the ice, paused, and dropped in with a faint splash, like something falling down a well. Molly cheered. Tina joined her. Janet leaned, staring. The hole in the ice seemed to go down forever; and yet this was not a deep stream.

"It's cold," she said to her roommates. "Let's go home."

The next evening was Thursday, which she always spent with Nick in his room. Robin and Molly would betake themselves to various places, as the mood took them; several times Janet had come home to find them lying on the floor of the room in Eliot, studying or arguing. After she and Nick had made up for a week of neglect—he was taking one of the dread twenty-four-credit terms, having decided on a double major in Music and Classics or possibly Music and English, and it left him even less leisure than usual—Janet told him about Tina and the pills.

"I'm not sure that was wise," said Nick, lying back amid the disarranged bedclothes and looking very sober. His sheets were dark green with huge sprays of lilac on them, and as a background to his wild dark hair and odd features made him look distinctly faunlike. "And it doesn't bode well for Thomas, does it?"

"Why does everybody persist in thinking Tina's the only girl for Thomas, when everybody including Thomas agrees they never really suited one another to begin with? Tina says every girl in the folk-dancing group has a crush on him, and they were all dreadfully disappointed that he didn't keep on attending after she broke up with him, even if he couldn't dance and couldn't learn to."

"Have you told him so?"

"No; I don't see much of him—privately, anyway. Why don't you tell him? He lives next door."

"He's not there much," said Nick, "but I'll make a note of it." He wound his fingers in a stray lock of her hair, and smiled. "This is getting nice and long."

"If I keep it long all summer, you'll know I take you seriously."

"If I thought you did not," said Nick, "I should be very upset."

Janet looked at him. His expression was earnest but not overly concerned. Having brought the conversation to this point, she was not sure she would be wise to go on with it. She remembered what Thomas had said. There had certainly been no time this term.

"How's the corrupt and despicable Classics Department?" she said.

Nick was leaning on his elbows; on the word "despicable," he flung up both his hands with enough violence to push his head and shoulders into a crevice between the pillows. "I'd really rather you said you didn't believe me, than to take that tone about it," he said in a muffled voice.

"I do believe you," said Janet, "at least, I don't think you'd lie to me about it—I believe you intellectually, but it's hard to get an emotional grasp on something like that with so little solid information."

"Do you think all those jokes about Classics majors being about in their heads are based on nothing?"

"Having met some of you," said Janet, giving him a poke in the ribs, "I know they're not. But—"

"It's been a quiet time," said Nick. "These things run in cycles. We are due for an unpleasantness in a year or two."

"Wonderful. Why don't you tell me about unpleasantnesses in the past: I'm sure they make wonderful gossip."

Nick didn't move. After a moment he said consideringly, "From time to time somebody's spouse finds out about Medeous."

"Finds out what about—oh." Janet started to ask for names, and stopped. Brilliant, cherubic Professor Ferris, with his dry-spoken wife; the intense and humorous Janie Schafer, who had switched to the History Department but whose jokes Peg and Kit still remembered, who had a husband; even Melinda Wolfe, who was not married at all—did she really want to hear about the eruption of their private lives into the violent public light? "Gossip is mischievous," said Hesiod, "light and easy to raise, but grievous to bear and hard to get rid of." She remembered it so well because it had fallen to her to sight-read it in Medeous's class. "Wait a minute. You say it's all Medeous's fault, but how long has she been here?"

"Five years, so."

"There were jokes about Classics majors long before that."

"True for you."

Janet sighed. When he got Irish, there was very little to be done with him. She was greatly surprised when he sat up suddenly and said, "The head of the department has often been a trifle odd."

"Victoria Thompson was a Classics major," said Janet, struck by a revelation. "Was it the head of the Classics Department who got her pregnant?"

Nick began to laugh, in much the way Robin did instead of with his own usually moderate chuckle. "Oh, dear dear dear," he said at last, wiping his face upon the blanket. "My dear girl, the head of the Classics Department in 1897 was our own Professor Medeous's grandmother. Think of the outrage of the biologists."

"Maybe she just hounded her righteously, then," said Janet, smiling a little sourly.

"She was not at any time a righteous woman," said Nick. "Why are you brooding over poor Victoria?"

"Tina's pills, probably," said Janet, giving up on rational conversation and lying down again. "If Victoria had had any, she never would have gotten into trouble in the first place."

"If she'd lived in a time that made any decent provisions for such trouble, she'd have got out again."

"Well, maybe."

The term wound to its close. The February thaw came in March, and having melted every flake of snow and icicle in sight and covered all available surfaces with a thin film of water, withdrew again in favor of an arctic cold spell that froze everything solid.

The Biology Department canceled Biology 13, obliging Janet and also Nick, whose distribution credits were in rather worse shape than hers, to sign up for Physics 20. This class was thrillingly titled, "Revolutions in Physics," but was referred to by Kevin, witheringly, as "Physics for Poets." It irked him that majors in the humanities should have a physics course tailored for them, while the hapless science major who needed a couple of English or history courses had to take English 10 with the terrifying Evans or History 12 with the incalculable Wallace like anybody else. Sharon suggested that the College must figure science majors were smarter than humanities majors, but this only got Nick and Robin as irked as Kevin.

Janet was amused, having heard the entire argument in every possible form every year since she was ten years old. It was her private conviction that anybody could be taught to read a poem usefully but that some people could not be taught mathematics no matter how you went about it. She kept this theory to herself, knowing already the sort of trouble that expressing it would cause.

She also registered for her father's class in the Romantic Poets and, after a struggle with Melinda Wolfe, for Greek Lyric Poetry. Melinda Wolfe wanted her to have one, or preferably two, of the tragedians under her belt before tackling lyric poetry; she also recommended Plato or Herodotus or Thucydides. But it became clear fairly early in the interview that she would rather Janet took the wrong Classics course than no Classics course at all. Janet thought this was odd, but was happy to employ it to her advantage.

She was in fact a little worried about the lyric poetry class, Homer having shaken her confidence in her linguistic abilities. She had gotten an A, but at the expenditure of roughly three times the effort she had expected to use. She dared Greek Lyric Poetry largely because she was certain she knew everything her father would be teaching. Even if she didn't, she had certainly read everything he would assign. So the lyric poetry could be given the attention due to two classes.

Thomas and Robin were both in the Romantics class. She asked Nick why Robin should bother, and was told rather shortly that Robin was rethinking his position on Keats and thought he would like some help doing it.

"I hope your father's a ruthless realist," said Nick.

"What *have* you got against Keats?" said Janet, closing her Shakespeare and glaring at him.

It was the afternoon of Dead Day, a cold and rainy one, and they were sitting in Janet's room with Molly, ostensibly studying for the Shakespeare final. Miss Davison had had a brainwave and occupied the last class period with a group reading of *Richard III*. She had given Nick the part of Richard, which had annoyed him. He had done a very quiet and melancholy Richard, reminding Janet of Hamlet's description of himself—Richard had lost all his mirth, forgone all custom of exercise, and was delighted by neither man nor woman. This did not work very well.

Molly had been stuck with the part of Anne, and she told Janet later that being seduced over her father's coffin by a mournful puppy dog who appeared to have done all his murders in his sleep had made her want to smack Nick with the Penguin Shakespeare and end everybody's misery. Janet assumed that this was Nick's revenge on Professor Davison. She had feared he would exact it in his oral report on Bacon, but that turned out to be a lively and well-researched performance indeed; its conclusion being that nobody who thought the evidence for Shakespeare's authorship dubious had any business putting forward any other candidates. All this excitement had not only squeezed *Measure for Measure* out of the syllabus, but left certain gaps in everybody's understanding of the third part of *Henry VI*.

"I bet Keats is too swoony for Nick," said Molly.

"He is not swoony," said Janet, indignantly. "*Swinburne* is swoony."

"He is, though," said Nick. "You will go on about how he's the only poet remotely like Shakespeare to come along; but when Keats swoons, it's in dead earnest—"

Molly burst out laughing and fell off her bed, and remained on the floor, still laughing, until Janet went and got her a bottle of Coke out of the machine.

"I am sorry," she gasped, sitting up and wiping her eyes and accepting the bottle. "All I could think of was that horrible joke about necrophiliacs."

"When Keats swoons," said Nick, smiling but dogged, "he is entirely serious about it. In Shakespeare, people swoon only in the comedies."

"Haven't you read *Venus and Adonis*?" demanded Janet.

Nick looked considerably startled, but after a moment he said, "It's not the same sort of swooning."

"Have a heart," said Molly. "He was ten years younger when he started writing than Shakespeare was when he started—I mean, Keats was nineteen and Shakespeare was twenty-nine."

"And Keats," said Janet, "never even *got* to twenty-nine."

"All right," said Nick. "If you really want to know what I have against Keats, that's it. Everybody is always weeping over him and talking about how great a poet he'd have been if he'd lived. If he *had* lived he'd have written a lot of third-rate swoony plays and nobody would mark him in the least."

Janet opened her mouth, and caught Molly's warning look. Molly was right, of course, because it was the same in Molly's dealings with Robin—when either of them got this way, there was no use in arguing. And at least she had managed to find out what Nick had against Keats.

Exams went by; people went home for spring break, or to northern Minnesota with Medeous. Janet retired to her bedroom and read mystery novels. It snowed three times during the ten days the college was closed; but the sharpness of deep winter had vanished from the air. Lily had discovered horses and was making a predictable and very reassuring nuisance of herself. Andrew had actually learned to play recognizable music on the flute, and was deeply disappointed that Nick was not going to come over during break and hear him demonstrate it.

Janet's father received the lists of his forthcoming students in campus mail, and was horrified to find his own daughter in his Romantics class.

"Don't do this to me," he said to her over the breakfast pancakes on the last Saturday of break. "For heaven's sake, I won't know where to look. Take Romantics from Simpson next winter; she'll make a fine job of it, and she likes Keats better than I do."

"I can't. I have to take Victorian literature next winter, because I took Shakespeare last winter instead."

"Well, take 'em both; it will give you a nice continuity."

"I can't. I have to take Spenser from Brinsley and I want to take Euripides."

"What do you want to take Euripides for? Isn't that the fellow who invented the deus ex machina?"

"I'll let you know," said Janet.

There was an obstinate pause, during which Lily and Andrew had a vociferous argument over who was supposed to take the dog for a walk, and Janet's mother went into the kitchen, where she would probably stay until it was all over.

"I'll be unfair to you," said her father. "I won't be able to help it. I'll overcompensate."

"Fine. I look forward to it."

"My head aches," said her father, getting up, "and a drowsy numbness pains my sense. I suspect Keats had a teenage daughter."

"No, he was one. A teenager, I mean. I won't be any trouble, honest."

"I know you won't, my child—but I will. Oh, well, perhaps they will be a dull lot and you'll liven it up."

"No, they won't. You get Thomas and Robin both."

"Not Nick?"

"No—I think he's settled on Music and Classics."

"Probably just as well," said her father; "it saves competition in the family circle."

He went into the kitchen and began to talk to his wife. Janet sat staring after him, and only Andrew's upsetting the syrup pitcher made her move from the table.

She went to the first session of the Romantics class with a certain trepidation. It was a bitter March day with a blinding sky and a wind that made you long for February. The class was on the second floor of Masters Hall, in the back, with a bleak view of the mottled brown-and-white playing fields and the bare gray trees of the Lower Arboretum. Janet met Thomas coming up the stairs; Robin was already in the classroom, making Diane Zimmerman and Anne Beauvais laugh by imitating Charlie Caspar's struggles with the optative mood. He chose to sit, however, with Thomas and Janet, who had retreated with one accord to the very back of the small classroom.

There were nineteen students in the class. Janet's father trudged in about five minutes late, wearing the despised gray suit he always began his terms in, and an orange-and-purple tie given him by Andrew and Lily three years ago. He said the combination of the chaste suit and the profligate tie weeded out the faint of heart. Janet tried to watch Thomas and Robin at the same time. Thomas's eyes got big, but he kept them resolutely turned away from her. One of Robin's dimples appeared, briefly, and vanished.

Her father sat down on his table and began, in his mild voice, a short speech of praise for the poetic tradition overturned by Wordsworth and Coleridge. The Romantic Revolution, he said, like the French, had perpetuated a number of excesses that half defeated its purpose, though it had not, at least, ended up with the literary equivalent of Napoleon Bonaparte and the subsequent Restoration of an Augustan Age now decadent, forgetful, and mindlessly autocratic.

He moved briskly through the French and American Revolutions, the accession and defeat of Napoleon, the restoration of despotism throughout continental Europe, William Godwin's *Inquiry Concerning Political Justice*, Jacobin hysteria in England, enclosure, the Industrial Revolution, the beginning of the outrages Charles Dickens was to suffer and write about half a century later, Disraeli's Two Nations. He spoke briefly on the Preface to *Lyrical Ballads*, which they would read; and listed the schools into which contemporary critics of the Romantic poets had divided them: the Lake School of Southey, Wordsworth, and Coleridge; the Satanic School of Byron, Shelley, and their lesser followers; the Cockney School of Hunt, Hazlitt, and Keats. Each of these was colored differently by the politics of the day.

Janet, as always when considering history, felt oppressed and miserable. She looked at Thomas, who was scribbling impassively, his mouth set rather hard; and then past him at Robin. Robin's face held a kind of impatient resignation. Then he, too, looked at Thomas, and went on looking until Thomas lifted his eyes from the notebook. Robin smiled. Thomas's hair hid his face from Janet; but after a moment Robin laid a hand on his wrist. It was the first time Janet had ever seen him touch anyone of his own accord.

Thomas's neck and ear turned red. He picked up his pen again, wrote a line or two, and pushed the notebook toward Robin. Robin read what he had written, while Janet valiantly did not try to.

"Does anybody have any questions?" said Janet's father.

Thomas jumped, Robin removed his hand unhurriedly, and Diane Zimmerman asked about the Peterloo Massacre.

Janet stayed after class for a few minutes, waited for the people who had questions about the midterm and the weekly papers to clear out, and said to her father, "That wasn't so bad, was it?"

"You held your hand, that's all," said her father. "When we get to Keats, you'll spear me with some question I've never thought of. If you were anybody else I'd be grateful; but if it's you I'll say something unforgivable."

"Phooey," said Janet, and went out into the hallway.

Robin and Thomas were waiting for her, and seemed still to be speaking to one another. Thomas was at the end of a long and impassioned speech; Janet had been aware of his voice while she was still in the classroom. He was saying, ". . . the whole reason I quit Political Science. It's fucking intolerable; people have been doing the same damn stupid things, collectively and individually, over and over and over, since—"

"Adam delved and Eve span," said Robin amiably.

"I wish I thought they ever had," snapped Thomas.

"This world uncertain is," said Robin, a little less amiably, as you might offer a five-year-old a bowl of ice cream after it has already refused cake, cookies, and candy.

"Fine!" said Thomas, with such force that people starting down the stairs at the other end of the hall turned their heads and stared at him. "*You* say farewell earth's bliss, then."

He slammed his book bag over his shoulder and stalked away. The bars of thin winter sunlight lit up his hair as he flung through them. The gapers disappeared hastily down the stairs.

Robin, staying where he was and not raising his voice, said, "An thou takest it not on thyself, knave, I may well."

Thomas's shoulders jerked, but he walked on.

"You know you shouldn't quote Shakespeare at him when he's upset," said Janet.

"What?" said Robin, vaguely; Janet thought it was probably the only unguarded utterance she had ever heard pass his lips.

"What's the matter?" she said.

"Life," said Robin, in a sepulchral tone that was just on the edge of parodying itself.

Janet rather dreaded the next class, but aside from making her sit between them, Thomas and Robin made no sign that anything out of the ordinary had happened, or ever would.

It was the unregarded physics class that actually caused the trouble. The theoretical part of it was fine. Professor Livingston was a brisk young man with an arid sense of humor, and the material he was presenting was the scientific side of Mr. Soukup's philosophy class. It was very satisfying. But every other week he devised some laboratory work for them.

Janet and Nick had naturally agreed to be partners. Janet was even eager to get into something nice and clean like a physics laboratory, which contained nothing either dead or explosive. On first glance, indeed, it contained a wholly delightful collection of weird objects that could be put together or smashed together: inclined planes for rolling little steel balls down, to replicate the experiments of Galileo; bits of two-by-four fitted up with the wheels off roller skates and wired up to an ingenious harness that would draw a line on a graph for you; flat, transparent, and mysteriously marked pans of water that could be made to vibrate at various speeds, for the study of wave mechanics.

But as they had once had the bakery write on Molly's cake, it didn't work. They had agreed that Nick would write up the reports but Janet would do the actual experiments; Nick had seemed thoroughly alarmed by the notion of a physics laboratory. But after they spent six hours with the inclined planes and steel balls, and two weeks later seven hours with the pans of water, and in both instances had to reason backward from what they already knew to discover what they were supposed to be proving, and then fake up some data that was not too perfect, he suggested that Janet let him take a hand.

And when he was performing the experiment, the equipment submitted meekly to him and they finished deducing the law of conservation of momentum (that was what the bits of wood with roller-skate wheels were for) in an hour and a half.

"Let's just try those balls again," said Nick; set up the apparatus in about ten minutes, and was merrily rolling balls down its Escheresque windings and demanding that Janet record the data.

"It's bewitched, that's what it is," grumbled Janet. She had a large and recalcitrant chunk of Pindar to read for Friday and did not relish the notion of having to write up lab reports.

"It's nothing of the sort," said Nick, so sharply that she stared at him. "It just wants a little sensible handling."

From the man who could not change the tire on his own bicycle and had let Janet put up the hardware for hanging his curtains, this was abominable. If he had shrugged and said he was lucky; if he had been as smug as he liked about the roller-skate experiment but had not insisted on trying the others over again; if he had even refrained from speaking to her in that tone of voice—but he hadn't.

Janet had no legitimate cause for complaint. "Look," she said, "it's no use doing those again; we've turned in the reports and I don't suppose you really want to go confess that we faked them. Let's go; I've got Greek to do."

"I just want to make sure we were right," said Nick.

"We got an A on the first report and a B+ on the second; what do you want?"

"You go ahead; I'll see you later."

"You can write up the lab report," said Janet, and left in a hurry, before she said something regrettable.

She was willing to forgive him by dinner; but he clearly felt innocent of any crime, and he continued to be so pleased with himself over every lab they did that Janet felt perpetually cross with him. He did eventually notice that, though the original incident seemed to have gone right over his head. He became snappish in his turn, and it made for a very uncomfortable term. When he told her, on a rare walk in the woods at the end of May, that he would be spending the summer in England with his family, she was a little relieved. Nick seemed genuinely regretful, which made her feel more kindly toward him. She decided not to try to sort out all the squabbles they had had; it would only spoil the little time they had left.

* * *

She got her job at the greenhouse back. Molly went back to Maine and wrote long letters on lined yellow paper. Robin had sent Molly a four-page letter to the lab, so that it was waiting for her when she arrived. It analyzed their relations, mourned over his own faults, and exalted her virtues. Molly was delighted, and found her old high-school flame much less of a temptation.

Tina wrote short letters on white paper with pink borders. She sounded much the same as she had last summer, but Janet was interested to see that the examples of journal writing seemed to at least have taught her how to express her sense of humor. Several letters describing lunch with ill-assorted feuding colleagues in the company cafeteria made Janet laugh so much that Lily pounded on the wall shared by their rooms and demanded that she be quiet. Lily had taken up meditation, and the least little thing disturbed her.

Nick wrote once a week, three or four very thin sheets covered with small writing in peacock-blue ink. He did a fine job of describing England, seeming to know just what she most wanted to hear about. He spent four pages on Tintern Abbey and only one on Brighton, which showed a good sense of proportion. But he hardly mentioned his family, and his letters were rather weak in romantic or even affectionate passages. He did say he wished she had been with him to see a production of *Measure for Measure*, but he could probably have said the same thing to Robin.

Janet spent three weeks reading the most mindless literature she could lay her hands on, including a pile of awful teen romances that Lily had tossed into the garbage can. She helped her mother in the garden and proofread three essays of her father's; but she was beginning to find time very heavy on her hands. Danny Chin was taking a summer seminar in nineteenth-century German philosophy, and would not be home until a week before Blackstock started up again.

On June 23 after supper she walked over to Blackstock; it was too hot to bicycle up that last hill. There was a thunderstorm threatening in the northwest; after a rather dull and dry spell, and she thought she would like to go stand on the veranda that encircled Eliot, and watch the lightning. She walked slowly along the southern edge of campus, admiring the wild roses that lined the walk to the chapel and were now in full riot. The College had put out big wooden tubs of white carnations on the plaza of the Music and Drama Center; Ericson was surrounded with lavender, which was not generally hardy in Minnesota; Forbes had foxglove, which was, but seldom bloomed this early. Eliot, where they would be living again next year, one floor down, rose out of a nest of bridal-veil spirea. That at least was blooming when and where it ought.

Somebody had left a couple of folding chairs on the western side of the veranda. Janet carried one along to the north side, and sat down to watch the storm come in. She had a fine view of both lakes, and the new concrete bridge between them, and on their left the steep hill with the larches. The wind was picking up. The dark clouds boiled up over the Upper Arboretum, over the willows on Mai Fete Island, over the larches and the lake and Eliot. There was no lightning yet, but there was a steady roll of thunder. No, that wasn't thunder. Janet jumped out of the chair and leaned on the balustrade. It was horses. They were coming over the hill beyond Dunbar, down the asphalt road and, one by one at what had to be a completely reckless speed, down the narrow sidewalk between Dunbar and the lake. Six black horses pelted down the hill, pounded over the wooden bridge with a noise like an avalanche, and flung themselves up the hill between Eliot and Forbes, tails streaming. It was very dark all of a sudden, but the riders carried a light with them. Janet saw Medeous's flying crazy hair.

It started to rain. Behind the black horses raced six or seven brown ones, and behind those five or six white ones. They were going much too fast for the riders to be discernible; they were going much too fast altogether.

There was a tremendous clap of real thunder, and the last white horse rounded the corner of Forbes and disappeared in the driving rain.

Janet was already wet. She skidded along the veranda, leapt down the steps, and ran for all she was worth. The riders had cut back between Forbes and Ericson and were apparently breathing their horses; at any rate, the horses were milling around in some confusion. Having gone too fast altogether, they had now stopped far too quickly. Janet slipped in the wet grass and herself slowed to a walk, gasping. And as the last few white horses went past Ericson and pulled up with the others, a rain of books shot out of Ericson's fourth-floor windows. Janet couldn't see what, if anything, they hit; but they upset the horses, which took off galloping wildly up the next asphalt road, and disappeared behind the Fine Arts building.

Janet walked through the rain to the first book. It was a thin volume bound in dark red, a little larger than a trade paperback. She opened it up, trying to shield it from the rain with her head and shoulders. "Shakespeare's MIDSUMMER NIGHT'S DREAM. THE FIRST QUARTO, 1600: A FAC-SIMILE IN PHOTO-LITHOGRAPHY." It had been published in London, by William Griggs, in 1880. Janet tucked it under her shirt and went to the next one. Liddell and Scott. *The Scarlet Letter*, in a very handsome edition. Janet thought of her battered Signet paperback, and grinned. A little green book. Yes—*Legendary Ballads*. All according to spec. She hunted a little more in the grass; it had looked as if dozens of books were falling, but that might have been just excitement and the scattering effect of the rain, or the light from the riders. *Tess of the D'Urbervilles*. But there had been no Hardy in the Thompson Collection. She picked it up anyway. The front of her shirt was beginning to fill up.

She ranged back and forth a few more times, but found only

sticks and pine cones and somebody's math paper. Math 11, B+. She kept that too; but a huge streak of lightning cut the sky to pieces just then, followed by an ungodly crack of thunder, and she decided to seek shelter. The side door of Ericson was locked, but its main door, which she tried more or less in passing on her way to trying Olin, opened placidly under her hand. It was gloomy in the entrance hall. Janet dumped the books on the disused monitor's desk, wrung her shirt out, and investigated. The door to the stairway and the swinging glass doors that let onto the first floor were shut and locked, which unfortunately meant she had no access to a bathroom, or to the pay phone in the basement. But she could sit out the storm in the lounge. She certainly had reading matter.

She found the hallway's light switch, and in its dim glow was sorting the books to find the driest, when behind her a door opened and Melinda Wolfe's voice said, "May I help you?"

Janet dropped Liddell and Scott with a dreadful bang on the stone floor and turned guiltily. "Hi," she said.

"Oh, it's you," said her advisor, and smiled. She was wearing a long and voluminous robe with running horses appliquéd on its hem and the opening at the throat. It ought to have clashed with her hair; but it was a very dark red. Janet's throat was dry. Melinda Wolfe said, "Are you having second thoughts about your schedule?"

Janet thought that was irony, since she had registered for Boswell and Johnson, Herodotus, and Sociology 11 with no discussion at all. But she answered, "No, I just got caught in the rain. I thought I'd sit it out in the lounge; I didn't mean to disturb you."

"You didn't really; I just realized I'd forgotten to lock the front door. We never do it in term time, and it's hard to get back into the habit. Why don't you come in and have a cup of tea? What have you got there?"

"Just some books," said Janet, picking up Liddell and Scott, which mercifully had landed without damage. "They can dry out here."

"Bring them in; you'll want to blot them dry at least, I think."

Janet gathered them up, resignedly, and carried them into Melinda Wolfe's living room. Behind her she heard Melinda Wolfe shooting the bolt on the main door of Ericson.

"Carry the books on through to the kitchen," said her advisor, returning and shutting the door of the apartment. "There's a vinyl cloth on the table; put them on that. I'll get you a towel."

Janet did as she was told. You could not tell a great deal about Melinda Wolfe's personality from the apartment, which was furnished by the College with objects only a little more elegant than those they gave to the students. But the wreaths of herbs and the little Persian-looking carpets, as bright as jewels, were probably hers. Janet laid the books one by one on the table. The color was running a little from the cover of the Shakespeare. Janet had just found a paper towel and was carefully lifting the pink stain from the first page when Melinda Wolfe came back, carrying a large green towel for Janet and a rather ragged yellow one for the books.

Janet dried her hair and face and arms and tried to rub some of the water out of her shirt. Melinda Wolfe said, "Let me get you a dry one," did so, and sent her into the bathroom to put it on.

The bathroom smelled of apricots. The borrowed shirt, a gauzy white muslin affair with long puffy sleeves and a thick embroidery of flowers, also white, on the yoke and cuffs, smelled of lavender. If Melinda Wolfe had planted the lavender outside, Janet should ask her how she managed to keep it going. She shook out her damp hair, hung her own limp green cotton tank top over the shower rod, and went back to the kitchen.

Melinda Wolfe had stood all the books upright, covers open and pages spread to dry. A collection of stains on the yellow towel showed that she had probably prevented the worst of the damage. Janet opened her mouth, and Melinda Wolfe looked up and saw her. Her glance was as cold as a Gorgon's. Janet stood perfectly still.

"Did you check these out of the Thompson Collection?" said Melinda Wolfe, as if she were asking how many children Janet had murdered today.

"I found them on the grass between Forbes and Ericson."

Melinda Wolfe's gaze grew colder still.

"Somebody threw them out the window," said Janet. She walked forward; if she was dead, then she was dead, but there was no point in being a coward about it. "I wanted to check—see, look, they don't have the library markings on them."

"Of course they do," said Melinda Wolfe, picking up the copy of *Tess* and holding it out.

It did have the white library letters on its spine.

"Maybe I need glasses," said Janet.

"It's the rain in your eyes," said Melinda Wolfe, kindly. "Sit down. Herb tea, or caffeinated?"

"Caffeinated," said Janet. "Please." She sat down and stole a surreptitious look at the Shakespeare and the Liddell and Scott, whose bindings had been so fair and empty when she looked at them thirty seconds ago. Library markings, as clear as you pleased.

"May I use your phone?" said Janet. "I should call my parents."

"Help yourself," said Melinda Wolfe, rummaging in a cupboard.

The telephone was on a wall in the kitchen, which was unfortunate, though Janet was not at all sure what she would have said in privacy if she had had it. She dialed her home number, got Andrew, talked him into calling Lily to the phone, and cajoled Lily into telling her parents, who were shut up in her father's study with the June bills, that she was sitting out the storm with Melinda Wolfe and would be home when it stopped raining.

She took a hopeful look out the window as she was hanging up the phone, but the rain was beating the huddled larches like fury, and another smash of thunder made her shrug and go sit down again. Melinda Wolfe brought the tea in big glass mugs: Earl Gray with lemon for Janet, and a repellent greenish-yellow brew for herself.

Melinda Wolfe, in the most prosaic possible manner, asked Janet how her summer was being. Janet said she had been catching up on her light reading, and they discussed mystery novels peacefully for a while. Melinda Wolfe admitted to reading Mary Stewart and an occasional Ruth Rendell, which made Janet think more kindly of her. "But you can only read so many," said Janet, "even of the best ones."

"Hence the trip to the Thompson Collection," said Melinda Wolfe.

Janet looked at her, taking a large gulp of tea as an excuse for not answering immediately. Somebody had thrown those books out the window, and nobody was going to talk her out of believing that. She was quite certain also that those books had not had the library markings on them when she picked them out of the grass; but that was something it would have been easy to make a mistake about. What did Melinda Wolfe want? "I've got my own Liddell and Scott at home," said Janet. "There wouldn't be any point in checking it out of the library."

Melinda Wolfe sipped her tea and said absolutely nothing. Her face was serene enough. "Is that Hardy from the Thompson Collection?" said Janet.

Melinda Wolfe tipped the book toward her and shook her head. "No. An underslept student helper on a work contract might have put it back in the wrong place, though. The numbers are similar."

She sat there blandly drinking her tea and waiting for Janet—to do what? Finish the tea and fall over? Finish the tea and become suggestible? She didn't feel suggestible; she felt extremely stubborn. And what she really wanted to do was to ask Melinda Wolfe if she was really sleeping with Professor Medeous. That was the single most fascinating piece of gossip Janet had ever had out of Blackstock—which was saying a great deal. But there was no way of asking it; and no way of forgetting it. A mental bow for Hesiod. Janet found herself inclined to giggle, and took another swallow of tea.

"It would be entirely natural to check out books from the Thompson Collection," said Melinda Wolfe. "These handsome old editions are much more satisfying to read. I never thought the feel of a book was important, myself, until I was given the special edition of Medeous's translation of *The Odyssey*. It's enormous; the Greek letters are about as big as your thumbnail, and the footnotes are the size of normal type. The pages are thick as cloth. It smells scholarly. Here, let me show you."

She got up and went into the living room, leaving Janet with a wild impulse to laugh. When she got back, lugging a black-bound, gold-lettered volume with the dimensions of *Life* magazine, only much thicker, Janet said, "Is this our Professor Medeous, or the other one?"

"This is ours," said Melinda Wolfe, clearing the tea things away, drying the table with the yellow towel, and laying the book down. "The nineteenth-century one didn't translate anything in her field; her translations were all done for pleasure." She opened the book. "There. Isn't that something? Go ahead, you can touch it."

Janet wiped her hands on her napkin and turned one of the huge creamy pages. The black letters were as sharp as if they had been engraved. Janet rubbed her thumb over the first two lines. They had been engraved. It must have cost a fortune. The book had English on the right and Greek on the left. Professor Medeous had used a fairly free blank verse for the English—rather like the Fitzgerald translation, except that it didn't sound at all like that. Fitzgerald was modern in idiom and rather cinematic in his images; he put in a lot that wasn't there, though the additions were rarely jarring. Medeous's sounded uncannily like the Greek.

"Why doesn't Professor Ferris use this in his classes? It's gorgeous."

"Professor Medeous won't let him; and he has been known to admit that it would probably discourage the students. Fitzgerald isn't literal, Lattimore's a terrible plodder if you don't know the Greek; any diligent student can improve on their work here and there. But what can you do with that, except admire it? Now, he might use it in Thirty-three, except he's always hoping most of the kids in that class will go on to take Greek."

"And Professor Medeous won't let him?"

"That, too."

"What a shame."

"He did put it on the list of additional reading one year, but she almost took his head off. Here, why don't you borrow it?"

"*This?* No way. Isn't there a paperback or something?"

"Yes, but it deserves this housing. I can run you home in the car, and maybe your father could return it later in the summer."

Her father usually rode his bicycle to campus in the summer, but he would certainly get out the car for this object—always supposing they were not all tempted to flee to some foreign strand to live in poverty and gloat over it for the rest of their lives.

"I really can't."

"Of course you can. There are few enough people who appreciate things like this. Go see if your shirt is dry, and I'll run you home."

Janet woke up at four in the morning, to a renewed assault of thunder and rain, and remembered that all the books she had picked up out of the wet grass were still sitting on Melinda Wolfe's kitchen table. Well, no doubt Melinda Wolfe would return the books to the library, whence it would be easy enough to take them out again.

But she had Medeous's *Odyssey* to read first. She read it a book at a time, every night before bed. It was not quite so fine an experience as reading *The Iliad* in the original; but she could read this in the original her senior year, under the kind but ruthless eye of Professor Ferris. This was a very different story from that of the wrath of Achilles. Quite apart from anything else, it had some sympathetic and clever women in it. Janet remembered Professor Ferris's saying, in Greek 33, that *The Iliad* was a tragedy and *The Odyssey* a comedy. She thought of the women in Shakespeare's comedies, and of those in the few tragedies she had read; and wondered if she had hold of something; if the women in comedies were always more real than those in tragedies.

About halfway through July and *The Odyssey*, she remembered that in junior high school Danny Chin had always been nagging her to read it. She wrote him a letter about it, and entered upon the most satisfying correspondence of the summer. Danny was, in some unpejorative way, a nice ordinary person, who moreover had acquired, from what he said, a nice ordinary girlfriend, who was passionately interested in Depression glassware and espionage thrillers. He said what he meant; he was not difficult; as long as you didn't mention ghosts to him he was as patient and whimsical as anybody could wish for. He was an enormous relief. When he got home they made one visit to Sheila's, one to the used-book stores in the city, and one to see a movie; and Janet felt September as something of a shock when it landed her back at Blackstock.

CHAPTER 18

Robin and Thomas were rooming together. They had a double on the ground floor of Eliot, because Nick had let his Room Draw number go to his head, and had secured a single—a rather narrow and utterly unprepossessing single, but his own—in Holmes.

He and Janet had a very satisfactory reunion in it, among the unpacked boxes shipped from England—a reunion that he spoiled almost immediately by telling her he was adding Music Theory to his schedule to make another twenty-four-credit term. This would be like his senior year in many regards, because as a student with two majors he had to take his comprehensives in one of them. He had decided it had better be Music, in which he felt he had a head start. The Listening Test was administered in the winter, so as not to interfere with the Senior Recital in the spring; so he expected to spend those moments not used up in class or in studying sitting inside a pair of headphones in the Music Library. He already looked tired and harried: England must be less restful than Wisconsin with Medeous.

"Shall we make a date for once a month?" said Janet acidly.

"Yes," said Nick, with the utmost seriousness. "That's a fine idea." He reached over the edge of the bed for his jacket, which had ended up on the floor, and extracted his pocket calendar from it. "I'm glad you are taking this so calmly."

"I'm not, actually," said Janet.

"Certainly you are. Nine girls out of ten would have set up a terrible wailing. Are Friday evenings good for you, or have you got Saturday classes?"

Walking back to Eliot under a mild autumn sky, Janet tried to fume, but found herself laughing instead. She was not sure what she was angry about—not the neglect of her for education's sake, which she sympathized with; more, she thought, the form of Nick's announcement and the failure of that usually ironic young man to understand irony when he heard it. He had not appeared in the least distressed at the prospect of giving her up for the pleasures of sitting in a stuffy room and analyzing classical pieces of music for hours on end—that was what stung, and that was what was funny, too. She remembered Thomas's advice about time. She and Nick hadn't had any time, except for that first summer, which she had squandered mooning over Christopher Fry and feeling put-upon. I wasted time, and now time doth waste me. And what was she in such a hurry for, anyway?

She climbed the stairs to the second floor of A column, went into their room (much like last year's, but with a very shabby blue carpet, and one wall painted bright red by departing students who had been supposed to repaint it white and preferred to pay a fine instead), and poured out her troubles to Molly and Tina, whom she found swearing and agonizing over their fall-term schedules. Since Tina was still enjoying her loverless state and Molly had been putting up with Robin's sulks and absences and general unaccountability for going on three years, neither of them was very helpful, though Molly seemed willing to be indignant; she said she would have thought better of Nick.

"But why better?" said Janet. "That's how I feel, too, but it's not reasonable. What are we here for, anyway?"

Tina burst out laughing, and Molly said solemnly, "'It is concerned with facilitating the continuous self-development and self-fulfillment of each individual, as well as with the natural and social environment in which the individual must live and work.'"

"*What?*"

"That's what it says in the catalog about a liberal education."

"You have got to be kidding."

Molly tossed her the 1973–74 catalog, bound in royal-blue paper and checkered with pictures of college life. Medeous stood in front of a blackboard looking quizzical; Anne Beauvais slept in a library chair with *Pride and Prejudice* open facedown on her stomach; Kit Lane sat in a larch tree, holding a paper airplane and grinning like a maniac; the rest of the pictures were of strangers.

"Page six," Molly said. "It's been in all the catalogs, we just never bothered to read it."

"Jesus Christ," said Janet, reading. This was worse than the anthropologists. "It gets worse, too. 'To develop an appreciation—often by doing—of the creative arts and literature.' Who *wrote* this—President Phelps? I don't believe it."

"Have a heart," said Tina. "He's an administrator, not a writer."

"Well, my God, couldn't he have asked his own English Department for advice? A freshman turning in prose like this would get blasted clear to Wisconsin."

"Oh, come on—it's grammatical, at least."

"So what? My gosh, what does the stuff at the beginning of the English section look like—no, that's okay. I bet Evans wrote it; there's something about the parallelism of the advice to majors."

"*Anyway*," said Tina, "romance is part of your natural and social environment, isn't it?"

"How should I know? What is my natural environment? Is he talking about the Arboretum, or what?"

"You know perfectly well what he means," said Tina.

"Well, if I do, I shouldn't. If I do, it just means my mind is every bit as murky as his."

"You are mad at Nick, aren't you?"

"I'd hate bad prose whether I was mad at Nick or about to marry him," snapped Janet.

Tina looked at her.

"All right, all right, I might hate it but I wouldn't yell at you about it."

"You'll feel better without him," said Tina. "You'll have time to yourself."

"That reminds me," said Janet, giving up on the whole discussion. "I want to keep a watch for the Fourth Ericson ghost this Hallowe'en."

She had photocopied and brought along her father's notes and chapters on Victoria Thompson's manifestations. Tina and Molly, who were already worried about taking Microbiology and Biochemistry in the same term, repudiated the documents with cries of dismay, but consented to be told all about them. They then wandered off on a discussion of how to make a really scientific study of a ghostly apparition. Janet wished them well of it, but there was something about Victoria Thompson's ghost that she was trying to remember. She had still not remembered it when they went to bed.

She missed Nick acutely at times: when somebody came whistling up the stairs and turned out to be Tina; when the Old Theater put on *Richard III* and even Molly had no time to go see it with her; when she walked along the river or through the autumn wildflowers by herself, or with Molly and Robin or Peg or Sharon and Kevin or Tina and Susan or Diane Zimmerman, who had taken up with Jack Nikopoulos but complained about not seeing him either; and when she watched the yellow leaves sweep the bright air clean and carpet the woods with gold.

The Friday once-a-month dates with Nick were very pleasant, but they could barely keep one another up-to-date on their mundane doings, let alone engage in anything like intimate confidences.

She could not fret for long over these problems, being engaged in a very busy term herself. Evans could have filled an entire term all on his own, especially with Boswell and Johnson. Diane Zimmerman was taking that class with her, and they gossiped about Boswell's youthful excesses as if he lived down the hall from them. Janet hoped Hesiod's strictures did not apply to historical characters.

New Testament Greek, though linguistically maddening in the way it collapsed its vowels together and slurred its endings, was taught by Mr. Fields, who was even-tempered, energetic, and fond of Hebrew poetry; and Sociology 11, while all its textbooks had obviously been written by the star graduates of the Mangled-English School that had taught all the anthropologists, at least had an articulate teacher. Hallowe'en came along with astonishing rapidity.

Molly had borrowed a Polaroid camera from a boy in her American history class. Tina had wanted to bring a thermometer, but since nobody had reported a sudden drop in temperature before the appearance of the ghost—or rather, of the ghost's books—this was deemed unnecessary. After being questioned, the afternoon of Hallowe'en, for half an hour by Molly and Tina, who seemed to feel that one Polaroid camera did not a collection of scientific apparatus make, Janet finally said, "You know what it is. Whenever *I've* seen the ghost, somebody always comes and takes the books away. Peg did it; and then Melinda Wolfe did it."

"All right," said Molly. "Books to be retained at all costs. Did you talk to those girls on Fourth Ericson?"

"They obviously thought I was crazy, but they said two of them will be in studying, and they'll keep an eye out for books flying around."

"Well, I guess that will have to do."

"Did you enlist Robin?" asked Janet.

"Nope—he's got to play the bagpipes for Medeous's party."

"It sounds as if we should have assigned somebody to keep an eye on Peg and Melinda Wolfe," said Tina.

"We're not being very efficient, are we?" said Janet. "I can ask Sharon to deal with Peg. I don't see how anybody's to do anything about Melinda Wolfe."

She went and called Sharon, who first laughed, and then allowed as how Peg did often sleepwalk on Hallowe'en. "You want me to keep her awake," she said, probably with some humorous intention, "or just follow her around if she sleep-walks?"

"Whichever is more convenient," said Janet.

She went back to the room.

"Look," said Molly the moment she got in the door, "what *time* on Hallowe'en does this poor girl throw books?"

Janet dragged her photocopies from under her bed and skimmed through them. "It was eleven forty-five the first time," she said, "and midnight the second. Dr. Bishop was assaulted much earlier in the evening; but that might have been real students."

"It would explain why we missed her the first Hallowe'en when we lived in Ericson," said Molly. "We were chasing pipers after our party, between eleven and midnight."

"We should start at ten or so, just to be safe," said Tina.

They accordingly betook themselves, a couple of blankets, some flashlights, the camera, a thermos of tea, and an empty knapsack to put the books in, out to the grassy space between Forbes and Ericson, and sat down far enough from Ericson to be out of the range of flying books. The windows of their old room were lit; the present occupants had bright red curtains with white lace around the bottom.

At eleven-fifteen, the mournful noise of the bagpipes swam over the roof of Forbes, from the direction of Dunbar and the lilac maze. "Do you want to go find Robin?" Janet asked Molly. "I can work the camera."

"No, not particularly. You can go if you want a glimpse of Nick."

"I think I do," said Janet, slowly. "I think—" Yes. The last time anybody had thrown books out of Ericson, they had been thrown at Medeous and her riders. So if she just waited, they might show up here; but the last Hallowe'en she had seen them, they had not come this way.

"Yes, I'm going," said Janet, dropped her empty tea mug onto the blanket, and took off down the hill, over the wooden bridge, up past Dunbar, down and up and down again, to the highway. She crossed it in a hurry and dropped into the bushes beside the gravel path that led down to the bridge over the stream.

She had just managed to quiet her breathing when she heard the sedate *tock, tock* of horses crossing the bridge. It felt for some reason far more frightening to be noticed when she was the only spectator than it would have been when she was accompanied by her entire Hallowe'en party; she lay flat and pulled her turtleneck over her nose and mouth and her green beret of Scottish wool, a belated birthday present from Nick, over her forehead.

It was not a very useful angle, unless you wanted to study the undersides of horses. But she was able to see that all their trappings were jeweled and glowing right around and under, and by twisting her neck very uncomfortably, she was able to distinguish Medeous, and Melinda Wolfe, and the Beauvais sisters, as well as the usual remote and foreign-looking people one never seemed to see around campus. There were more brown horses this time; and surely that was Nick on one of them—yes. Nick, and Jack Nikopoulos, and Rob Benfield, when the hell had *he* come back? And two other Classics majors who had graduated last year; and Kit Lane and bad-tempered John. Here came the white horses, just two—one of them ridden by Professor Ferris, who looked ghastly in the greeny light—unless it was just the angle she was viewing him from—and the other one, which Ferris was leading, with an empty saddle. Who was playing hooky this year, then? Nobody Janet knew.

They walked gently over the bridge, and up the path, and gathered on the highway. Medeous said something in her lovely voice. Janet almost jumped out of her skin; she knew what that word meant. It was Greek. It was one of the interrogatives—damn, which one? No, not that—whither, that was it. There was a chorus of answers, which might or might not have been Greek; and then they let out that same horrendous yell, and took off down the highway straight for the center of town.

Janet scrambled up and watched them around the corner. They could still, if they wanted to stay on the pavement rather than ride over the outlying fields of the campus, come back upon Ericson by taking the service road behind Sterne Hall. If they did, Molly and Tina would see them, and perhaps somebody would throw books at them again; fine. The bagpipes were still wailing and complaining in the woods. She would wait for Robin.

He was playing the Ceol Mohr again; no doubt about it. Tom, Tom the piper's son had been far more reassuring. Janet walked onto the bridge to meet him, and thought for a moment he was going to walk right into her. Then the pipes stopped with a wheeze, and Robin peered around them and said, "What are you doing here?" He was wearing a doublet of dark red with braid on it that glimmered, and high boots. Janet thought it might be a costume from *The Revenger's Tragedy*. It was nervewracking for other reasons entirely: Robin had a figure that was unprepossessing in jeans but suited these outlandish garments all too well. As Lussurioso he had made you feel he lived up to his name; as Robin, he was alarming.

She said, "I'm catching a glimpse of Nick. I don't get to see him for another two weeks, you know."

"I think it's a very foolish arrangement," said Robin. "You haven't brought Molly, have you?"

"No; she and Tina are lying in wait for the Fourth Ericson ghost."

Robin said nothing. Janet felt unwelcome. The stream gurgled below them, and a few leaves drifted down onto the boards of the bridge. "Do you have to follow the riders?" she said.

"No," said Robin. "They'll be racketing up and down for a bit, and then we all meet at Medeous's house and carouse until dawn."

"You sound tired of it."

"It doesn't suit an academic schedule so well. Walk back to Holmes with me, why don't you, and we'll see if Thomas is moping at home instead of going to the party."

"I didn't see him with the riders. Doesn't he like horses?"

Robin made a noncommittal noise, and then said, "May I go on playing, if it's melodious?"

"Certainly; just let me fall behind a bit so I'm not deafened."

She did so, and Robin began another of his unsuitable tunes; he seemed to play either the very esoteric and unbearable bagpipe music, or else things that would have been far better on a guitar or a piano. This was one that he and Nick and Anne sang. Janet found herself mouthing the words with the sound of the pipes: "Seven days are in the week, in almost every circumstance; And there's four seasons in the year, or so we learn in school; But never count your chickens when you're dealing with the women, For many a wise man fell asleep and wakened up a fool."

Hah, thought Janet, following the incongruous noise down the hill to Dunbar, you think it's any better dealing with men?

Eliot, when they got to it, was lively with parties, many of which had spilled out into the halls. The costumed and celebrating students had a number of things to say about Robin and the bagpipes, but he only smiled in his beard and refused to stop and play for them. He and Thomas lived in one of the big and much-coveted two-room doubles, with a bay window to it. There was a light under the door when they got there; Robin knocked, and was answered with a querulous, "What?"

"I've brought Janet," called Robin, and flung the door open.

Thomas was sitting cross-legged in the middle of the clean blue carpet of the main room, completely surrounded by Tinker Toys.

"What on earth are you doing?" said Janet.

"That's a fine greeting," said Thomas, smiling up at her. She was almost used to the shock of his appearance. The eyes and mouth and face were merely familiar now, for the most part; but the hair, its mixture of rich and subdued yellows all shining in the light, was still alarming. She suffered an acute wave of longing for Nick's pleasant, normal face. "It's all right," said Thomas; her face must have mirrored her thoughts. "I'm just trying to make a model of a molecule of muscarine—good Lord, that sounds just like Gilbert and Sullivan—for this goddamned physics course."

"Fucking," said Janet. "That is the proper adjective for physics courses."

"I beg your pardon," said Thomas. "Well, Robin, did you wake the dead?"

Robin, putting his bagpipes away in the closet, did not reply; nor did Thomas seem to expect it.

"Are you coming along?" Robin said to Thomas, slinging a red cloak lined with gold, no doubt also from *The Revenger's Tragedy*, over his doublet. In the cold fluorescent light of Thomas's desk lamp, the colors were as rich as on stage; but

Robin's face, what you could see between the thick fringe of brown hair and the beard, looked rather sharp and pale.

"No," said Thomas, without looking at him.

"It would be better if you did."

"If it be now," said Thomas, still not looking at him, "it is not to come. If it be not to come, then it will be—"

"Oh, for Christ's sake!" said Robin, and left, slamming the door with a violence that shook the windowpanes.

"Does he always get that way when you quote *Hamlet*?" said Janet. "And what are you talking about? Is Medeous going to kick you out again if you don't go to her party?"

"Robin is like that no matter what I quote. I suppose Nick's gone to this party like the good child he is?"

"I guess. I only see him once a month."

"Well, stay and have some coffee with me, then. I have a lot of real cream to put in it, frozen on the windowsill; and I've got a box of chocolate-mint cookies I've been saving for some great occasion. Help me pick up these damnable toys, and we'll have a mild sort of orgy."

They used up the entire pint of cream and ate the entire box of cookies. They discussed Keats, Shakespeare, the diabolical nature of all physics classes, how many times in a row it was possible to watch *Butch Cassidy and the Sundance Kid* before the mind rebelled, whether Tina had actually slept with Jack before hurling her pills into the stream, why Peg Powell never went out with anybody, and just how guilty President Nixon might be in the matter of Watergate.

In a daze of sugar and caffeine, Janet told Thomas all about the Fourth Ericson ghost. Thomas seemed vaguely horrified by the whole business. "I wonder why she threw *A Midsummer Night's Dream*?" he said.

"Well, I've been thinking about that, and it was Midsummer's Eve."

"Because all the other books are either connected with

Classics, or else they're about women who get pregnant out of wedlock and suffer for it."

"McGuffey's *Reader*?"

"I've never read them; who knows what's in there?"

"Maybe she threw the Shakespeare because somebody says in it, 'Lord, what fools these mortals be.'"

"Maybe," said Thomas.

"Do you actually believe in ghosts?"

Thomas smiled a very unpleasant smile. "No," he said. "But then, I don't want to."

"But you'll discuss them?"

"In my present disgusting state, yes. As if they were characters in a poem."

"That's what I've been doing, too. And all the reports of what she actually said are interpolations by an inept editor."

Thomas smiled, less unpleasantly:

"Dr. Johnson thought there must be ghosts, because he felt disparate human cultures could not independently evolve similar ideas unless they were true."

Thomas snorted.

"But he could never find any actual evidence that satisfied him."

"No fool he."

"Nick believes in them, too. It turned out to be one of those things you can't talk about, because it never occurred to him to think they might not exist."

"Has *he* got any evidence that satisfies him?" said Thomas, almost angrily.

"I didn't think to ask. It would be like asking me if I had any evidence that satisfies me about supernovae."

"And have you?"

"Yes—but it wouldn't come to much under determined examination. I don't mean I think there isn't any, I mean I don't know enough to satisfy a real skeptic."

* * *

Janet overslept the next morning, and got up feeling as if she had a hangover. She had to skip her shower, and she was too late for breakfast at either Eliot or Dunbar. Taylor was still serving toast, juice, coffee, and cold cereal. She did not feel capable of facing Boswell and Johnson—let alone Professor Evans—without any breakfast. She flung on the first clothing that came to hand, and rushed over to Taylor.

She had forgotten how very depressing it was. She piled a few items of alleged food onto her tray and walked along the wall, trying to find a table under a window. It was a bright November day out there; surely a little sun must be coming in even to Taylor's basement.

Yes, it was. It fell, dim and dusty but dazzling in the murk of Taylor, on a scratched table for two, and on Peg Powell's shining light brown hair and white ruffled blouse, where she sat smiling like Patience on a monument and holding hands with Nick. Janet stopped dead, spilling half her orange juice into her glazed doughnuts. Then she backed slowly away until she was safely behind one of Taylor's massive pillars, after which she put the tray down carefully on an empty table and bolted out of the building.

She arrived in her classroom fifteen minutes early, and sat staring at somebody's metrical analysis of Wordsworth's "Milton! thou shouldst be living at this hour" on the blackboard. The class gathered. Evans came in, brisk and a little sardonic; he had not found their last batch of papers inspiring, and set himself to explain how they might do better next time. Janet wrote down everything he said. She never felt quite the same again about the excellent advice not to generalize from fewer than three examples; she thought that another two examples of what she was generalizing about at the moment would probably kill her.

Then they discussed the entry in Boswell's *Life* for 22 March 1776, in which Johnson, encountering many years after their first meeting the first woman he had been in love with, laughed at the notion that a man never can be really in love but once, and said furthermore, "I believe marriages would in general be as happy, and often more so, if they were all made by the Lord Chancellor, upon a due consideration of characters and circumstances, without the parties having any choice in the matter."

The problem with literature, thought Janet crossly, while Evans delivered one of his more sardonic speeches relating these opinions to Johnson's actual behavior and then to the profound foolishness of students, the twentieth century, and humanity in general, was that either it applied not at all to your private concerns, or else you wished it wouldn't.

When she went back to Ericson, she found both Molly and Tina rather cross in their turn, on account of having been abandoned the night before in the midst of their ghostly researches—fruitless researches, as it turned out. They had sat out in the grass until twelve-thirty, unmolested by flying books or reckless equestrians, and then given up and gone home. Sharon had called at one o'clock and said Peg was sleeping like a log and could Sharon also go to bed, please? Janet apologized abjectly; Molly asked her if anything was the matter; Janet opened her mouth and surprised everybody, herself most of all, by bursting into tears. They patted her on the back and gave her Kleenex.

When she had explained the cause, both Tina and Molly looked relieved. "That doesn't mean anything at all," said Molly. "Peg's always melancholy; he was probably just cheering her up."

"If he's got time to cheer Peg up, why hasn't he got any time for me?"

"I think that's the problem," said Tina. "You wouldn't be so upset and suspicious if you guys were having a normal relationship. Maybe after he has the Listening Test—"

"Then he has to study for the written exam and practice for his recital. It's hopeless."

"Well, if he has time to comfort Peg, it can't be too hopeless," said Molly.

Janet perceived that she had failed to convey some element of what she had seen, and decided it was probably not communicable anyway. She blew her nose and consented to go to lunch, since this was not a day on which they would see Peg.

She found herself looking forward to seeing Nick with a feverish impatience; but when she knocked on his door on the appointed date and heard him call, "Come in," she felt suddenly incapable of either ignoring the matter or dealing with it. She went in. Nick had ordered a pizza, and was trying to cut it with a Swiss Army knife that had seen better days.

"Hello, my lass," he said. "Sit down and put on a bib, if you can find such a thing. This pizza would suit somebody on a liquid diet, but it smells all right."

"Nicholas, I can't stand this anymore."

Nick looked up, wide-eyed. "Do you want to go eat soggy sandwiches at Sheila's? I don't mind." He started to get up.

"No, I mean this. Seeing you once a month. Can't we do something?"

"I don't see what, until I've got these exams out of the way."

"Well, I can't stand it, that's all."

"Would you rather not see me at all?"

"Yes," said Janet, "I think I would."

Nick put the knife down, very carefully, on his purple-flowered pillow, and stood looking at her. Janet, advising anybody else in such a situation, would have told her to go ahead and confront him with Peg; it could not do any more harm than she had done already. But she could not do it. There was, after last spring and this summer and fall, so huge a collection of unspoken thoughts between them that no single one could fight its way out of the tangle. And what had he been thinking and not saying all that time? She blinked, hard. He would not begin; if there was anything to be said, she had to say it. She opened her mouth, but her throat had closed. She refused to break down crying on his bed. Nothing in all their relations had made that a possibility.

She turned and walked out of the room, leaving the door open. She was afraid she would fall down the stairs. Holmes was a modern building with an elevator, so she stabbed the button. She could see the open door of Nick's room from where she stood, once she had let the first rush of tears run out. The bell rang; the elevator came; she got into it and pressed 1. It was possible to beat the elevator by running full tilt down the stairs; they had had a few races that way. The elevator jerked to a stop and opened its doors. The modern, cheerful lounge, full of angular furniture in purple and blue, was empty. Janet pushed open the doors and went outside.

It was a dark night with a heavy overcast. The wind hissed in the remaining oak leaves. Janet leaned against the bicycle rack belonging to the Women's Gym. She had been thinking about doing this for months; why was she so upset now that she had done it? "Of the passion of love he remarked, that its violence and ill effects were much exaggerated; for who knows any real sufferings on that head, more than from the exorbitancy of any other passion?" Thanks a lot, Dr. Johnson. She could hardly call to mind any other passion. "Youth to itself rebels, though none else near." And you can shut up, too, Will of Stratford. "And truly in my youth I suffered much extremity for love, very near this." I just bet.

She went into Eliot and used the first floor's telephone to call Thomas. She could hear the telephone ringing faintly one level down, and a door opening, and the footsteps of the person going to answer it. An unfamiliar female voice, very pleasant; Janet heard its owner go along the hall and pound on Thomas and Robin's door, pause, pound again, and return to tell Janet over the telephone that nobody seemed to be there.

Janet declined to leave a message, thanked her, and walked over to the library. It was about half full of people who were not terribly harried yet, but Thomas was not one of their number. She didn't want to go back to Eliot: Molly and Tina were studying their Microbiology, which always made them fractious; and even if they were in the jolliest possible mood they would still tell her she had been an idiot, and urge her to call Nick immediately and reopen negotiations. Thomas was the only person she could think of who would really understand the small shiftings of unspoken thought and feeling, minor tremors that might suddenly expand into an earthquake.

What I want, thought Janet, standing in a portion of the library apparently devoted to the storage of biological works with titles longer than seven words, is something really esoteric or really depressing. Both, for preference. She wandered vaguely in the direction of the stairs, since incomprehensibility was not one of her requirements, and found the modern poetry. She hesitated a little between Pound and Eliot, but remembering again about the incomprehensibility, she took out *The Waste Land* and retired to a padded room containing a tall girl with a chemistry book and a round boy with three volumes of the Close Rolls.

"April is the cruelest month, Mixing memory and desire." It was just what she needed. The allusions melting into one another, the entirely poetic, utterly alogical connections, the sweep from free to blank to doggerel verse, the mind behind it steeped in everything anybody had ever written. Professor Evans had once told them that if they ever wanted to feel the immediate benefit of majoring in English, they should read *The Waste Land*. He had been making a rather sour joke about people who didn't understand the purposes of a liberal education, but he had a point. Chaucer, the Bible, Shakespeare—Shakespeare more than anybody, maybe—Virgil, Ovid, Middleton, Dante (she had to use the notes to discover those, but at least she knew who they were, and might read them, next year, or in graduate school), Spenser, Shakespeare again, Homer. "These fragments have I shored against my ruins."

"You said it," said Janet, half aloud; the girl reading chemistry never stirred, but the boy delving in the tiny print and frustrating dead ends of the Close Rolls glanced up and smiled.

Janet made a deprecating face at him, returned the book to the shelves, and went back to her own Eliot.

Her roommates were up, and seemed annoyed that she was not cheerful once more. Molly was very tiresome about it all; Tina, however, seemed to understand what had happened, though she could not express it well enough to satisfy Molly.

"It's odd," said Molly, sitting up in bed in her University of Pennsylvania sweatshirt, worn enough now to be used only as sleepwear, "that Robin and I should be the last ones left. Remember when there were six of us?"

"You make us sound like one of those mystery novels where they kill off half the characters," said Janet, rather crossly.

"I wonder what went wrong," said Tina.

"If you could know," said Janet, mangling Tennyson a little, "you should know what God and man is."

"Are."

"Nope. It's got to rhyme with crannies."

"Sure," said Tina.

Because she was feeling fed up with the Classics Department, when Janet declared her major she opted for a simple English degree. She was accordingly removed from the custody of Melinda Wolfe and given not to Professor Evans as she had earnestly hoped, but to Professor Fleisher, a kindly man from whom she had never taken a course, largely because he specialized in the modern novel and occasionally taught modern poetry as well. He looked like a slovenly and dissipated version of Professor Ferris, and in fact had Ferris's sweetness and brilliance without possessing the cutting edge that made Ferris so formidable a teacher. Janet thought he would make a good advisor, if he didn't take against her for avoiding modern literature. Maybe he would give a seminar in Wallace Stevens, or let her take an independent study. She was beginning to feel a little bewildered and oppressed by so many lectures. Maybe some quiet research would help.

In the meantime, Professor Fleisher gently brought to her attention the deficiencies of her distribution, and made her map out the schedules for all five terms left to her. Winter term of this, her junior year, was left largely alone: she got to take Victorian Literature, Euripides, and Spenser. But for spring he made her agree to take Chemistry 13 (Concepts of Chemistry, the Chem Department's offering for nonmajors) as well as French 1 to help get her into graduate school and American Literature I to balance her courses in the English Department. Worst of all, he persuaded her to consider Math 10 for fall term of her senior year. ("Donald Brunner can explain math so *I* can understand it," he told her.) She also ended up stuck with American Literature II that term, though American literature was an area she had been assiduously avoiding. Fleisher was not encouraging about Aristophanes either, but since she had given in on the math and sacrificed Shakespeare's tragedies and romances to the dubious pleasures of Jonathan Edwards, Nathaniel Hawthorne, and Theodore Dreiser, she clung stubbornly to her Greek, and he gave in.

Emerging from this conference, Janet was aware of a profound lack of tension. On some level far below the surface, Melinda Wolfe had been very difficult to deal with. Mr. Fleisher, while he had talked her into several less appealing terms than Melinda Wolfe had ever managed, was nevertheless simple and human and seemed to have her welfare at heart. What Melinda Wolfe had at heart Janet had never ascertained.

On the last day of exams, Thomas called.

"Robin says you broke up with Nick," he said, without preliminaries.

"Yes."

"Are you all right?"

"Not especially."

"Why didn't you call, dimwit?"

"I did; you weren't there."

"Well, I can't hang around twenty-four hours a day in case one of my friends does something stupid, now can I? You should have left a message."

"I called too soon; I was too upset. Then I wasn't upset enough, and it was exam week, so I didn't."

Thomas sighed heavily. Even his nonverbal expressions were almost too much for the telephone. "Look, I've got a plane in three hours and I'm not packed. I'm getting back January second, and I'll probably catch the seven-thirty bus. Why don't you meet me at the bus station and we can go eat awful sandwiches and you can tell me all about it?"

"Okay."

"See you in ten days."

"Thomas?"

"What?"

"Thank you."

"Don't be silly," said Thomas, and hung up.

CHAPTER 19

Thomas neither scolded nor lectured; but he did treat Janet as if she were recovering from some obscure sort of nervous breakdown. He made her compare schedules with him, and they settled on Tuesday lunch as a meeting time. He called her at odd hours during the rest of the week, to see how she was doing. Janet was at first exasperated, and then amused, and finally touched. A nagging worry that Thomas was going to go all romantic on her now that they were both free metamorphosed gradually into a certain irritation that he showed no signs of it. She caught herself making tentative motions in that direction herself, and pulled herself up sharply. Nobody who knew as little as she did about how she felt or what she wanted had any business entangling anybody else. It would only spoil the friendship.

Having decided this, she called up the gynecologist that the Women's Caucus, after months of exhausting negotiation, had persuaded the College to hire to come down once a week and minister to those needs that the Health Service proper refused to deal with. Dr. Irving, a thin, gray-haired woman who grumbled constantly in such a way as to make you feel part of the solution rather than of the problem, assured Janet that all her parts were in working order and gave her a prescription for birth-control pills. Janet had specifically asked not to be given the sort Tina had had and Molly still used, and was gratified to have Dr. Irving refer to them as, "Goddamned water-retaining stuff, silly dosage," and give her something else.

The something else made Janet's appetite erratic but did not actually make her sick. Taking the pills comforted her; ever since she walked out on Nick that evening, she had had the sensation that there was no telling what she might do next. The pills would guard against the worst consequences; and it was pleasant to have one's period be so predictable.

She did not make a TAKE PILL sign to join the battered one Molly still put above her bed; instead she put up the passage Nick had quoted long ago: "I would there were no age between sixteen and three-and-twenty, or that youth would sleep out the rest; for there is nothing in the between but getting wenches with child, wronging the ancientry, stealing, fighting." This was effective as a mnemonic device. It also made her think more kindly even of the beer-drinking, football-playing, practical-joking segment of the student body, mostly but not entirely male, that periodically interrupted everybody's peace. They stole nothing, fought very little, and seemed to feel that the ancientry were not worth bothering with. Clearly, however annoying they were, they might have been far worse.

Besides, the quotation always made Thomas laugh, though he did not know its actual purpose.

So winter arrived, and deepened, and departed to make way for a blustery spring. When their class schedules changed for spring term, Thomas and Janet changed their meeting time to Friday dinner. Robin gave Molly a bracelet of silver crocuses. Janet chose a moment when Tina was in class and Molly in the bathroom, and asked him if he thought she should return the necklace he had made for Nick to give to her. She knew what normal etiquette said on the subject; she had been ignoring that mostly because the process of returning the necklace would so painfully combine the ridiculous and the melodramatic. She kept remembering the stiff little couplet with which Ophelia had returned Hamlet's presents; she was sure her own effort would be no better and had no wish to be laughed at.

"I made it for you," said Robin. He was thumbing through Molly's math book, and did not look up. "What would he do with it?"

"Give it to Peg?"

"It wouldn't suit her."

"Why not? She's all fragile and Victorian, isn't she?"

"You're better off out of it," said Robin. He lifted an entirely sober face to her. He so seldom looked right at you, or seemed to see you when he did, that the impact of his attentive blue gaze was appalling. Janet felt the hair rise along her arms, and remembered that Nick had asked her if she didn't want to go to bed with Robin.

"Out of a kind of subterranean ménage à trois?" she said, with an extreme sharpness intended for herself, not for Robin. "Yes, I'm sure. But—"

"But the necklace was for you," said Robin; her tone had not so much as made him blink. He went back to the math book. "Do you keep it."

"Yes, I suppose I do," said Janet.

That weekend Tina bicycled out to a nearby farm with Susan to look at somebody's genuine crinoline, and returned with a gray tiger kitten with three white feet and no manners. He would begin to purr the moment you picked him up, which made it difficult to scold him. He was passionately fond of Robin.

"And I must say it's a relief," Molly said one evening, when Robin had stayed an hour past everybody's bedtime in hopes that the kitten sleeping on his shoulder would wake up. "I sometimes wonder if Robin is human; but if the monster here likes him, he must be at least benign."

After ten days of wrangling, they called the kitten Amoeba, because he seemed to divide himself and be in many places at once. This was rapidly shortened to The Meebe. Thomas called him Pyewacket, but it was not a name he would answer to.

Summer came; everybody went home. Molly wrote faithfully, long philosophical letters, interspersed with accounts of her loony family and the antics at the lab, on lined yellow paper. Tina wrote on purple paper with kittens rollicking across the top. She had taken The Meebe home with her, where he charmed her family, terrorized the family dog, and grew huge without altering his behavior in the least. From Nick, to whom Janet had hardly spoken, she got a couple of witty postcards, one a caricature of Mark Twain and the other of Samuel Johnson, their postmarks smudged and unreadable.

From Thomas came letters typed on erasable bond, much smudged and bearing unmistakable evidence of a mind that moved faster than the fingers it drove. He was still fretting about Tina, which gave Janet license to fret back about Nick, and they used up dozens of pages of paper and innumerable typewriter ribbons. Thomas's last letter, received three days before the start of fall term, said he would be arriving on September 18, probably by the one-fifteen bus, and that he was grateful for all the discussion of romance its vicissitudes that she had allowed him. "I think I'll abandon the entire business for the remainder of my time at Blackstock," he wrote, "except for a judicious selection of drama. I have obtained two sets of Student Season Tickets at the Old Theater, and hope you will find time to occupy the other seat."

Janet moved herself into the room she and Tina and Molly had secured on Second Ericson, on the seventeenth of September, and had hardly put down her suitcases before she was assailed by a violent melancholy. This was her senior year. It was her last fall at Blackstock. All this time had gone by like a dream. You couldn't stay, unless like Thomas you had managed to muck up your graduation requirements. You could sometimes come back; there were scores of Blackstock graduates working here as instructors and librarians and counselors and secretaries and anything you liked to name; but that was different. It might in some way reproduce the social atmosphere, but it would not make up for the history courses you had not taken and the English courses you had failed to extract the best out of and the Latin you had completely forgotten to think about.

"Our revels now are ended." If you could call them revels. Yes, they had been that. Evans, Medeous, Ferris, Davison, Fleisher, had all served as Master of the Revels, each in his own manner, with her own flourishes, using his own language, her own music.

Janet shook herself, and began to unpack her clothes. There were three terms left—three appallingly heavy terms finished up, for English majors, by a six-hour written examination concocted by all the formidable teachers in the department, not to mention people like Mr. Fleisher who were vague and kindly in appearance but death on paper; and, if you survived the written exam, a three-hour catechism conducted by three members of the department for each one quavering student, so that they might catch you out if you were not very quick-witted. Revels, indeed. It was probably very much as her mother described pregnancy—by the end you were so fed up with it, you positively welcomed the labor and delivery that had scared you silly eight months ago.

Neither Molly nor Tina had come back by one o'clock the next afternoon, when Janet left to meet Thomas at the bus station. Tina's mother was driving her up from Chicago, because of the cat. Molly was coming on student standby to save money, because she wanted to go on the Biology Department's winter seminar to Bermuda. That was depressing, too: only two more terms with Molly, and the College might put somebody else in the room with Janet and Tina.

It was raining, spottily and not very hard: the sidewalk outside Ericson was wet, the walkway up to the chapel was dry, the sidewalk that ran by Murchison and so downtown was damp. The sun came out briefly from time to time and lit up the top of the chapel or gilded an elm branch here and a telephone wire there. The bus station was in the lobby of the Murray Hotel, a building that might possibly have been a cousin to Ericson or Masters, except that it had been coated with the kind of shiny pale gray paint you normally saw on basement floors, and then left to itself for about fifty years. Lily, Janet, and their mother used to wait here to catch the bus to the city and go shopping. Lily usually got sick on the bus.

When she heard the grinding and roar of the arriving bus, she got up and went outside again; it would do Thomas no good to have to peer about in that gloomy cave. He came out last, behind a group of giggling high-school girls and three more Blackstock students, with his luggage slung all over him like Robin's bagpipes. He waved wildly when he saw her, grinning all over his face. Janet went forward and relieved him of a duffel bag and the smaller of his two knapsacks. "Don't you believe in the luggage compartment?" she said.

"Not since they sent the rough draft of a term paper I'd spent all spring break composing all the way to Fargo and took five weeks to give it back so I had to rewrite the whole thing to make my deadline, I don't."

"What was it about?"

"The pattern of revolutions in the Dominican Republic. I was still in Poli Sci. How are you? You look glum."

"I'm being foolish," said Janet, as they crossed Main Street and went up the steep hill that led to campus. "It struck me, while I was unpacking, that this is my last fall term here. All around me I feel the ghosts of lost opportunities."

"I know what you mean."

"You've had seven falls here, at least; I was dumb enough to be obedient and allow myself to be booted out in a mere four."

"Since," said Thomas, "to look at falling leaves, Fifty years is but a sieve, About the woodland we will run To see the elm gold in the sun."

Janet dropped his duffel bag and sat on it until she could stop laughing. "I hope," she said at last, "that A. E. Housman's ears are sufficiently stopped with earth that he did not hear that. Are you suggesting that we take a walk, or merely commenting on the vanity of human wishes?"

"Both," said Thomas, mildly. "Get off that bag, it's got cheese and apples in it."

They went along to Forbes, where Thomas and Robin had a room on the second floor. Robin would not be arriving until tomorrow. "Thomas," said Janet, dumping the knapsack on the nearest desk, "have Nick and Robin had a falling-out?"

"I think so, but you know Nick and I never really got along, and you know Robin never says anything germane if he can help it. Do you want some of this cheese, or shall we just go walking?"

The rain had stopped. The trees and grass were still green as summer, but the air and sky had thinned indefinably, as they did in autumn, and the first few leaves, dropped from what trees you could never tell, were drifting downwards in the sunlit air.

"Did they have it over Nick and Peg?" said Janet, as they walked by the stream in the Lower Arb and apologized to the ducks.

Thomas did not pretend that he could not construe her sentence, which was decent of him. "I think so," he said.

"So Nick and Peg comprise an entity that Robin might object to."

"You wretched girl," said Thomas, sitting down abruptly on a rotting log and plucking a black-eyed Susan with unnecessary force, "if you wanted to know that, why didn't you just ask?"

"I thought it was easier this way." Janet sat down too. "Robin seems to take his friends' love affairs very seriously. You should have heard him trying to bully me into making Tina take you back—what a sentence—after she broke up with you."

"He's trying to forestall fate," said Thomas. "Having beyond all expectation found the one woman in seven or eight thousand who would put up with him, he feels uneasy in his luck, and thinks that by maneuvering the affairs of his friends, he will be able to put off the disaster that inevitably attends on good fortune."

"You've been reading too much Greek tragedy."

"Maybe," said Thomas. "Supposing this to be possible. Look. What sort of a schedule have you got this term?"

"Aristophanes, Math 10, American Literature (bah). And Outdoor Fitness."

"Rather light, for you, isn't it?"

"Mr. Fleisher is a dangerous man. He talked me out of Shakespeare."

"It's probably just as well. Look. Since you're feeling nostalgic already and I'm feeling terrified at the prospect of actually leaving this place, shall we take a month off and be frivolous? Walk and bicycle to all those places we always meant to get to, and attend the extracurricular activities of which we always said, who has time to do *that*? We could collapse exhausted at the end of October and catch up on all our classes and curse one another."

Janet looked at him. There was a feverish note in his voice that she did not altogether like the sound of. He had bent his head over the flower as if he had never seen one before, and his fine straight profile and waving yellow hair told her nothing. Since what he wanted to do was very like what she wanted to do, she answered, "I'd love to. May we have Molly and Tina sometimes?"

"Certainly," said Thomas. "I wasn't proposing to monopolize you. Robin, too, I imagine. Speaking of which, when do your roommates get back? Molly owes me a letter."

"Tina's probably there now, feeling neglected. Molly's coming standby, so God knows."

"Well, let's go and see. I want to renew my acquaintance with Pyewacket."

Tina was there when they got back, unpacking with the assistance of Amoeba, who had become all legs and tail, in the manner of adolescent animals everywhere. He had not lost his charming disposition. Tina hugged Janet while the cat swarmed all over Thomas; then she solemnly shook hands with Thomas, which he appeared to find amusing, though he only asked her how she was.

"I'm fine now," said Tina, plugging in her desk lamp, "but as soon as classes start it's going to be awful."

"Does that mean you don't want to come gambol with Janet and me?"

"I don't play Bingo," said Tina vaguely, from the depths of a box full of tea mugs and dusty black enamel bookends.

Janet laughed, affronting the cat; and Thomas explained.

"Well," said Tina, "let me know when you want to go gambol, anyway. Where should we put the litter box, Jan?"

Janet found the month of September alarming. The only classes she had ever skipped had been Modern Poetry and Mr. King's anthropology class when he wasn't talking about Malinowski. She refused to skip Aristophanes, because it had only seven students and Professor Medeous, who was teaching it, had a way of looking at you, the first time she saw you after an absence, as if you had just sold Athens out to the Persians. But Math 10, even under the competent and humorous aegis of Mr.

Brunner, and American Literature, even under the dry and articulate flag of Mrs. Simpson, saw her once a week at best.

She and Thomas bought children's books in the college bookstore and read them in the Arboretum; they went to amateur puppet shows at the public library downtown; they attended every movie the Blackstock Student Association chose to offer them; they canoed on the river, rode their bicycles to an allegedly haunted house that Janet had been hearing about for ten years (it was sad and dreary, but not apparently haunted); they went, with Tina and Molly, to see Amoeba's mother's next litter, and barely escaped returning with two more kittens; and in the third week of September they went up to the city to see *The Lady's Not for Burning* at the Old Theater. Molly couldn't come with them, having a lab the next morning, but she charged them with getting her a ticket for later in the term.

It was a peculiar performance, being understated in the extreme and performed in modern dress, which rather seemed to miss the point. But its cumulative effect, whether owing to the overwhelming nature of Fry's verse or to the director's having more sense than was immediately evident, was still powerful. When Jennet Jourdemayne told Thomas Mendip that she would let him go after another fifty years, and Thomas Mendip agreed to put up with "hypocrisy, porcous pomposity, greed, Lust, vulgarity, cruelty, trickery, sham And all possible nitwittery" because he was too well brought up not to see her home, even though nobody knew where in the wide world it was, the balance of tears and laughter canceled itself and produced in the theater a perfect silence. It occurred to Janet that, more than any author she had read in her admittedly still small experience, Fry had the knack of showing you the tragic but allowing the comic to prevail. He was a little like Jane Austen in that regard, though possibly in no other.

She offered these observations to Thomas on the bus trip home; he received them pleasantly, but with no apparent desire to enter into a discussion. Janet fell silent herself. She ran her mind over the production and felt increasingly wrought up and distracted. She had not noticed before that it was about two people named Thomas and Jennet. It had a highly unsympathetic Nicholas in it, too. She knew perfectly well that, if examined with the eye of logic, these associations would unravel, since the plot of the play bore no relation to the events of the last three years. She did not cast the eye of logic over her ruminations. She shut the eye of logic up in the back of her head, where it could look on darkness and sigh over the exigencies of human folly.

And she said to Thomas as they were walking up the hill to campus, "I know you don't want fifty years of me, but do you think you might like fifty minutes?"

There was a long silence. They paced past Murchison, turned right, walked by one end of Taylor and past the red sandstone building, put together from a hundred curlicues of stone, that made up the old library.

"Fifty days, even," said Thomas, taking her hand. His was cold. It always had been. "Fifty days just about exactly," said Thomas, and laughed.

"I beg your pardon?"

"Never mind. We'll try the fifty minutes first, and see if you want another fifty after that. The question is, where? My roommate is wrestling with angels, in the form of New Testament Greek; yours are suffering agonies from Genetics and Statistical Mechanics—though why Tina is taking that I'll never know—yes, I know I'm babbling, dear heart, and so should you be, if I would shut up long enough to make you nervous."

"You can't make me any more nervous than this."

"Let's go where nerves are ravaged, then. Chester Hall is open, and the practice rooms are soundproof and have locks on the doors."

Janet burst out laughing.

"Have you got a better suggestion?" said Thomas, sounding less affronted than apologetic. "Or if you want to withdraw the offer, we can go drink milk shakes and talk about how we refuse to be the toys of irresponsible events."

"No, by all means let it be the practice room. It's a form of irony I especially like."

"Oh, for God's sake—Nick—"

"No, not once. That's why. Come along."

Outside the doors of Chester Hall, Thomas said, "Wait a minute," and began digging in his pockets.

"What are you—oh. Don't worry about it. I'm on the pill."

"After all the lectures I got for subjecting Tina to—"

"I spoke to you about it exactly once. Anyway, this is a new modern formula that causes me no trouble at all."

"All right, then," said Thomas. He put his hand on the bar of the door, but did not push it. The light from the building cast half his face into shadow. "You don't come anywhere near my bottom lip," he said. "More like the collarbone."

"Excellent. Then you won't have to reconcile yourself to a dark world."

"That's true," said Thomas, as if she had hit him, and shoved the door open.

Janet followed him, hoping he was not going to suffer a return of his temper in the next fifty minutes. He didn't, even though it was rather longer than fifty minutes, mostly because each party tended to burst into hysterical laughter and affect the other. Janet realized gradually that this was due not to nervousness so much as to the fact that the coldness of Thomas's hands, the sweatiness of her own, the hardness of the floor, the scratchiness of the carpet, the inconvenient placement of the piano so that it took up more than its rightful share of floor space, and the recalcitrance of all material objects were in fact funny, and that both of them, even in so delicate a situation, had to wit to realize it.

Thomas had not learned love from whatever masters—

mistresses, really, thought Janet, and started another round of laughter—had taught Nick; but he had one valuable quality that made up for any amount of clumsiness, uncertainty, and ignorance: he was indubitably present, bodily and mentally, at any given moment. She had not realized until now, having no basis of comparison, in how many ways Nick had not been.

"Does one always think unkindly about former lovers while having a new one?" she asked, while they were setting the room to rights.

Thomas sat down on the piano bench and gave vent to one last gurgle of laughter. "One tries to, I suspect," he said, wiping his eyes. "I'd think it would depend on the lovers. And on one's personality. Some people fool themselves about the present, and others prefer to exercise selective memory on the past. Why do you let me pontificate like this? Let's get something to eat."

They called Bartholemew's, which would deliver pizza until two o'clock, and had a large one sent to Eliot lounge, where they sat talking until four in the morning. Janet then lay awake for another hour, trying to decide what she had done. All modern philosophies would advise her to think of it as an incident, now over; but you could not disconnect events, even irresponsible events, like that. Amoeba, unaccustomed to human beings' walking about in the middle of the night, abandoned his post at the foot of Tina's bed and came and sat on her chest and purred, which eventually did send her to sleep.

She slept through her math course the next morning, which made her feel very guilty, even though she had been skipping it with abandon since it began. Thomas had proposed behaving frivolously until the end of October, but Janet wondered if three weeks of this might not be enough. She ought at least to go to her classes, even if she still cavorted outside the classroom rather than doing her background reading and starting to prepare for her comprehensives.

At the thought of the comprehensives she shuddered, and decided to read some James Joyce before lunch. Into this unproductive exercise walked Thomas, announcing his presence by shooing the cat, who had learned to open the door, back into the room, and then shutting the door loudly.

"Good morning," he said.

He looked ill at ease. He was probably wondering what to do, just as she was herself. Leaping up and kissing him seemed indecorous. Janet felt that she had made the first move, and he should make the second. He, of course, was probably wondering if she was regretting the entire business, and talking himself into letting her decide how to proceed.

"Lord," said Janet, "what fools these mortals be. Did I forget to tell you I'd respect you in the morning?"

"Not exactly," said Thomas, sitting down on the end of her bed and winding his long fingers up into knots. "It did occur to me that the effect of good literature may be as dizzying as that of alcohol."

"If it is, I haven't been sober for years. I am of the same mind as I was last night. If you are having any second thoughts, you'd better say so. Don't prolong the agony, for God's sake."

"There isn't any agony to prolong," said Thomas, rather sharply. "What do you say to fifty days?"

"What is this, a limited-contract marriage?"

"If you like. We could see what we thought at the end of it."

"Well," said Janet, "it makes a change from Nick, who implied and assumed a whole lot of things but hardly ever stated anything."

"Is that why you went after me in that downright way just now? It's hard on the nerves, you know."

"That's my natural approach, I'm afraid. But Nick was very good at stifling it—I don't think he meant to, but he had a different set of assumptions and—I don't know—there was something awfully powerful about them. He made you feel like an idiot if you tried to go contrary to them."

"Robin's much the same."

"Yes, only it's impossible to figure out what Robin's assumptions are, so you just go on as usual."

"You can afford that; you don't live with him." This might have been an automatic remark, but it sounded heartfelt.

"Is he giving you problems?" said Janet.

"Nothing serious," said Thomas.

Having been just chided for being downright, Janet didn't press him for details; she gave him a kiss instead.

Ten days later she was rummaging on the top of her dresser in search of Amoeba's flea collar, which he knew how to take off and enjoyed hiding, when the sign above her bed caught the corner of her eye. "I would there were no age between sixteen and three-and-twenty, or that youth could sleep out the rest." She felt extremely cold. It was not that she had missed a pill—it was that she was five days into the seven days on which one was not supposed to take any, and her period had not begun.

Janet sat down on Amoeba's tail, got up again so he could hide under the bed and complain, and stood in the middle of the room staring at Tina's picture of a bust of Beethoven. Don't panic, she told herself, this could mean many things, and the one you're afraid of is the least likely of the lot. She got out her Penguin Shakespeare, since rereading *Much Ado About Nothing* had been what she planned to do after finding the collar. She found herself looking up *All's Well That Ends Well* in the table of contents instead.

She went out into the hall and called Dr. Irving's office in the city. They put her on hold for ten minutes. Dr. Irving did not sound at all concerned, but her instructions were less than reassuring. "You shouldn't go back on the pill if there's any chance you might be pregnant. Use some other form of contraception—I can fit you with a diaphragm next Tuesday, if you want to make an appointment—until you can get a pregnancy test. Yes, I do them. No, not till you've missed your next period. Yes, I know that's another three weeks—it won't hurt you to use some other contraception for that long—even abstention wouldn't hurt you for that long. Yes, make an appointment with the nurse down there if you want to see me Tuesday."

Janet hung up carefully, and found herself muttering as she shut the door of her room. "Abstention is not the problem," she told Amoeba. She sank down on her bed and picked up the Shakespeare again, leafing through its preliminary pages with shaking fingers. These were facsimiles of the opening pages of the 1623 Folio; she had pored over them from time to time, but the erratic spelling and the old-style *s* that looked like a misconceived *f* made them difficult. She thumbed through "To the Reader," the picture of Shakespeare, which had always looked a little startled to her; past the elaborate dedication to William, Earl of Pembroke, and Philip, Earle of Montgomery; past the closely printed, wandering essay addressed "To the great Variety of Readers," from which one learned that Shakespeare's friends had scarcely received from him a blot in his papers; past the laudatory poems by Jonson and Holland; past the table of contents (they called it a Catalog) with its decoration of cupids and peacocks and hunting dogs; past more laudatory poems; past the page containing the Names of the Principall Actors, to the opening lines of *The Tempest*.

Janet thought she saw Robin's name go by, and turned back to the list of players, wondering what might look like "Robert Armin" out of the corner of a distracted eye. There were two Richards in the first column, but no Roberts. Samuel Gilburne, Robert Armin. No, it really did say that. William Ostler, Nathan Field, John Underwood, Nicholas Tooley—surely not. No, that was what it said, in nice clear italics, and the *s* at the end of the first name, where it looked normal to modern eyes. William Ecclestone, Joseph Taylor, Robert Benfield. "For pity's sake," said Janet. Richard Robinson, John Shancke, John Rice.

She looked at the first column again. No Thomas Lane; no Jack Nikopoulous; no Melinda Wolfe, of course, women didn't act in Elizabethan times. Just those three names. They were fairly common, except maybe for Armin. But for there to be three of them—and the way Robin and Nick talked. Not aliens but—what? Time travelers? "You *are* pregnant," said Janet, "and you're having fancies." Saying it aloud made her perversely certain that she was not pregnant; but that meant, of course, that she was not having fancies.

She got Tina's copy of *Webster's Biographical Dictionary* down and looked up Robert Armin. Nothing. Nicholas Tooley. Robert Benfield. Nothing. She looked up Hemmings and Condell, who had put together the Folio, just to make sure she had not wandered suddenly into some alternate universe. Yes, Webster's did admit their existence. She checked the index of Tillyard's *The Elizabethan World Picture*. Nothing. She had read the General Introduction to this edition of Shakespeare several times; she read it again. And there on page twenty-four it was, a list of the actors who had comprised "a vital core" of the Lord Chamberlain's Men, Shakespeare's company. Robert Armin was the last name listed.

She pulled a box from under her bed, and found the little stack of books Professor Davison had recommended as additional reading. She had read most of them, and Robert Armin and Nicholas Tooley and Robert Benfield weren't in them. But there were several she had never gotten around to. "Robert Armin, actor," was in the index of Harrison and Granville-Barker's *A Companion to Shakespeare Studies*, and from the three references there she learned that he was an author of plays himself, that he had replaced Will Kempe as the company's comedian, playing parts such as Feste and the Fool in *Lear* and perhaps somebody called Autolycus in *The Winter's Tale*. He could sing, said the essay, because the parts he played called for music; Shakespeare had not written any singing clowns until he had Armin to play them.

He could sing all right. He had definite and peculiar opinions about *Hamlet*; he talked familiarly of Shakespeare; he was certainly an actor. Janet shut the book and looked around the room, at the familiar scarred oak furniture; the red carpet; the four-year-old curtains, looking a little faded across their middles; Tina's sewing machine in the corner; the gray cat asleep in a patch of sunlight on top of Molly's biology notes. This was much harder to believe in than the Fourth Ericson ghost. And Nick, whose name appeared in no reference she had—though he was probably in the library somewhere, if she wanted to look him up—was a greater enigma than ever.

Janet began to laugh. Why in the world was she rummaging through all these books? Why was she thinking of looking people up in the library, when they were walking around to be talked to?

"What's The Meebe done now?" said Molly, coming in the door and tossing her armload of heavy books onto her unmade bed.

"He's asleep; I was laughing at myself."

"Want to share the joke?"

Janet opened her mouth; and after a moment, she closed it again. She thought in terms of looking things up in the library not just because of her upbringing and her training, but because if those people walking around to be talked to had wanted her to know what she would be looking up, they could have told her. Nick's curious reticence was suddenly explained, though it didn't necessarily make much sense. None of it made sense, really. Why should four-hundred-year-old actors, if they were that old, come to a midwestern liberal-arts college? If they weren't old, but just time travelers, which made more sense, because they didn't *look* old—no, she was dreaming; she was crazy.

"Molly, have you ever missed a period, while you were on the pill?"

"No, worse luck."

"But some people do?"

"Usually while they're getting adjusted to them, in the first few months. Why don't you call Dr. Irving?"

"She said go off the pill till it's time to do a pregnancy test."

"Oh, wonderful. You're probably not, you know—unless—have you missed any pills lately?"

"Nope."

"Well, you're probably not, then."

"Right."

"I know it's no use telling you not to worry about it, because you're going to. So just thank God it's not last year. Utter a grateful prayer to the Supreme Court. And you could call the Women's Caucus and see how much they've got in the abortion fund."

Janet felt sick.

"Yes, I know that's cold-blooded. But think about the worst, if you have to worry, and get it over with."

"Is that the worst?"

"Abortion? You aren't thinking of having the baby?"

"Now you're talking as if there were one."

"That's what we're doing, looking at the worst. Have you talked to—" Molly closed her mouth.

"Thomas, yes, you're right. No. Why should we both go quietly crazy?"

"Misery loves company."

"Would you tell Robin?"

"No," said Molly, "but that's a different kettle of fish. Why don't you go call the Women's Caucus?"

"I don't think they should have to pay for my sins, when my parents are perfectly capable of it."

"Well, they don't think you should have to apply to your parents if you don't want to. Do you think you've sinned?"

"I didn't—but it feels as if Nemesis has come to live under the bed. You remember the last Laura Ingalls Wilder book, the one about her marriage? I knew she'd had a daughter, and I wondered, when I bought the book, how Laura would ever talk about sex. You know what she thought, when she found out she was pregnant? She thought, Ma always said that those who dance must pay the fiddler. Well, I've danced, and now I'm paying."

"At least she seems to have enjoyed it."

"At least she was married."

"If you're going to go on like that, I think you should talk to Thomas."

"No. If I'm not pregnant, I don't want to force all those issues. It's only been three weeks."

"If you mean you and Thomas, it's been three years."

Janet stared at her. "That's a very interesting theory, Miss Dubois," she said, in her best imitation of Evans's manner. "Would you care to support it from the text?"

"I leave that," said Molly, imitating Professor Davison back at her, "as an exercise for the student. Come and have lunch with Robin and me."

"Robin won't like that."

"Nonsense. He can't talk about anything but New Testament Greek, which he hates for being different from Classical Greek; he'll love having a knowledgeable audience. I keep trying to compare all the verb changes he's raving about with mutations in the typhus bacillus, and it drives him crazy."

"The Elizabethans are supposed to like weird metaphors."

"Well, Robin doesn't imitate them in every one of their strange ways. Come on, he's got a class at one."

Janet moved through the next two weeks feeling as if she were carrying a large, ill-balanced tray of priceless china. It was easier than she had expected not to tell Thomas that she might be pregnant. She had thought of no good way to explain why she was no longer on the pill, and it would have been the height of idiocy to get pregnant because she thought she was already. But Thomas was not importunate, and did not seem surprised that she was not, either. He called or dropped by or suggested walks and movies as often as before. When she called him, he was agreeable to her own suggestions. His attitude, while it made matters easier in the short run, filled her with a certain dread when she thought about the future.

What was far more difficult than she had expected was refraining from telling him about the list of the Principall Actors in All the Plays. He was the best person to tell: the best person to talk the issue into its component parts if it were true, and the best person with whom to discuss its beauties and flaws if it were a fantasy. But she felt that by telling anybody she would somehow disturb the balance of the universe; and she did not want to do that, not now, when she might, still, not be pregnant. Thomas did ask her once if she was all right; she said she was still depressed about leaving Blackstock next spring, and as a result they took even more walks.

She did start attending all her classes, a move Thomas approved of and also undertook himself, being, as he told her, unhappy at having missed Professor Evans's initial remarks on Swift, which seemed to be the key to all later lectures. Janet lent him her notes from her own sojourn in Eighteenth-Century Literature; but Thomas said Evans had been using a different set of metaphors then.

American Literature was not as annoying as she had feared it would be. Mrs. Simpson, a tall, thin woman with a great deal of gray hair braided and wound around her head so that she looked rather like a statue of Athena that Professor Ferris had shown a slide of in Greek 33, was a delight. Like Evans, she was as sharp as a razor and had apparently memorized every work with which the class had to deal; like Fleisher, she was gentle and patient with all but the most obdurate stupidity. Janet would have preferred to take Chaucer from her, but she made American literature interesting if not entrancing. Janet did look forward to what she might have to say about Mark Twain, the only American author (of those commonly taught in college English classes) Janet had any use for.

The homework for Math 10 was tedious in the extreme, but Mr. Brunner had not only announced his intention of explaining calculus in metaphors, with no mathematics higher than high-school algebra, he seemed in a fair way to achieving it. His class was peculiarly complementary to Medeous's approach to Aristophanes as a series of linguistic puzzles that included prizes for those discovering the greatest number of (linguistically and culturally verifiable) dirty jokes.

Janet was still puzzled by Medeous. Only in her enjoyment of the more salacious aspects of Aristophanes did she demonstrate any characteristics in conformance with Nick's assessment of her. She was so dignified that it was three weeks before anybody laughed in class, a class on one of the greatest comic dramatists of all time; nobody would have dreamed of taking any liberties of any sort with her; she did not abuse the powers vested in her as professor or treat any student with other than impersonal courtesy. It made no sense. Nick made no sense. Too much cogitation in this area always led Janet back to the list of Principall Actors, from which even *The Rise of Silas Lapham* provided a welcome relief.

CHAPTER 20

Janet did in fact dream one night in the middle of October of Silas Lapham's daughters, who had turned up as Celia and Rosalind in a production of *As You Like It* that was set in Elsinore Castle and also included Pekuah from Dr. Johnson's *Rasselas*, solemnly reciting the first paragraph of Johnson's Preface to his *Dictionary*, and adding, after Celia had spoken a few words in New Testament Greek, "Inconsistencies cannot both be right, but imputed to man, they may both be true." This all seemed natural at the time; but Janet woke from it, slowly, to a sensation of vast interior discomfort.

"Oh, hell," said Janet, sitting up and wishing she had not.

Amoeba made a querulous noise from Tina's bed. Janet's roommates slept on. Janet groped her way to the door, blundered down the hall to the bathroom, and stayed there the rest of the night because she was too depressed to move.

No, depressed was not the word. It was a cold panic that paralyzed every nerve but left the mind free to concoct the most horrible scenarios it was capable of. Not, I'll not, carrion comfort, Despair, not feast on thee. Oh, get hold of yourself. You're not Tess; you're not Hester; you're not Mary Hamilton in the ballad, who slept with the King and had his baby and put the baby in a little boat and sent him out to sea, and was hanged for murder and the only satisfaction she got out of the whole thing was being able to tell the King to hold his tongue and let his folly be.

You're not Victoria Thompson. I suppose she thought her parents would throw her out in the storm. You're lucky, Janet Carter, that's what it is, lucky. You are the beloved daughter of tolerant parents with plenty of money, living in a society that has just declared it's none of the government's business if a woman has an abortion in the first trimester. I wonder if it's their business if you have the baby? Well, they can't put you in jail for it. *Is* it illegal to have a child out of wedlock, the way it still is in lots of states for unmarried people to have sex? But oh, God, why me? There are people around here who sleep with somebody different every night of the week, and *they* don't get pregnant.

There was a crack in the tiled wall behind the toilet. Somebody had written in large black letters on the plaster wall above it, "I read [history] a little as a duty, but it tells me nothing that does not either vex or weary me. The quarrels of popes and kings, with wars or pestilences, in every page; the men all so good for nothing, and hardly any women at all: it is very tiresome; and yet I often think it odd that it should be so dull, for a great deal of it must be invention."

No attribution, despite the businesslike and scholarly use of those square brackets. Janet spent a relatively pleasant fifteen minutes trying to remember the source of the quotation, and finally tracked it to *Northanger Abbey*. Catherine, who was so silly, and read only gothic novels, had said it, which meant perhaps one was not supposed to take it seriously; and yet it would be exactly like Jane Austen to put something like that in the mouth of a character like Catherine; it gave her the pleasure of saying it and the probability that nobody would take her to task for it.

It was an odd thing to put on a bathroom wall, which might explain why the people whose job it was to remove such effusions had not cleaned it off. How long had it been here? This was the first time she had been in this stall, which was the farthest from the door. Her primary feeling, running into the bathroom, had not been to accommodate her rebellious stomach so much as to hide herself.

Which was impossible, of course. Janet got up slowly, flexing her cramped knees. It was five-thirty. A dull gray light was beginning to suffuse the bathroom and drip into the hallway. Janet went back to her room, fetched her toothbrush and paste, and spent some time brushing her teeth. Then she took a shower. Out, damned spot. Virtue cannot so inoculate our old stock but we shall relish of it. Without gold and women, there would be no damnation.

I wish I'd read some modern poets, thought Janet, rinsing shampoo out of her hair. Some of them might have written about being pregnant out of wedlock, at the very start of your life, just when you began to think you might be a good critic—the most moral job in the world, if you can believe Pope—and thought of going to graduate school to see about it. But no, they're all men, too, except Sylvia Plath—and if I read *The Bell Jar* right now I *would* kill myself. How in the world did I get into this? I was so sensible. I wonder if one could sue the drug company for maintenance of the baby? Oh, God, what's Mom going to say? Well, she already said it: no form of birth control is completely reliable. I know just how those medieval monks felt about the treachery of the body—except theirs never did *this* to them. Men, men, always men. Not that it's fair to blame Thomas; the woman tempted him. He can go *away*, that's what's so galling, while nowhere I can go would be far enough. Which way I fly is Hell, myself am Hell.

I don't believe it. Birth-control pills don't fail like that; they just don't. My lord, the chances of conceiving from *unprotected* intercourse are only about one in four. Something has gone all wrong with the world, Elizabethan actors attending colleges, people getting pregnant while on birth-control pills. Maybe if I go out I'll see the sheeted dead all squeak and gibber in the American streets. No, that doesn't sound at all likely. Victoria Thompson never squeaked or gibbered; she just threw books.

Good God, Victoria Thompson. Is that it? Am I doomed to relive her tragedy, because I lived in her dorm? What was that Tina said about the girl who killed herself and made Nora buy a copy of the *PDR*—in consequence of which, I mean, Nora did it; there are less drastic ways to make people buy books, I'd hope. Oh, God, I'm going crazy. Though Mr. Evans would just say it's the damage caused by too early an exposure to thought. I wonder how much exposure to thought would have prevented this mess?

She went back to the room with her ears full of water and got dressed in her dearest old smock and green denim pants. Luckily Tina woke up before Janet had to decide whether to wake her. For the first time in their acquaintance, she was glad that Tina was a morning person. She put her question while Tina was shrugging into her bathrobe.

"I can't remember. You could ask Sharon."

Sharon lived with Peg. "Think."

"You shouldn't get up so early," said Tina, "it's bad for your disposition. I'll think in the shower, okay?" She made a dignified exit, but came tearing back ten minutes later, wearing a pink towel and a great many soapsuds in her hair. "Margaret," she called in the door, so loudly that Molly rolled over. "Margaret Roxburgh. I remember somebody going on and on about how Roxburgh was the same as Rochester, and then they got on to talking about *Jane Eyre*. Nobody around here can ever stick to the point. Can I take my shower now?"

"Go, go," said Janet, rather in the manner of Lady Macbeth.

Tina vanished; Janet ran to the door and yelled, "Thanks!" down the hall. The bathroom door swung in answer.

Janet grabbed her old green jacket and ran to the library, which was of course closed until eight-thirty. Janet sat down on the low brick wall in front for perhaps twenty seconds; she could not seem to keep still. She slipped between the library and Masters Hall, skidded down the dewy hill, ran across the field and the highway, and trudged up the highway until she came to the gravel patch and the wooden bridge, where she stood dropping sticks into the water and trying to think of something cheerful, like Lewis Carroll or the wonderful habits of Dr. Johnson's sentences.

It was a curious thing that, while bad prose was invariably maddening (unless it was funny), good prose was not invariably cheering. She said aloud to the burbling water and the dragonflies: "'That praises are without reason lavished on the dead, and that the honours due only to excellence are paid to antiquity, is a complaint likely to be always continued by those, who, being able to add nothing to truth, hope for eminence from the heresies of paradox; or those, who, being forced by disappointment upon consolatory expedients, are willing to hope from posterity what the present age refuses, and flatter themselves that the regard that is yet denied by envy, will be at last bestowed by time.'"

She had heard students reading Dr. Johnson aloud and laughing; but since these people invariably liked either Kahlil Gibran, Richard Brautigan, the anthropologists of the Mangled-English school, or the prose of James Fenimore Cooper, she was not impressed. That was a gorgeous sentence. The balance and clarity of it were a wonder. And it was true, too. She thought of Nick and Keats.

She rolled the syllables of "consolatory expedients" over her tongue again. That was what she needed, some consolatory expedients. She thought again of the women in Shakespeare. Shakespeare was full of bastards, but very little time was given to their mothers. The only young woman in Shakespeare who was pregnant out of wedlock, at least that Janet could remember, was Juliet in *Measure for Measure*; and while the suddenly oppressive rule of Angelo had made Juliet suffer, the real concern of the play seemed to be with Mariana, who couldn't get her husband to sleep with her, and Isabel the nun, who had to choose between sleeping with the abominable and hypocritical Angelo or having her brother executed, and who later ended up engaged to the Duke. And Ophelia—everybody argued about Ophelia, but surely it had been virginity that Hamlet had condemned her to. The thing you remembered about Ophelia was Gertrude saying, "I thought your bridebed to have decked, sweet maid, and not have strewed thy grave." Shakespeare fussed about lust, but he also worried about virginity. It wasn't his pregnant characters who went crazy.

Janet leaned her forehead on the rough wooden rail and laughed. There, then, that's all right, she thought. If you were a character in Shakespeare, you wouldn't go crazy. She looked at her watch. It was eight-twenty.

The student assistant who unlocked the main doors of the library gave her a sympathetic smile; he thought she had a paper due later today and was beginning to panic. If that were all, she thought, making for the room where they would hand you microfiches of old newspapers. She had forgotten to ask Tina in what year Margaret Roxburgh had killed herself, but if Nora had been at Blackstock it would be 1969 or 1970, probably, or the spring of '71. She poked about in the indexes to the two tiny local newspapers and to the Minneapolis and St. Paul papers, though she doubted the event would have penetrated their august attention. There was no index to Blackstock's own student paper, but at least those were only eight pages. She handed a depressingly long list of articles to the young woman behind the counter, adding a request for back issues of *Taking Stock* for the years 1966 through 1971, just to be certain.

Most of the student suicides turned out to have happened at various branches of the University of Minnesota. Margaret Roxburgh merited a paragraph in the Minneapolis paper, four paragraphs in the less agriculturally centered of the two local papers, and two columns, with picture, in *Taking Stock*. She had killed herself on Hallowe'en in 1967. She had been two months pregnant and had known it. She possessed a pleasant face, straight dark hair, a pair of the silly-looking glasses people had worn then, and a lot of freckles. She had been, as Molly or Tina had already mentioned, a Classics major.

"You don't get *me*," said Janet to the wobbly viewer. She sat staring at it, trying to think. The birth-control pills that were supposed to work had not worked; therefore she needed to try something that was not supposed to work, because it would. This was not very useful: there was, after all, a huge number of activities and substances that did not induce miscarriage. It should be, then, something that people had once thought would induce miscarriage but in fact did not. She thought of Nick's herbal tea, which probably ought not to have worked but had. She went upstairs and thumbed a little feverishly through the card catalog; then she went back downstairs, collected six or seven books, and sat down at the nearest table.

She started with Nicholas Culpeper's *Pharmacopoeia Londinensis*, because it was the oldest book there. It had been published in 1683, and this was not a reprint or a facsimile, but the thing itself—sitting around in the stacks for anybody to check out. She looked in the index. It gave her a certain amount of trouble; she finally realized that it was arranged by letter, in normal alphabetical order, but that within each letter the headings were in no order at all—or possibly the order in which they appeared in the book. She found "Abortion hindereth," and "Miscarriage," and dutifully copied down all the herbs listed. Then she surveyed what she had left, and settled on *Rodale's Illustrated Encyclopedia of Herbs*, which had a reassuring look to it.

Unfortunately, most of the herbs Nicholas Culpeper thought caused miscarriage did cause it, according to Rodale—in many cases, it appeared, by being poisons of such virulence that they simply killed the mother. Some of the herbs he thought hindered abortion actually encouraged it; most of the rest of them were dangerous in other ways. Janet looked in turn at rue, angelica, pennyroyal, and tansy. None of them was considered really safe.

She sighed, stretching with both hands thrust into the pockets of her jacket, which she had forgotten to take off. Down in the bottom of one pocket was a hard crumbly dry thing. Janet pulled it out. Brown and withered, it was nevertheless still recognizable as the flower of yarrow that had fallen out of Melinda Wolfe's wreath two years ago.

Janet looked for yarrow in Culpeper, but he had not dealt with it. Given the nasty things he did deal with, this was more encouraging than otherwise. She looked it up in Rodale. It had a long and honorable history. Culpeper was said to have recommended it for wounds, which must have been in some other book. Research from the 1960's, said Rodale, showed that yarrow contained some thujone, which in sufficient quantities can cause abortion. But yarrow was not generally considered toxic, though some people were allergic to it. Only the American Indians were listed as having used it as an abortifacient.

"All right," said Janet, to the line drawing of yarrow's lovely fernlike leaves and tiny clustered flowers, "we'll try you. If I have to I'll steal Melinda Wolfe's wreath off her door."

She put the books back and emerged into the air again. Yarrow was said by Rodale to grow on roadsides and in fields and waste places; but she was practically certain she had seen some flowering on the south side of Chester Hall. It had been hidden behind the lavender for most of the summer, but the lavender had stopped flowering in late August and was now, after two mild frosts, beginning to droop a little. And indeed, on the south side of Chester Hall where the sun came in between two larches, she found a large patch of yarrow, in full flower and still, this late in the year, buzzing with bees.

Janet approached cautiously, and began plucking it down near the ground, holding it at arm's length, and shaking the bees from it. Some of them departed, and some of them zoomed back to unmolested flowers. Janet wasn't certain how much of this stuff she would need; she went on picking it.

"What the hell are you doing?" said Thomas's resonant, shaky voice.

Janet dropped her armful and stood looking at the south wall of Chester. The sun on its windows glared back at her. "I was picking yarrow, until you scared me half to death."

"What for?"

Janet turned to look at him. He was unwashed, uncombed, and extremely pale. She said, "You wouldn't look like that if you didn't know."

"Molly told me she thought you thought you were pregnant."

"I do think so."

"What are you going to do with that?"

"Make it into a tea and drink it."

Thomas let out a long and wavering breath; he looked on the verge of tears. He also looked like a man who could not make up his mind what to do, like somebody who saw no way out. Since he wasn't pregnant, there seemed no cause for this. Nobody was going to come along as Angelo had in *Measure for Measure* and haul Thomas off to jail and threaten to execute him. Janet bent and picked up the scattered stalks of yarrow. It was used to cast the I Ching. She wondered what future she had just scooped up unread.

"Look," said Thomas, "I know it's your body. But will you at least talk to me before you do this?"

"Do you think it will work?"

"Talking? I certainly—"

"No, the yarrow."

"I thought you knew, or why are you picking it?"

"Because the pills didn't work."

Thomas frowned, painfully; more as if he had a headache than as if he failed to understand her. "I've sent Robin away for a few hours. Come up to my room and talk."

"I didn't want to talk," said Janet, "I just wanted to get it over."

"Look, if you want to get it over, I'll help you. But I want to tell you something first. Oh, Christ," said Thomas, "I didn't mean this to happen. I should have known Chester Hall would do this."

"Do what?" She had every dropped bit of yarrow back up, and they were walking toward Forbes. Janet felt the last of her momentum leaking away. She ought to go now and brew this tea and drink it, but she was too tired. Damn Molly anyway.

They went without speaking up to Forbes's second floor and into Thomas and Robin's room. Robin's side was as neat as a nun; Thomas's was in a state of wild confusion. Thomas flung the bedspread over his unmade bed and made Janet sit down on it, and sat down himself.

"Let's try to start at the beginning," he said. "You asked me to go to bed, not the other way around."

"I know that! I wasn't blaming you. I was just trying to fix things." Janet realized she was still clutching the armful of yarrow, and laid it to one side.

"That's not what I mean. Look. I'm in a mess so terrible that I can't even begin to describe it, and if you would have the goodness to stay pregnant until after Hallowe'en, you would help me more than I can say. I know you don't want to help me, you hate my guts; but if you do, I'll stand by you any way I can, whatever you decide to do."

"I can't possibly still be pregnant on Hallowe'en."

"Why not? It's only four days away."

Janet told him, not altogether coherently, about Victoria Thompson and Margaret Roxburgh.

"They killed themselves because their lovers betrayed them," said Thomas.

"How do you know?"

Thomas stood up and began prowling the paper-strewn carpet as The Meebe did when he wanted to go run up and down the hall. His voice filled the room. "Because I knew their goddamned lovers, that's how, the bastards. Picking out nice sensitive intelligent neurotic types because it's easier to pull the wool over their eyes, and then cackling like some fucking Victorian villain and saying, ha-ha, you're pregnant so you have to do what I say. Every once in a while Medeous picks somebody who deserves it." Thomas stopped, rather as if he were a tape recorder somebody had pushed the STOP button on—which Janet thought was a fine idea.

She closed her eyes. "Begin at the beginning," she said, "go on until you get—"

"And they didn't see any way out." Nobody had pushed the STOP button; he had just been musing. He stood by Robin's desk and rattled at her, "You've got a way out. You've got dozens. I won't desert you. I didn't mean to get you pregnant at all; I thought I'd just go through with it."

"With what, for pity's sake?"

"I don't know where to start."

"I'm easy these days," said Janet sourly. "I half convinced myself that Nick and Robin were some of Shakespeare's actors. What can you tell me that's half as silly as that?"

"They are some of Shakespeare's actors."

"They are?"

"They are."

The world opened out suddenly, replete with possibilities. "They knew Shakespeare?"

"They won't talk about him much. Nick said he was the sweetest-tempered man in England, but they don't really remember all that much." Thomas sat down on Robin's desk and hugged himself.

"Why on earth not?"

"It's been a long time, and they've changed."

"Into something rich and strange?"

"Yes," said Thomas. "And—she wanted Shakespeare, too, but she couldn't get him, and I think they hate to think he may have had the right of it. And that's why Nick can't abide the mention of Keats—and if you'd tried him with Langland or Chatterton or—hell, not Brooke, the other one—Owen—or whatshisname, you know, the epitaph on Maria Wentworth—"

"Campion. No, sorry, Carew. 'Ask Me No More Where Jove Bestows.' He did some nice stuff. Now Campion—Campion wrote songs. 'When Thou Must Home to Shades of Underground,' that's Campion. It's really spooky." Janet began to listen to herself, and tried hitting her own STOP button by smacking herself in the side of the head. This made her stop speaking, but did not make her mind any clearer. "What are we talking about?" she said. "Who wanted Shakespeare?"

"Medeous." Thomas stood up again.

"And all those other poets, she didn't get them either?"

"No, she got some of them."

"Oh, hell," said Janet, "what does it matter?"

"It does matter. It's why Victoria Thompson threw *A Midsummer Night's Dream* out the window."

Janet stared at him. It was exactly as if she had spent four years reading a poem, probably by Keats, and had gotten to the end and seen, finally, what relation all the pieces bore to one another. Not aliens. Not time travelers. Not science fiction at all, but a far older idea; remnants of things she had read in her childhood. And this did make sense. If you were in the habit of vanishing under a hill into a realm where time stood still, then, supposing you wanted to live in the world again—and after all, one must do something—you might very well decide to go to college to catch up on what the world had been doing. Adolescents are awkward; they know nothing; nobody is surprised at any ignorance they display. Mingle with college students and nobody would notice you twice.

The horses and the shining jewels; the distorted reflection of *The Revenger's Tragedy*; the presence of living men who should have died centuries ago; the skill at translation, the easy terms on which the literature of classical antiquity was dealt with; the fascination with poets and poetry and music; the pale stern people. She said, "Professor Medeous—"

"Go on."

"I won't. It's ridiculous."

"Yes, I know it is, but that doesn't prevent its being true. Look. I wrote it all down after it happened. Do you want to just sit here quietly and read it? I can make you some tea."

"No," said Janet. "I can't read your handwriting. And I don't want any tea. Thank you," she added; she could tell not so much from what she had said, which she could hardly remember, but from the trapped and furious feeling in her stomach, that she was being rude. "Just tell me. And sit *down* first. Please."

Thomas came slowly across the room and sat down at the head of the bed. "Seven years ago," said Thomas, "it was fall term of my freshman year. I was going to major in Political Science and change the world. I was going to make history behave itself. The people in Govy 10 were having a Hallowe'en party, but I already didn't really like the looks of them; I figured they were going to think up something worse than climbing the water tower. So I went up to the farm and asked for the friskiest horse they had. That was athletic, you see, and manly, but I could do it in solitary splendor.

"They were having a party up there, too, a whole bunch of Classics majors, waiting for Medeous to come so they could ride all over town and feel superior—never mind. Johnny Lane was minding the stable, and he tried to warn me. If it had been Kit, it might have worked, but Johnny's got an awful way with him, the minute he tells you something's a bad idea you think it's the unified field theory and you have to try it."

"Excuse me. You say, 'Johnny Lane' as if—I don't know—isn't he your brother?"

"No, he isn't, that's one of Medeous's little jokes. He's a great-granduncle, or something like that. She likes the resemblance. He really did try to tell me, but nobody's going to persuade me to take a nice placid old mare by referring to my pretty face.

"So I referred to *his* pretty face—it's the same one, more or less, except for the chin; he's got a dimple and I haven't, thank God. He was all in red and green velvet, and he had a cap with a feather in it, which of course I envied like hell, but I wouldn't have admitted it if my—well, anyway, he drew himself up and he said—I remember the exact words, because it was the only dead-serious thing I ever heard him say—he said, 'You ride at your peril; this is the night for ambition; distraction comes later.'"

"He alluded to Lewis Carroll?"

"Yes, he did. And he spoke indirectly, the way they all do. He was trying to tell me that this was a night for recruiting—"

"Addition."

"Yes. And that the sacrifice came later."

"Subtraction and distraction too?"

"Uh-huh."

"So what happened?"

"I said that the uglification and derision were already right in front of me; and that was that. Never cap the quotation of somebody who's helping you against his instincts, that's all I can say. He gave me one of the black horses. It was a mare, and I thought he'd foisted off on me the very placid old horse I'd said I didn't want. But we rode off, down the shoulder of the highway, past the bridge and the Lower Arb and all the playing fields, and along a path there used to be, before they put up the New Men's Gym, and down to the river. And I could tell that she wasn't placid, but I thought she had very good manners, at least. We had a gallop along the river path, which was suicidal; but she managed, and I managed. We stopped in that sort of sunken meadow you can see from the bus, right after the good view of campus. She ate some grass and I lay down and stared at the stars until all the bugs still left came and bit me.

"We went back along the river path, not even galloping; and I heard horses coming, and bells, and tried to rein her in. She wasn't having any of it. She had me off her back in a second, down there by the river. I landed stupidly and sprained my wrist, and I was sitting there in a clump of goldenrod swearing at it and the horse, and I looked up."

Janet felt as if she had turned the page of a book in the middle of a sentence and found herself staring at the Afterword. Thomas was looking over her head, into his chaotic closet. "What happened then?" she said, not loudly.

"You know what Thomas the Rhymer said when he met the Queen of Faerie? He said, 'All hail thou mighty queen of Heaven, your like on earth I never did see.' But she didn't look like that to me. I knew who Medeous was, because she'd been the speaker at Convocation. But I didn't recognize her. All the red in her hair was glowing. There were fireflies all around her, in October. I thought, one or the other of us shouldn't be here; this is a meeting that shouldn't happen; it's against the rules. She frightened me more than anything ever has. I was more scared then than I am now, when I know what's going to happen. I don't want to die, but it's a thing people do. But I should be dying for some human thing, even if it's folly or stupidity—not for her. Not for them. They're not evil; even that is comprehensible; people can be evil. They're foreign. They're like Linear A. They look as if they ought to mean something, but you can't tell what it is."

"What did she do?"

"First she reamed me out for stealing one of her horses and blistered Johnny for giving it to me; and then she took me up on her own horse, in front of her, the way you'd do with a child you were giving a ride to; and we rode back through campus and into the Lower Arb, to that place where the river makes a huge bend and there are those gigantic willows. They built enormous fires there, and sang and ate and drank, and she bound up my wrist with her headband. She made Johnny take me home, which scared me almost as much as she did. I looked pleadingly at Kit, and he came along too.

"The next morning the swelling was gone from my wrist. And my advisor started trying to persuade me to major in Classics."

"Who was your advisor?"

"Janie Schafer. She hadn't gone over to History yet. I thought that was the key; that if you wouldn't be a Classics major, they couldn't have you. But she had me from the minute I fell off that horse. And every seven years, the Queen of Faerie pays a tithe to Hell. It's seven of her years, not of ours; it depends on what she does and where she goes, but she's been teaching at Blackstock for seven years, and this year is the time. She doesn't pay with one of her own; she pays with one of us."

"Do you *believe* in Hell?" Janet wanted Danny Chin here as she had never wanted anybody.

"I believe in something nasty that Medeous needs to feed me to."

"What could scare *her*?" said Janet involuntarily. When she saw Thomas's face, she wished she had kept quiet.

"Guess I'll find out," said Thomas.

With extreme care, Janet steadied her voice. If Thomas wanted to treat this as a nice academic discussion, he should be allowed to do so. It was his fate they were analyzing. "What happens if she doesn't pay?"

"I'm not sure. Nobody is. They have all these theories on how one escapes. But the only method anybody has ever seen actually work was to have a pregnant woman come and drag the intended victim off his horse on Hallowe'en and hang onto him for dear life while he turned into everything under the sun."

"So what happens to Medeous then, if she fails to pay her tithe?"

"They think she has to pay more next time. They aren't sure. Some of them say there were two victims, one year, and some of them say that was something else; I don't know what. Robin says it's harder for her to control the department after she's missed a payment. Kit says that's nonsense, but Nick agrees with Robin. I don't know. It's like researching Renaissance Italy."

"And you think it's you this time?"

"They give us a little time to get shriven."

"Did you know it was you when we—"

"Yes, long before that. Why do you think Nick let you go so easily?"

"Do you really expect me to believe you didn't get me pregnant on purpose?"

"Allow me to remind you that you suggested the action that made it possible."

"Allow me to remind you that you took me to that play."

"You said you were on the pill."

"I was on the pill. Do you expect me to believe you didn't know Chester Hall would—would counteract it? Chester Hall, that's got lavender growing around it all summer when you can't *grow* lavender in Minnesota this far north; Chester Hall that's got yarrow blooming next to it in October when yarrow stops blooming in September."

"I don't expect anything," said Thomas. "I've been trying to tell you that."

"My God, no wonder those girls killed themselves. Why don't *you*—" Janet stopped, horrified. What had she become? Before she could frame an apology half abject enough, Thomas answered her.

"I thought of it," he said. "I'm informed, by people who have reason to know, that that only makes it worse. And besides, if I shuffle off this mortal coil before the proper time, she's got time to choose somebody else; and I don't like to think who she might choose to keep me company. All right?"

"And whoever she chooses won't have a pregnant woman handy."

"No."

"Can't you just go get one at the hospital?"

Thomas made a noise that might have been partly a laugh. "Oh, no, you don't fool them that way. It's got to be my child—or the victim's child, whoever the victim is."

"And you really expect me to believe—"

"Stop saying that, for God's sake. If you don't know me it's too late to start collecting testimonials now. I don't expect anything. I shouldn't have said anything. Go drink your yarrow tea."

"Do you want to die?"

"As I observed once before, you are the *dimmest* intelligent woman I have ever met."

This enabled Janet to get up and leave, which was perhaps what he had intended.

She went outside. A patch of pennyroyal flaunted itself next to the sidewalk, mingling with the petunias the Blackstock gardeners planted every spring. Janet plucked a leaf and smelled it. It was minty, but bitter. There were foxgloves nearby, too. She thought of the conversation with her father, with her mother, about pregnancy and being sensible. It is easy to promise to be sensible, she thought, when one is in a sensible situation. She looked, half in accusation and half in belated sympathy, across the grass to the high windows of Ericson. She remembered another conversation; the result, in fact, of the original discussion of Margaret Roxburgh's suicide.

Whatever else fairy tales might be good for, they taught you to keep your promises. Janet went back to Eliot without noticing how she got there. Tina was in the room, ironing a patchwork skirt for folk dancing. She chattered cheerfully about her physics professor, who had spent most of the class period telling funny anecdotes about mountain climbing and then related them all to statistical mechanics in the last ten minutes. Janet lay on her bed and listened, smiling when it seemed appropriate.

Molly came in just as Tina unplugged the iron. "Did you talk to Thomas?" she demanded.

"It's pink curtain time," said Janet.

"I thought those were looking a little faded," said Molly, "but is now the—"

"Oh, *Molly*," said Tina. "You've got a brain. Use it." Molly glared at her. Tina said, with a certain smugness, "Pink curtains means an emergency. What's happened?"

"She thinks she's pregnant," said Molly, without missing a beat.

Tina sat down hard on her bed.

"I also think I'm haunted," said Janet. She could not bear to contemplate the results of telling them that Professor Medeous was the Queen of Elfland. But she told them about Margaret Roxburgh and Victoria Thompson. After all, it didn't matter if she really was haunted or only thought she was; they would want to keep an eye on her either way. It was a subject far less vulnerable to endless and agonizing discussion. "Do you think you guys could possibly stand watches?" she said. "I know it's getting late in the term—"

"Of course we can," said Molly, "but where's the other party in this disaster? Can't he stand some watches?"

"I don't want to ask him."

"Did you talk to him?"

"Yes, but I don't—"

"What did he say?"

"He said it was my body, but he'd do anything; whatever I wanted to do he'd stand by me. I don't want to be stood by, that's all, okay?" Janet was obliged to stop and gulp several times.

"Certainly," said Molly. "We shall stand over you instead. Come and compare schedules, Tina; do you get up early tomorrow?"

"Shouldn't you see a psychologist or something?" said Tina doubtfully.

"Tina, I really do think I'm haunted and psychologists don't believe in ghosts and would just try to talk me out of it. I don't want to be talked at; I want to be kept company until after Hallowe'en."

"Okay. I've got folk dancing Hallowe'en night, Molly; can you take then?"

"Certainly," said Molly again. They sat murmuring over their figures and drawing up little schedules on some of their lab paper. Janet lay down on her bed and, much to her own surprise, fell asleep.

Molly woke her up for dinner. "Thomas called to say he won't be joining us," said Molly, while Janet was brushing her hair and Tina was changing the cat's box, "but you're to call anytime if you want anything."

"I want to change the past," said Janet gloomily.

CHAPTER 21

Janet had expected to find Tina irritating; as a matter of fact, Tina, who would talk endlessly if you let her and was also willing to read to Janet from mindless men's adventure novels with hardly an English sentence from the first page to the last, was very soothing. Molly would, it was true, read from Dr. Johnson's *Rambler* essays, which Tina refused to do because she never knew when, if ever, the sentences were going to end. But Molly insisted on discussing Thomas and the baby and what they planned to do about it and why Thomas was never here and why Janet wouldn't call him, until finally Janet, who had thought of something, got up in disgust and did call him.

He answered the phone, breathlessly.

"It's Janet."

"What can I do for you?"

"Were you suggesting that I save your life and *then* have an abortion?"

"If you want one. It's up to you; I won't go away."

"I don't think I could do that."

"Do what? You thought yarrow would *produce* abortion, I thought."

"I mean I don't think I could use your baby to save you and then kill it."

"I don't know if it is a baby yet and I don't know if it is killing, but I do see your point. It's the kind of nasty problem that comes back to haunt you."

"So it's both or neither."

There was a long silence. Janet shifted the receiver to her other ear. Her hand was sweaty.

"Look," said Thomas in a stifled voice. "I understand that I have put you in an impossible position. But I don't think anybody's interests are served by your trying to put me in an equally impossible one. I can't say anything to you that you won't interpret as self-serving. Maybe I can't say anything to you that *isn't* self-serving."

"That understood," said Janet, whose own voice was also clogging up, "say something."

"Do you want to get married?"

"Don't be an idiot."

"As a response to the only proposal of marriage I'm ever likely to make," said Thomas, "that lacks something." And he hung up.

Janet went back to the room and said to the watchdog of the moment, "I have to go home and talk to my family. If I'm not back in an hour, you may institute whatever procedures seem good to you."

"Shouldn't I come with you?"

"No, stay and study your genetics. I'll get my dad to drive me back, thus thwarting suicidal impulses on the way home."

"I'll walk over with you and walk back again by myself, then," said Molly, and did so.

Having herded both parents into her father's study and wept all over her mother, Janet managed to tell them that she was pregnant. Her father, shedding all modern and enlightened attitudes in about twenty seconds, was disposed to blame the young man, and intermittently during the ensuing discussion demanded to be told who he was.

They both told her that money and support would be forthcoming for whatever she might decide to do, and, like Thomas, infuriatingly left this entirely up to her. Her mother, pressed for advice, finally said, "Do you want to go to graduate school?"

"Yes. There's not much else I'm good for."

She noticed with interest, in the part of her mind that went on operating despite all disaster, that they were sufficiently upset not to pursue this point, or even to mark the attitude as uncharacteristic.

"If you attended some school close by," said her mother thoughtfully, "you could leave the baby with me. I wouldn't mind another."

"Mom!" said Janet, horrified. "Andrew's just gotten to the age where you have some time to yourself. You don't want to be cluttered up with another kid."

"Believe me," said her father, "your mother knows what she wants and always has."

"So if you don't want to marry this boy—"

"Who is he, for God's sake?" said her father.

"—that might be a solution."

"You don't think I should give it up for adoption?"

"My first grandchild? It's up to you—but no, I don't think you should."

"And you don't think I should have an abortion?"

"I don't know. It seems the simplest solution—but I'm afraid you'd always wonder. Sometimes the road not taken really is different."

The discussion wound around several more times and ended where it had begun. Showered with hugs and reassurances, Janet climbed into the car and was driven back to

Blackstock—by her mother, who did not want her father to worm the name of the baby's father out of Janet on the way.

Hallowe'en came; Tina, after a number of worried glances and falsely cheerful remarks, left for her dance. And Molly started in on Thomas again.

"Will you stop it!" said Janet.

Molly looked angry for a moment; then she turned red. "I'm sorry," she said. "It's just things are so weird with Robin, I want to tie somebody's love life up neatly, even if it can't be mine."

That impulse worked both ways, thought Janet. Because her affairs were in a complete tangle, she wanted to make things easier for Molly. She said, "If I knew something about Robin that he didn't choose to tell you, would you want me to?"

"To what? Tell me? I don't know. It would depend on what it was. If he's sleeping with somebody else I don't want to hear about it."

"No, not that." He probably was, or had been, thought Janet; but that was not the important thing.

"Well, what? Robin doesn't choose to tell me anything, so—"

"Is that the problem?"

"Part of it."

"Well, what I know will explain the problem but I don't know if it'll solve it."

"Just say it," said Molly.

Janet got out the Pelican Shakespeare and turned to the proper page. "Just read the names," she said.

Molly read them. She went on staring at the page for some time, the heavy black-and-green book open over her crossed legs; she was sitting on the floor.

"Far out," she said. "Three of them." Finally she looked up. "I can't say I believe this. But I'm willing to treat it as a hypothesis. You know—it's like looking up the answer to a physics problem in the back of the book. For one glorious moment you think everything fits together; and then you stop and think, and it doesn't, because you haven't done your homework and you don't know as much as you think you did. But I don't know what the homework would be in this case. It seems to explain Robin all right, I'll admit that. But how did they *get* here?"

"They've been to Elfland," said Janet. "And they awoke, and found them here, on the cold hillside."

Molly looked at her. Janet told her about Medeous. And then she told her about Thomas.

Molly said, "How does Thomas know it's him? What if it's Robin?"

"It had better not be, since I don't believe Robin's gotten anybody pregnant."

"I never heard of anything so crazy."

"I did, actually, and I've been trying to remember where. Wait a minute—" Janet got up, pulled Volume I of her battered *Norton Anthology of English Literature* off the shelf, and leafed through the section titled "Popular Ballads."

"Here it is," she said. "No—damn it. This is about Thomas the Rhymer. The Queen of Faerie got him, too, but she took him home after seven years—I wonder if that was to keep Hell from coming for him and now they're onto that sort of trick?"

"I don't believe in Hell," said Molly, a little wildly.

"Why, this is Hell, nor are we out of it."

"You're just depressed. Not that I blame you. Look," she said, sounding like Thomas. "It would be much better to be wrong about all this and look silly, than be right about all this and not do anything. Let's go out tonight—remembering the flashlights for once—and you can pull Thomas off his horse. If nothing happens, then people will talk for a while. If something happens, then it's worth it, isn't it?"

"But then I can't have an abortion."

"Say that again."

Janet explained.

"I don't guess you could think of it as a life for a life?"

"No, it's not that. I don't know what I think about abortion; but I can't take advantage of being pregnant and then just go merrily off and not be pregnant anymore. Those that dance must pay the fiddler."

"You read too much."

"Such men are dangerous."

"Huh."

"So instead of having two months to decide if I'm going to have an abortion, I get about another two hours."

"You know you don't want to have one," said Molly. "You just want a little longer to get used to the idea of being stuck with a baby."

"I can't believe this is happening to me."

"Think how Thomas feels."

"Will you stop harping on Thomas?"

"What happens if he doesn't show up?"

"I'm not sure he can not show up." Janet frowned, remembering. "He's stayed away the last two times I saw them riding, though."

"Has he thought of that?"

"Probably. He said if he killed himself first they'd choose somebody else, so if he *could* stay away, I guess they'd choose somebody else."

"Like Robin."

"Maybe."

"If I were Thomas and I thought you weren't coming, I think I might very well chicken out. I'm going out there; they aren't getting Robin without a fight."

"Well, if you're going, I'm not staying here."

"Fine. If Thomas isn't there, we can both pull Robin off his horse. A lover and a pregnant friend surely can't fail."

"I don't think Thomas will chicken out, though."

"If you think that highly of him, why don't you just make up your mind to marry him?"

"Cut it *out*!"

"Lord," said Molly, "what fools these mortals be."

It was a chilly night, clear but tending to mist in the hollows.

Eliot and Dunbar were bright with lit windows and noisy with music and laughter. The road up past the lilac maze seemed very steep, and once they had passed the tangle of bushes, there was a vast silence in which their every step made Janet's scalp twitch.

"Damn!" said Molly, as they started down the long hill to the highway.

"Shhh! What?"

"We forgot the fucking flashlights."

"We always do. It's okay. I don't want anybody to see me coming."

The grass of the hill was soaking wet. The highway seemed impossibly wide. Janet broke into a run to cross it, and then skidded to a stop in the gravel. Molly, following, said not a word of protest. It was only eleven o'clock; they had come in plenty of time, in case the legions of Faerie kept a different time in this matter, as they certainly did in others.

"Do we hide in the bushes, or block the bridge and yell at them to stand and deliver?" said Molly.

It was clear which she preferred. Janet said, "We'd better hide in the bushes. The white horses come last, and I don't know what Medeous would do if she saw us."

They crawled into the bushes and sat shivering under Janet's old green blanket. Janet's ears kept turning the distant sounds of revelry into bagpipe music; but when it finally came, there was no mistaking it. It was rather labored, and definitely some sort of march; not the Ceol Mohr.

"That's not Robin playing," whispered Molly.

"I know. Maybe you'd better get ready after all."

"I am."

Tock, tock, tock came the first horses over the bridge: black as jet, darker than the night, with the beads and ribbons streaming in a tangled glow behind them. Medeous; Melinda Wolfe; the pale, stern people. Who will go with Fergus now, thought Janet.

The black horses passed. The stocky brown ones came. Professor Ferris; Jack Nikopoulos; Anne and Odile and Kit; Johnny Lane, whose fault this all was; and Nicholas Tooley, sitting very straight, with a face like a mask. The brown horses joined the black ones in the road. Janet wished they were farther away. Her heart was so loud she could barely hear the piper, though he was now just the other side of the bridge.

Tock, tock, tock. The white horses came. Robin was on the first one, looking so grim Janet did not recognize him for a moment. Behind him, with his hair all braided with shining beads and a painful smile on his face, rode Thomas.

Janet scrambled out of the bushes, and ran at the horse, which not unnaturally sidled sideways. Janet made an enormous leap and caught Thomas around the leg. His hands caught and lifted her. The horse was still trying to go somewhere. Janet wound her arms around Thomas and simply leaned backwards until they both fell off the horse; sideways, because Thomas twisted so as not to land on her.

"Hold on," he said in her ear.

Janet did. There was a confused outcry from the other riders, and the sound of footsteps, and a complicated thud, underlaid with some gasping, that was probably Molly dragging Robin off his horse for safety's sake. She looked at Thomas's face, wondering how long she was to hold on, when there was a suffocating incursion of hot air and animal smell, and instead of having both arms wrapped firmly around a tall, thin boy, she found her hands sliding off a huge rough-coated muscular shape that snarled in her face. Janet gripped it as hard as she could and stuck her head under its chin. Somewhere nearby Thomas's furious and neglectful voice said, "What fucking difference does it make to you?" *The Romance of the Rose* slapped to the library floor. The lion made a resonant growl in her ear that was as much struggle as sound. Good question, dimwit, thought Janet.

But she hung on grimly, and there was nothing in her arms

but air. A dry, cool thing slithered over her shoulder, and she grabbed it just in time, dragged it into her smock, and bundled it up. It flung its head free, opened its mouth impossibly wide, and hissed at her. Janet struck its head away from her face and, inspired vaguely by the men's adventure novels, held it hard with both hands just behind the head. Odile Beauvais, in the oil-smooth voice she had used for Gratiana, said right into Janet's ear, "I'll give you this, that one I never knew Plead better for and 'gainst the devil, than you." The snake closed its mouth and flicked its tongue thoughtfully at her wrist. Janet decided not to slacken her grip.

The next moment she had a firm grip on nothing at all, and a madly flapping white shape was beating her about the head and delivering small sharp blows to her forehead. Janet batted it into the smock, too, where its terrified struggles were worse than the threats of the other shapes. She was afraid it would break its wings. "I'm not going anywhere," said Thomas's carrying voice, somewhere very distant.

Janet tried to make more room in the smock without letting the dove out. The smock filled suddenly with a flailing thing, light but very strong. The cloth ripped, and a long white head with a yellow beak and an evil eye snapped at her nose. Janet wanted to laugh. The snake and the dove had joined forces. She caught the swan's neck as she had the snake's, and it twisted free and bit her finger. "Fine!" said Thomas, very close. "*You* say farewell, earth's bliss." Oh, no, not that, thought Janet. She was more angry than frightened now, and that was dangerous: if she hurt any of these abominable beasts, what would she have done to Thomas? Not that he didn't deserve something—but she could not tell what it would be.

The swan got one wing free and beat her on the head with it. Janet sat down, not quite intentionally, and smothered its biting head in the smock again. There was a *whoosh* like the lighting of a Bunsen burner multiplied by a million, and she was holding not a living body but a burning brand.

Somebody was screaming. It was herself. She could not hold this thing any longer; nobody would; her arms were going to fling it from her of their own volition, as one's hand jerks back from a hot stove before the message of pain even reaches the mind. Janet rolled over so the fire was underneath her; and with a sudden thought went on rolling, until the blessed icy water of the stream engulfed them like a bed. The fire went out. The thing she was holding was suddenly heavy. She opened her eyes, and hastily dragged Thomas's head out of the water.

He was naked, which probably boded pneumonia if Medeous did not render the matter moot. Janet snagged the blanket she and Molly had brought from a bush that it had become involved with, and stood up. "If you'll get up," she said, giddily, "you can have this nice blanket."

Thomas stood up, his teeth chattering. Bony, thought Janet, definitely bony. Well, he's yours now. You can feed him up. Thomas' expelled a shivering breath, and she wrapped the blanket around him. They climbed out of the stream, stumbled over some branches, and stood dripping on the gravel.

All the horses stood still on the highway, sparkling and gleaming with jewels. The glittering riders had dismounted, and made a silent clump, some holding the horses, and some just looking. Robin was standing a little to one side, looking disheveled. He had the only immediately recognizable expression: he was desperately trying not to laugh. Kit Lane's was similar; it might be that he was hiding a face of great and catlike smugness. Anne and Odile might have just watched their team win at some bloodless and polite sport—tennis, perhaps. Professor Ferris had put his hands over his face. Melinda Wolfe was so still and so devoid of expression that she looked like a statue. The pale, stern people were remote and indecipherable, as always. Johnny Lane might have been horrified; Nick might have been astonished. He avoided Janet's gaze, but seemed to be trying to catch Thomas's.

But Thomas was not attending to any of them. Professor Medeous, her red and green rags hanging straight down and all their edges shaking as if with flame, stood two feet away and looked at them. No: looked at Janet.

"Oh, had I known," she said in her own voice, but with a wild note and a wilder accent, Scottish flavored with Welsh or French or something nobody knew; she said this much straight to Janet, and then jerked her head to address Thomas. "Tam Lin," she said, "what this night I did see," and she looked back at Janet, "I had looked him in the eye, and turned him to a tree."

She would have; and she could have. It was in her voice: wood; a slow vegetable life rather than a bright swift animal one; a kind of blindness; a kind of deafness; and some death of the heart. Linear A: the alphabet no one knew. Janet clutched at Thomas, who was cold and wet and slippery, but still flesh and blood.

"There will be two then," said Medeous, still with those wild-flavored vowels, but otherwise for all the world as if she were correcting somebody's sight-reading. "In seven years, we shall have two." She looked hard at Thomas. "And two dearer," she said, clearly.

She turned, and without a word or another sign from her all the riders mounted. She climbed onto her horse as if she were one drop of water joining another on a windowpane; and silently, with no shout and no sound of hoofs, all that troupe rode up the long hill and vanished around the bend. They stood and looked at the empty black road. The stream lapped at the rocks. The wind picked up.

"Listen," said Thomas in a shivering voice. "I couldn't say it before, it wasn't fair. I love you. Will you marry me?"

"Don't be an idiot," said Janet, but she put her arms around him.

"'Had you rather hear your dog bark at a crow?'"

"Nobody else in the entire world," said Molly, coming up

behind Janet, "would stand out here freezing to death so they could quote Shakespeare at each other. Come in."

"Where's Robin?" said Janet.

"He's gone riding," said Molly lightly. "It's safe now, you know."

They started walking.

"If we'd known," said Molly, "we could have brought you some clothes."

"I didn't think anybody was coming." Thomas said this with perfect composure, allowing for the chattering of his teeth. But Janet let her imagination, for the first time, consider what had been happening to him. She took his cold hand in her cold hand. Behind them, belatedly, the bagpipes made sounds as of an asthmatic giant, and lumbered into music.

"Robin didn't play," said Molly.

"He wouldn't," said Thomas. "Not for my funeral procession."

"Was that all he could think of to do? Make you die to the sounds of inept piping?"

"You don't know what it's like," said Thomas. "You don't know what it's like in that Court. It's like being wrapped up in cotton. And it's been going on for thousands of years. And they're all old, and you know, they don't get bored or tired; the older they are, the more they want to go on living. Robin remembers Shakespeare, at least a little. Why shouldn't he go on remembering him? Who do I remember? Besides—he tried to warn me about *The Revenger's Tragedy,* and after that he washed his hands of me. If he saved me, it might be him they'd take instead; it might be Nick. And they are all so remote there. Things take years to work their way through the cotton. They'd have wept for me, I calculate, around the year 3000. Getting a B.A. at one of the best small colleges in the country is like a vacation to them; it's like going to the beach for a week."

"Has anybody ever told you that you talk too much?" said Molly.

"I'm sorry," said Thomas. "I don't mean you should give up on Robin. He is human—and my God, Shakespeare wrote Feste for him. But you should know what you're up against."

"What did she mean, about there being two next time?"

"What she said," said Thomas.

"So she might mean Robin and Nick?"

"Well—two dearer. Anne and Odile? Or Kit and Johnny. I'm Johnny's fault; that's how she'll think of it now."

Janet thought of two other people Medeous might mean; but she said nothing. Dearer to whom, that was the question. Seven years was a long time. In seven years she might be dead, or the baby might. She was not sure she could get through the next seven minutes. Her finger was still bleeding from the swan; her whole back smarted; there was an entire network of stings on her head. No burns, though, for what that was worth. And now she was stuck with having a baby.

They went into Forbes, garnering a few comments from students dressed, for Hallowe'en, in garments hardly less strange than Thomas's. Of course, none of them was dripping wet. Thomas let himself into his room and emerged after a moment in his bathrobe. He gave Janet a Blackstock T-shirt and a pair of Robin's jeans. He distributed towels, both his own and Robin's, which made Molly laugh, and made sure Molly had a book. Then he pointed Janet in the direction of the women's bathroom, and walked down the hall to the men's.

Janet was cold, but there was no lingering smell from the water, only a little sand and gravel painfully ingrained. She was going to be all over bruises tomorrow, and she had to stand under the water a long time before she stopped trembling. "Sorry, kid," she said to her flat, swan-clawed stomach. It was hard to believe there was anybody in there. She had no idea what was bad for embryos, except alcohol. She could research the matter. That would help.

Robin's jeans smelled like lavender. Thomas's T-shirt smelled like rue. Janet wished they would wash with chemicals like normal people.

Thomas made them tea when they were all assembled in the room again. They talked a little about Victoria Thompson and Margaret Roxburgh. "I feel as if I ought to write a book about them," said Janet, "but who would believe it?"

"Even if you left out the faerie element, it could be a very good book," said Molly. "I suppose that's bad scholarship, though, isn't it?"

"It might be good sense," said Janet. "I don't want some modern version of Pope satirizing me the way he went after Bentley."

"There are no modern versions of Pope," said Thomas.

"More's the pity."

"Who's Bentley?" said Molly.

Janet said, "He was a very great classical scholar. He also appears to have been an unpleasant person—"

"Yes," said Thomas, "when he was Master of Trinity College he was tried and very nearly tossed out for what they called despotic rule."

"Yes, I know, and what he did to Milton passes belief. That, of course, is why he's in *The Dunciad* with Colley Cibber and Nahum Tate and—"

"Robin's Colley Cibber?" said Molly. "The one who mucked with Shakespeare? Robin despises him."

"That's him," said Janet. "And Bentley did that with Milton—except it was even worse, in a way, because Cibber just said he was improving Shakespeare, while Bentley said he was restoring what Milton meant to write, only his secretary wrote it down wrong and the printer screwed up. Milton's secretary, that is. I'm glad Evans can't hear me now."

"What's *The Dunciad*?"

Janet and Thomas looked at each other. Thomas said, a little helplessly, "It's a mock epic on the history and nature of Dullness and its eventual conquest of the world. It's hilarious if you've read Homer." He pushed his wet hair out of his eyes and recited, "'Turn what they will to verse, their toil is vain. Critics like me will make it Prose again.'"

"I thought you had trouble in that class," said Janet.

"I had trouble with Swift. Pope is a wonder."

"*Anyway,*" said Janet, "regardless of all his bad qualities, Bentley really was a very great classical scholar, and he invented practically single-handed the science of textual criticism—except he hadn't the tools for it, which is why he made such a mess of Milton—and he was responsible for one of the most important discoveries ever made in Homeric scholarship. But Pope couldn't see that."

"Was it fair to expect him to?" said Molly.

"Maybe not. Similarly, it's probably not fair to expect anybody who might read any book I might write to give credit to the parts they think are sensible while pooh-poohing the supernatural elements."

"This is far too hypothetical for me," said Molly, yawning and standing up. She set her teacup neatly in the middle of Robin's open volume of the Greek New Testament. "I am going home to my cold couch."

Janet got up.

"You stay right here," said Molly. "If you come home in less than an hour I'll kick you out. The Meebe and I." She scooped up her sweater and effected a majestic exit.

The door clicked behind her. Janet looked at Thomas, who cleared his throat. "If," he said, "I did my best not to be an idiot—"

"Don't. Let's take this one thing at a time, okay? I understand that you don't want to marry me just because you got me—we got me—what a silly language—pregnant. Well, I don't want to marry you just because I'm pregnant. Let's make it easy for those disgusting people who count the months between the wedding anniversary and the child's birthday, shall we? Let's get married on the kid's first birthday, and put the kid in the wedding pictures. If I'm going to make myself a scandal and a hissing, I might as well enjoy it."

"What should you like to do in the meantime?"

"Finish my senior year, and you should do the same. Oh, God, I'll be eight months pregnant when I take my comprehensives."

"Take a leave of absence and finish up the following fall," said Thomas. "You wanted another autumn at Blackstock." He looked thoughtful. "Maybe nobody will throw any books," he said. "Maybe Victoria and Margaret are avenged."

"What will you do? Don't you want to go to graduate school?"

"Having taken seven years to get my B.A., I won't be thought odd at all for taking a year off between undergraduate and graduate work. I could get a job; I understand babies are expensive."

"This really isn't going to work, Thomas; there's a recession, for God's sake."

"I understand that the publishing industry is unaffected by recessions," said Thomas, still thoughtfully. "We might look into that. I might like digging ditches—you never can tell."

"You're hopeless."

"Not as hopeless as I was earlier this evening."

Janet looked at him. "I'm sorry I hesitated for a minute," she said. "It's not as if I had Robin's excuse."

"Don't. You didn't more than half believe me; and if you resented being suddenly bullied into the female role, who could blame you?" He rubbed his eyes.

Janet got up from his desk chair and walked over to the bed, where he was sitting. She put a hand on his damp head. Two next time, Medeous had said. By then, if all went well, there would be three of them. No, you don't get us, thought Janet. You had your chance. She wondered about the rest of them. But when Medeous said two next time, she thought, nobody said a word of protest.

"It really would be better," said Thomas from under his hand, "if youth *could* sleep out the rest. But since we can't, let us tell one another stories around the campfire until the sun of maturity rises over the hills." He dropped his hand and began to laugh. "God, what would Pope say about that metaphor?"

"I don't know," said Janet slowly, "but—" She made a bound at the desk, flung herself into the chair again, rummaged a pen out of the center drawer, and found a piece of typewritten manuscript with a line drawn violently across its diagonal. She turned it over; the back was usefully blank.

"Janet, for God's sake come to bed."

"In a minute," said Janet. "I'm writing you a poem."

AUTHOR'S NOTE

Readers acquainted with Carleton College will find much that is familiar to them in the architecture, landscape, classes, terminology, and general atmosphere of Blackstock. They are earnestly advised that it would be unwise to refine too much upon this. Blackstock is not Carleton. It has its own history and its own characters, and even some minor physical differences: those who trouble to consider such things will notice, for example, that Davis Hall has disappeared, that the old Music Building has taken on considerable grandeur, and that a number of distances have been altered.

The people who occupy Blackstock are entirely imaginary. In particular, I never encountered at Carleton, in the Classics Department or outside it, anybody remotely resembling Melinda Wolfe or Professor Medeous. It would also be unwise, though certainly in accord with human nature, to identify the author with the protagonist.

I do not mean to denigrate my debt to Carleton, which is

enormous: what little I may be said to know about the joys and responsibilities of the intellect and the glory of literature Carleton, and in particular its Classics and English Departments, has taught me. My errors, of course, are my own.

AFTERWORD

This is the hardest part of the book; what I had to say about "Tam Lin," I've said already. But there are a few bare facts that may be interesting. "Tam Lin" is not in fact a fairy tale at all, but a member of that curious class, the sixteenth-century Scottish ballad. You can find it in Volume I of Francis James Child's invaluable work, *The English and Scottish Popular Ballads*—it's Number 39. I was first introduced to it by Fairport Convention, who included a rather sedate (by their later standards) rock version of it on their album *Liege and Leaf*.

The song had fascinated me for years. I liked the fact that the girl got to rescue the boy; the way she went straight to Carter Hall the moment somebody told her not to; the fact that she was the one who plucked the rose; the shape-shifting; the ominous and ambiguous ending that gives the Faerie Queen the last word.

I was still fascinated when Terri Windling told me about the Fairy Tale Line, and after delving among all my much-loved fairy tales and mumbling to myself a lot, I finally confessed to her that I wanted to adapt a ballad instead. It had enough fairy-tale elements in it to satisfy her. She thought I might set it in Elizabethan England, which seemed to be a splendid idea, except that I couldn't get anywhere with it. I was scowling over all the alternate versions in Child (they go from A to I), when I came across some verses that are not included in the song I knew.

Four and twenty ladies fair
Were playing at the ba',
And out then came the fair Janet,
Ance the flower among them a'.

Four and twenty ladies fair
Were playing at the chess,
And out then came the fair Janet,
As green as onie glass.

And suddenly it all reminded me of college, where the fear of getting pregnant collaborated with the conviction that you weren't nearly as smart as you'd thought you were, that you would never amount to anything practical even if all the professors thought you were a genius, and that the world was going to hell so fast that you'd be lucky to have a B.A. to show the devil when it got there, to produce a sub-clinical state of frenzy; where juggling your love life with anything else was almost but never quite completely impossible; where we all did any number of foolish and peculiar things while surrounded by and occasionally even absorbing the wisdom of the ages.

This was a song about adolescents. I could set it in a college. I did; and everything else, including the ghosts, who had no part in the original outline, sprang from that.

In many versions of the song, the last verse reads, "O had I known at early morn Tomlin would from me gone, I would have taken out his heart of flesh, Put in a heart of stone."

At the moment, if you asked me, I would say that this book is about keeping the heart of flesh in a world that wants to put in a heart of stone; and about how, regardless of the accusations regularly flung at them from all quarters, learning and literature can help their adherents accomplish that.

If you asked me tomorrow, I might say something else.

Pamela Dean
Minneapolis, Minnesota
8 July 1990

TAM LIN (CHILD 39–A)

O I forbid you, maidens a',
That wear gowd on your hair,
To come or gae by Carterhaugh,
For young Tam Lin is there.

There's nane that gaes by Carterhaugh
But they leave him a wad,
Either their rings, or green mantles,
Or else their maidenhead.

Janet has kilted her green kirtle
A little aboon her knee,
And she has broded her yellow hair
A little aboon her bree,
And she's awa to Carterhaugh
As fast as she can hie.

When she came to Carterhaugh
Tam Lin was at the well,
And there she fand his steed standing,
But away was himsel.

She had na pu'd a double rose,
A rose but only twa,
Till up then started young Tam Lin,
Says, Lady, thou's pu nae mae.

Tam Lin

Why pu's thou the rose, Janet,
And why breaks thou the wand?
Or why comes thou to Carterhaugh
Withoutten my command?

"Carterhaugh, it is my own,
My daddy gave it me;
I'll come and gang by Carterhaugh,
And ask nae leave at thee."

Janet has kilted her green kirtle
A little aboon her knee,
And she has broded her yellow hair
A little aboon her bree,
And she is to her father's ha,
As fast as she can hie.

Four and twenty ladies fair
Were playing at the ba,
And out then came the fair Janet,
The flower among them a'.

Four and twenty ladies fair
Were playing at the chess,
And out then came the fair Janet,
As green as onie glass.

Out then spak an auld grey knight,
Lay oer the castle wa,
And says, Alas, fair Janet, for thee,
But we'll be blamed a'.

"Haud your tongue, ye auld fac'd knight,
Some ill death may ye die!

Father my bairn on whom I will,
I'll father none on thee."

Out then spak her father dear,
And he spak meek and mild;
"And ever alas, sweet Janet," he says,
"I think thou gaest wi child."

"If that I gae wi child, father,
Mysel maun bear the blame;
There's neer a laird about your ha
Shall get the bairn's name.

"If my love were an earthly knight,
As he's an elfin grey,
I wad na gie my ain true-love
For nae lord that ye hae.

"The steed that my true love rides on
Is lighter than the wind;
Wi siller he is shod before,
Wi burning gowd behind."

Janet has kilted her green kirtle
A little aboon her knee,
And she has broded her yellow hair
A little aboon her bree,
And she's awa to Carterhaugh
As fast as she can hie.

When she came to Carterhaugh,
Tam Lin was at the well,
And there she fand his steed standing,
But away was himsel.

She had na pu'd a double rose,
A rose but only twa,
Till up then started young Tam Lin,
Says, Lady, thou pu's nae mae.

"Why pu's thou the rose, Janet,
Amang the groves sae green,
And a' to kill the bonny babe
That we gat us between?"

"O tell me, tell me, Tam Lin," she says,
"For's sake that died on tree,
If eer ye was in holy chapel,
Or christendom did see?"

"Roxbrugh he was my grandfather,
Took me with him to bide,
And ance it fell upon a day
That wae did me betide.

"And ance it fell upon a day
A cauld day and a snell,
When we were frae the hunting come,
That frae my horse I fell;
The Queen o' Fairies she caught me,
In yon green hill do dwell.

"And pleasant is the fairy land,
But, an eerie tale to tell,
Ay at the end of seven years,
We pay a tiend to hell;
I am sae fair and fu o flesh,
I'm feard it be mysel.

"But the night is Halloween, lady,
The morn is Hallowday;
Then win me, win me, an ye will,
For weel I wat ye may.

"Just at the mirk and midnight hour
The fairy folk will ride,
And they that wad their true-love win,
At Miles Cross they maun bide."

"But how shall I thee ken, Tam Lin,
Or how my true-love know,
Amang sa mony unco knights,
The like I never saw?"

"O first let pass the black, lady,
And syne let pass the brown,
But quickly run to the milk-white steed,
Pu ye his rider down.

"For I'll ride on the milk-white steed,
And ay nearest the town;
Because I was an earthly knight
They gie me that renown.

"My right hand will be gloved, lady,
My left hand will be bare,
Cockt up shall my bonnet be,
And kaimed down shall my hair,
And thae's the takens I gie thee,
Nae doubt I will be there.

"They'll turn me in your arms, lady,
Into an esk and adder;
But hold me fast, and fear me not,
I am your bairn's father.

"They'll turn me to a bear sae grim,
And then a lion bold;
But hold me fast, and fear me not,
And ye shall love your child.

"Again they'll turn me in your arms
To a red het gand of airn;
But hold me fast, and fear me not,
I'll do to you nae harm.

"And last they'll turn me in your arms
Into the burning gleed;
Then throw me into well water,
O throw me in with speed.

"And then I'll be your ain true-love,
I'll turn a naked knight;
Then cover me wi your green mantle,
And cover me out o sight."

Gloomy, gloomy was the night,
And eerie was the way,
As fair Jenny in her green mantle
To Miles Cross she did gae.

About the middle o the night
She heard the bridles ring;
This lady was as glad at that
As any earthly thing.

First she let the black pass by,
And syne she let the brown;
But quickly she ran to the milk-white steed,
And pu'd the rider down.

Sae weel she minded what he did say,
And young Tam Lin did win;
Syne covered him wi her green mantle,
As blythe's a bird in spring.

Out then spak the Queen o Fairies,
Out of a bush o broom;
"Them that has gotten young Tam Lin
Has gotten a stately groom."

Out then spak the Queen o Fairies,
And an angry woman was she:
"Shame betide her ill-far'd face,
And an ill death may she die,
For she's taen awa the bonniest knight
In a' my companie.

"But had I kend, Tam Lin," she says,
"What now this night I see,
I wad hae taen out thy twa grey een,
And put in twa een o tree."